FANTASTICLAND

A NOVEL

MIKE BOCKOVEN

Skyhorse Publishing

This is a work of fiction. Names, characters, places, and incidents are either the product of the author's imagination or are used fictitiously. Any resemblance to actual persons, living or dead, events, or locales is entirely coincidental.

Skyhorse Publishing books may be purchased in bulk at special discounts for sales promotion, corporate gifts, fund-raising, or educational purposes. Special editions can also be created to specifications. For details, contact the Special Sales Department, Skyhorse Publishing, 307 West 36th Street, 11th Floor, New York, NY 10018 or info@skyhorsepublishing.com.

Skyhorse® and Skyhorse Publishing® are registered trademarks of Skyhorse Publishing, Inc.®, a Delaware corporation.

Visit our website at www.skyhorsepublishing.com.

12

Library of Congress Cataloging-in-Publication Data is available on file.

Cover design by Erin Seaward-Hiatt

ISBN: 978-1-5107-3788-4
Ebook ISBN: 978-1-5107-0946-1

Printed in the United States of America

For Sarah, my companion; for Stephanie, my advisor and friend;
and for Chad. Burnt toast Bigfoot.

TABLE OF CONTENTS

AUTHOR'S NOTE

By now the details of what happened in FantasticLand during the thirty-five days dubbed "The Battle of the Tribes" have been dissected, obsessed over, and satirized so thoroughly by the public and the media that returning to what we *know* to have happened seems simultaneously a waste of time and a refreshingly new take on the story. With the sheer number of images and stories that defy belief and with the story occupying so dominant a place in the public consciousness, I feel it is a vital exercise to establish the facts.

In the simplest terms I can use, this is what happened.

On September 15, 2017, a hurricane more powerful than any in history fully broadsided the eastern coast of Florida. The effects of the hurricane, dubbed Hurricane Sadie, were felt along the totality of the Florida shoreline. The wind and subsequent flooding destroyed power grids, battered inland businesses, and left hundreds of thousands homeless. Local authorities were instantly outmatched. The National Guard was dispatched but were in over their heads. The Red Cross could only help so much. By November 1, thousands of people had died, not of drowning or the direct effects of the storm, but of neglect, exposure, and a lack of fresh water. Some smaller communities were not contacted until almost a month after the storm, in most cases far too late to do any good. Before the FantasticLand story broke, the phrase "America's Shame" had been attached to the response effort and was gaining traction.

It was only when the situation came under a reasonable amount of control and billions in federal government aid had been disbursed that the story of FantasticLand hit with a crash that shattered all other news stories about the disaster. It sounded like an urban legend at first—far too "out there" to be real. Only after the ruins of the once mighty amusement park appeared in online video footage did it become clear that the worst stories were true. Shockingly true, unbelievably true, but undeniable.

Of the 326 employees who stayed behind in the park, 207 were eventually evacuated. The fate of the 119 missing souls may never be known, but evidence of death and slaughter was immediately apparent. Photos soon emerged: heads on spikes outside of rides, corpses floating in detention cells, and viscera decaying in the humid Florida sun. FantasticLand, where "Fun Is Guaranteed!", was covered in blood. There were human bones littering the gift shops. It was all the country could talk about. The coverage crossed all media, breaking records for hits, views, likes, clicks, and shares.

The most indelible image, the one most of the public saw first, is among the most haunting photos of the past fifty years. Snapped on a cell phone camera by Sgt. Richard Hammell of the Florida State Patrol, who was among the first thirty members of law enforcement through the gate after the site was cleared by the National Guard, the photo shows the seventy-five-foot-tall FantasticLand logo, a bright red Exclamation Point at the center of the 2,200-acre amusement park, shattered into thousands of jagged pieces on the ground. In its place, a crude yardarm stretches between support towers that once held the Exclamation Point in place. Hanging from the plank are five bodies, strung by their necks. Two nooses are empty, the bodies visible on the ground. One has simply fallen. The other has been decapitated. Behind the bodies, a sign boasts in bright red letters, FUN IS GUARANTEED!

Reinforcements were called immediately. By the time employees broke their silence and began telling their stories, the media were scrambling and desperate to get on the scene. Unfortunately for FantasticFun Inc., the legal owner of the park, an uploaded video showed National Guard troops entering the park the very day a press conference downplaying the carnage was held. The footage aired side by side on most networks. Details began to emerge, bringing with them a flood of unanswerable, terrible questions.

How could a group of survivors, mostly children, commit such terrible acts? How could survivors with the best possible circumstances in which to weather the storm and its aftermath produce the worst possible result? What does this say about our children? Ourselves? Is every American teenager just a few short steps away from bloodthirsty savagery? How do we prevent this in the future? Was an American institution that had provided joy to children since the 1970s fatally harmed by this incident, or is redemption possible?

Many of these questions are answered in the following interviews, but I will warn you—many questions remain, and the answers I found only led to more questions. I was able to speak with almost all of the key players, from FantasticFun Inc. representatives to evacuated employees to rescue crew. And, as you've probably heard in the publicity run-up to the release of this book, there are multiple interviews with employees inside the park, as well as interviews with five of the seven members of the infamous "Council of Pieces." If there are answers, these are the people who would have them.

Yet as I turned this book over to my editor, I felt I understood the events either only as well or slightly less well than I did after the initial news articles had been written and all the trial dates had been set. I knew facts. I knew locations. I knew the players, and I looked into their eyes. With one notable exception, none of these (some very young) adults are monsters. I'm convinced of that. I know now what I suspected then—that a cocktail of immense fear, absolute freedom, rising uncertainty, boredom, and raging hormones turned an amusement park into a tribal battle ground. I've read dozens of think pieces that have dissected every aspect of this story, from academics giving thoughtful criticism, to "take away their phones, and kids turn into killers" hysteria. I've heard the players describe what they were thinking, and I still can't answer the most awful question everyone has asked themselves.

What would I have done?

What if I were a scared twentysomething, just getting my feet under me, more concerned with my Instagram account than my 401(k)? What if I had the entirety of human knowledge and experience at my fingertips and were suddenly plunged into the Dark Ages? What if I were cold and wet and scared and sick and bored to the point of losing my mind? Would I have followed someone? What if that someone asked me to kill?

Most of us want to believe that we would have acted more reasonably if trapped in FantasticLand. You would like to believe that you would have hidden, or you would have calmed things, or you would have found some nonviolent way to ride out the events that led to so many dead bodies. On some level, we all need to think that about ourselves. So allow me to share one story before we dive into the interviews.

There are many reasons I was unable to interview nineteen-year-old Alice Barlow, who, my sources tell me, was an archer for the ShopGirls Tribe, one of seven tribes that formed over the time FantasticLand was cut off from humanity. There were only four archers in the entire park, two of whom were ShopGirls. Of the ninety-two bodies recovered, an incredible thirty-four were killed by arrows. It is possible, albeit unlikely, that Alice didn't fire any of the killing shots. More likely that there were moments, perched on roofs of confectionaries and clothing stores and year-round Christmas shops, when Alice shot arrow after arrow after arrow into the heads, necks, chests, and legs of her coworkers as they bled and screamed and died below. It's not a stretch to speculate that it became somewhat normal for her, and that she was rewarded every time she spilled blood.

Alice was a good student (3.7 GPA in high school) and had a promising future in veterinary medicine. Beyond that, her digital trail paints the story of an all-American sweetheart. She loved movies and music, but her Facebook page (now deleted) had over two hundred photos of her with animals. One photo shows Alice holding a baby duck, gingerly, as if to protect it, on a stormy, windy day. If I were to interview Alice Barlow and ask her how the girl who protected a soft yellow duckling with only her hands could turn around and kill with impunity after only a few days cut off from civilization, what would she say? What could she say? I don't know that she knows the answer herself or that we would know the answer if it were staring us in the face.

It is my hope that this book not only sets the record straight on some pretty irresponsible reporting but also that for every arrow shot and every corpse viewed, you remember Alice and Joy and Alan and Tamera and Reggie and the other human beings who were in a situation most of us cannot fathom. There are many, many facts about the events at FantasticLand found in these pages, but there are also stories of human beings who started off as something else and were sometimes led, sometimes forced, sometimes coerced into acts of unspeakable savagery. Remember the victims. Remember those who are left alive. Most of all, remember the children they used to be. Because while many of them are still children, for a few weeks they were monsters. Most likely, you would have been, too.

A quick note on the format of this book: I have removed my questions from the conversations, streamlined the stories, and made a few editorial tweaks and edits to keep the subjects on point and their narratives flowing. In some cases, large parts of the interviews were cut for relevance or clarity, but at no point do I believe I have misrepresented anything said by the subjects. In many cases, I have preserved the conversational flow by keeping transitions and other verbal tics as markers left for the ease of the readers. A few chapters are presented in their original, uncut form, and the original audio of the interviews are available at my website. I encourage you to listen to them for yourselves.

—Adam Jakes

INTERVIEW 1: JESSICA LANDIS

FantasticLand Historian, Author of *Fun Is Guaranteed! An Authorized History of FantasticLand.*

My daughter told me the only time she ever heard me swear was when I was watching the media coverage of the FantasticLand situation. I told her it was the last time I remember really doing it, too, because nothing, excuse me, nothing pisses off a historian more than seeing context thrown out the window because people were too lazy to ask questions. Also, if they're too stupid to know to ask those questions to provide that context in the first place, that's just as bad. Either way, when you look at it, the novelty of this whole thing is that it happened at FantasticLand, but the history is the key. In order to put the whole "tribes" thing in any sort of context, you have to start with Johnny Fresno and the way he did things, and to my mind, nobody in the media bothered to do that.

That wasn't his real name, obviously, but a persona he created. You could tell just by looking at him and by his posture that he thought a lot of himself and his place in the world. He was a short man, but he had a strut, for lack of a better term. After talking with Johnny for a few minutes, it was clear that he had the ego, but he could back it up. He was creative, he was enthusiastic, and he was fun. He was every inch the legend, never a disappointment. He was born Mohammad Assad Kassab, and he grew up in several locations across the Middle East. He was privately educated, as his father moved their family around while working in the oil business. Fresno, he insisted on being called Fresno. He never told anyone exactly what his father did and there aren't great records on the guy, but we do know the Kassab family was known to have lived in Egypt, Lebanon, and Saudi Arabia for the first eight years of Johnny's life, then Canada, and finally the United States.

All of his family freely admit that little Mohammad was the black sheep from the get-go. He was the youngest of four brothers and the only one not to follow their father into the oil business or to choose a career in the military. The father, Youssef, ran a very strict household and didn't let the boys consume a lot of media. Mohammad didn't see his first movie until he was eight, but well before that it was pretty clear he was going to go a different direction than the rest of his family. His mother used to call him "my little dreamer," while his father didn't know how to relate to him at all. That meant a lot of yelling and the occasional beating when Mohammad would spend all his time writing or drawing instead of more masculine pursuits.

So imagine this situation. You've got a strong, rich man; his sophisticated jewel of a wife; three older brothers who were built like tanks and whose lives were dedicated to impressing their father; and then you had Mohammad in the corner, playing with dolls he made out of grass and twigs. He was creative in the least fertile environment you can think of for an artist, but what that upbringing accomplished was to make him single-minded and absolutely sure in his vision. When he latched onto something, he didn't waver until he was done with it. He obviously inherited his father's sense of pride in his work and his sense of indomitability. He barely got in to UCLA, as he wasn't a great student, but the second he left the front stoop of his parents' home he ceased thinking of himself as Mohammad Assad Kassab and started living his life as Johnny Fresno.

I asked him about it before he died. Where did that name come from? It's patently ridiculous. It's phony as a three-dollar bill, and I don't want to traffic in stereotypes, but he was obviously of Middle Eastern descent, his accent would come and go, and there aren't a lot of Fresnos in Jordan or Syria. When you say "Johnny Fresno" I immediately conjure up a blonde surfer type from North Beach, but when I posed the question to him, he answered matter-of-factly, "That's who I am." No "I met this girl in Fresno" or "I thought it would appeal to Middle

America." He said he was more Johnny Fresno than he was Mohammad Assad Kassab. In a strange way, you can't argue with that logic.

I might be making him out to be a tortured genius type, but he was not an unpleasant guy—just the opposite. He was often described with words like "generous" and "kind." We also don't know exactly how much of what Johnny Fresno said was—to put it diplomatically—bullshit, because the guy was first and foremost a talker. That was his skill. When you look at recent historical figures, the main challenge is to figure out what they were good at. Steve Jobs, for example, was the guy who took the foreign language of technology and made it look and act like "the future" in a way everyone could understand, but by all accounts, he was awful to work for. Fresno was the opposite. He would make you feel brilliant, and his employees would take a bullet for him. But for every great idea he had, and he had a few, he had twenty terrible ideas, and if you weren't careful, he'd start insisting on implementing those bad ideas. That's where Ollie Tracks came in.

Tracks was the CFO of FantasticFun Inc. and one of three people in the world who could tell Johnny what was what, the others being his mother and his wife, Cassie. When Johnny Fresno said, "I want to build a giant fantasy land in the middle of New York City," Trolly—that's what everyone called him—he steered Fresno to toward cheaper land. When Johnny said, "I want to build in Disney World's backyard," Trolly got him to move it a couple hundred miles away. When Johnny said, "I want an actual street made of gold," Ollie was the one who pointed out that it would cost more money than the GDP of most countries and everyone would try to steal it. They eventually settled on that thin line of gold in the street that goes from the gates to the center of the park. It's all encased in plexiglass, but everyone still feels special walking the "Golden Road."

But every now and then there was something Trolly couldn't talk Johnny Fresno out of, and this, this one thing, is what you need to understand when you look at what those kids did to each other. Johnny Fresno said he had a dream where he was in a restaurant in the clouds where he could look one way and see nothing but trees and another way and see nothing but the ocean. By now, it was 1971 and Disney World had just opened and they needed to make a decision about where to build the park. The media at that point was starting to speculate that two giant theme parks couldn't exist in the same state. Johnny was desperate to make sure FantasticLand stood out, that it had some sort of identity. Then he had this dream. A month later they broke ground on a site between Daytona Beach and the Lake George Conservation Area near Seville, not far from the beach and not far from the trees. A year to the day after they broke ground, Fresno was sitting on the top of the Point Café, eighty stories up. There's this great video where he looks at the trees, then turns and can see the ocean way off in the distance and he says, "It's not as good as I imagined, but it will do."

Tracks was livid about it. Just livid. There were meetings where the two men threw things at each other. Tracks even had to go to the hospital when Johnny got in a particularly good shot with a glass tumbler to his temple and Tracks needed a few stitches. One secretary got so fed up with listening to them fight about where to put FantasticLand that she transcribed one of the arguments where they were screaming at each other and circulated it around the offices. It soon became a pre-Internet version of a meme.

Author's note: Here is the transcript she is referring to, emphasis in the original document:

FRESNO. IF YOU COULD ONLY SEE WHAT I SEE!!
TRACKS. Please, listen to me . . .
FRESNO. THE OCEAN! They HAVE to SEE THE OCEAN!
TRACKS. YOU have to see this is FINANCIALLY IMPOSSIBLE!
FRESNO. That's why IT'S A DREAM, TROLLY! If we can build the dream, everything else will work out!
TRACKS. If we build this, you won't have a company, Johnny. You'll have nothing but rusted roller coasters and soggy corn dogs.
FRESNO. FUCK YOU FOR PISSING ON MY DREAM!

[Loud crash, muffled grunts]

TRACKS. Goddammit, you bit me!
FRESNO. AAAAAAAHHH!

Some of the staff made T-shirts that year that said FUCK YOU FOR PISSING ON MY DREAM. My kids can't stand it when I tell that story *[laughing]*. It kind of became the unofficial slogan of the FantasticLand senior staff to this day, so I hear. But, in the end, Johnny got his way and they built the thing not far from the ocean over the objections of Tracks and the shareholders.

Remember, this was before climate change was understood and before we knew that the oceans were going to rise. Tracks knew that there would be storms because there are always storms, and that one of them would be huge and would barrel through and likely do some significant damage to the park. The market bore him out on this, too, because insuring a nearly billion-dollar project a few dozen miles away from the coast was almost as bad, in his mind, as building a golden road at the entrance to the park. But on some things, Johnny Fresno could not be moved, and in the end, well, before all this happened, it looked like his gamble had paid off. Before all this happened, the privately held FantasticLand Inc. was worth well over two billion dollars, most of which went right to Johnny Fresno.

I mean, you know this as well as I do. FantasticLand is a blow-for-blow competitor with Disney and Universal. Each one of them does something unique. Universal has Harry Potter, Disney is . . . well, Disney, and FantasticLand has the immersion factor. The different FantasticLand worlds are truly different, and everyone from the planners to the snow cone salesman thinks of absolutely everything. The food is different, the music is different, and they even pipe in different smells for each location, like seawater for the Pirate Cove and cotton candy for the Fairy Prairie. Turns out there was not only room for three theme parks, but each one would challenge the others and force them to innovate. And they would share some of the audience. I don't need to tell you about the tens of millions of people and hundreds of billions of dollars the theme park industry brings in.

The difference is, Universal and Disney had the good sense to build away from the ocean. FantasticLand did not.

Part of the reason why each section of the park was so different was due to the plan that Tracks put into place after that famous yelling incident. He totally shifted gears away from convincing Fresno to change his fool mind to focusing on safety and infrastructure. He ended up spending more on levies and emergency preparedness than he ever would have on insurance for a mammoth semi-coastal theme park. People thought he was too obsessive. The park was near Daytona Beach, which hadn't taken a direct hit from a hurricane in fifty years. The thing is, they were absolutely right. He was obsessed. Tracks brought in experts and then went to other countries and brought in their experts, and then he went and found the intellectual enemies of those experts and brought them in. It reached such obsessive levels that the elaborate network of tunnels under the park doubled as bomb shelters that could withstand a ten-megaton explosion. The emergency plans were just as elaborate, some running seven hundred pages. I vividly remember a photo of one of those huge binders labeled DISASTER PLAN FOR THE FAIRY PRAIRIE floating in the water after the front gate flooded.

Fresno let Tracks plan and overplan and redo the plans, basically without limit or, really, supervision. Fresno told me once that "it made a valued member of my team feel like he was prepared. Who was I to deny him that?" See what I mean, that he could make you feel important? So these plans existed, and the park was a big success when it first opened, and little by little the emphasis on disaster preparedness started to fade away as management changed. Then, of course, Tracks died in September of 1999, and Fresno died in 2001, and his son, Ritchie, took over. These safety plans were in place, and they were as much a part of the park as the beams that held the giant Exclamation Point logo in the center of town, and upper management let them be. My impression, and that's all it is, is that they thought they had safety covered and didn't feel the need to update or train people on what was, in essence, the most sophisticated disaster manual ever created by a private company. If you have something like that in your pocket, it's easy to see it as an asset as opposed to a living document that had to be refreshed from time to time.

OK, the different worlds. As you know, FantasticLand is set up in six distinct areas, the first being the Golden Road when you first enter the park. It's full up with shops and info stations and topiaries and whatnot. Then there's the Fairy Prairie, which is for children six and under, Fantastic Future World, the World's Circus, the Hero Haven, and the Pirate Cove. Then there are the many parts of the park that aren't open to the public, like the tunnels that run under the park for maintenance and janitorial and the multiple offices and work spaces that were hidden away behind the facades in many of these places. The offices where executives worked were divided by the themed lands as well. Operations were along Golden Street, Park Development was in the World's Circus, HR was in the Fairy Prairie, which was a constant source of ridicule and bad feelings, and Marketing was in the Pirate Cove. The point of Trolly's disaster plan as it stood when he died was that everyone, from the janitor in the tunnel, to the executive behind the facades, to the actors working in the rides, would follow the same plan, and that plan happened to be one of the most comprehensive and thick and, in many ways, impenetrable documents I've ever come across. There was no easy way to look up what you were supposed to do if your officc was filling up with water. And it never got updated. Add Ritchie's lack of focus on disaster planning, and that's a recipe for something bad happening.

When my daughter caught me screaming at the TV, what I was screaming about was the overall tone of the news coverage. People seemed to think this was some sort of metaphor, that "the veneer of American happiness has been stripped away," and that young adults murdering each other in terrible ways was what was truly underneath. I have sworn more in this interview than I have in the past three months, I promise you, but that analysis is pure bullshit. It just doesn't wash. Given the history I've laid out, let me give you some analysis, OK? There are three major reasons why the "tribe" thing happened and got so out of hand and so violent so quickly.

First and foremost, these six parts of the park, the Circus and the Fairies and the Pirates and all of that, they all existed in very distinct geographical, tactical, and operational sections of the park. The Pirate Cove is not like the World's Circus is not like the Golden Road, is what

I'm getting at. The cultures are different, the landscape is different, the tools they use are different, and the clientele is different. Hell, the smells are different. The employees, they all carried around devices, they were smartphones, basically, that told them everything they needed to know for the day and that they used to communicate with each other, and even those devices—RADs, they called them—were only coded to certain sections. It was like that on purpose. Johnny Fresno wanted a unique feeling for each location, and he wanted visitors to feel like they'd been to four or five different parks in a day, when really it was one big park. He accomplished that and people worked like that. Please try and hold that in your head when considering points two and three.

Point two—I just got done telling you that each section was different, but the disaster guide was kind of a mess in terms of what was section-specific and what was mandatory for the entire park. Parts of the disaster response were a mess inside the park, but there was fresh water and food and medical supplies for everyone who was not evacuated. There was plenty to go around. This might sound counterintuitive. If there was plenty for everyone, why did they start fighting? They weren't starving; they had enough water, right? The way I see it, if you come up to someone and say, "I'm thirsty and you have plenty of water. Can I please have a drink?" most people are going to be a human being and share. If it was a personal thing, if Susie from the gift shop came to you and said "please," then Susie is likely not going to be shot with an arrow or strung up in the center of the park. But everyone had enough and they were staring across the park at five different groups who could potentially come and take what they had. Instead of needing to coexist to survive, the disaster plan Ollie Tracks had put in place twenty years before bred contempt and paranoia. Basically, you had six little groups who felt like they were Israel, beset on all sides by those who wanted their extermination.

Which brings me to the most obvious but least talked about reason why so many people died in FantasticLand. They were kids. They were scared kids. Some of them had never been away from home for more than a few weeks. These were the kids that would complain when they don't have Wi-Fi and couldn't get on Facebook. What do you think happens when it's suddenly life or death? People want to make this out to be a great American failing, but try this experiment: Take one hundred kids from that age group from any country, separate them on islands, give them the cocktail of constant affirmation and stimulation these kids were getting pumped through their brains, and one hundred times out of one hundred you have bloodshed. I guarantee it. Put yourself in the shoes of any of these kids, with their peers yelling "kill or be killed" in their ear, coaxing them, begging them to swing that sword or shoot that arrow or . . . or stab that other kid tied up and . . . sorry. I'm sorry. Those images that came out of that park, I don't want to admit it, but they got to me. FantasticLand was a place of dreams, and to see it in disrepair was bad enough, but to see the big Exclamation Point destroyed and the faces of dead . . . of dead employees . . .

Did you ever go to FantasticLand? You should have been there with a kid. They see the line of gold in the street, and their eyes go to that giant Exclamation Point, bigger than you imagined for all those weeks, and then you decide where to go first and you get there, and *that* is better than you imagined. It was special. It inspired awe. Johnny Fresno was a talker, and on some level a huckster, but he built something magnificent. And that magnificent view, from the rotating tower? You could see the ocean. Clear as day.

[Laughing] And then you go home and your daughter hears you swearing at the TV.

INTERVIEW 2: MIRANDA TOTS

Former director of the Palm Beach–Treasure Cove Region of the American Red Cross.

Hurricane Sadie was the first hurricane to hit the Daytona Beach area since 1960. Let me get that out of the way up front. Most hurricanes are going to make landfall around the Miami or Key West area, and when you have limited resources, that's where you concentrate your preventative efforts. That's where you set up shop. Up until last fall, there seemed little to no point in putting manpower and resources in the Daytona Beach area. This was the major issue with the response. When you're guarding your head, you don't expect a blow to the breadbasket.

The other issue was that no one, not in their wildest dreams, expected a storm anything like Hurricane Sadie. The laws of how hurricanes are supposed to behave seemed to no longer apply. The basic protocol for even the most severe hurricane is to evacuate everyone within ten miles of the coast where the storm is going to make landfall. That's the worst-case scenario any human being has ever seen. Get everyone ten miles away from the coast, and then you just have 150-mile-per-hour winds to deal with. But when they were tracking the storm, immediately things started to look . . . "wonky" was the term we used around the office. Everything was happening faster than normal. Development off the coast that should have taken a day took nine hours, and before we knew what had happened, the storm had strengthened, and then it just kept getting stronger as we watched. We'd never seen anything like it, and by the time we realized what was going to happen, it was too late to reposition resources. All we could do was warn people and try to get as much information to the public as possible.

What did it feel like? I asked one of the forecasters from NOAA about it. I'm not going to give you his name, but I asked him something like "how did we not see this coming?" and he told me that what he was feeling must have been similar to what the CIA agents responsible for keeping tabs on bin Laden felt on 9/11. He said it was a combination of intense regret that he hadn't done more to figure it out and dread because, at that point, we knew it was coming and we knew it was too late to properly prepare. We were sitting there before the storm was even visible from the coast, and we knew this was going to be one of the worst disasters we'd ever seen. We knew the storm would kill people, and because of my job, I knew that the aftermath was probably going to kill more people than the storm. I was right.

But, like I was saying, ten miles. That was the protocol. Turns out with the waves and the infrastructure not up to the task and the way the storm was pounding Florida so far north, ten miles wasn't even close to adequate. Buildings fifteen miles away were blowing apart and we could only watch as the amount of rain went up and up and up, ten inches, twelve inches, fifteen inches. I can tell you now, at the height of the thing, I was on the phone to the Navy, and I told them, only half joking, that they might be able to find boating lanes all the way to Orlando. I could go on, but I don't like reliving it, to be honest. Besides, you're interested in Daytona Beach and FantasticLand, right? OK. Let me start with the hurricane, because some people don't understand what caused these conditions in the first place.

Hurricanes are rated on a scale from 1 to 5, 5 being the most severe. A level 5 hurricane hits you with 150- to 180-mile-per-hour winds if you are in its path. With Sadie, we saw winds that high seventy-five miles inland, which is rare. What 150-mile-per-hour winds do, effectively, is blow small buildings off their foundations and rip off the roofs of larger buildings. You would expect to see tons of roof damage for a storm like this, and what we were seeing was less roof damage and more roof removal. If someone was out in something like that, they would certainly be lifted off their feet and thrown into the nearest solid object.

If you hadn't taken shelter, you would certainly be injured or killed, and we saw our fair share of that.

Anyone who's had to respond to a hurricane will tell you the absolute worst moment isn't huddling in a bathtub hoping your siding isn't in Louisiana. It's the moment after the storm dies and you walk outside and realize you need help. Most Americans aren't too happy asking for help, to be honest with you. It's part of our national character. I used to run a Red Cross chapter in Iowa, and we had to deal with tornadoes. You'd think it would be a straightforward idea—the tornado hits; some houses are damaged; you feed, house, and provide resources for those affected. As it turns out, there is no point opening shelters after a tornado. The folks who lost their homes, they are too proud to sleep in a gym or a church. They'll come in for a drink and a meal and to cool off or warm up, but they will not stay in a shelter. It's not part of the character there.

I'm on a tangent. What was I talking about? That moment, right. That moment when you come out of your house, you are alive, but you realize your house isn't structurally sound and you have no electricity or water and there's nothing you can immediately do about it. The absence of self-determination is a terrifying prospect for most people, and then coupled with the lack of preparation many of these people had, it was a bad situation. Some of those affected by the storm were more than unprepared. They were dumbstruck. We saw that particularly in more affluent neighborhoods. Some of them had generators, but not one of them had thought about water, you know? I ran across more than one family who had a generator but had never turned it on or they didn't have gas for it. "Unprepared" is an understatement, but I'm digressing again.

In that moment, when you realize you need help, that's when we're supposed to fulfill our main purpose: to be there with that help. And we were ready to help . . . in Miami and Key West, even with two feet of water on the roads. We were fine there. But up north, we knew we were in trouble. That moment of silence after the storm was a bad moment for a lot of people, but I think it was the worst for me and my volunteers. We realized we were out of position and that hell might break loose before we got there. Some locations weren't nearly as bad as we were worried about. People were civil and were helping each other. The weak got help first. It was the best of America. Then you'd go to the next location and it would be out-and-out looting and every man for himself.

No, I don't want to talk about those three nursing homes that made the news. Not at all.

FantasticLand was an interesting case from a number of perspectives. We knew, from dealings with the company going all the way back to the 1980s, that they kept ample water, rations, medicine, and other survival gear at multiple locations around the park as well as an internal communications system to communicate with their employees. The idea, as it was relayed to me, was that they could survive for a couple of days of being cut off from all civilization with a park full of people. I was able to speak with some of their board members a couple weeks after Sadie hit, and I was assured that they were staffed with something like three hundred employees and that those employees would be able to stay alive for another month if they needed to. I know this point is in dispute, but I have the conversation on the record, so I don't think I'm telling you anything you don't know or haven't heard for yourself. I was also assured that all the visitors had been transported inland and that we were dealing primarily with employees. At one point, the board member raised the issue of his visitors' luggage, which was way, way down the list of relevant topics. I don't want to make this sound like he didn't care about his employees. He clearly did from an administrative and personal standpoint, but in disasters, people react differently. It's not uncommon for people to focus on one thing they can control amid a sea of chaos and hyperfocus on that one thing. If you ask my opinion as someone who's worked in disaster preparedness and response for three decades, I think he was scared and didn't want to think that his employees would be in any danger. Of course they were in danger. We all were.

What this conversation with representatives from FantasticLand did right away was bump FantasticLand way down the list in terms of which locations we were going to tackle and in what order. When you have five thousand locations in need of assistance, it only made sense that FantasticLand cede its place in line to more immediate concerns, and trust me, we had more immediate concerns. We had a million people homeless. We had over ten million people without power. We had rescue efforts and aid distribution and truckloads of unwanted aid to deal with. Volunteers flooded in faster than we could assign them duties. FantasticLand had water and food and relative safety for three hundred employees. We knew they were there, and we were going to get them. It was just going to take some time.

The other aspect of FantasticLand that made it an interesting case was the way the park was set up. It's one huge, several-thousand-acre park divided into different sections, but topographically, it's on a decent piece of land as far as flooding is concerned. It wasn't going to flood easily, is what I mean. Also, Mr. Tracks, I believe his name was, had built detention cells around a few areas, the thinking being that they would either prevent flooding altogether or lessen the effect, which they certainly did. That was another reason we put FantasticLand behind other locations where people were drowning and fighting over resources.

What we didn't account for, and what no one could have accounted for, was that the rain kept coming. After Sadie finally blew herself out, we could not catch a break for weeks. September is the wet season in that part of the state anyway—well, one of the wet seasons—but that year it was beyond what we expected. Some locations around Daytona received up to twenty-four inches of rain in the three weeks after Sadie, which had a very negative effect on rescue efforts.

We don't deny that a lot of people died, but when you only have so many boots on the ground and only so much air support and more places to evacuate than you ever have in the history of your organization, and you get two feet of rain on top of that, everything is not going to go as planned. What you must understand about the world of disaster response is you do the most good you can with the full understanding that you can't get to everyone quickly and that, because this is a disaster, people are going to die. Now that I'm no longer in a leadership role with the Red Cross, I can also point out that consolidations led to less volunteer training and fewer hands to work with in my particular case, but to be fair, we wouldn't have had enough hands if we had suddenly found ourselves at double our funding levels. It was a massive, massive undertaking, and we started from behind. Then, like any disaster, managing the people who want to help becomes a big job. We had busloads of Boy Scouts and mission groups show up every day and we had to tell them, "It's not safe here. Turn around." We were going through neighborhood by neighborhood, and some of them were a completely inappropriate environment for volunteers. I remember one day a semitruck full of stuffed animals showed up. Everyone had a million things to do and all of a sudden we had tens of thousands of stuffed animals to deal with. The families who could maybe use them had no place to put them. Everyone wants to help, but oh man, when that truckload of stuffed animals showed up I was about ready to kill someone. We ended up dumping them in a detention cell and commandeering the truck to ship supplies. I remember shots of the thousands of stuffed animals floating in filthy water showing up on the news.

I'm sorry; I keep veering from the subject. We first approached FantasticLand on September 29 from the air. We had surveillance planes in the sky hours after the storm broke, and again, FantasticLand was an interesting case. We could see the front had flooded, and we could see the swamp-like conditions all the way around the park, but we could also see most of the park was dry and there were no obvious signs of distress from the survivors that we could see. All the buildings seemed structurally intact and there were no bed sheets with Help Us messages hanging from windows like there were in many other communities. That was uncommon at that point in the relief effort.

When we flew over on the twenty-ninth, we did not see the yardarm, and the bodies hanging and had received no outward cries for help, so we bumped FantasticLand down the level of priorities. It's quite simple. When you have places screaming for help and news helicopters flying over and getting hours and hours and hours of footage of the job you're not doing, it becomes very easy to let lower priorities slide down the list. We stopped flying by FantasticLand, and with the help of their management we made plans to get to them after we had taken care of business in several nearby townships. The risk certainly was there that things could degenerate, but—and I hate to sound callous—we simply did not have the resources to worry about that. If things were going to go bad in FantasticLand, and they obviously did, we were not in a position to provide aid.

When the large Exclamation Point at the center of the park fell, I was alerted to it, and it did seem strange. I passed the information along to the command center and urged someone in the office to contact FantasticLand again to see if they had any information we didn't have. We never heard back. By that point, FantasticLand had its own internal problems, and it was hard to figure out who was in charge. Yes, the fact that nobody could tell who was in charge meant that FantasticLand was left to sit, and that's probably part of the reason it wasn't breached until October 20, with the National Guard going in guns drawn, as they had every right to. Then the media showed up, and heads started to roll.

I'm sorry. That was in terrible taste. I wish I hadn't said that.

Yes, Mr. Fresno was as helpful as he could be. Mainly, he was in shock.

I will not comment on what happened inside the park. I don't know what went on there, and I don't care to know. I had spent thirty-five days before this FantasticLand situation dealing with one of the worst natural disasters mankind had ever had to deal with, using tools that were invented on the spot because nobody thought anything like this was possible. I understand why you're focusing on this, Mr. Jakes. It's sensational, and it's amazing, and it speaks to the human capacity for evil. I would just beg you, after you're done with this glitzy story, go out and talk to other people who survived Sadie. You'll find just the opposite of what you'll find here. You'll find so many stories of people who worked and worked to help their fellow man until they literally collapsed, people who went without a drink for days to give their water to dying babies. You will find heroism and horror in equal measure that will put this story of well-off kids killing each other to shame, sir. You will find stories like you wouldn't believe.

I have enough stories of my own to last a lifetime.

INTERVIEW 3: AARON HOFFMAN

Husband of Suzanne, father of Kendall and Keinan. Evacuated from FantasticLand as Hurricane Sadie hit.

At first, the toughest part of our trip to FantasticLand was just figuring out where to go.

Kendall—he's seven—was desperate to go to the Pirate Cove first, while Keinan, she was all about the Fairy Prairie. When you first go into the park, you cut right from the Exclamation Point, and you find the Fairies. Left for the Pirates. Suzanne was all like "you kids settle it," but of course they weren't going to settle it. They just screamed "Fairies" and "Pirates" at each other until I finally said, "Neither of you are getting your way. We're going to the robots first," and then they cried, and my wife shot me a "you're an asshole" look. I didn't see her coming up with a better idea.

We'd been saving up for a couple months to go. We didn't want to go in the summer when it was so damn hot and when there's a million freakin' people. Suzanne's dad, Carl, he had taken Suzanne and her sisters there, like, six times, and she had been on me since Kendall was five, wanting us to go. It was always a money thing. FantasticLand is cheaper than Disney, that's for sure, but I can think of a couple hundred better ways to spend $3,500. She said I could golf twice, that's why we decided to eventually go. That and the kids wanted to.

So we get there, and everything you see is "Isn't it great to be in FantasticLand!" It's really over the top. They've got three huge hotels, the most expensive one is right next to the park, and there are signs all over the place that are like HAPPINESS IS OUR JOB or something like that. We get to the hotel, and Suzanne is thrilled and I'm a little more reserved. I was like, prove it to me if you're so great. The room was nothing to write home about. I mean, it was clean, and there was a pull-out couch for the kids so we could have our privacy. It was also a five-minute tram ride to the park, but for what we were paying, I don't know. I expected a big breakfast or something. But there are fairies on the walls and immediately Kendall wants a room with pirates, so we call to the front desk and the best they can do is a pirate pillow. That made him happy for a minute before he lost his mind again.

We were going to be there for a week and we left home on the twelfth. I didn't want to fly on September 11. Who the hell would? It's stupid, if you ask me. So we get there on the twelfth and we spend the first night in the pool. You've got an entire theme park five minutes outside your door, we pull up at 6:45, and the kids want to swim. I was all for going downstairs, but Suzanne was like, "Let them swim, we'll hit it tomorrow." I told her, "We're paying to go to FantasticLand, let's *go* to FantasticLand." I mean, we can swim at home. They do swim at home, all the damn time. What's the point of traveling halfway across the damn country to swim in a pool? Let's go to the park, right? Good thing the hotel had a bar with Heineken on tap, you know what I'm saying.

I have to hand it to them, the park really was something. Suzanne read a blog that had all this insider info on it, and what they tell you to do is follow the Golden Road to the big red Exclamation Point and then you can go right to the Fairies, right and up to the Future World place, straight for the Big Carnival place, left and up for the Super Hero part, and straight left for the Pirates. I like that because it's simple. You can see the Exclamation Point from anywhere in the park, so you always know about where you are. It's a good system, and they really did think of everything. We only got lost one time and had to ask an employee about where we were, and he pulled out this interactive phone-looking thing and showed us exactly where we were. It was pretty cool. Then there are these arches in each place that tell you where you are, and the second you're on the other side of the arches, the whole thing changes. My favorite was when you hit the Pirate Cove, you could immediately hear the ocean. I don't know how they did it, but a cool breeze hit your face, and you heard the ocean, like I said, and there was music and dancing girls, and it was just great.

But of course the kids were still fighting about what land to go to first. Kendall didn't want to go to the Fairy Land or whatever you call it at all, and he wouldn't let it go. He was too old to be such a brat about it so the whole time we're in Future Land, he was teasing Keinan, saying "We're going to Pirates next" and "I'm going to buy a sword and stab you," and then she'd cry. I told him if he kept it up, I'd give him a swat on the behind, and we'd do the Pirates last. That worked, but he sulked all the way through Future Land. The only time he really loosened up was when we went on that ride where you shoot aliens. Have you been on that one? It's kind of great because they use a lot of black lights so when the stuff pops out at you, it comes out of nowhere. It scared the hell out of Keinan, but Kendall was yelling and shooting and just loving it. He beat my score on that ride.

So we did the Future World, and we did the Circus, which was actually kind of good, and we did the Super Hero Land and we got a lot of great pictures there. Two of the heroes actually picked Keinan up and she was laughing like I hadn't heard her laugh before. We left that place in a good mood and then it was dinnertime, so we decided to leave for one of our scheduled fancy dinners and then go back to the hotel and finish with the superheroes in the morning. Suzanne was making a map of places we missed so we could double back later on. That was a good plan, but then dinner didn't go as well that night. We had booked it in this restaurant in the carnival part where there were actual trapeze artists doing their thing overhead as you ate. It was cool, but the kids got distracted and didn't eat their dinner. I was paying for this big fancy dinner with farm-raised chicken and, like, grapes that grow in only one part of the Himalayas or something, and they were watching women in spandex do flips over their head. Do both, you know? The food was great but we got frustrated really fast.

At that point, there was no mention of the weather at the park or on my phone or anything. I'm not much of a news guy, but I have this weather app on my phone that alerts you if there's severe weather in the area, but it didn't go off or send me an alert. There was some talk in the park, stuff like "looks like Miami is in for a doozy, huh?" and I would sort of shrug it off. So, when the kids finally fell asleep, I did turn on the Weather Channel and watched a bit about Hurricane Sadie. They said, basically, don't mess around with this storm, and I took it serious enough, but it didn't look like it was going to go near us. Besides, if we got some rain, big deal. We'd have fun and get wet. It'd become a family legend, you know? It would blow over by the time our plane left on the seventeenth, and we'd be home before we had to worry about it. That's what I was thinking.

The morning of the fourteenth, it's already cloudy and a little colder, which is fine. We brought jackets. But the kids were still complaining about which park to go to, Pirates or Fairies. We pick back up in Super Hero World, and there weren't too many people there. Apparently it takes a couple hours to get going, so we ride some of the rides, one of which really freaked out Keinan, and then we had to make the decision. Pirates or Fairies. And they were still at each other about it. Keinan would start crying, and Kendall would scream, "*We're going to see the Pirates,*" and Keinan would cry more, and they wouldn't listen to any sort of plan about it. Finally, we decided to flip a coin. The kids didn't want to do that, but I was sick of it, and there wasn't any other option as far as I could tell other than straight up leaving the park, and it wasn't even lunchtime yet. So we flipped a coin, and it came up Pirates, which was probably for the best because Keinan screamed and cried, but two minutes past the Pirate gate she was having fun. Little kids are good like that. They tend not to hold grudges. Kendall, he would have carried that grudge past his high school graduation.

We spent the rest of the day doing Pirate Land and go home happy. We tell Keinan tomorrow is the Fairies, and she is all smiles before she goes to sleep. Kendall was decked out in a hat and a sword, and we got this photo at the Grog Pit where he was surrounded by seven guys dressed head to toe in these great pirate outfits. He slept with a sword that was plastic, but it was kind of sharp. He slept with that. Suzanne and I had some alone time, and we got to sleep about 10:30, which isn't too bad. Then, at four o'clock in the damn morning, we hear our hotel phone blaring like an alarm. At first, we have no idea what's going on, and we couldn't make it stop. It just kept blasting this really irritating sound. It's the kind of thing that makes your stomach drop because you don't hear that tone unless someone is dead serious. I had that thing happen where, when I first heard it, I was so disoriented that panic set in for a second, and once you figure out what's going on you have to deal with your heart pounding so fast that you feel like you're going to pass out. At one point, Suzanne stuck her head out in the hall and the same alarm with the same tone was blaring. The kids were crying at this point. Suzanne was, too. Then, after about two minutes, it stopped.

That silence, man. That silence was something. It was . . . deep. That's the best word I can come up with. No one in my room said anything, no one in the other rooms was saying anything. It was just dead. After having that alarm blare for however long, everyone was listening hard to hear what came next. Then we hear this clicking noise, and the manager of the hotel starts talking through the speakers of every phone in the place and through the intercom.

Author's note: Here is the transcript of Mighty Maiden General Manager Matt Krenk's words to the hotel in the early morning of September 15, as verified by multiple sources.

> "Hello, guests of the Mighty Maiden, FantasticLand's premier family resort. I am Matt Krenk, the general manager of the hotel. The alarm you just heard was a test we are required to run by park security. As you likely know, Hurricane Sadie is off the coast of Miami right now, and we are required to test this alarm in case she takes a turn in our direction, which is very unlikely. We apologize for waking most of you. We will be providing our free 'Fantastic Breakfast' as a way of making it up to you—it can be redeemed starting at 6:00 a.m. Again, we are sorry to have disturbed you and hope you enjoy your time at FantasticLand, the place where fun is guaranteed."

At least I got my free breakfast.

I had turned my phone off because sometimes it boops and beeps at me in the middle of the night, even if I set it to silent, and the weather app is throwing alert after alert at me. I turn on the TV, and the stations are all on the same channel and it's this woman going on about the hurricane. That's enough to put Suzanne into a fit. She's saying things like, "We've got to get out of here" and "This isn't worth dying over," and . . . that . . . that made me mad. I'm not going to lie, I was seeing red. We had such a good time the day before. Seriously, I was never 100 percent onboard with this trip, but that last day in the Pirate section, that's everything I had wanted. The kids were happy, Suzanne was so happy she ate an ice cream bar. I haven't seen her eat ice cream since Keinan's birthday last year. She and I were holding hands, and the kids were laughing. I guess I didn't think it was going to be like that. So I may have put down a "my way or the highway" sort of attitude. I told her, "We paid for this, and the kids had such a good time, and we're so far north this thing isn't going to hit us," and I really laid it on thick. I convinced her, in the middle of the night, 1,500 miles away from home, to at least wait until the free breakfast and see how things looked then. Turns out, most of the hotel decided to get the hell out of Dodge after that first alarm. We . . . we should have done that. It would have saved us a lot of trouble.

There were about one hundred people there for breakfast, and I think seating was something like 350. It was awesome food, I've got to hand it to them. I don't think I had a bad meal while the park was running. The sausage was just spicy enough, and the eggs were fluffy; it was a good breakfast. That guy on the intercom, he was there making sure everyone was OK. When he came to our table, he asked Keinan if she was going to see the fairies today. She was wearing a T-shirt that said Believe in Fairies, so he zeroed in on that. Suzanne asked if the park was still open today because of the hurricane, and he said, "Oh yeah, it's open. If they haven't told us it's closed, it's going full steam, and we have the best weathermen in the country" and this and that and the other. That was enough for her, but I noticed the whole time his phone was beeping and throwing alerts at him, just like mine was. I wish I could tell you I had a bad feeling in my stomach or something, but I really didn't. I wanted to get into the park. It just made sense. We had spent all that money to get there.

We finished our breakfast and went and got on the buses that take you to the park, and right off the bat there's not a lot of traffic going into the park. There's a ton going away from it but not a lot going toward it, which was the opposite of the day before. Suzanne looked nervous, so I got on my phone and was going to show her what the weather was doing when I saw which way the storms were headed. The night before it had been threatening to hit Palm and Martin counties, but the alerts were getting further north and further inland, and soon they were putting notices that Okeechobee and Cecelia counties were in the path of this thing. The kids, they didn't notice, but I went up to the driver to show him my phone, and he was very concerned, too. He said we were going to pull up to the gates, and if there were instructions, we'd get them there. It's a twenty-minute ride to the front gates of FantasticLand, and in that twenty minutes, things had gone from "it might get bad" to "it's going to get bad." The clouds were dark, and the wind picked up, and Suzanne and I were ready to get on the nearest bus the hell out of Florida.

Once we pull up, there's a crowd of people waiting to get on the bus. There are some employees and some early birds and some maintenance folks. It was all kinds. The word had gone out: we're going to get hit, we're closing the park. Get out if you can. There was a woman there in a security outfit reading off who had a spot on the bus and who had to wait for the next one. She had this big, booming voice and was yelling, "If you need medication, if you are over sixty years old, if your family has already evacuated" and stuff like that. No one was listening. Every square inch of that bus was prime real estate at that point. The bus driver throws open the doors and I hear Suzanne yell "*Kendall*" and he's off the bus a split second before all the people desperate to get on start pushing their way in. I see him get knocked down and at that point instinct took over. I look at Suzanne and I say, "I've got him," and I go into beast mode. I'm pushing and shoving and using my legs to pry people apart. I take an elbow to the eye, and I swear someone grabbed my stomach and just twisted as hard as they could. I had a bruise, and it looks more like a kick, but it felt like someone was twisting my skin, but I didn't care. I got in a few good shots, too. I used to play sports in high school so I can dish it out if I need to, but it had been a while. So I fight and I fight, and it takes me a couple minutes to get to him, and when I do, it's already started to rain. So here's me, fighting this crowd trying to get on, and when I find Kendall he's wet and crying and saying, "I want to go see the pirates again," between sobs. I hadn't heard him cry like that since he had night terrors when he was three, just gulping and gulping for air.

Then, out of nowhere, this guy shows up. He's tall, and he's got this weird beard and mustache thing going, and I recognize that he's one of the pirates from yesterday that took his picture with Kendall. I recognize him and he sees me recognize him and he sort of comes up behind and puts his hand on Kendall's shoulder and says, "Ahoy, there, little man," in his pirate voice. Kendall looks up, and it takes him a second but he recognized the guy too, and the pirate says, I'll never forget it, "We've got some rough seas ahead, boy-o. A pirate can be scared, but a pirate don't quit. Got it?" Kendall, God love him, stops crying, or starts crying less, anyway, and says, "A pirate doesn't quit." Then Kendall asks, "Where's your costume?" and the guy, without missing a beat, says, "I had to leave it in Davy Jones' locker," and then he keeps walking to wherever it was he was going, like it wasn't a big thing. But it was a big thing. I don't know who that guy was, but if I ever meet him, I'm going to shake his hand. Hell, I might give him a hug. If I ever meet the guy who allowed buses to go to the park until ten that morning, I'm going to kick him in the fucking nuts.

I quickly text Suzanne because the bus was long gone at that point, and I tell her we're OK and to let me know where she's going so Kendall and I can get there too. Keep in mind, there's this giant wave of people and other folks in security outfits yelling instructions no one can hear over the rain and the wind, which started coming up. I tell Kendall to hang on to me, and we muscle our way to the front where I explain to the lady in the security outfit what happened, and she said, "You're on the next bus. Don't let anyone tell you different," which pissed off some guy a row back who started screaming, "*You fucking bitch,*" at her as loud as he could. I told Kendall to cover his ears and I laid into the guy right back, calling him a selfish asshole, and how dare he swear in front of my kid and that kind of thing. My Irish was already up after fighting my way off the bus, so I wasn't going to hold back. Not with an asshole like that. The security lady kind of smiled at me, which made me feel good and made me feel like we were sure going to get a seat on the bus. Other people from the crowd kind of calmed everything down, and it was OK until the buses showed up. Then I knew we were in trouble.

There was this fleet of buses. I stopped counting at thirty-five. They just kept coming in a straight line. The thing that I noticed was they weren't all, like, luxury coaches. There was every kind of vehicle you can think of that can hold more than eight people. There were big vans and trams, and I think I even saw a limo in there. It was obvious what was happening. It was an evacuation. The sight of all those vehicles calmed everyone right down, and they just started packing on. We got on the next bus, just like the lady said. Kendall was sort of jabbering the whole time, but he was OK and it wasn't until our bus was pulling out that I noticed how many people were behind us. There were thousands of people covering the entire parking lot and going all the way back into the park. The good news was there were thousands of seats. I didn't think, "Oh, there are way too few buses," or anything like that. It seemed to me like everyone was going to get a seat.

Once we get on the road and things calm down a little bit, I realize something. Kendall is singing, and it takes me a minute, but he's singing this song they have in the park about pirates. And he's singing kind of softly and then a little louder and soon it's totally quiet in the bus. It's just the rain hitting the windows and wet people breathing and this kid singing. Then the guy next to us, not the pirate guy that talked to Kendall but another guy, he starts singing too, and since we're on a bus filled mostly with employees and visitors, pretty soon the whole bus was singing. What are the words? It's . . . just a second . . .

Fire off the cannon
Blow my boat to bits
I'll swim with all my might 'cause
A pirate never quits

I use my ruthless cunning
My learnin' and my wits
To be the best companion
'cause a pirate never quits

I was once to be married
My bride, up there she sits
But I ran back to my mateys
'cause a pirate never quits

A pirate gets what he wants
and what he wants he gets
He's dependable and manly
And a pirate never quits

I'm not sentimental, but I'm going to remember that moment as long as I live because it changed the entire mood of the bus. Before we were kind of panicky and tired, you know? Everyone was thinking, "This is an emergency," and I was thinking, "I'm going to do whatever is necessary to get back to Suzanne and Keinan and protect my son," but as soon as he started singing, you could feel the mood get better. Even the driver joined in, and he was getting increasingly bad reports over his radio and his phone. I heard one guy say the road was starting to flood, and his voice was not calm.

But we got out. We got out fine. The buses took us to this conference center about thirty miles west where the rain wasn't so bad. We had no trouble finding Suzanne and Keinan. I told you I'm not sentimental, but man, finding her and holding her again. It's strange, but our marriage has been better since then. I'm less . . . kind of . . . resentful, I guess. We feel stronger. We screw all the time. *[Laughing]* She's going to kill me for saying that.

The problem after we found each other was getting back to Kansas City. We were in a small town, I forget the name, and we didn't have a lot of options. It had a small airport, but any rental car was long gone, so I got the bright idea to find someone who looked respectable and pay them $1,000 to drive us home. Screw our luggage, screw the souvenirs, my kids needed their own beds, and I needed everyone to feel safe again. We found this guy whose name was Paul. He worked on a road construction crew and said they had canceled things for a couple days so he was basically free, so we all pile in to his Windstar and drive straight through. The kids slept most of the way, which was good. We paid for gas, I gave him $1,500 and told him to watch his back. We were asleep in our own beds a few hours later.

From what I hear went down, we were lucky.

INTERVIEW 4: PHIL MUELLER

Head of Park Personnel at FantasticLand.

The first thing I would like you to know is that I very much respect Ritchie Fresno and his company. I worked with some great men and women keeping the park in shape, and we kept it tip-top, I'll tell you. It was one of the hardest jobs I've ever had and one of the most rewarding, which makes the fact that I'm the only one willing to talk to you just a downright shame.

I did know Johnny Fresno, now that you ask. He was a special guy. Ritchie, he's got some of that *pizzazz*, but not the way his old man had it. Johnny Fresno made you feel good and you wanted to please him in return, which is how I ended up working at the park in the first place. I remember, I was a teacher at a community college in Central Florida, had been for about five years at that point, and Johnny showed up out of the clear blue sky one day. No idea he was coming. He comes in and says, "You must be Phil. I'm told you're the guy to talk to around here," and he shook my hand, and by the time we were done talking, he had me convinced to go work for him. I was thinking teaching was a pretty sweet racket and I might sit there until I retired, but in forty-five minutes, he convinced me to stop whatever I was doing and go work at an amusement park with fairies and robots. *[Laughing]* My wife was not pleased when I told her. I introduced her to Johnny, and she came around.

How'd he do it? I guess it was a mix of being very specific about what he wanted me to do and convincing me I was the only one that could do it. I taught construction management at the college, basically how to be a crew chief or head up a large-scale site. I had some experience in that area and had sort of made my money in the business. I took the teaching job because I was good at it, but also because it was more time with the missus. Running a site, it's a mix of pointing workers in the right direction and making sure they have what they need once they get there, that's what I always told people who asked about it. Johnny Fresno, he told me he needed someone like me, that he'd pay me a good wage, which he did, and that I would be doing something . . . something not just special, but magical. Man, I can't pull it off, but when it came out of his mouth, I'll tell you. You believed it because he believed it.

I was there when the park opened, yes sir. Started as a security manager, if you can believe it, and worked my way up to head of personnel. It's not HR, thank God, but I had a seat at the big boy table along with the park's operations manager and a bunch of other folks. And with Mr. Fresno. I was there when he died in 1999, too. His funeral was one of the saddest but also one of the most amazing things I'd ever seen. They held it in the center of the park because all the employees wanted to attend. They weren't told to. The *wanted* to. At the end, everyone held up an Exclamation Point balloon over their head and let it go. It was amazing seeing them all go up at once. It changed what the sky looked like for about ten minutes. Johnny would have liked that, his final tribute doing something like changing the way the damn sky looked.

I'm off on a story. I'm sorry. I know why you're here.

Part of being the Head of Park Personnel was, like I said, pointing your workers in the right direction. It was a little more than that, though, because instead of making sure they had bricks to put down or drywall to put up, I had to make sure of three things. I had to make sure they were trained, I had to make sure they knew the safety protocol, and—and this is one of Mr. Fresno's things—I had to make sure they wanted to be there. Believe it or not, we got requests to work at FantasticLand from all over the world, and Terrance, he was my main interview guy, he had to make sure they "had the spirit," so they said. Had to make sure they were there to serve and to make sure everyone left there better than they came in. To be honest, I don't know what questions they asked to make sure they were the kind of folks who would work in the park. All I know is when I got them, they were ready and eager to get out there.

Yeah, it was mainly kids who worked in the park. A lot of older folks like myself worked behind the scenes, but the ride operators and the food vendors and the store sales force and the actors on the rides and the people in the mascot suits, they were by and large under twenty-five years old. Part of that was due to the program we had where we wouldn't just do a job fair, we'd find kids who fit a certain profile and send someone to talk to them. It was the personal attention that got them. We had some old fogies like me pushing brooms and taking out the trash, and even they had to "have the spirit." Mr. Fresno's orders. He checked on you, too. He had this Fisherman's Wharf cap that hid his kind of bushy hair, so if you didn't look close, you wouldn't recognize him, and he would walk up and down the park at least once every day or so and make sure things were going the way he wanted them to be going. I'm proud to say, usually, they were.

The safety protocol was the hard part for some of these kids. There was a lot to memorize, and then Trolly, he was the CFO and one of the only guys who could get important business stuff through to Mr. Fresno, he made sure they applied it. He was a hard-ass on these things, and to hear him tell it, he had to be because no one else was doing the job. I don't want to get into that, especially not that nasty episode between Trolly and Mr. Fresno that was so popular around the office, but what it meant was anyone who worked at FantasticLand, anyone and everyone, they knew the protocol. We always joked that it was a fun place to work but we all knew the emergency exits and how to work them. We all knew where the first aid kits were and if someone collapsed in the heat, they had water within ninety seconds. A few years ago, we installed a system-wide RAD program that stood for "Response and Directives," which was basically a smartphone that let us talk to all the employees at once or one employee in any part of the park. It was an innovative thing, and it lessened the need to memorize all the safety protocols. After a while and after getting to know Trolly, I was proud of what we had. Again, point the workers in the right direction and make sure they have the tools to do the job when they get there.

So, the hurricane. OK, let's talk about the hurricane. We have our own weather team, a group of three guys that take eight-hour shifts to make sure there's never a second when someone isn't watching developing weather patterns and the like. The reason we employed three meteorologists at great expense was that someone did the math and figured out that if we were able to do a few simple things before storms hit, like cover the tables and put up the shutters out front of the stores and some other stuff, then we would not only be safer but we'd save money overall on the deal. Plus the stores could start pushing rain slickers and all that fun stuff. Allan B—we had two Allans and a Jeremy on the weather team—he was working the overnight shift, which he liked doing, and was keeping a really close eye on Sandy. Sadie? Sadie. I get my big girls mixed up some times. Allan B was all over it, and he did a good job, that boy. We called him in to the every-other-day staff meeting we have to go over the park operations, this was the day of the fourteenth, and he told us Sadie was tracking further north than they thought, but there wouldn't be any way it would get up as high as Okeechobee county, but that he would be keeping an eye on it anyway. Either way, he said, we should schedule a test of our emergency alarms just in case something went a little goofy, which means certain managers and key personnel were responsible for a live sounding of their alarm when there were people around. It was one of Trolly's things. He would say, "Train like it's real as much as you can," so we did. Well, something went a little goofy.

I don't live far from the park, about fifteen minutes is all. That means I get calls all the time to come in and settle this, that, or the other thing, but I knew when I got a call later that night, the night of the fourteenth, that it was going to be a little different.

I know we're getting to the part you want to talk about, but there's one more thing you need to know about how the park is set up, OK? It won't take long. We house about 85 percent of our workers in dormitories we call FresnoVille. It's about a ten-minute walk away from the park, and looks a heck of a lot like a college campus. It's got a cafeteria, recreation areas, even a fountain in the middle of the dorms. We can house 800 people there at one time, and we were right up close to that because we were just coming off peak season. We had 690 folks in the five dorms that we just called Alpha, Beta, Theta, Pi, and Zeta. We always used to joke that creativity ran out when you left the park because whatever you have in your head 'bout what these places looked like, you're exactly right. It was concrete and stone and a few green spaces, and that was it. That was FresnoVille. That name, I'm not sure where it came from, but it was called FresnoVille before I started, so it must have come from somewhere. Why'd I tell you about that? You'll see in a second.

So, Allan B, he sounds the alarm the night of the fourteenth and by then he called up the senior staff and started screaming that Sadie was a monster and she was going to hit us and this and that. He was laying it on pretty thick, but he wasn't the sort to yank our chain, so I load up in the car and head down there. The first thing I did was check who had done their emergency alarm test, and we had a bunch of slackers who didn't follow through, so the first call was to them. I like to be friendly when I can, but this was one of those times where I had to put on my Big Bad Wolf voice and make a threat or two in the right places. The hotels were always the worst about that. The manager of the Mighty Maiden wasn't happy at all, complaining that we'd wake everybody up. I told him he should have thought of that before he blew off the test when he got the notice yesterday afternoon. Don't procrastinate on this shit, you know? Do your job. So we got the alarm tests done, and everybody was on alert, and while I was setting that up, Allan B was showing other senior staff what was going to happen. When I was done with my part and walked into that room, I thought I had walked into a room full of ghosts. No one was freaking out. Not a single person. They were ashen, but that shook off after a while, and people got to work. Again, do your job.

I know you're gonna have a lot of questions about what decisions were made about opening the park, who made them, and when. I'm afraid I can't help you. What I can do, the only thing I can do, is tell you what I did and what I saw, which I'll remember as well as I can. You can ask, but I don't have a lot of the answers you want.

You've been to the park, what would you say it's worth? Not in an abstract sense. If a mob descended on the park and ran off with all the merchandise and the food and the fixtures and all the rest, what do you think they'd get away with? Can't guess? Well, we guessed. We commissioned a study that wasn't the best, but it gave us a ballpark estimate that $580 million would be lost if something bad happened and gangs of looters busted into an unmanned FantasticLand. So that's why Operation Rapture was in place. Yeah, that's what they called it. I wish I had picked a better name, looking back. The basic idea was that the park had some of the safest storm shelters in all of Florida that weren't built by the military. Trolly, he saw to that, and he succeeded beyond what anyone thought was reasonable. So, the thinking went, if you can be sure you have a safe place for folks to ride out the storm, you're going to need people on the grounds after the storm to make sure the looters stay out and all that $580 million worth of "vulnerable assets" are locked down. I knew Trolly, and he set me onto this idea personally. The idea was never "fight off the barbarians at the gate"—rather, have a skeleton crew onboard to safely and voluntarily keep everything in its place. And pay them to do it.

When folks first came on to work, we would explain Operation Rapture to them and give them a choice: if the need should arise, do you want to stay behind and look after the park? They would be given certain designations, and if the need arose they would not evacuate the park but hit the storm shelters and then be given a very specific set of duties once the storm let up. In return, they would be paid their hourly wage every hour they were in the park. It might not sound like much, but being paid $12 an hour to sit in a storm shelter, do a few chores, play cards with your friends, and then *still* be making money if you had to spend two or three or four days on grounds, even while you slept? That was really appealing to a lot of youngsters. Some of the older guys saw through the deal and said there was no way, no how they were going to deal with all the shit that was sure to come down if we had to evacuate the park. They were smart enough to know that if we evacuated and lost all that revenue, that the fan would have long since stopped running 'cause of all the shit that hit it. But for a young person it wasn't a hard sell. We had tons of them sign up, so once the alarms were sounded, it was my job to help with evacuation and then implement Operation Rapture.

Of course, you can't make anyone stay, but most everyone who signed up was still onboard. We had a few key folks stay behind too, especially in the maintenance department, as there are very bad things that could happen if parts of the park were left unattended. Yeah *[laughing]*, like the Exclamation Point in the middle of the park falling over. That would be a big thing.

Why did the park open on the morning of the fifteenth? Good question. I'm not entirely sure, to this day, why the park gates were open after evacuation had been called for, and if I ever figure out it was one person's decision and that person opened the doors after having the information that he or she should have had, words are going to be exchanged. Lots and lots of words, yes sir. I got there about four in the morning, and Allan B was freaking out and squawking like a chicken on a hot plate. Evacuation, by my recollection, was called for by 6:00 a.m., when it was crystal damn clear that the storm was going to take a big ol' dump on us. The park opens at eight, and we open an hour earlier for guests staying in our four resorts. I can count on one hand the number of times we opened earlier than that, and those were big fat hairy deals with big corporate money behind it, something we all would have heard about and been ready for. The park should not have opened, period. But there was someone in charge of that, and all information of this nature flows from one person, and I'll leave you to figure that out. I don't want to go on record as saying anything more about that.

Author's note: Robert Digby, the head of Intergrounds Transportation, has claimed, under oath, that he was never told not to bring visitors to the park on September 15. There is some legal dispute over whether or not he should have been told by a superior not to run the buses or whether he should have checked before running the buses given the park's heightened state of readiness. The civil case against Digby remains ongoing.

The first problem I saw in trying to organize the evacuation was that everyone was thinking small. One guy, whose name I won't mention, thought we should just run the buses, and I piped up, "Where do you think they're going? To the hotels?" That shut him up. We had to move people inland

and stay there, this wasn't a route we were running. These vehicles were going to move and stay moved, so I kind of powered through and took charge of the efforts. I had a guy tell me I sounded like Tommy Lee Jones from *The Fugitive*. "I want every transport van, work van, employee van that can hold more than six people; I want every limo and every luxury van and every tram that can limp out of here on a busted radiator and no muffler at the front in fifteen minutes getting people loaded up so we don't have a riot on our hands!" I guess I sounded like I knew what I was talking about because everybody hopped to. I'm kind of proud of this: we didn't have any problem finding a ride for everyone at the park who needed to leave, even those who came to the park first thing in the morning because some complete moron forgot to stop the buses. To the moron's credit, the buses were really important to getting everyone out. We headed west because Allan B said if we could make it just thirty miles or so west we'd be OK, and turns out he was right on the money. We ended up taking over the gymnasium of a school in some small town, I forget the name. We got a hell of a rain storm once we got there, but that real damaging wind, Allan B was right. It missed us. It was remarkable.

OK, so, the Rapture kids. Making sure we had a seat for everyone took most of the time we had before the storm hit. The shift managers had herded all those staying behind into the Dream Pop Star Amphitheater, and they were already getting rained on and were miserable and pretty damn grumpy. I don't want to brag, but I was out there saving folks; they could sit in the rain for a minute. Plus, if they'd read the disaster manual, they would have known where to go, which was the damn storm shelters. We put out a call on the RADs, and that finally got the ball rolling. Like I said, someone's got to be there to point the workers in the right direction and give them the tools they need, so it was up to me.

Author's Note: Here is the text of Phil Mueller's speech as recorded on a camera phone by a worker in the crowd who wishes to remain anonymous.

"All right, calm the hell down, everyone. We've got a lot to do and no time to do it. I need you to listen closely, I need you to understand what I'm saying, and I'm sorry to say, we won't have time for questions as Sadie is about to beat the holy shit out of us. When we leave here, you are to go to the main storm shelter just off of Golden Road. If you don't know where this shelter is, find someone who does and stick to their ass like glue, because if you make it to the storm shelter in the next forty-five minutes, you will be safe. Again, if you are in the storm shelter in forty-five minutes, you will be safe. Inside the storm shelter is power, food, water, bathrooms, and everything you're going to need to ride out the storm inside that shelter. Once the storm lets up, and you will know because you will have weather radios, you will all leave the shelter and report to your section of the park. There, in the storage areas, you will find food, water, toiletries, and everything else you will need for your stay, along with a disaster manual. You will be bored in the shelter, so I would recommend you spend your time reading the manual as to what you are supposed to do next. You will be paid for every hour at the park *[cheering]*, and you will be told to leave by management personnel, who will come back as soon as we get the all-clear. I expect you to be here no more than seventy-two hours. All right, all of you, head to the shelter now."

I made my speech, I sent them off, and that's when the bad news comes over the radio that the last buses are leaving. I had made a deal to hitch a ride back to my house with a fella I knew, and he was screaming at me to get on the bus, so I literally sprinted back to the front gate. Did we have a hierarchy among the workers who stayed behind? Well, we were supposed to! Everyone had a level based on their experience, pay, and something we called "job vitality," which basically means how important you are. As I was sprinting back to my ride, I wasn't thinking about that, honestly. I knew there might be an issue or two to clean up when we got back to the park, but I was mainly concerned with how fast the wind was whipping already. We were about out of time.

A lot of people ask me when I knew things were going to go bad. That's pretty easy to answer, if I'm being honest with you: right away. I gave that speech to the kids staying behind, and I knew they were going to be alone in the park for a few days, at least that's what I thought, and I kind of had a moment of clarity, as it's called. I knew this was a bad idea, but I also knew that my wife hates storms and that she would be freaking out and that my sixty-two-year-old body was going to need some time to make it to the front gate and to catch my ride, even though, as you can tell, I take care of myself. So I left. What else was I going to do?

The other time I knew we were in trouble, I am hesitant to tell you about. You have to understand, FantasticLand reinvested a lot of money back into the park. A lot. More than our shareholders and our board of directors wanted, and we did that because that's what Johnny Fresno did and that's what Ritchie kept doing. They called it the "competitive advantage," and Mr. Fresno, he's going to be super hot under the collar that I'm telling you this, but we had a contract with a private company that gave us live, up-to-the-second satellite imaging over the park. We did it because it gave us great data in terms of park traffic and where the lines were. Well, I had access to that satellite imaging, and I kept an eye on it, and I knew we were in trouble when I saw three things happen.

First, we saw Golden Road flood about eight hours after we evacuated. That blew my hair back because it meant that even with all our planning and all our improvements, no one ever thought this level of water would get to our front gate. Turns out there's a big dip going from the top of the main [parking] lot to about the first row of stores which means, eight hours after we left, there was a small lake between the park and the road. Second was when the same thing happened between the park and FresnoVille. There was damn lake between these kids and their beds and their phones—we don't allow those in the park. I knew the sides of the park would be hard to get through, but I always thought those employees, I need to stop calling them kids, those employees would have a back door out of the park.

Last thing was when the power grid went down. I honestly did not see that coming. Once the power went out, I was thinking to myself, "We're fucked. We are good and proper fucked."

INTERVIEW 5: SAM GARLIEK

First-shift manager of FantasticLand.

Before FantasticLand, I had been in a hurricane before. Hurricane Leo glanced off the coast near Miami when I used to live down there. I was working as a manager of a hotel restaurant and had to herd everyone out when it was evacuated. I was the last person out and ended up spending the night in a walk-in freezer, of all places. It was not pleasant. My doctors told me I had frostbite in a couple of my toes, but I told them it was fine. I'm rugged like that.

FantasticLand wasn't nearly as bad an experience at first because everyone knew the protocol and knew where to go. I made sure of it. Mr. Mueller talks a lot in training about pointing workers in the right direction, and that's exactly what we did, and everyone from the girls in the shop to the guys in the rides reacted exactly like they were supposed to. It was my job to keep the head count. That was important, because even though we had over four hundred people who had signed up to stay at the park—we called it "Operation Rapture"—we needed to know how many actually stayed. It's human nature to want to run in the event of an emergency, and we saw our fair share of that. I was told we would have between 420 and 450 people, and we ended up with 326. The space was equipped for more than that, so we weren't even "cozy." Everyone had their own space, and I noticed right away that groups sort of clustered together. Everyone realized right away that as far as storm shelters go, you could have done a whole lot worse. The biggest hardship everyone went through was that the park's Wi-Fi didn't work in the storm shelters.

Mr. Mueller had given a speech that let everyone know they were in a serious situation. That was so important because many of the employees who live in FresnoVille, they might not be the most up to date on current affairs. Some of them are partiers, some of them are studiers, some of them constantly have their nose in a phone or a tablet. You get that with any group. My fear was that one or two of them wouldn't make it to the shelters, and we'd have employees in the park, and they would have to fight to survive or get stranded someplace, and then they'd find themselves in a really bad situation. Luckily, we didn't have to deal with anything of the sort. Everyone showed up, everyone listened to Mr. Mueller, and everyone made it to the shelters. No exceptions, I'm proud to say, at least none that I'm aware of.

We were down there for about fifty hours, when all was said and done, and we could have stayed down there longer if not for . . . OK, let me walk you through it.

The shelter was designed almost exactly like the tunnels that run under the park. I can't take you down there anymore, but you can find cell phone pictures online. Picture long, concrete walls and hard concrete floors with rooms full of supplies about every 150 feet. There were only two entrances and exits, at either end of the shelter, and we had managers posted at those spots 24/7. Inside the doors along the edge of the tunnels were bathrooms and supply stations with water and crackers and other rations, storage areas with sleeping bags and pillows, and one big room that ran on a generator and had all the contacts to the outside, like radios and satellite phones and radar. The managers called it the Command Center, but one of the employees thought it looked like one of the bunkers from the first season of *The Walking Dead*, so you might hear it referred to as the Zombie Center. I don't know why it stuck but it did. It's not very clever if you ask me. I kept referring to it as the Command Center, and a couple times I got blank looks until I called it the Zombie . . . my point is no one was lacking anything they needed. All the diabetics had their insulin, all the hungry had food, and we all had community. I'll put it that way.

I remember, quite clearly, once everyone got to the shelter, there was a moment when we had to shut the doors. By then it was raining, and the wind had really picked up, so another park employee and I stood there and took a last look out to make sure everyone had gotten inside. The employee, I don't remember his name but he worked in the Pirate's Cove, asked me if there was anyone else out there, and I said, "If there is anyone out there, we'll be able to see them." Then I shut the door, and he made this weird growling noise and I asked him, "What was that?" and he said it was Chewbacca from *Star Wars*. Apparently there's a moment in one of the movies when they shut a gate and . . . I don't know, I didn't remember the scene, but it's weird what you remember in situations like that. There are probably a hundred other things that were more vivid that day, but his stupid noise is what sticks in my head.

We quickly established a couple ways of communicating with everyone since the RADs didn't work and personal phones were prohibited in the park. At each 150-foot marker there was a whiteboard, and every hour I would have managers write a new piece of information on that whiteboard. For example, one hour might say GROUP DINING IN SECTION C, 11–1 if we wanted people to come eat together. We set a sleep schedule, which was important because there was no night or day down there. We put up information about the storm. We told people where they could find first aid. It was all very orderly that first day, and we really didn't have anything that stood out by way of problems. We had one fight on the first day, and it turned out to be a long-standing thing, nothing about the evacuation. I tell you, it was downright comfortable. The bathrooms even worked. Everyone seemed to be getting along, but when you're a manager, you can see the seeds of discord in the different ways people act.

Let me give you an example. What we saw was that once we were all down there, the employees separated into two camps. There were those who were really interested in what was happening outside—they crowded around the Command Center—and then there were those who hung back. Mostly they were preestablished groups of friends, from what I could tell, though there was certainly a loner or two in there. Mostly what I saw was a lot of nervous employees. Some of them got over that nervousness with information about the storm, and they were the ones who hung close to the Command Center. I had one guy tell me, "I'm used to tracking storms on my phone in real time. Now I can't even look out a window," so it was natural to be curious, I guess.

At first it was kind of cute. Whenever there was a development it would be passed down the line like a game of telephone. The problem with that was there were some things that we didn't want getting out there for mass consumption, you know? Like the situation at the front of the park. It was deteriorating quickly. At first it was just a few puddles, but then they sort of . . . coalesced, if that's the right word, and started getting bigger. Soon there was sort of a small lake at the front, and after about twelve hours it was clear there were not going to be any vehicles, rescue or otherwise, coming into the park for quite some time. I had never seen anything quite like it. I remember going to bed that night and thinking, "This is a pretty big problem," and then waking up and wondering if the ticket booths had blown away in the night. Turns out they were mostly underwater.

After that first night, we shut the door to the Command Center and only allowed a few key people to watch the screens, which was an unpopular decision, but you could see why we would do it. The absolute last thing you need in an enclosed space is panic. But, again, there were two groups: those who were glued to every piece of information we put out there and others who couldn't be bothered. So it was really only that one group that was upset, and after the first night, they started getting vocal about it. We started hearing whispers of, "We have a right to know," and "fascist" and that kind of thing. I'm in management, so I've been called a lot worse. Good managers know how to shake that sort of thing off, and I'm a good manager.

So, you've got the picture? A bunch of employees crowded around the Command Center and a bunch of other employees sort of doing their own thing. What kind of thing? Lots of card games. I know there were many decks of cards in the disaster packs, and a lot of folks tore into those right away. For a short time there was even a game of old-fashioned charades going, if you can believe that. One group of girls started a "selfie" contest, only they didn't have phones, which was kind of weird. They were doing that thing where they all get together in a group and smile and say, "Heeeeey," and then they'd laugh as one of them "took a picture" with a box of candy, then another group would pose, and it went on like that for a while. Other people chose to read. One or two people had snuck in weather radios—I don't know where they got them—but they mostly didn't work down in the shelters. You couldn't pick up anything. Our radios in the Command Center were connected straight to antennas outside, so we had a great signal, but that only added to the feeling that we had the information and those outside didn't. I remember there was this one girl, something Flynn, I don't remember her first name, but everyone called her Flynn, she was the one who would speak up whenever I went out to give more information to the crowds. She was always up in the front and always made eye contact and always asked me the same question: "Why did you shut the door?" After the third time, I tried to take her aside to explain the situation, but she wouldn't have it. She was adamant that if I talked to her, I had to talk to all those gathered around the door to the Command Center. I wasn't about to concede that point, so I kept giving updates, and she kept asking why I shut the door. She would just stare at me, all self-important, like I was the one who put her in this situation. I know folks like that, who have no sense of the greater good, you know? Whose agenda is the only thing that matters. I don't mind saying, it pisses me off. You see it on the Internet and on the news all the time, someone says something a little off-color and then you have a steady stream of professional victims and attention-grabbers demanding they apologize in the way they want you to apologize. It makes me sick. Look, I know I'm making the situation down there sound heated, but it was actually pretty civil. Until we lost power.

The power went out overnight. I'm not sure when. I'm sure whoever I had on the overnight shift at the Command Center could tell you, but all I remember was waking up to shrieks and not seeing anything at all except the frantic flicker of flashlights. No one was taking the flashlight and pointing it at what they wanted to see, like it laid out in the disaster manual. Everyone was waving their flashlights around, wasting power and acting like it would produce more light by waving it around. It was stupid and panicky, and I knew things were sort of bad at that point.

If we'd lost lights, we'd lost everything in the Command Center and basically all contact with the outside world. I don't mind telling you, it took me a moment to get a hold of myself. I was dealing with over three hundred employees, most of them five years or so out of middle school, in a pitch-dark concrete bunker, and I was in charge. Tell me you wouldn't have panicked a little. Once I left my little room where I was sleeping and walked into the main area, it was absolute bedlam. It was dark, and people were flailing around. People were desperate to see where they were, so anyone who had a flashlight was likely to have it snatched from them, and then they would try to try to snatch it back, and some people were still asleep and being stepped on. Hell, if you tried to get out of the way, how would you know where to go? Most of the injuries that happened in the tunnels, it happened right then when the lights went out and people didn't stay put, like they should have. They panicked, and people got hurt. There was nothing huge, just a few split lips and the like, but again, the only thing worse than being alone in the dark is being in the middle of a big crowd of people in the dark. Yeah, we did have room in the shelter, but no one could find it.

After I calmed myself down, I figured I had two options. I could make my way to the Command Center and try to find the protocol on how to turn on the emergency generator, or I could throw open one of the doors to the storm shelter and at least get a little bit of light in there and maybe calm some folks down a little. I had no idea what time it was, but my body was telling me I'd gotten a little bit of sleep, probably five hours, so it was as likely as not that there would be some sun if I did open the door. But then you run the risk of people running into the storm and getting hurt. I decided that the door would be the better idea because even if the storm was still raging, a visible way out would calm everyone down, at least for a bit. Then I could work on the generator. That was the plan. Finding my way to the nearest exit was another matter entirely. I had a flashlight in my pocket, so my strategy was to keep it off for as long as I could. What I could see was whenever a light came on, people flooded around it and the light would bounce all around and then eventually go out amidst lots of yelling and screaming. It was really loud in there, as you can imagine.

I picked a direction, said a little prayer, and started pushing. I did not know where I was going, not even close, but I knew I had gone to sleep in Section B of the shelter, and there was one exit in Section A and one in Section D. I was praying my luck held out and that I was going the right way so I wouldn't have to fight my way through two sections. Truth be told, when I started out I thought, "I'm never going to make it." I was immediately hit in the lip and tasted blood, and my eye took a really good shot. I'm not accustomed to being beaten up, so I don't know if this is true or not, but I think I actually felt the one side of my face swelling where I had been hit. I also took one in the ribs, but I didn't drop and I didn't stop. I pushed until I found the back wall, which was almost deserted. I figured most people were stuck to the sides of the shelter and not to the back. I was able to feel around for the door and push through without much interference into another section full of screaming, punching mobs. I figured at that point there was very little accountability, so I sort of barreled forward and went on the offensive a bit. I was either going to get to the end of the section and find the doors to the outside or I had another whole section to fight through. Either way, I sort of . . . what's the expression . . . girded my loins and plowed forward. I honestly wish I could describe it for you better, but it was a totally dark mosh pit in there. The music was the yells of scared people, and I gave as good as I got, I can tell you that much.

I have no idea how long I was pushing or shoving, but once I found a wall I clung to that sucker like it was a lifeline and kept plowing forward. I ran into a lot of people who were hugging the wall, too, but they didn't know where they were going. I did. I had a direction. So I pushed and came upon the end of the tunnel and hallelujah praise Jesus, I had gone the right way. I was in Section A, and I felt around, found the lock on the door, pulled out my keys and my flashlight, and before anyone could attack me I had the door open. Well, partially open. I had to push with everything I had, and then the wind caught this big metal door and damn near blew it off the hinges. The storm was still very much going on.

But I was right about the time. It was light out but it was mostly gray. That's a damn sight better than black, I can tell you. Light flooded

Section A, and soon B was coming up too and the word spread. This was when I put my plan into effect.

The idea was to open the doors, despite whatever was happening outside, and use the opportunity to bolt to the Command Center and figure out the generator before the situation got worse. My plan worked, and it worked extremely well. The Command Center is in Section C, and the light from the door spread all the way into B, so everyone immediately started crowding toward A. It wasn't hard to get to the Command Center after that. I was able to turn on my flashlight without getting mauled, even though there was still a lot of pushing and shoving in the area. Like I said, it was a good plan.

I got to the Command Center door in short order, and it was locked, which I knew was bad. When we shut the door and started partitioning off information, we didn't lock the door. It seemed like a bridge too far. I had keys, but it made me nervous to go inside for some reason, but I went. Let me clarify quickly, the Command Center was not where the generators were but where the information on how to run the generators was kept. These weren't the sort of generators you buy at Home Depot. These were state of the art, large-scale generators meant to run for a long time, and they had start-up sequences and checklists. You couldn't just go press a button and turn them on, so I was looking for the instruction manuals. Once I got inside, it was deeply spooky to see all the screens blank. I don't know how to describe it other than I got a knot in my stomach. It was a tangible thing, you know? Our situation was so bad we couldn't turn on the computers. That's when I felt something hit the back of my head. It was dark, so that sort of white light flash that you get when you're hit really hard? That was really pronounced. I also remember hearing a distinct clacking noise, like a bunch of plastic hitting the ground. I dropped my flashlight and was able to turn around before the next hit came.

I had no idea who was hitting me at the time. No clue. I . . . I don't want to sound like I'm justifying what happened, but I was scared, I was working to save people, I was ostensibly in charge, and I had just been on the receiving end of a cheap shot. It was fight or flight and fight kicked in, and I can tell you, if you've ever been in a fight in near pitch blackness, I don't recommend it. You have just as good a chance of punching the wall really hard as you do of hitting anyone, but I got lucky. OK, so I got hit, I turned around and got hit again, but the second hit was more of a glancing blow, it sort of bounced off my shoulder and neck. I was aware I was being hit *with* something, it wasn't just someone punching me. This was a full-fledged attack, so I . . . I didn't hold back, let's put it that way. I was able to get my hands around something that felt like a head, and I threw it as hard as I could into where I thought the wall was, and then I just kept coming. I grabbed the head and hit it three or four more times, then I might have shouted a question, but you have to understand, it was still really loud outside. Really chaotic. I wasn't getting hit anymore, so I refocused and started trying to find my flashlight. It took a really long time, but I eventually found it, under the desk, of all places. I was pretty beat up between fighting my way through the dark to getting into that fight, so I wasn't surprised when I turned on the flashlight and saw a lot of blood. It wasn't until later that I realized it wasn't mine.

I feel kind of callous telling you this, but the first thing I did was find the manual. That was the whole reason I was there and it's where my head was at. I was about to leave before I decided to shine my flashlight at the ground where the fight had been. I can't explain it; I just felt like that was one more obstacle and I was over it. When I did shine some light down there, I wasn't terribly surprised that I didn't find anyone. They had run off while I was looking around. What I was surprised at was the amount of blood on the floor and that the weapon was still on the floor. It was a keyboard. What a stupid thing to attack someone with, right? He could have grabbed a chair or a flashlight or something with some heft to it, but a keyboard? It just supports the theory that it wasn't a planned thing but a random thing, I guess. Someone got it in their head to perpetrate some violence, and that was it. I gave them a good thrashing, and they realized they were bleeding, and they ran away. I don't really care that we never found out who it was. It's pretty clear that there was nothing to it other than some kid being afraid of the dark.

I got the manual and gave it a quick once-over. The lucky thing was the generators were in a utility closet just a hundred feet from where I was, so it wasn't like before where I had to fight my way to the next point. All I had to do was slide along the wall until I found a door handle, use my keys to open it, and there I was. The sequence took me about fifteen minutes, and no one bothered me except for the noise on the other side of the door. It was a lot of arguing, lots of one person yelling and then someone yelling for them to shut up and then people taking sides. Some people were crying, others were being ironic about it and yelling stuff out like "sandwich" and singing kiddie songs from the park. It was pretty nuts, but the work was pretty straightforward, just time-consuming and detailed. But once those lights came on, that felt really good. I felt like once the lights came up, everyone immediately calmed down. The loud ruckus outside stopped, and I took off like a shot down to Section A and to where I had opened the door. At least, that's what I had meant to do. Instead, there were at least three people on the floor. I know now that at least two of them were dead. One of them was that Flynn girl, Maria, her name was. I recognized her because she was face up, but I didn't stop to help. I knew I was needed up at the front where the door was open.

There was a crowd to fight through, but once they recognized who I was, it wasn't hard getting through. It got harder the closer I got to the door because Sadie wasn't done with us yet. The wind was still howling, and there was water everywhere along Section A, just everywhere. I tried yelling but no one could hear me, so I ran back to the Command Center and got on the PA.

Author's Note: Mr. Garliek's speech was recorded on camera phone and is as follows:

> "Employees, I need your attention. Attention, please. *[Pause]* The generators are now working and will run for the next forty-eight hours. There is an exit door open in A Section. If you wish to leave, no one but Hurricane Sadie is going to stop you. If you choose to stay you will have lights, food, and a dry place to sleep tonight, but I need your help, and I need it without question. Looking at the radar, it looks like we're in for at least another

twelve hours of rain and high winds, and we've got a lot of hurt people. I need everyone who's going to stay, please help your injured coworkers to D Section, where the medical supplies are kept. I need park managers and anyone else with first aid training to please report to D Section. I'm going to leave this door open for another hour, and if you want to leave, make your way out right now. If you plan on violence in my shelter, I would strongly recommend you taking your chances with the storm, because if I find out you were responsible for any of the chaos down here, you will get more sympathy from the storm than you will from me. There will be order here, and order involves clean spaces and everyone getting their fair share of food. If you have any questions, see me or your immediate supervisor, and we are all out of here, probably tonight. That is all."

I sounded like kind of a badass, huh? *[Laughing]* I guess I was kind of jacked from fighting my way through the crowd. The good news is, the speech worked for the most part. I was able to get the weather computers back up and running, and we were able to leave en masse about twelve hours after we started the generator. Our managers, they responded like champs, and the place was in pretty good shape in just a couple of hours. Soon we had a proper infirmary going. Well, infirmary and morgue. I'd never seen a dead body before, much less five of them. Three had been beaten or trampled to death, including Maria Flynn; one had gone into some sort of shock and died, at least that's as near as we could figure; and another poor guy needed his inhaler and couldn't get it in the dark. He couldn't find help over the shouting, and he was just out of luck. He suffocated in that part of the shelter. That's the one that gets me. He must have been terrified. It wasn't until much later that I learned who he was, and I didn't feel so bad for him anymore. It was Bryce Hockney, he was the one who died. Yeah, *that* Hockney. I mean, if your brother is a monster, how far does the acorn fall from the family tree, right? He didn't get his inhaler, and it probably saved us some issues in the grand scheme of things.

No, I don't think the person who attacked me was Maria Flynn. Why would you ask that? Didn't you hear the story? I was the only one working to save people. I was it. Without me, who knows how many more would have died? Hundreds maybe. I don't want to say I'm the hero, but you could certainly read it that way. Plus, even if it was that Flynn girl, what would it matter? I was attacked and I defended myself, that's the entire point, that's always been the point, not just in the shelter but in the entire park. Look at it this way—if you consider what happened after the bunker, I am the only one who was able to keep order at the beginning, and I spent my entire time in the park fighting and scratching and bleeding to try to keep any amount of order that I could, OK? I don't care what others tell you, that's the God's honest truth.

It doesn't matter who attacked me, and quite frankly, I'm not the bad guy here. I was saving people when we were in the shelter, and I was doing my best to keep order and keep the peace after we got out. Given all the violence that came later, I feel pretty safe in saying I'm the closest thing you're going to find to a good guy in this clusterfuck.

INTERVIEW 6: STUART DIETZ

Maintenance employee at FantasticLand, Mole Man.

Sam? Oh yeah. He definitely killed that girl. At least that's what everyone thought, and that's all that matters, isn't it? I don't have any information that you don't have 'bout that, but I can tell you getting out of that hole was one of the best goddamn feelings I've ever had, bar none. How 'bout we start there?

Part of it was because I'm quite a bit older than most of the little farts who work in the park, so all us old guys, we hung around together, and because we hung around together, we were constantly getting asked questions on how to fix things. Us maintenance guys and gals, we knew more than anybody about what makes that place run. Shit, I knew more about fixing the park in my little finger than anyone in charge does. You think any one of those assholes could change a safety arm on any of those rides? If they were in charge of my job we'd have kids falling from the sky and splatting on the ground, and then I'd probably have to clean it up. That's anywhere, I guess, but the good news about this whole thing was people who knew how to get things done, we were finally getting asked to help make decisions about everything. That's how it shook out when Sam and the rest of his little group realized how fucked we were. They came running to the guys with the big ring of keys.

Once Mr. Mueller—he's one of the good ones—once he was done telling everyone to duck and cover, we headed to the shelters, and I'll tell you, it was not where anyone wanted to be. The one thing worse than being stuck somewhere you can't leave is being stuck there with a bunch of half-wits twenty minutes out of middle school. Most of those kids, you could size them up in a few seconds. You had the criers and you had the jokers—they're the worst because you can't give them enough attention for them to shut the fuck up—you had the ones who try to be in charge of something to make themselves feel big. Me and my guys, we played cards and practiced the fine art of riding it out. If you've ever worked on a construction site, you know what I mean. People think guys are just standing around not doing anything, but the truth of the matter is more often than not we're waiting for another guy to finish his job so we can do ours and go home. Until then, you stare and wait, stare and wait. There's an art to it, but you gotta be prepared when it's your turn, and that's how we were down there. We were waiting, but ready in case anything happened.

Me and a group of guys, about twenty of us, we knew once we headed to the shelter that if things were going to go bad they were going to go real bad real quick, so we all camped out as far on one end as we could. All the way to one end of Section D, up against the door. We figured if we needed to live to fight another day, if you will, we could leave the shelter and take cover somewhere else. The storm was bad, and there was a lot of water, but you weren't going to take flight if you stepped outside. There are over five hundred goddamn structures in the park, and nobody locked up. We would have been OK. An escape route was absolutely necessary and us old guys, we had one. Well, not just guys. Janet and Jill, they were on the clock and in the shelter and were madder than hell about it. Some women sure can complain when given the opportunity.

When it went dark, we had the door cracked within two minutes. Every one of us maintenance folks had emergency keys, it's part of the protocol, so the only holdup was who was going to unlock that heavy-ass door and let in the fresh air. To be honest, there was a lot of pushing and pulling, and I'm not sure how we got that big son of a bitch open, but we did. Problem was, after we had the door open, the wind caught it and blew it open hard, making it an absolute bitch to close. We had these two guys, Carlos and Miguel, both great guys, who stepped out into it and tried to pull the door shut. They're a couple big boys and couldn't make it budge. The wind got to them too and they were inside within ninety seconds. That Sadie was a big old bitch, let me tell you.

Once we cracked the door everyone calmed right down, no fussin', no fightin', no problem. Most everyone sort of crowded toward the door to get a look at the storm and, oh man, was there something to see. Even the jokers shut their yaps for once. The Section D door was hidden under some fake buildings, but you could make out the Golden Road if you squinted, and it was not in good shape. There was shit flying everywhere, awnings and decorations, and I thought I saw part of a roof go. I never got to take a closer look. Never made it that far along the Golden Road until we left the park, and by then I wasn't too interested in checking out the storm damage, but I swear it looked like it took part of a roof on those Golden Road shops. It's one of those things where, as a maintenance guy, part of you is thinking, "Jesus Christ, that's going to take forever to fix," even as you see it happening, you know? Anyway, it was pretty bad. Thing about it was, the wind was whipping and the rain pounding, we didn't hear much of what was going on in Section C, much less B or A. The doors that separate the sections, they were pretty thick and hard to open, I'd guess. I figure that's why no one from C made it in our direction. I'm not sure why no one thought to open the door from our side, to be honest. It's just one of those things. No one thought of it. Wish we had.

The shelter was built to not let water get in, even with the door open, so a few rain drops aside we kept pretty dry and just let the door be wide open until the power came back on. We heard about the fighting and the bodies and all of that. Everyone on our side was hunky dory, so we were really surprised when that little Garliek asshole who thought he was in charge got on the intercom and tried to sound like Charles Bronson. He was shitting his pants, we could all tell. Then he tells everyone who's hurt to come to Section D, where we all are. I guess it made sense looking back on it, but at the time the thought was, "Why are you dragging your mess to my section?" Still, everyone jumped up and helped and there was enough work to go around. Like I said, wait until it's your turn and then do your job. You remember me talking about Carlos and Miguel, those big guys? They were the heroes. They were the ones who went into the other sections and brought back the bodies, and they were the ones who covered them up and kept watch over them. I got the impression it was a Catholic thing, I don't know for sure. I've been attending Bedside Baptist since the late '80s, if you know what I mean.

To be honest with you, it didn't take that long for everything to calm down. Sam Garliek, he was strutting around like he was in charge, and he'd occasionally throw shade in someone's direction to prove he was in charge, but other than that it was a pretty quiet twelve hours. They gave hourly reports on the intercom about what Sadie was doing, and most of my crew even got some sleep, which is good. A lot of people slept, actually. Not me. Charlie and me, we were mapping things out. Charlie was a good guy, another one of the good ones. It's hard to peg down what makes a leader, but whatever it was, Charlie had it. He and I, we both had the same set of priorities, get out or hide, because shit was already bad and going to get worse. We could see it coming. A bunch of scared kids with no rules and more resources than they know what to do with, a lot of them without mommy or daddy looking over their shoulder for the first time? Didn't take a genius to figure out things were going south and no one would be looking out for the guys in the work shirts. Us old guys, we needed a plan.

This is what we came up with: Once the storm broke, we were going to check the back exit, the employee parking along the west side, and the route to FresnoVille. We knew the front was flooded, and all around the park there were acres and acres of trees. They did that because Johnny Fresno said he wanted people to feel like the outside world couldn't intrude on the park. What it meant for us is we didn't have any damn access roads to about 70 percent of the places that needed access roads, so we had to get creative. Every time we expanded, which was every two or three years, those trees had to be uprooted, and we had to save the ones we could and replant them and get new trees. Those assholes didn't care. If you have enough money, moving a forest was no big deal. OK, sorry, off on a tangent. The idea was to see how bad it was around the park. I knew that if the employee parking lot was flooded we were in some trouble because those forests are nothing but mud up to your asshole on a dry day. It's basically the most tree-filled Florida swamp you can imagine. I didn't think it was impassable by any means, I was just thinking if all the concrete was flooded, we were in for a really rough go of it. So Charlie and me, we talk it out, and we decide that if the only way out is through the trees, we ask for volunteers to see how bad it is. Then, worst-case scenario, we figure out where these kids are congregating, and we get the hell away from them. We saw eye to eye on that. These kids were unsupervised, some of them were strong, and there were more of them than there were of us. Like I said, you don't have to be a genius to see where this was headed. The proof was right there in that shelter. Five dead bodies tend to get your hackles up.

Slowly, we spread the word around. We told everyone to meet in the maintenance break room off of the Golden Road, and we were going to talk this out, just us maintenance folks. Most of them had the idea that once the storm broke they were heading right home, and I had to remind them that we were kind of stuck here. Just how stuck we didn't know, but stuck. So I told them, come to the maintenance break room off the Golden Road and we'd hash it out. I don't want to make it seem like they were a bunch of simpletons, but when you're in a situation like this and someone has a plan, they seem pretty ready and willing to follow it, you know? Especially when it was Charlie who had the plan. Like I said, leadership.

The storm broke a little after lunchtime on the sixteenth, and by broke, I mean went from dangerously rainy and windy to not quite so rainy and windy but still pretty goddamn rainy and windy. But you could walk around. Before we left, Sam, he comes up to me and Charlie and asks me all these questions. "What's unlocked? What's not unlocked? Where should we move the bodies? Is there power in the park?" To which Charlie tells him, "Why are you asking these questions now? Couldn't we have done this ten hours ago?" But that little shit, he was having none of it. He was ordering Charlie around. At one point, he said, "Follow behind me so we can survey the damage," to which Charlie replied, "Yes sir, Sergeant Shitstain!" which got a big laugh from the group. Old Sam, he didn't like that. He walked away to find someone else to yell at, and by then the rumors about him and that Flynn girl had started. He had what you could politely call a "credibility gap." From Sam's perspective, he must have felt like he was in charge, but as far as anyone with a brain was concerned, he was in charge of Jack and Shit at that point.

Once we got out, first thing we all noticed was there was no way we were getting out the front. No way. The water stretched from the first store on the Golden Road as far as we could see, past the parking lots, past the trolley stands, past the two hotels we could see out the front, past everything. I remember Charlie saying "this is not good," and he was goddamned right. It wasn't good. Neither were the south exits to the employee parking lot, where there was just as much water as the front gate. The road to FresnoVille, that was a little better, but once we got down that path a little further it was clear that we could almost get to campus, but not quite. If you really wanted to, you could get there, but you would be exhausted and wet to the bone. I don't care if you were a competitive swimmer, you weren't making it more than a couple miles in that muck, and most of us were not competitive swimmers. It was a slog and a half, so the only option left was to go for the trees.

We met up with everyone in the break room off the Golden Road, and there were a hundred questions. Being the good guy that he is, Charlie calmed everyone down, told them what he knew, and then answered every single question, even the rock stupid ones. Then he told them the plan. We were looking for volunteers to see how far they could get through the trees, and the rest of us, we would stick together. There was plenty of food and water, good food as it turned out, and if we all stuck together, rescue would be along in a day or two. That was before we knew the dumb-ass board members had called off the rescue for us. If I ever meet those rich assholes . . . they better be faster than me. That's all I'm saying.

Sure enough, Carlos and Miguel step up and volunteer for our little expedition to see how far we can make it through the trees. I need to describe these guys to you. Carlos was a spark plug, about five foot eight but wide and strong. If you were carrying something heavy, he's the guy you wanted on the other end because you knew he'd carry his weight and then some. Miguel was a little taller, a little lankier, but a good guy. Always on time, always ready to work. I wish I'd known him better. Once they volunteered, Charlie and I had a bit of a tussle over which way they should go. Charlie figured the boys should head out straight into the trees behind the Pirate Cove on the east end of the park. His thinking was the nearest civilization that wasn't run by FantasticFun Inc. would be that way, and if there were rescue tanks or boats or whatever that's where they would be coming from. My thought was everywhere was underwater, it was just a matter of degree, so why not head toward the parking lots and see if you could find something to get us out of here? I didn't know at that time that they had used every available vehicle to move folks out. Turns out, when we did make it down there, it was as empty as hip-hop night at the bingo parlor.

Charlie won out because of course he did. He had a way of talking you into things, and he talked me and Carlos and Miguel into heading toward civilization. The thought was they'd wait until morning and then head out to give the rescue efforts a chance to get their shit together. That was the thought, anyway. We spent that morning packing food and fresh water for them and planning out where they were most likely to run into someone. They were pretty upbeat, and everyone thought for sure they'd run into someone who knew what was going on. Thinking back with hindsight and all that, it was kind of stupid. Word was, and I don't know if this is true or not, but word was Ritchie Fresno got out on a helicopter before the winds got nasty, and if that was true, or even if it wasn't and he drove out in a limo, the disaster folks would be looking to him to figure out how urgent our situation was. Honestly, thinking back, I don't know what we thought Carlos and Miguel would find other than water covering everything. I don't mean to go off on a thing here, but us Mole Men were resourceful and smart, we weren't killers, and we looked out for each other. We were, by far, not the worst of the group, but when I look back on it with, like, a rational head, we were acting like numbskulls. Idiots without a brain in their fucking head, that was us, and I wish I could tell you why. I kind of tell myself Carlos and Miguel didn't have to go, but then a little voice in my head tells me, "you didn't have to let them."

It was raining when they headed out, but they were still feeling good about it. Miguel didn't talk much but Carlos was talking big, about how they were going to come with the cavalry, though he pronounced it

Calvary like the place Jesus died. Again, Catholic. He was all smiles and said, "See you in a day or two, boss," to Charlie when they headed out. Then we waited. A wise man once said it's the hardest part.

We kept our little plan a secret, obviously. If we hadn't, someone would have had some brains and tried to put a stop to it, but nope. We knew best. We had the big ring of keys. Charlie pulled me aside once they were gone and said, "If they don't come back with good news, we could be here a while." I remember it clearly, we were sitting in the covered picnic area in front of Pirate Cove, one of just a few acres of the park that are general space and not dedicated to any one theme. The rain was hitting the top of that candy-green awning and I remember thinking, *No way. We're out of here in time for the weekend*, but like I said, Charlie had a way of talking you into things. He said everyone kicking and biting and killing each other in the dark, that was going to happen again, and, "There's a lot of dark around here with no power," was how he put it, and of course he meant it two ways. I don't know what it was, but that hit me hard in the chest, and I knew he was right. He was goddamn right. It wouldn't take long, and these kids who sold trinkets and pushed the buttons on rides would start all sorts of bad around here, and we had to plan for it even if nothing ended up happening. Charlie's plan was simple: "Lie low." Head to the tunnels, take some of the beds from the shelter, and sort of hunker down. We'd have access to every part of the park, we'd be able to lock the entrances and exits from the inside, but most important, we knew the tunnels, and these little shits didn't.

The tunnels? Every major theme park has them. You ever been to Universal Studios or Disney and see someone lugging a bag of trash for blocks? Of course you haven't, and the tunnels are why. They get the support staff to and from where they need to be without the public having to look at them or smell what they're carrying. If I had to describe them, they're exactly what you're picturing in your head—lit with fluorescent lights and long and narrow. The power was out, but one thing we didn't lack was flashlights and batteries. There were tens of thousands of hours of flashlight power down there. The park was big on that. Sure, it was dark, but it's not like there was very much to see when the lights were on. They were tunnels, but like I said, we knew them, and if you knew where you were going you could get anywhere in the park in fifteen minutes, from one side to the other. We knew where the tunnels went and what direction got us where and where to hide if need be. It turned out to be a pretty damn good idea almost immediately.

Sorry, I keep getting off track. Charlie and I just started going around to all the maintenance folks and saying, "We're headed for the tunnels. Please think about coming with us." And they'd ask why, and we'd lay it out for them, and most of them packed up and headed for the nearest utility entrance. Beautiful part was there was a big central work area that had a skylight, so that room and everything next to it had natural light, and that's where we all congregated. The reason there was a room like that is it's part of the exclusive "behind the scenes package" where you could see folks taking out the trash and tour part of the tunnels. Some folks are weird like that, but if someone wants to pay an extra ninety-five bucks to watch me work, more power to them, I guess. That's where we all gathered and Charlie laid it out. What I remember about it was he basically said "pucker up buttercup," because those kids were going to start grabbing and punching any second, and it was up to us older folks to take care of ourselves and each other, and the tunnels was how we were going to do it. Someone shouted, "But we're going to be rescued soon," and Charlie, I remember, he said, "If so, then all this is no big deal, but if it takes a while, you're going to want a plan, and if you got a better plan than this, we are all fucking ears, my friend. Lay it on us." I remember because Charlie hardly ever swore. He saved it for special occasions, I guess.

The good news was everyone sort of got it. A lot of them had either heard bad stories about the storm shelter or had been in the middle of it, and even the folks who didn't want to stay in the tunnels, they recognized we were in danger and needed to do something about it. Someone said, "What about Carlos and Miguel?" and it occurred to us that was going to be a problem. They would either come back with help, which was looking less and less likely the more we surveyed the condition of the park, or they would come back in bad shape having tromped through water for God knows how long, and we had no idea where they would come back. If they came with help, great, but if not, we wanted them in the tunnels with us. What we decided to do was set up camp in the tunnels. Everyone would set up their bunks in whatever tunnel they wanted, there were plenty to choose from, but we would meet in the mornings at 9:00 a.m. to make sure everyone had what they needed and no one was going out of their minds. The "morning meeting" ended up being a really good idea because it allowed us to keep track of our people. I don't know about the rest of the tribes, but we knew when someone was sick, we knew when someone was unexplainably gone, we knew when someone was late, and we had a good group of guys and girls who knew everyone else's business. We watched out for each other, I can say that much. All told, there were thirty-eight of us down there, not counting Carlos and Miguel. That was us. That was the Mole Men.

Carlos and Miguel turned up three days later. Well, Carlos did. So I hear. I've heard from people I trust that Miguel never made it back, that he got too sick and dehydrated and couldn't go on and that when Carlos stumbled back into the park, the Pirates got him. Either way, we never heard from either of them again.

INTERVIEW 7: JILL VAN MEVEREN

FantasticLand Character, Deadpool Soldier.

I used to get called Jill the Soldier all the time. There was this popular cartoon when I was a kid called *Major Pummel and His Army Elite,* and I remember I used to put my hair in braids like the Jill in the show and run around the neighborhood with the boys. We used, like, sticks for guns and pretended to shoot people. It made total sense that when I went to work at FantasticLand, one of the first jobs I tried out for was Jill the Soldier in the Hero Haven. I tried three times before they finally gave it to me, and then I learned that's pretty standard. No one gets the character they want right out of the gate. They want to make sure you have, you know, tenacity.

It was a great gig, no doubt. There must be, literally, ten thousand photos of me pointing my guns at the camera while some little girl or boy used their fingers to make it look like they had guns too. That was the standard pose. We told parents to post pictures to their Facebook pages and hashtag it "#FantasticFun." That was a "success metric," how many mentions we actually got on social media. I remember at the beginning of the summer the "social media manager" of the park came and gave us this big speech about how this was the new "word of mouth," and "word of mouth" was the best advertising there was. We were supposed to "harness the power of social media" by encouraging the parents to use hashtags and shares and retweets and any other way we could think of to get our product out there. Then he told us if we didn't meet our goals in terms of mentions, that we'd be hearing about it and he wasn't kidding around. There was a fairly big flatscreen in most of the break rooms that had the running tally for the day and it was always the Fairy Prairie or the Circus, always always always. It was a lot harder for us in the Hero Haven because a lot of the characters in the Fairy Prairie or the World's Circus were characters you hugged. Sometimes there would be lines over half an hour to hug somebody in a stuffed costume or to take a selfie as a trapeze artist or whatever they did over there, but it wasn't like that with the Pirates or with us. We had to work a lot harder to get mentions and we did work harder. We got a lot of high fives and struck a lot of poses, which was OK with me. Less chance some adventurous little boy would feel you up, you know? *[Laughter]* But other than having that pressure to get some parent to share their photo, it paid really well for a summer job, and I got a bunch of stories out of it.

You remember that viral video last year when a little kid dressed up as ToBor the War Lord and pretended to take down the entire Army Elite? I was in that video. It was an awesome day. Tons of hashtags. You also got to interact with a lot of kids. It hit home with me rather quickly that some of these kids had really built up this meeting and you actually have a great amount of power. Some kids, just by telling them some stupid catchphrase like, "There's a warrior inside you," or "You make America shine," was enough to make these kids so, so happy. And it made their parents happy too, which meant our bosses were happy, which meant I could keep my hair in braids and put on my fatigues and go out there every day and get paid better than working at a Dairy Queen or something.

After my first year of playing Jill the Soldier, I decided to take some martial arts classes through UT, where I went to school. It was an elective, so I figured it was, like, no big deal. I thought it might help me with the job, that it would make me look more like I knew how to handle myself. I loved it. Like, loved it, loved it. I went through my first four belts in one semester and planned to go back. The instructor told me I had a natural talent for martial arts and I could earn my black belt by the time I was out of school, which I really wanted to do. After I got out of FantasticLand, he called me and asked how I was doing, and I told him he had either saved my life or kept me from getting messed up pretty bad. He said he was proud of me and the truth is, I'm proud of myself. I played Jill the Soldier in the park, but I had to become Jill the Soldier to get out alive.

Oh God, that sounds so stupid. Cut that out, OK? Seriously, that just tumbled out of my mouth, and it's really stupid. I'm embarrassed I said that.

OK, I'm serious now. Want me to start when we got out of the shelter? OK, everyone's already told you that, basically, it never stopped raining, right? The storm hit, and we didn't see the sun hardly at all, and it was always raining or about to rain. Keep that in mind, that's the backdrop. Once we got out of the tunnel, everyone sort of looked around, and it was clear no one knew what they were doing. That Sam guy who thought he ran the place, everyone was talking behind his back and in front of it about that girl he killed. I remember one time he tried to stand on a bench and get everyone's attention and someone shouted, "Shut the . . . f— up, killer!" and he got really red in the face and got down. Can we swear here? Well, you get the idea.

So you've got the one guy in charge with absolutely no credibility still walking around like he was in charge of something, and you've got a couple hundred kids like me who suddenly have no idea what they're supposed to be doing. After all that excitement, kids got really bored. There was no texting, no Instagram, no nothing. Some kids literally did not know what to do with themselves. There was this one group of kids who claimed they could hack the RADs to pick up Wi-Fi, but that never went anywhere, at least not that I saw.

During one of the really boring periods, I actually read some of the disaster plans, and it said that shift managers were supposed to start giving their workers direction and tell them what specific jobs to do, but no one did. There was just this giant sense of "no one is in charge and no one knows what to do." What do you do when you're in an empty amusement park and you can do what you want because no one's going to stop you and you're bored out of your gourd? Turns out, there are a lot of different answers. Some people started taking things from the shops, but the people who worked in the shops kind of shut that down. Some people started hanging out with their groups of friends. I remember one guy started climbing up on some of the roofs and making Batman jokes, like, "I'm the hero this park deserves," in that stupid growly voice, and like, some people would cheer him on, and others would yell for him to get down. There were a lot of people milling around trying to figure out what to do. Some people kind of naturally migrated back to their section of the park to see what sort of damage there had been, but there was a big group of people who just sort of milled around the center of the park waiting for some sort of direction. Sometimes a sing-along or something would break out, but mostly it was groups of people hanging out in the rain or under awnings or going back to their sections where they knew where the shelter was. Some of the shop girls, or the employees who would later become the ShopGirls, I noticed they were protecting their shops from getting looted, kind of aggressively in some cases. There were a lot of locked doors just minutes after we all got out of the shelter.

The first bad thing I remember happening was over food after it became clear no one was going to feed us lunch. There was no cafeteria, so at first people raided the food that was already there in the shelter, and there was plenty of it. You would think that over three hundred people would mow through that food pretty fast, but people were pretty calm at first. I even heard one person say "slow down, we need to make it last." This girl who worked in the Hero Haven that I knew, her name was Riley, I heard her whisper, "bullshit," and I asked her why. She said there were more than seventy restaurants in the park, and all of them were meant to serve 1,500 meals a day. This food might last three or four days, she said, but people would start raiding the restaurants pretty soon, so I said, "Hell yeah, we should definitely do that!" You know, get the good stuff. At this point, we thought we'd be there, like, four days tops, so that "make the food last" line seemed really stupid at the time.

I asked Riley what restaurant she worked at, and she said the Muscle Man Grill, so she grabbed some of her friends and I grabbed some of my friends, and we headed over there. There was me and Tom and Shelly—we were all characters. Tom was Shooter Adams and Shelly was Crackin' Kate, the explosives expert. And Riley brought Braden and Allie who she worked with at the restaurant, so there were six of us all together. She had keys and everything, but nothing was locked, which bothered Riley because she had told everyone to lock up when we made for the shelters, and someone clearly hadn't. It made me wonder if the whole park was like that. By the time we got there, we looked like we just got out of the shower, and I was still in my full Jill the Soldier outfit. I hadn't had time to change and it's . . . it made my boobs look huge, OK? There's a reason I'm telling you this, I don't just suddenly start talking about my boobs. I'm not nearly the D cup the costume made me out to be. In the shelter, I was wearing a sweater, but a wet sweater is a terrible thing so I had it rolled up under my arm, and I was ready to get into some different clothes, but when we went into that kitchen, it was awesome. I mean, it was dingy and like any other kitchen, and it was sort of hard to see because the power was out, but there was more food than we could eat and no one to tell us not to eat it, you know? I'm not a big eater because of my job, but I had a great time making my own desserts from the dessert bar and ripping into a giant turkey leg. It was awesome until we heard the door open and those three guys walked in.

I had never seen them before, which is easy when you work at a park that employs 1,700 people. There were four of them, and they had been laughing about something. They saw me first because I was up at the front case to get some more root beer from the bottles because the machines weren't working with the power off. Everyone else was in the kitchen eating, so it looked like I was there by myself if you didn't know better. These guys, the second they see me, they get what I call the "bully look." I . . . I was bullied in middle school because I, um, developed early, you know? I "filled out," my mom called it, and the boys in school, some of them would leer, and that was gross, but others would get this different look. It was like a mix of . . . I don't know, of smugness and joy but in the worst way. Like they were saying "I'm going to hurt you and you're not going to do anything." You know, bully face. The grins were always bigger when they were in a group, and they hurt you more in a group, too. Well, this was a group, and they all had the same face, and I was instantly uneasy. They came in, and the first thing out of one guy's mouth was, "Holy shit, check out the tits on Jill the Soldier," and that was funny to the three other guys, and they all started laughing. Other rude things were said. I'm not, like, a prude, but this wasn't about that. It was pretty damn clear I was being threatened, and I started to panic until I started remembering my martial arts stuff about when to fight and when not to fight, and that helped calm me down.

I could have called for the rest of the group, but part of me wanted to see if I could handle this. It's hard to describe why, exactly, but I felt like this was my deal and the others didn't need to take part. Slowly, I moved behind the register. I was figuring, if I moved quick they would move quick, so I moved slow and kept my mouth shut. Plus, I wanted something between me and them. The main guy comes up and leans against the register, and the three others close in around him. He said, "You gonna take our order, Jill? I'll have the grilled breast and some tater tits." This sent them all laughing, of course. I kept my mouth shut and my heart rate down. His friends kept up with the jokes, and I kept waiting. I knew eventually one of them was going to try to grope me and when he did I was going to break his arm. Finally, after three or four more jokes about my boobs, the main guy says, "Why aren't you talking, Jill?" and I busted out the old, "When you can't say anything nice . . ." but I said it really slow and deliberate. I wanted them to know I wasn't scared even though my heart was beating pretty fast. The main guy was the first who realized I had insulted them, and he was the one who made the move. I think he was going for my braids, but I grabbed his arm under my left side and twisted really hard. His whole body moved in the direction of the twisting, just like in class, leaving his face right over the table, so with my free hand I punched the back of his head as hard as I could with my open hand and busted his nose on the counter. It was quicker and easier than I imagined it would be, and when I let go of his arm, he didn't stagger back, he fell. And his friends stood there with their mouths open. At that point, Riley and Tom and Shelly and all of them came running from the back and the guys, their magic bully spell was broken, and they left. Sure, they threw a bunch of swear words my way and called everyone all sorts of names, but they knew I wasn't scared and I was smarter than they were. To be honest, it was the first time I had ever gotten the better of a bully, and it felt really, really good.

I told Tom and Shelly and Riley and the rest of them what happened, and suddenly I'm a hero. I was getting all sorts of pats on the back, and my group was taking turns telling me what a badass I was, but Riley was really quiet. I asked her what was up and she said, "First what happened in the shelter and now this? Things are going to get bad before we get out of here." Tom said, "We should stick together then," and Riley was like, "Yes we should, but, it's got to be more than that. We've got to recruit." She laid out what we should do in the restaurant, and we talked about it for a long time, but basically, this is what she meant—she wanted to get as many folks from the restaurant together and kind of make it a base, and I said I could probably get the costumed characters together, too, and we shouldn't meet in the Muscle Man Grill, but in the costumed character lounge in the back of the false cityscape. My thought was that place was big, it was more or less hidden, and you could access seven or eight different locations in the Hero Haven pretty much in secret. Everyone thought that was a good idea but that we had to move fast. The plan was Riley and Tom and Shelly and I would head back toward the center of the park, and when we saw people we knew, we would tell them there was a big meal at the characters' lounge and to go there now. Braden and Allie would stay behind and actually cook something up. They had the buffet stuff for corporate events; the Muscle Man Grill was one of the twelve restaurants in the park that could set up for what we called "mass feeding," but what that meant was corporate events or parties, so they were going to move that stuff over to the lounge and start cooking. Once we got a group together, Riley thought we could take everyone who was at that meeting, and they could recruit their friends, and it would go from there.

She was really smart because she said what we would do is form a preliminary council. The six of us, this was our deal, she said, so if there was anyone who seemed like they were going to cause problems, we could vote them out. We would make a decision and then, in private, go tell them that they were . . . that it wasn't going to work out and they should seek shelter somewhere else. We would try that and see how it went, you know? The idea behind it was, what if those four guys showed up at the meeting and wanted to eat our food and take shelter from us? I remember Tom saying, "Fuck that!" Sorry, Mom, if you're reading this, but that's what he said. He was really shaken up by those guys. He wanted to go find them, but I asked him, "What would you do then? How would you hurt them?" and that calmed him down. I learned that from a friend of mine, who was a Buddhist in my dorm at UT. She said, if someone wants to commit an act of violence, walk them through it, and once they see the consequences, most of the time they'll back down. It worked that day. Not so much later, though. God, I'm talking so much and I'm off on so many tangents! You're going to edit this so I don't sound completely stupid, right? Oh my God.

OK, so we headed back to the main part of the square, and immediately it was clear something was wrong. There was a big crowd on one side of the Golden Road, and they were all gathered around something. It turns out that idiot guy who was climbing on the buildings pretending to be Batman had fallen while trying to climb down, and he had hurt himself really badly. I was to the back, so I didn't see it myself, but what I heard was he hit his head, and I guess first aid was, like, not going to help. He had liquid coming out of his ears, which means there's significant brain damage, someone told me. I could hear a couple of people yelling, one was screaming, "Help him," and another was yelling, "There's nothing I can do," that sort of thing but with more swear words, and other people were pushing to see, and it was just sort of an ugly scene. Then this guy, he starts pushing his way through the crowd, really aggressively. He pushed past me and hit my elbow with something metal. It turned out to be one of those big metal stanchions that hold the ropes up so people can get in line, you know? He pushed his way through the crowd and lifts the stanchion over his head, and I hear people start screaming. You can guess, right? It took all of ten seconds for him to walk through the crowd and crush not-Batman's head in with that big metal pole. Just like that. Everyone shut up and watched him, and, even from the back, I heard him mutter, "Someone had to do it." Then he walked away, and nobody followed him or questioned him or nothing. He left the stanchion on the ground, and I heard it clang—it was the loudest thing anyone could hear—and there was this trail of blood coming off it. It was . . . look, we're talking about Brock Hockney here, I figured you'd have guessed by now, so I don't want to make it sound like anything he did was good. He was a fucking monster, sorry, Mom. But of all the terrible things he ended up doing, that was probably the most understandable, you know? Not-Batman, I never learned his name, if he was hurt as bad as everyone was saying and he was going to die anyway and was in a lot of pain, someone sort of did have to do it. He was suffering, you know? I didn't walk up to see the aftermath. I don't even know what happened to his body. He . . . he deserved better as a person, I guess is what I want to say. Please, don't make a stupid joke about "the death he deserved" in a stupid Batman voice, OK. I'm being serious.

Whatever the, like, morals of the situation, seeing that lit a fire under my ass, and I had found seventeen people I knew in about half an hour and told them to get to Hero Haven and what we were doing. Nobody asked me any questions. They just went. They were scared, and I think they could tell I was getting scared, too. Plus, this is hard to describe, but everything just felt really "off." There was no one in charge, no structure, no phones. I mean, I'm not glued to my phone, but I check Facebook and Instagram once every two hours or so, and when you aren't connected it's just . . . weird. Recruiting wasn't hard. Riley and Tom and Shelly, they had the same sort of reaction from the people they talked to. All the clocks in the park were stopped, so we couldn't say, "Meet us at 9:30" or whatever, so people trickled in to the characters' lounge, and we had over fifty people present when we started talking.

Riley, she wasn't what I'd call a good friend of mine, but I knew her well enough to say that girl really stepped it up at that meeting. She was amazing. She was clear in what we wanted to do, which was start a group that could protect its members. She said, if you have friends who you want to have in the group, you have two hours to find them and bring them here and that after sundown, things would start to get hairy, that's what she said, hairy. She said get them here and we would work out where to sleep and where to eat and what space belonged to us and how to keep it safe, and everyone agreed. The story of Hockney killing that kid with the stanchion, that had spread like wildfire, and folks were understandably scared. Then along comes Riley with a plan for sleep and food and safety right away, and everyone jumped at the chance. I did notice that one of the four of those guys who had bullied me at the Muscle Man Grill was there, but he left quietly when he saw who was running the meeting, and we didn't have to tell him to leave. Turned out, we should have at least talked to him. He ended up in the Pirate Cove.

See, what happened was word of this group and what Riley and the rest of us were doing spread almost as fast as news of what happened to not-Batman. It spread the old-fashioned way, too, which means it became a game of telephone, I think. People may have . . . what's the word, embellished a bit. In the two hours between when the meeting ended and when we "closed enrollment," that's what Riley called it, we had a visit from Mr. Garliek, who was still sure he was in charge of something. He said we didn't need to form this group, that the park was safe and that he was trying to get everyone to the Dream Pop Star Amphitheater so he could tell us all what to do. That went over like a lead fucking balloon. Tom kind of laughed at him, and I told him what had happened to me in the restaurant, that I would have been assaulted had I been in there by myself. He said everyone would be safe, the disaster manual had protocol for this and yadda yadda. We didn't take him seriously, and it was Riley who hit him with what he had done in the shelter. She said something like, "If we don't come with you, are you going to kill us in the dark like you did that other girl?" and that shut him up. We didn't hear from him much after that.

But what we did see was that the people at the meeting went to find their friends, and they were finding that their friends didn't want to leave their section of the park. Apparently our story was not unique. Someone in each section of the park knew where the food was and got their friends together, and even if they weren't organized, they had gravitated to their own section. That was fine with Riley, because she said, we want people who will fight for themselves and their friends if they have to. What we didn't want was a lot of freeloaders, that's what she called them, a bunch of freeloaders eating our food and running when it was time to stand up and protect ourselves, which is what we were convinced was going to happen. Personally, I was still in love with the idea that your friends standing up with you would run off all the threats we were going to face. I got my heart broken on that one.

OK, that was stupid, too. Just make it sound like I was normal there, OK?

I finally, finally found some different clothes in a locker, but I decided to keep on my Soldier Jill beret because of the rain. Keep your head covered, you know? All of Private Pummel's platoon wore berets, so there were a ton of them in the characters' lounge, and people just started putting them on. I hesitate to say they were our uniform, because people wore them to keep the rain off their heads, not to identify themselves, but just so you know, most of us wore berets, and that might be my fault. Anyway, things kind of took shape fast, and it seemed like, in the early stages, things were going to be OK. Braden and Allie were in charge of food distribution, and they were good at it. Tom and Shelly and I figured out the bathroom situation, which wasn't pleasant. It was a bucket system, OK? The less said about that, the better. Also, most of the toilets for visitors and employees had backed up during the storm. The less said about *that*, the better. Riley was sort of the general, in charge of it all. She sent some folks to the other restaurants and snack bars to gather up food, she met with Braden and Allie to figure out what would keep and what we had to eat right away, we figured out water and how to ration it and we figured out where to sleep, all before it got dark, which was pretty impressive, thank you very much.

It was Tom who thought that a patrol would be a good idea, to send five or six people out every so often just to have a look around. It was Tom who talked about what we should call ourselves. The idea was most of our section was about superheroes, but we had this great comic book store in the middle of the Hero Haven, and it had absolutely anything you'd want to read. It was weird because they featured all the comics that had characters in the park, but you didn't have to look too hard for niche items or some really weird stuff. I remember one time a couple of us played a game to see who could go in with ten dollars and come out with the weirdest piece of literature, drawn or otherwise. My friend Jackson won when he found some Japanese tentacle porn, which means they sell that stuff in FantasticLand. That's pretty far out there. The reason it had such niche stuff, rumor had it, was that Johnny Fresno told this owner of a great comic book store in

Los Angeles that he would have autonomy if he opened the store in the park, and the guy agreed, which is why you have the Private Pummel and all the kids books in one part of the store and then *whatever* in the bulk of the store. The store had the FantasticLand Exclamation Point logo outside, but when you go inside the first thing you saw was this giant sculpture of the character Deadpool from Marvel comics coming out of the wall. It was really big. You couldn't miss it. So much so that a lot of people would say, "Meet me under the Deadpool if you get lost," so that's where the name came from. Deadpool was also a really rude and caustic guy in the comics, which is why Tom suggested the name. Some people said, "How about the Justice League or the Avengers?" and Tom said "The Deadpools," and everyone was like, yeah, that's it. Tom was good at stuff like that.

So the first night, everything is going better than you would have thought. Some people are playing cards, other people are just talking, and there's a real community atmosphere in the characters' lounge. Nobody had gone to their assigned places to sleep because no one was tired. Everyone was kind of juiced. We had candles lit, and there was a very soft glow in the room. It was after dinner when Tom picked his group to go out on patrol.

Real quick, how much of this have you heard? I don't like going over it if I don't have to.

OK, Jill, deep breath. The Hero Haven, it's not that big. It's probably four to six city blocks of walkable space, so it was a no-brainer that Tom and the rest of them should have been back in less than fifteen minutes. We started getting nervous at twenty, and just when Riley and I were going to get a group together to go looking for them, we heard an explosion outside. A couple of us threw open the door and saw a firework exploding, which was kind of unexpected because it was still raining. Not hard, but kinda drizzling. I also remember it was really dark and everyone was having a hard time seeing what was going on. What we were able to see was a bright light and what looked like a flare. Later we found out it was some sort of flare gun. Let me back up, the second we opened the door, the flare went off. What we saw was that Brock Hockney guy and two of his friends standing, each with a candle. Tom was there, and he was on his knees with his hands tied in front of him on a wooden block. At least, that's what it looked like.

I'm going to remember this as long as I live. Brock held the flare above his head and yelled, "You think you're safe. You're not." Then one of his friends made this movement, and we heard Tom scream. Just like that the flares go out, and all you can hear is Tom screaming and screaming and people inside the lounge are screaming too, and there's lots of jostling and people scrambling around. It was like the shelter when the power went out, but worse. It was more frantic. Thank God no one knocked over any of the candles because the next thing I'm able to make out is Riley holding Tom. By that point, someone grabbed one of the flashlights and turned it on, and we all saw what happened. They had cut off Tom's hands. He had blood gushing out of both wrists and . . . nobody knew what to do. There was a first aid kit but it had Band-Aids and heat packs. What the fuck were we supposed to do with those? I ran over and grabbed Tom's head and was whispering whatever I could think of to him, but he was already really cold. I was whispering, "I know it hurts," and "It's OK baby," and stuff like that, but like I said, no one knew what to do. God damn it, all we could do was watch him bleed and scream and cry. At some point, someone got the idea to stop the bleeding by making tourniquets out of belts, but by the time two people got their belts off and got them around Tom's wrists, he had lost consciousness. Maybe that was good.

It wasn't until the morning that we noticed the stanchion. That monster left it, there like some fucking calling card. Tom's hands were . . . on top of it, and one of them, one of the Pirates had taken the time to make the middle finger stick up. There wasn't even any blood. The rain had washed it away. All the blood was all inside, on us.

I . . . he lived another nine hours or so. During that time, we had folks running around trying to find anyone with medical training, but everyone was in their tribes by then. There was no one to help. Tom would occasionally make noise and struggle around, but he never opened his eyes. There has not been a day since then when I didn't think of him. Mostly I hope he wasn't in pain. I . . . we tried things to help but we only hurt him more, I think. No one knew what they were doing.

I can't tell you how bad it was other than to say I've never felt so helpless, but so in need of help. We were grasping onto anything. Someone would have an idea and say, "We have to put his feet up, so he doesn't go into shock," and no one had a better idea so we put his feet up, and he would get worse, and then someone would say "we need to get him water," so seven people would go and get him water, and there would be these bottles of water lying around. Someone even convinced us if we could get the Internet back up we could go to WebMD and figure out what we needed to do. It was that kind of desperate.

We were still missing another one of the guys from the patrol. I heard later they went and joined the circus, as it were. Tough to say. I don't really care. I had something else on my mind, something bad. Riley felt it too and she was, once again, the leader we needed. When the sun came up but before Tom died, she went into the comic book store on her own and grabbed a real sword off the wall. Everyone gathered for breakfast, like we had talked about the night before, and we all looked like a bunch of drowned rats, wet and tired and miserable, and I remember when the sun came up you could see just how much of Tom's blood had gotten everywhere. Riley went to the center of the room, took the sword, and drove it hard into one of the tables. It stuck there, wobbling a little bit. She said what we all were thinking.

She said, "No, we're not safe. But neither are they."

INTERVIEW 8: CRISTOBAL ABASOLO

Concession Manager in the Fairy Prairie, Eventual Robot Soldier

I was the guy who left the Deadpools. It was nothing personal, and I had my reasons. I wasn't going to be anywhere near the Pirates, not after what happened to me and then to Tom, you know? The Deadpools and the Pirates, they were right next to each other in the park. I wanted to be as far away as possible. I believe the phrase in English is, "Fuck that noise."

I came for the summer from Chile. They say in America they love men with accents, and I can lay it on thick if it's to my advantage. FantasticLand, they recruit from certain countries very aggressively because they like having an international flavor. I remember seeing ads all over my Facebook page the summer before I came to work. They get visitors from all over, so why not come here and work for the summer? The money is good, the people are good, and it's just as hot as it is where I live on the equator. I came the summer before the storm, and the people, they really liked me. I don't want to go into too much detail, but I was lucky a lot. Is that how you say it? I was lucky? I don't want to say too much. My parents will likely hear this. They will insist I go right to church after, I think.

Because I came back and because I encouraged others to come, they made me a manager at one of the restaurants in the Fairy Prairie. I oversaw four of the snack stations. There were two cupcake stands, a smoothie station, and a place that sold nachos. I, uh, I never really understood the nacho station, but who was I to judge? Americans, they love disgusting cheese. They were all very profitable. I was in charge of making the schedules and handling the deliveries, that sort of thing. No problem. At least, not until I met Travis. He worked in the Hero Haven and he played Radio Roger, who was one of Private Pummel's group. He and I became very good friends. We were together all the time we could be together. Sometimes, if I could manage, I would go over there to watch him interact with the visitors. He would do this thing where he would give the kid one of his radios and run to the other side of a building and try to talk to the kid and tell him where to go. It was very cute to watch. We were very good friends.

Mostly, in the Fairy Prairie, it is girls. Nothing against girls, but after getting out of the shelter, I felt like it would be a good idea to be with guys who could protect each other if they needed to. Let me back up. After the shelter and after that Pirate leader killed the boy who fell off the roof, everyone I talked to felt like they needed to protect themselves and groups were the easiest way to find protection. The girls who ran the shops, they were not happy to have people there. They started making lots of noise and saying, "You can't stand here," and "You need to find somewhere else to go." It all got worse after that boy fell off the roof. People started going their separate ways and looking for a group. I could have gone back to the Fairies, but I didn't have a lot in common with those girls. I was their boss, but I didn't think they would listen to me. We didn't listen to bosses after we got out of the shelter.

Why? I have thought about this. You know Mr. Garliek, the man who was supposed to be in charge? Everyone thought he killed that girl, yes? You've heard about this? He had a group of people around him who were supposed to help him be in charge and when everyone got out, they all immediately decided they didn't want to listen to him anymore. I wouldn't have listened to him either. He was very rude to everyone around him. He had no authority because everyone believed he had killed that girl for disagreeing with him. Instead of everyone being afraid that he would kill them too, everyone ignored him. I think that when everyone ignored him, all the managers on all levels decided they had no authority either. They joined a group, and other leaders stepped forward.

That's how it worked and how you got the tribes. The leader became a joke; no one cared enough to step up and try to lead. I wasn't going to risk anything for a nacho stand and two cupcake stations. Those girls who worked in the concession stands, they never showed me respect, anyway.

I decided to not go with the Fairies and followed Travis. He was good friends with Riley, so he had a group who would welcome him. Everyone was very welcoming at first, but Riley looked at me like I was not right. After the first meeting but before everything went bad, she came to me while I was playing cards with Travis and some of his friends. She asked if I would like to go on the first patrol and that it would be a good idea because I could get to know some of the other people who worked here. I remember saying, "Most of my friends are here, so it's OK," and she left me alone, but she pulled Travis aside and talked to him. When he sat back down, he told me it would be a really good idea to go on patrol. I did it because Travis asked.

Please remember, no one thought this was anything dangerous. I was comfortable in the lounge, I was with my friends, I had a full belly, one of Travis's friends had stolen several bottles of wine from one of the restaurants, and we had started drinking them. It was starting to feel like an adventure or like a camp where there's no Internet. I didn't want to leave because I was warm and dry and felt good, but Travis said it would "grease the wheels" and that I would make new friends. I did what Travis wanted.

Riley introduced me to Tom, who was a nice guy. I will say that about him. The other girl, named Shelly, she was going to go, but Tom told her not to. He told her to save her strength for the next patrol. He had two other people selected, one named Sam and one named Adrienne. Sam worked at the Hero Haven and Adrienne, she didn't say much. I learned she was from the shops on the Golden Road, and her English wasn't as good as mine. She was from Venezuela and was very scared. When she saw me and I spoke to her in Spanish, her eyes lit up and she began speaking very quickly about what had happened to her. She got as far as the shelter and broke one of her fingers when the lights went out before Tom asked that we speak English so we all could talk to each other. I told him her English wasn't great but we promised not to talk about anything important. He wasn't mad, but he told me it was rude to speak in Spanish. I didn't want him to be angry with me, so I agreed. She spoke in English and told me what happened to her finger. She wanted to see a doctor, and when Tom wasn't looking, I whispered to her that she was a strong girl and that she could get through this but I did it in Spanish so only she would understand me. She was a little more confident after that, but we didn't speak Spanish any longer.

Adrienne was very sweet but was very scared. I remember she kept reaching into her pocket. She didn't put her hands in her pocket and leave them there; she would put them in, then take them out, then put them in again. When I asked her why she did that, she said, "I keep feeling my phone vibrate," even though they had taken our phones away. Then she said, "I keep hoping it's a message saying they are going to rescue us." I remember feeling very sad when she said that.

The patrol shouldn't have taken very long because the Hero Haven is less than a hundred acres, but everything is slower when there are no lights. I want to impress upon you how dark it was. There was no electricity at all—there were no street lights or exit signs or anything to light the way. It occurred to me, at that time, that a patrol was absolutely worthless when you're stumbling around in the dark. People could be right in front of us and we wouldn't have known it, plus we didn't exactly see the point. What would we have done if we had run into someone? I asked Tom this, and he said we would "assess their intentions," which didn't make much sense to me. We had flashlights, but they were no match for the size of the area we were trying to illuminate. I noticed after only a few minutes that our group would instinctively move toward any light we were able to find. We found some battery-operated signs that were starting to go out, and we found a lit public toilet that was hooked up to some sort of generator. Of course it was raining, so between the dark and the wet we were very miserable, and Tom wouldn't tell us what it was we were doing out there. We were blindly following the lead of this man, moving toward any light we saw, which was how we ended up in the Pirate gift shop.

I don't know what Tom was thinking, and I've thought a lot about it. I could only come up with two ideas. The first was that he wanted to take people to the Pirates to see how they would react. The second is that he wanted to feel like he was in control, and this patrol was the way he came up with to do it. Either way it was a bad plan. The lights that we saw, and we saw them from quite a distance, belonged to old-fashioned lanterns that had been lit. They were part of the park's decor, is that the right word? Decor? They were always there but hardly ever used. They put out a lot of light, and when we got there they were lit but no one was there. Only us and lots of souvenirs, T-shirts, and cases of pop and energy drinks. There were also chocolate bars by the register but no other food that we could see. Tom and Sam grabbed a few bags and stuffed some drinks and chocolate into them. They were in a hurry, so they didn't see what was happening outside, but I did.

A flash of light made me turn my head. I didn't know what it was at the time, but I started speaking to Adrienne in Spanish. I told her to "*Ocultar!*" which means "hide," and she very quickly jumped into a rack of T-shirts. It was the round kind, and it hid her very well, especially in the dark. She was a petite girl, so she made very little noise, but Tom and Sam, they were very loud. They were so loud, they didn't hear the tapping right away, but it got louder quickly. It started as the sound of metal on wood, not a "clang" but a "thud" and then it got louder. I looked to the area with the most light, and I saw several boys with swords, and they were banging the swords against the side of the building. Soon, they were all banging their real, metal swords on the wooden gift shop walls.

Tom and Sam stopped and realized there were at least twenty people surrounding the shop. The banging kept going and got louder, and I could hear Tom and Sam talking to each other very quickly and quietly. They never thought to include me. I don't know what they said, but they spoke very hurriedly, and I could tell, in the low light, they were worried. Then one of the Pirates yelled, in a deep voice, "Time to come out. There's nowhere to hide so you might as well face us." Please remember, at this point, things were tense but not what I would call dangerous. I had heard rumors of someone being killed, but it was described as a mercy killing, I think is the phrase. There was no reason to think we were in real danger. I had been beaten up a few times in Chile, and that was what I was expecting. I was prepared for a few hits to the stomach and maybe to the face, and I think I said to Tom, "Let's let them hit us, and we can go back to the others." He didn't say anything, but he yelled back at them. He yelled something like, "Sure, no problem," and he and Sam went out the front door. I went out behind them.

There were three boys outside, and one of them had a big pirate hat. They had lit torches and put them behind them so there was enough light to see. I knew one of the boys because I had seen him at a training earlier in the summer, but the other two I didn't know. I was only able to piece it together afterwards. It's funny, how the mind plays tricks on you. I saw some of these same boys on the news not all that long ago, and I remember them as tall and muscular, but on the TV, they were the same size as me. In the light of the torches, which were not going out in the rain, they were gigantic, and I could also tell they were not happy. As best as I can remember, they told us we had been caught stealing. Like I said, there were twenty or so boys with swords all in a circle, and they would react to whatever the three in the front would do. When they said, "You've been caught stealing," there were whoops and grunts of approval. That was the scariest to me. They never let us forget how many of them there were or that they had swords. They never let them rest or put them away. They were front and center the whole time.

The one Pirate to the right of the leader in the big hat, he came up to the three of us and said, "You have a choice." He said, "You can join us and take a test of loyalty, or you can accept your punishment and go back to your people." It sounds ridiculous to say it out loud, but he was very serious, and so was everyone else. They grunted in approval. Tom had chosen a lighter tone and was smiling and trying to reason with them. He would say, "Sorry guys, I didn't know I was stealing," and offered to put back everything in the sack he had. He did this a few times, saying things like, "Come on, guys," and "This is stupid, we're all employees of the same park." It was the third or fourth time he tried to appeal to them that the leader in the hat quietly stepped forward and smashed Tom's nose with the handle of his sword. There was enough light for me to see Tom fall to his hands and knees and spit blood onto the ground. The rain had matted his hair, and I remember his outline on the ground. It is a very clear memory.

The leader, he then said, "You don't understand where you are," and he kicked Tom in the ribs. Tom fell backward and lay on his back, breathing hard. He said something else that I didn't quite hear because of the rain, but it sounded like, "A pirate gets what he wants." I figured something like this was bound to happen to us next, and Sam thought so too. He jumped forward and said, "I want to join. What do I have to do to join?" They told him to stand still and then they came to me. The one I recognized from training got very close to my face and said, "What about you?" I remember my heart beating very fast, and for the first time feeling like this was something more than a beating. I felt in danger, like I was maybe going to die here. When they asked me what I wanted to do, I suddenly was very aware that they could kill me here in the rain, and no one would stop them or punish them. They had figured that out well before I had.

I said, "I will join." I am not proud of this.

After I said that, the leader in the hat started yelling to the crowd. He said, "We have two potential Pirates here and only room for one." Sam shot a glance at me and I at him, and I could see his fear. I'm sure he could see mine as well. The leader then said, "It's time for your test of loyalty. Whoever brings me the girl hiding in the gift shop can stay. Punishment for stealing from us awaits the other."

I had secretly been hoping that we would have to fight, as I might have been able to beat him, but once the leader made it clear what he wanted, I knew two things. The first was that Sam would give up Adrienne in a split second if he could and the second was I knew, for a fact, that he hadn't seen her hide in the T-shirt rack. I knew it almost for certain. After he looked at me, he turned and ran into the shop very quickly, and I followed. There was less light in the gift shop than outside with the torches, and once we got inside I immediately tackled Sam around the waist. He hadn't expected it, so he went down very hard onto the wet, carpeted floor. I tried to kick him, but there was even less light on the floor. I might have hit him, or I might have kicked a shelf or something, but after that first kick, I lost him. I heard him scrambling around, but it was too dark to get a good sense of anything. I ended up bumping into a shelf, and I heard him scrambling around, then he was quiet. He was hiding, and I didn't know what his plan was. To be honest, I didn't know what my plan was. If I found Adrienne, I was going to comfort her and try to figure out a way not to give her up, and at that moment, I didn't want Sam to find her. I was working on one problem at a time.

I made my way around the back of the register, and that's when I heard Adrienne. Sam was dragging her by the hair out of the T-shirt rack, and I ran at him. This . . . sounds more heroic than it is. I am not much of a fighter, really, and he punched me very hard in the face as I ran toward him. He was ready for me, even in the dark. It knocked me down, and Adrienne, who is small, couldn't put up much of a fight. Sam got her out of the shop before I could get to my feet, and I was bloody and in the dark. I heard some of the Pirates cheer when they came out of the shop, and I had no choice but to walk out as well. I stood there for a second trying to shake away the stars in my head and trying not to taste the blood from my lip. There were two exits from the gift shop with Pirates outside each one. There was no back door and no place to hide, so I walked out and stood behind them. It was hard to do, but not as hard as what was to come.

When I walked out, all the boys started yelling at me, but the leader put up his hand. He said that I was brave for coming out and facing my fate. He said, "That is no small thing," and told them to show some respect. Then two of them came with rope and tied my hands in front of me. It was dark, so they did not do a good job. As soon as they let go I realized it wouldn't be hard to free my hands, and with the darkness, I had a reasonable chance of escape. My blood was pumping very fast, but I decided to stay where I was for a moment and to see what happened to Sam and to Adrienne. I was very scared for her. I had lied to her before. I only knew two women from Venezuela, and they were not very tough.

Remember I told you there were two torches on either side of the three boys who were leading the group? One of the boys pulled a long thin piece of metal from his bag and held the tip to the torch. No one spoke as he did this. There were three of the boys holding Sam, and the leader walked up to him and said, "If you want to join us, you must know how to inflict pain, and how to handle it." In a strange way, I felt relieved. My biggest fear was that many of them would rape Adrienne while the others cheered. I . . . I did not want to see that and was thankful I wouldn't have to, but then my attention turned back to the torch. The leader had taken the piece of metal out and I understood. It was a brand, I think the word is. It is hot metal used to mark cattle, yes? They meant to mark Sam, but he didn't realize it until the leader told him to choose where the mark would be. He said "the arm is popular, but we've done legs too," and each of the Pirate boys started pulling up their sleeves or their pant legs to show that they had been marked. They all looked very fresh, which made sense since this was only the first or second night out of the shelter. They were already a tribe and they had the marks to show for it. The marks were all different letters. I couldn't see what letter they had chosen for Sam.

I can tell you what I think I saw because it was very dark except for the torches, but Sam looked like he was going to cry. He chose his shoulder as the place for the Pirates to put the mark, and the other boys gathered around him. They were saying things like, "It's going to hurt, brother," and "Brace yourself," and most of all, "After this, you are with us." They were all talking near his head and . . . this sounds silly, but it's like they were all giving him a hug. One of the boys took a rolled-up piece of cloth out of his pocket and asked if Sam wanted to bite on it, and he nodded. Then the leader came and said, very loudly, "We welcome our brother, Sam, into the Pirates. He will fight for us, we will fight for him." Then they all spoke in unison and said, "A Pirate never quits!" That's when the screaming started.

They held Sam very tightly, from what I could see, and his screams turned into whimpers, and he slowly started to calm down. I've had people ask me if I heard a sizzling sound or something like that, and I didn't. All I heard was Sam and the crackle of the fire. The second it was over, I started to very much worry about myself. If that was what they did to people that were in their group, what would they do to me? I made sure I could still get out of my ropes if I needed to, and I could. No one had noticed I wasn't tied up very well.

The leader handed the piece of metal back to another boy, who put it in the fire. Then he told Sam what else he had to do. He said, "Now that you've felt pain, you must inflict it. This girl is scared, Sam. She ran away, and she hid and those are two things a Pirate never does." He said because she was afraid of pain, that pain would find her or something like that. Then he whispered something to Sam, and a couple of the boys grabbed Adrienne, who immediately started to cry and say, "No, please don't." I don't know if she looked at me. It was too dark. I can only imagine her fear. She was wet, away from home, in the dark, and strange boys were pulling her into the middle of a circle and promising her pain. I can't think of many things more terrifying, and I knew my time was coming if I didn't do something.

I remember Sam had the brand and he walked toward her. She was on her knees, and three boys were holding her as she sobbed. I don't remember her saying words. They were more noises and sobs. Sam said, loud enough for everyone to hear, "Which side of your face do you want it?" and all the Pirates started to cheer. When they started to cheer, I let my ropes drop. I didn't move, because the hands of the two boys responsible for me, they were still there, but I was ready to run, and I had a sense of where I wanted to go. I was not the fastest runner, but in the dark, if you know where you're going and your enemies do not, well, that will make all the difference, will it not? But I wanted to see what happened to Adrienne and if there was any opportunity to help her.

By now, she was crying and, what's the word, hysterical. She was not making sense and wasn't fighting, so it was easy for the boys to push her head into the mud so Sam could do the deed and join their club. I remember, very clearly, that he paused a bit as he walked up to her with the piece of metal, and when he put it to her face, this time, I did hear a sizzling noise, and it didn't stop. Sam sort of jerked his hand around and then let go of the metal and it was stuck in Adrienne's cheek. He started yelling and saying, "Brock, Brock, it's stuck!" and jumping backward as Adrienne screamed and screamed and pulled at the metal piece sticking out of her face. The boys let her up, and the piece of metal, the brand, had gone through her cheek and into her mouth. It was still burning her tongue. I have thought about it, and what must have happened was she screamed and the brand must have gone through the soft part of her face and missed the teeth all together until it was in her mouth, burning her. I cannot imagine the pain or the panic she must have felt.

Everyone was in shock, and there were many people who ran toward Adrienne, including one of the boys who was supposed to be looking after me. I thought about punching the other one, but he was too wrapped up in Adrienne and her torture to even think about me. I turned on my heel and ran into the dark. I knew there was a restaurant fifty yards or so away and beyond that was a small shack used for storage. I was able to get into the shack by very quietly breaking a window and climbing in, and that's where I stayed until there was the first trace of light. Then I opened the door and ran as fast as I could to the center of the park where the Exclamation Point was, and then I kept running. I ran until I found my new friend Jeremy and I burst into tears telling him what I had seen. He was kind to me and I've never been so thankful for kindness in my life.

INTERVIEW 9: ELVIS SPRINGER

Security Manager at Fantastic Future World, Leader of the Robots.

We were having a great time until Cristobal showed up.

The kids in Future World, we're a pretty tight group. In the Science Dome, for some reason, seven employees are stationed at the entrance and exit to the ride, and then there are a couple safety and maintenance guys whose job it is to make sure everyone stays in their pods and nothing goes wrong while the ride is going. That's a dozen or so people whose job is to watch this machine that entertains guests. There's a lot of downtime, so they get to know each other, you know? It doesn't take long for coworkers to become friends and then they start hanging out during their off-hours. The whole section was like that. It was a constant, fun soap opera to watch these kids come through and fight and fall in love and get in Twitter beefs or whatever they called it. None of them were shy about introducing themselves so I knew everyone. I'm a people person. You can tell.

What you've heard is probably pretty accurate. After things went bad in the shelter, the most popular thing to do was go to your section of the park. You had some couples who were dating or people who had good friends in other sections, and they would sometimes end up in a different section, but by and large, everyone stuck to where they were comfortable. And that just makes sense. But Fantastic Future World, that was different. A few stragglers aside, it was forty or so of my favorite people. That's what I would say when I was on the job. One of them would nudge me as they passed by or yell at me when I was on break, and I would always go, "There goes my favorite person in the park." I don't play favorites. They were all my favorite, and I was sort of honored when they all started looking to me to solve problems. See, I'd worked at the park for eight years, which is an eternity for some of these kids fresh out of high school. Man, I've seen it all. I saw puke and blood and more puke and lost kids and teenagers screwing on the rides and puke and old ladies passing out. The job always kept me on my toes, but my favorite part was hanging out with these kids.

Now, I want to get something off my chest, and then I'll get into it, OK? If I'm a security guard, I bet you're wondering why me and the other guys and gals in my department didn't do anything when we first started hearing about the violence. It's a natural thing to wonder about, and I've got a couple of answers for you. First, the park is big. I mean, really big. You can scream your lungs out in one section and they won't hear you in another, plus the buildings have a way of swallowing sound. Plus, a lot of what we were hearing sounded like rumor. I'm not the type to go looking for trouble, but I'll take a good swing at it if it comes in my direction, you know? The second thing was, I inherited a shit-ton of responsibility once things went tits-up at the shelter. That Garlic guy, whatever his name is, he was supposed to be in charge, and it was clear by the way he acted and the stuff we heard about him that he wasn't up to the job. Scratch that, if everything I heard was true he was too stupid and full of himself to lead both hands to find his ass. Bottom line is you've got no structure, a huge area, no power, scared kids looking to you, and really no incentive to stick your neck out. At some point you make the calculation that it's easier to play defense and stop folks from hurting you than it is to stop what's already going on. It might sound a touch cowardly, but there you go. That's the answer. That make sense?

OK. So after the shelter we start trickling back to Fantastic Future World, and everyone's greeted with open arms. There's this big courtyard right off the main entrance where most people go to wait in line for the Star Slammer and Shoot the Shrieker rides. All the kids called it the "Big S." They're kids. What you gonna do? When I walked into the Big S, there were already about six or seven kids on the second floor of the courtyard, and they were yelling for me to come up. Once I got up there, they immediately had all sorts of issues. One of them thought she broke her nose, another lost his glasses, a third had really sensitive skin and the rain and the wet was a problem. I said, "Not broken but bloody, find some glasses at the gift shop near the bridges, and toughen up a bit and hang out up here where it's dry." All of these problems seemed huge to these kids, but they were nothing we couldn't handle at first. A couple of the kids who were a bit . . . how do I want to put this . . . whose mom and dad may have taken care of them a little too much, they were starting to get weepy. I heard a lot of, "I need to call my mom," and "My mom will be freaking out," but of course what could you do? No phones, no power, no nothing. Best I could do was to get us all together in one place. I wanted to make sure anyone from our group who came looking for us would find us, so some of the kids hung out in the public area of the park, and I moved the other kids who were there into the Shoot the Shrieker ride, which was shut down and dark, but I knew there was a spot with scaffolding that had skylights in the maintenance area. Most rides have a place where maintenance folks can go in case the power goes out, which happens more often than you'd think. One time on the Star Slammer, we had a major power outage, and it stuck people on the ride for twenty-five minutes. That might not seem like a long time, but try it hanging upside down. *[Laughter]* Anyway, then I told the kids, "Gather supplies. We're going to hang out here for a while." And we did. It was dry, it was isolated, it was good for that number of kids, and it was a short climb to the roof where we could see all the way past the big Exclamation Point in the center of town. Not to pat myself on the back, but it was as close to a perfect setup as we were likely to find, and I thought I had everything taken care of.

Now I'm back where I started. We were kind of having a great time. We had light during the day, all the food and drink we wanted, we even busted into some of the beer from the Future World Gravity Grill, and I swear, some of those kids hadn't touched alcohol before, but they were having fun that night. We had a talent show, and the kids quit bitching about their phones every five minutes. It was great. During the day, we hung out, we played cards, and we always had folks patrolling the Big S and other folks gathering supplies like water and such. By the time the third or fourth day rolled around, I was starting to think, "What's taking them so long?" I knew that some of the Mole Men, they weren't the Mole Men then but that's what we called them later, and I knew a few of them had set out into the forest surrounding the park, and from up on the roof we could see that everything was flooded beyond belief. I mean, you don't really get a sense of how trapped we were until you get up on that roof and saw all the water around the park. It was everywhere but I still thought rescue would be coming pretty soon. But the other thing I could see up on the roof of that ride was all the planes flying past us and absolutely nothing else going on. It's not like we could see to the highway, but I could tell nothing was moving out there. I sort of thought, in the back of my head, that we might be there a while, but I didn't let on. There would have been panic.

So the third or fourth day or whatever, we run into Cristobal. This really fun dude named Jeremy Neal, he was out hauling food for the night when this kid runs into him. To hear Jeremy tell it, he was babbling and talking about terrible stuff that was going on. Terrible stuff. He brought Cristobal to me since I was the resident fixer, and I took him into my office, and he told me the whole story about the Pirates and the Deadpools and the girl getting her face branded and all and it sounded really bad. But that's the other end of the park. There was no trouble in my place. We were keeping to ourselves and having a good time. It didn't track that other people couldn't get along just as well as we were getting along. I mean, how hard is it to hang out with friends, eat a bunch of free food, and wait for the cavalry? According to Cristobal, it was really damn hard. He was making it sound like some third-world hellhole where they chop off your head for eating meat on Saturday or whatever. It spooked me, so I figured we needed a bit more information. I mean, we hadn't even been to other sections of the park. No need, no desire. I knew the park, and Karen, who worked with me on the security beat and had been on the job a couple months, she was getting to know the park, so we figured we would take a look around, see what we could see.

I told Cristobal to keep his trap shut until we figured out what was going on, and of course he didn't. By the time we were getting ready to leave the next day, we had a full-blown game of "panic telephone" on our hands. Girls were asking me if the Pirates were raping anyone who went west of the Exclamation Point, and one kid came up and said we needed weapons and had started tearing big chunks off the Shoot the Shrieker ride to make the most ineffective clubs I had ever seen. I told everyone to calm down, we were in the information-gathering phase, and to sit tight until we get back. One kid yelled, "What if you don't come back?" and I yelled back, "Then do whatever the hell you want!" and everyone laughed at that. It was a nervous laugh, but I took it. Once we were clear, I told Karen what we were really up to, which was to go find the riot locker. I haven't told this to anyone yet, so you're getting the exclusive, pal.

I was looking for guns. Of course, we don't carry guns in the park. That would be stupid. We carry pepper spray and handcuffs and a small club if we want it, but it's made of shitty wood and is no good for anything other than looking like you're carrying a club. If what Cristobal was saying was even half right, there was danger coming, and I wanted the option of threatening to shoot someone if that's what it came to. You threaten most people with a loaded gun and they turn tail pretty fast, that's where my head was at. All the guns in the park were in the riot locker, and the riot locker was in the Fairy Prairie, which was south of where we were. That's where we started. We took off just after breakfast and walking through an empty Fantastic Future World was . . . I don't know. I want to use the word "stirring," but I don't think that's right. It changed the way I looked at the park. Every minute, I mean every single minute I'm working, there are people everywhere and you're never far away from an employee. Also, as a security guy, I'm watching for certain things like sudden movements that look like a fight, or smokers, or people running who shouldn't be running. Without the people around, the facades were really obvious, and every little crack was huge. The place was just a place, and it was sad but not in a depressing way. It was sad in a way that made me wish people were back here. What's a theme park without people enjoying it? Well, whatever that is, that's what I was walking through. Karen thought it pretty amazing and pulled out this little sketch pad she kept in her back pocket and sat right down and started sketching out a few of the details. I let her do that for about five minutes before I looked over her shoulder. She wasn't the best artist, but man, she nailed it. She caught the beauty and the sadness and everything. She said she was going to post the sketch on Instagram later once the Wi-Fi came back up. I don't know what happened to the picture.

We get to the Fairy Prairie, and it's crickets. There's nothing happening. Later, I learned where everyone was but there was no one we could see, so we waltzed right into the office under Wings and Things and into the security station. The door was wide open, which made me nervous, and when we went in, it was clear right from the first step that the place had been ransacked. There wasn't a gun or a bullet or a uniform or a club or a can of pepper spray or anything in that station, which was weird because I was worried that I wouldn't be able to get in the locker. You need a special key and security clearance that would have been shut down without power, but someone had been there, and the guns were gone, and my stomach was in knots. I knew this was sort of a game changer. Not only were there no guns for us, but someone had thought far enough ahead to grab all the guns and probably wasn't planning on sitting on them for very long. Karen agreed with me that this was a bad deal.

We headed across the Fairy Prairie to the big Exclamation Point and there was nothing there but water. Lots of water. I told Karen, let's go to the Pirates and work our way north to the World's Circus, but she was getting a case of the creeps and wasn't really interested. I told her it was OK, we could look out for each other. She didn't want to but she also didn't want to let me down. We kind of had a thing going. When you take shelter from a major storm with someone, it tends to tear down walls, you know? I have been single since my divorce a few years ago, and Karen, she was in a relationship, but she told me it wasn't that serious, and we really clicked. We sort of hooked up in the shelter and after that we got some alone time in the park. Not a lot, but enough to get to know each other. It was really nice to have someone looking out for you, watching your back in a bad situation. Like I said, it tore down walls. I'm glad, too, because the chances of me landing a girl like Karen outside of the park, that's pretty damn slim. She was out of my league, brother. Big time.

We weren't the only ones. A lot of kids were . . . not coupling off, but just sort of free and grabby with their coworkers. I know for a fact there was not a lot of straight-up sex, because I heard a lot of complaints that there wasn't a gift shop in the park that carried condoms. I asked one kid about it and he said, "I'm horny, not stupid," and I told him, "That's the same thing," and he said, "Don't worry. There won't be any knocked-up girls on your watch," and we had a good laugh about it, but there's something to that. These kids needed a release, really, so I wouldn't have blamed them if they were going at it like bunnies, but what I heard was there was a lot of other stuff, but not that one thing. Like that one kid said, horny, not stupid. In a way, I was sort of proud of them.

How the hell did I get off on that rant?

Anyway, no guns, past the Exclamation Point, Karen is nervous, right? That's where I left off? Right, so we're coming up on the Pirate Cove, and there are three guys visible when we come up on the gate. Each different section of the park has a large gate . . . you know this? OK, well, we come up on the Pirate gate, and there's this welcoming committee that's not really welcoming, if you follow me. Of the three of them, one turns around and runs, and the other two come up on us and we see they both have what look like pipes in their hands. They reminded me of the kind you see in Clue. I immediately put my hands up, like, "We aren't here to start nothin'," and they come up to us and it's clear they don't want us to cross through the gate.

I remember there was a tall one and a not-so-tall one, but the tall one was kind of chunky, and the small one was carved out of wood. He was solid and he was the one doing all the talking. He walks up to us and asks, "How much for the woman?" and at this point, it makes more sense to play it loose, I thought, so I kind of chuckled and said, "She's not for sale. What's going on here, fellas?" The little one, he didn't say anything, he just sort of did that thing where they hold the pipe in one hand and make it hit their palm over and over again, like they were getting ready to hit us. It was quiet for what seemed like a long time, and the tall one says, "Almost time now," and we look behind him and there are thirty or so guys all marching toward us. It probably took them less than two minutes from the time we walked up to the time all of the

Pirates were coming right toward us. They weren't running, either. They were walking, like, daring us to take off. I didn't need a dare, and neither did Karen.

She took off running north, toward the Hero Haven. I had about forty pounds on her, and she ran track in high school, so she was way out in front when I took the first hit. I remember hearing that getting shot feels like getting punched but then you have a hole in you, so when it felt like I had been punched in the shoulder, my brain immediately went, "You've been shot!" but I put my hand on my shoulder, and there was no blood there. They were just throwing rocks, but they must have had a couple of major leaguers because I got hit three times, and each time hurt like a bitch, I don't mind telling you. Karen was way out in front of me after I got hit and then I see her just drop. Her feet were over her head by the time she hit the ground, and she hit hard. I ran up to her and rolled her over, and there was blood everywhere. She had bitten through the bottom of her lip and her nose was all smashed up and she was moaning and going in and out of consciousness. I saw later what got her. We store all the Christmas decorations in the Pirate Cove when it's not that season, and they had taken the high-tensile wire we use to hang the decorations on the buildings and made a trip wire. It was just when you were leaving the Pirate Cove and could see the Hero Haven. I kind of looked up that way and that's when I got hit the second time with a rock, a big one it felt like, right along the right side of my back. That one hurt worse than the first. I have had back problems since high school when I wrestled.

The second rock hit me, and instead of knocking me down it pumped me up. I didn't know what the hell they were going to do, but I was now super fucking pissed off, so I bent over, picked up Karen, and kept going. Like I said, they were walking toward me, but once they saw that I was making a break for it, a few of them started running. Karen wasn't a big girl, but she slowed me down a bunch, and when I snuck a look behind me, it was really clear that a couple of the Pirates were going to get to me before I got anywhere near the Hero Haven. There was no chance I was getting away. No chance. There were three of them coming up on me, and the fastest was this skinny kid, and he comes up alongside me and says something I don't catch, and then he kicks the back of my knee, and I sprawl. I might have fallen harder than Karen, but I had her body to break my fall. She might have hit her head again, I don't know.

The Pirate kid, he's standing over me, and he's motioning for his buddies to hurry up, and I'm lying down looking up at him, and then, *bam*, he's just gone. Out of my field of vision. I have no idea where he went. I look to my left, and he's lying on the ground, blood coming out of his head, and I look to my right, and there's six or seven other kids throwing pieces of wood at the Pirates. One of them ran up and grabbed me, and I got to my feet and tried to pick up Karen. The one kid who got me up said, "We got her, get behind those barrels," and I look, and they've set up this barrier, and there are a whole bunch of kids on the other side of it. I pushed my legs as hard as I could, and that's when I got hit the third time, this one right on the back of my head. I didn't feel much pain, but I immediately started getting dizzy and losing my footing, and a couple of the Hero Haven kids, they grabbed me and hustled me behind the barrels. I passed out after that. I'm glad I did.

They didn't get Karen back. The Pirates got to her first. I . . . I choose to believe that she was in and out of consciousness a lot and she didn't know what was happening. I choose to believe that. There's some evidence that isn't the case, but I believe she didn't see it coming, and I didn't either. I was passed out behind those barrels or wherever they took me. When I woke up, they told me the Pirates had beaten Karen to death, right there in front of the other kids who were throwing bricks and logs and whatever they could at them. There was a lot of screaming and name-calling, they said. Their leader, a girl named Riley, said they got in some good shots, and a couple of her gang had been hit by rocks and whatnot. She wouldn't go into detail. I'm sort of glad she didn't, but at the time I was dizzy and mad and sick, and I wanted to know what had happened, you know? What happened to my girlfriend? Riley just told me to rest, and when I insisted, she walked me out of the lounge we were at and down the road, and she showed me the puddle of blood, then handed me some binoculars. I looked through them and saw Karen's body hanging from one of the high lampposts in Pirate Land.

The ones that are made to look like lantern hangers, sort of a gaslight district thing. She was on one of those. There wasn't a Pirate in sight.

Riley and I talked a long time, and I told her almost everything. I told her about the guns being missing and about how we were pretty happy in Fantastic Future World and how maybe they could all come and join us, and Riley said no. She said this was their section of the park and no one was going to take it from them. That seemed a little much. I tried to tell her, "Let's get out of here," you know, "Let's all join up in Fantastic Future World and not worry about these assholes," but she was having none of it, and neither were the people in her group. They were all about patrols and prepping for the next thing. My head was absolutely spinning, but Karen's death sort of hit me as I watched these kids move around like they were in the army or something. I mean, we were four days into this thing, and the kids were turning into murderers? How does this happen? What . . . Karen was a good person. A great person. There was no reason the last image I have of her is bloody and broken and moaning in pain. It didn't need to be this way, but it was, and I cried. I burst out there on a couch in some stupid lounge, and I bawled my eyes out. To Riley's credit, she left me alone and let me cry. It helped me pull myself together a little bit.

Riley's boyfriend got a hold of me on Facebook a while back. I should say, her fiancé. I didn't tell him any of what I'm telling you. I don't know why.

I was really nervous when I asked if I could go back to my group, but Riley was really cool about it. She said the more people who knew about what was going on over here, the better. I drank some of their water and said thanks, but not before promising to come back. I said, "Why don't we check on you in a couple days to see if there's anything you need?" and I think that cinched it that I would be able to go. It occurred to me as I headed back to my kids that I didn't know how long I had been gone. Two hours? A day or more? I didn't know, but I decided, if I had already lost so much, I might as well swing by the World's Circus and see what was up there. Maybe there were more allies there, you know? It was when I came up on it and saw the severed heads on pikes that I ran back to Fantastic Future World as fast as I could. I told the kids the whole story, and they got on the roof and could see the severed heads from up there with a set of binoculars. A lot of them were crying, and I told them to believe the worst until we heard otherwise. To trust anyone other than the Deadpools would be irresponsible. We had to come up with a plan, I told them. We had to defend ourselves, I told them. They were not going to end up hanging from some street lamp, and they were not going to end up on some spike outside the big top. That wasn't going to happen.

I remember telling the group all of that and walking up to one of the kids who had torn a chunk of metal off the ride. I told him to make it an effective weapon, you had to wrap the handle, or it would cut your hand when you used it. They listened to me. They didn't know their ass from a hole in the ground, but they listened to me.

Cristobal, man. We were doing fine until he showed up.

INTERVIEW 10: SOPHIE RUSKIN

Ride Operator in the Pirate Cove, Unaffiliated.

The only reason I'm here, and I mean the *only* reason I'm here, is to talk about Austin. Austin Rowland was the best hustler I ever knew. The man was wired to take whatever he had around him and make money out of it, and that's what he did. When he wasn't working or sleeping he was hustling, and that man could sell sand in the desert. Or water in FantasticLand.

Austin was my boyfriend. We met when I was running the Davy Jones' Locker ride in the Pirate Cove, and he was working maintenance. He didn't have much family. His dad ducked out on him early, and his mom didn't give a shit, I mean didn't . . . give . . . a . . . shit. About her own kid. He told me once he was five years old when he figured out no one was going to take care of him, so he had to take care of himself, and he started asking people on the street to take him to the grocery store. And some people would do it! This five- or six-year-old kid would come up to them and say, "I'm hungry, please buy me some food," and they would do it. It didn't take him long to start selling that food to some of the kids at his school who wanted snacks, then he made enough money to buy his own snacks and have some money left over, and he was off to the races, man. Off to the races. He was that kind of guy. He'd learn whatever anyone would teach him, and he'd use it. That's how a nineteen-year-old skinny-ass kid whose parents weren't worth a shit ended up working maintenance. He learned it from old guys who would teach it to him. He didn't need to go to a technical school or anything like that. He was just smart, and he hustled fast, and he hustled hard.

Like I said, I'm here to talk about Austin. Y'all don't need to know nothin' about me.

OK, I'll tell you this one thing about me. I worked the ride. So, working the ride, it's boring, right? It's mind-numbing, brain-crushing boring. *Bor-ing.* The same people doing the same shit over and over, and when they get to a spot you push a button and say your spiel into the microphone and then do that same thing a billion fucking times. They don't allow phones in the park, even though I knew how to sneak one in, and it was the only thing that kept me from losing my damn mind most days . . . just on Facebook or whatever. One day, it's way at the end of the shift on a day when not a lot of people are riding, and I see this guy get on, and I don't think much of it other than he's got a coat and a hat and, like, layers on. The coat was what got my attention. I don't know how well you know Florida, but it is fucking hot all the time. Even when it's cold it's muggy and hot and not anywhere you'd want to wear a coat, but there's this dude with a big heavy coat on. He rides the ride and gets right back in line but this time without the coat. He's still got all these layers, but his coat is gone. Then he rides again, but then his hat his gone. Then his gloves, then one of his shirts, then shoes, and by then, all us operators are gathered around the front of the line just watching this idiot get back on the ride over and over again losing all his clothes as he goes. He finally gets to where his shirt is gone, and he's this skinny guy and everyone is laughing at him. And he hasn't said or done anything, he's just riding the Davy Jones without a shirt. That's, like, super against the rules, but everyone was laughing so hard, plus we didn't really give a shit.

The next time around, my friend Samantha, she starts chanting, "Pants, pants, pants," like she wants him to ride without pants on. At this point he's shirtless, and all he's got on is pants and socks, right? He comes up and says, "If I ride this thing in my skivvies, you give me twenty bucks," and Samantha was totally down for that. So he said, "Give me a few more rides. Get your money ready," and I was already kind of thinking, "Damn, this guy's got game." He wasn't my type, necessarily, but he had a lot of charm. What's the word? Personality. The man had personality, and he had it locked up.

So he rides again with one sock, then with no socks, and then we're all gathered around to see if he's going to go through with it. So he comes up, no shirt, no socks, and Samantha has the whole group chanting, "Pants, pants, pants," again and even some of the visitors are getting in on it, they're cheering, and he saunters up all cool, undoes his belt, and drops 'em. As he pulled them off his right leg, he gave a kick, and his Levi's went flying over the car where people get on the ride, and I caught them. They were all damp because there were a couple of spots in the ride where you could get splashed if you were at the very front or very back of the car. At that point, I didn't even care, I pulled out my phone I had hidden and told him, "Smile, you goofball," and he, like, struck a pose. He gave me this wink, got in, put his arm around this lady who was laughing her ass off, and rode the ride again. He must have ridden over twenty times, man. That's a lot of the Davy Jones. That may be more than I've ridden the thing in my entire damn life, and I was like, I have got to get to know this dude who rode it without any pants on. Got to.

Turns out he was riding so many times as part of a bet. He collected over $300, well, $320 with Samantha's money. I said, "You could've lost your job over $300," and he said, "Nah. I knew you guys were cool." And we were. By the end of the day, we were so bored, we were desperate for anything to break the boredom. All he did was give us and some visitors one hell of a good story. No harm, right? I want to, like, make sure you understand, that was Austin. His hustle never hurt anyone or robbed anyone. That wasn't his thing. People who gave him money always did it with a smile on their face. Every time. He made people happy, that was part of his hustle. He made me happy.

We got together not long after that, and we were together a couple of months when the storm hit. Like I said, he was always looking for ways to make money and he had a mind that just would not stop taking stuff in. He read the rule book for the park. He read the disaster stuff. He read history books, and he could tell you all about the park and about where everything was kept. He talked me into doing the Operation Rapture bullshit. He said, "It's free money. If there's a disaster, they're going to come looking for us, and in the meantime, chill out, eat some free food, and make enough money to do whatever you want." Plus, he told me there was no better person to be stuck in the park with, and I kind of believed him. There was no one else I wanted to be with. I . . . I don't come from the best background either, though my mom, she tried really hard. I'm just telling you this so you understand, Austin was my world and I was his. I know it was only two months but if we weren't working, we were together. And it wasn't all about the sex, either, it was . . . we really liked each other. I mean, he was good in bed, too, but it wasn't just that. He was pretty great, and he thought I was pretty great too, and FantasticLand was where we could be together.

Austin, he had worked at the park for a little under two years, and the dude knew everybody. He knew the maintenance guys, he knew the ride operators, he knew who ran the snack stands, and he knew the poor bastards in the costumes. The only people he didn't know were the restaurant folks because they were behind closed doors, but Austin was sort of the guy who could get you stuff, and it didn't matter if it was supposed to be in the park or not. He got weed for people, he got special food for people, he would do favors for people, like the best spots to fuck in the park, or sometimes he would steal the schedule of the people in charge of FresnoVille, and he would say, "For ten bucks I'll tell you when the guards are coming," and he was always right. Always. And people loved his ass. He couldn't walk the park without getting high fives and, like, people coming up and begging him for stuff. One time, he was so busy I did his laundry and I emptied out his pants, and they were just busting with tens and twenties. Like I said earlier, best hustler I ever met.

When that hurricane started up, he came to find me at the ride. He ran over to me, and he said he had a plan for how we were going to get rich off this. He said there were three rules we had to follow from now until we got out of the park. Rule one was we had to be first everywhere. First in the shelter, first out of the shelter, first to wherever we went after that. Rule two was that we went together. We could separate, he said, but we always had to know where the other one was. We couldn't get too far away or bad things could happen, he said. The final thing was we rely on us and only us. He said the next little bit of time was going to be a bitch, and what we needed to do was hustle then hunker down, hustle, then hunker down. He said he guessed there would be beef between management and employees before too long, and he wanted to steer clear of that shit. We were the only ones we could trust, he said, and I believed him. So we ran to the shelter.

There wasn't much to do down there, so I'll skip ahead. There was a point where one side of the shelter started to pile out, and Austin grabbed my hand, hard, and said, "We're going. Don't lose me," and we shoved through as hard as we fuckin' could. We got to the front, and he turned to me and said, "Keep up, little girl," which was what he used to call me, and I said, "Don't you lose me, boy," and we started running. We head up to the Fairy Prairie, and he leads me to this, like, bunker underneath one of the snack bars. He had a key, and he kind of winked and said, "You don't want to know how much I paid for this," and we go in and it's this security station, but it's hard to see because the lights are out. He whips out a Maglite and says, "Start looking around for a bag," and I run up and find this big bag in the snack bar that they used to deliver chips and that nasty ass nacho cheese shit, and by the time I get back, he's got guns. Lots of guns.

I was kind of shocked because he was not a violent guy. Not violent. But he said, "Calm down. This is our ticket, baby," and we stuffed them in the sack I found. Turns out, he heard from a security guard drunk on contraband Hot Damn about where the locker with all the guns was. I asked him why, and he said, "Folks are going to be coming for these. It's best they don't get them." Then he said, if we needed to, we could sell them, and if we really, really needed to, we could use them to defend ourselves. I never fired a gun in my life, man. Not once. But he walked me through it, and it didn't seem so hard. I never asked him how he knew what he was doing, but I figured he read a book or hustled someone at a shooting range or something like that.

Next thing was to find a hole to hide in, and he had just the place where he figured no one would go. Just to the north of the big Exclamation Point before you hit the World's Circus is this big, stupid ride. It's for kids, and it's called Fantastic Folks from History, and it's this cheesy-ass thing where you get in this railcar, and you go through all these historic places like ancient Egypt and Rome and France and shit. He knew there was this storage area behind the Revolutionary War part where they kept all sorts of stuff they don't use anymore like broken ride parts and old costumes and all that. He said it was big and no one came there, and, most important, it would have light during the day because it wasn't far from the exit. The whole ride kind of looped around on itself, and he was right. When we got there, there was this little sliver of light, and once your eyes adjusted, it let you see everything in the room. It was old and sad and creepy, and we loved it. It was our nest, man. No one bothered us, but the most important thing was it was big enough to put everything he found. He said the first couple of hours were going to be super important because folks were going to start checking on things soon. He said we needed to raid the cash drawers, then the gift shops, and then get food and water. So we did.

That first day and night, we didn't stop moving. We found over $22,000 in cash, we grabbed flashlights and blankets and enough food to make it through a winter on *Little House on the* fucking *Prairie*. We finally collapsed, woke up, and did it again. We figured water would be a big deal, maybe bigger than the guns, so we started lugging pallets' worth of water that we found in the storage areas. I would carry for a while, and he would be the lookout and then we'd switch and we did that until we were achy and sore and couldn't do it anymore. The third night, he said it was time for the big haul, and I was like, "What, this isn't big enough for you?" and he said, we're heading to FresnoVille, up to the dorms. He had stolen a couple of hip waders from the maintenance guys, and his plan was to wade through the water that had rolled in between the park and the dorms and go through the rooms and bring back anything worth bringing. He said he knew there was weed and rubbers and cash and maybe more, and he wanted to be the guy who could hook you up with whatever you needed. That was why we worked so hard at the start. He said, "We need inventory if this is going to be a long haul." Always hustling. That was my Austin.

In order to get to FresnoVille, we had to go north up through the World's Circus. It rained every damn day we were in that park, and it was raining when we left. We get up there, and the first thing we see is a couple of the folks from up that way hanging out. Of course they know Austin. It's all, "Hey, man, we were hoping to catch up with you," and "Man, you gotta see what we found in the basement," but he really politely told them we had somewhere else to be. One of them pulled him aside and said he was dying for a smoke and Austin pulled out a pack, gave it to the guy and said, "The first one's free," had a good laugh about it. Everything seemed cool up Circus way. I don't know what the rest of those fools are talking about, killing and eating people and all that. It's bullshit if you ask me. People are stupid and believe anything.

We kept heading north and then we hit the water, and it was fucking cold and it got deep fast. You would be stepping, and it would be like ankle, ankle, waist, you know? Each step was a different water level. There were a couple times when I was worried that we'd have to finally give up the ghost and start swimming, but it never came to that. We made it to the dorms, and of course Austin's got a key. He was fumbling for it, and I'm like, "Man, you couldn't get that door open if you wanted to. There's too much water." So we busted out a window with one of those big pieces of concrete you see lying around sometimes. It was a trip, throwing a huge piece of concrete through a big-ass window and knowing no one cared, and you would never, ever get in trouble for it. Strange, you know? We work our way inside, and the first thing we notice is it smells just toxic. The water outside is different than the water in there. I'm sure there was some sewage or something mixed in with it, because the second we get inside we start coughing and choking on how bad it smells. We grabbed a couple of curtains and held them up to our mouths as best we could, but that place was unlivable. Totally.

But no one had been there, and in a couple hours we've got a giant bag full of what we came for, and the dorm, it had everything we wanted. We made a couple thousand in cash, we found enough rubbers for Saturday night in Miami, and we even found a suitcase full of weed. A fucking suitcase! Who comes to work at an amusement park with a suitcase full of weed? Didn't matter. It was ours now, and the suitcase kept the weed pretty dry. It was a nice suitcase. We also grabbed about a hundred smartphones. Whenever we saw one, *plunk*, we threw it in the bag. Might need them for later, you know? We headed back, and were home by dinner, like they say. We never did find out whose room it was that had the suitcase full of weed, but we did find some pretty freaky sex stuff in the rooms of some people we knew. I won't go into it, plus the toys were no good anyway. They had been in that shitty smelling place for too long. I wasn't putting them anywhere near my body.

The next morning we're still kind of basking in our good luck when we notice the rash. Both of us had it. We figured the hip waders would have protected us a little, but whatever was in the water in the dorms, it got through that rubber and was burning up our skin something fierce. It hurt. Both Austin and I had these red blotches, and it wasn't just like a rash, it was like, something is really wrong here. So the first order of business that morning was to head to the first aid station at the front of the park and pray they had something that could hold us over until the cavalry showed up and got our asses out of there. That meant walking up the Golden Road, but we weren't worried. At that point, we hadn't seen anything to make us worried. Nobody was threatening us. Everything seemed as cool as it could seem when you're talking about an amusement park after a big-ass hurricane. When we got there, we got our first idea that something bad might be happening. We got to the road, and there was a fucking dead body, right there. It was a guy, we could tell that much, but his head was bashed in, and it looked like he'd been there a little while. He was all white and kind of gooey looking because he'd been out in the rain, I guess. No one bothered to move him or nothing. Then we hear, like, these whistles and clicks, and people start yelling at us, like, "Who are you?" and "What's your deal?" and like that, and it's these girls yelling from the shops and out the windows. Austin put his hands up, and I followed him, and we were like, we're trying to get to the first aid station. Then Austin, I can tell he's trying to figure out his angle. Finally, he pulls up his shirt and shows part of the rash and yells, "We need help. Can you please help us?" It was the "please" that did it, and one of the girls came out.

Her name was Clara and she was a right and proper bitch, but Austin talked her down, and she eventually led us north a little bit to this tent where a couple of girls were doing first aid. They were busy with other folks so they let us rifle through some of the ointments and whatnot in the first aid station. It wasn't, like, a full-on doctor's office or anything, but Austin, the dude somehow knew what we were looking for, and he found it. Clara had followed us up to the first aid tent and she was going on and on about how they'd heard rumors of dead bodies over by the Pirates and someone getting their hands cut off and it all seemed really stupid at the time. Like, not believable in the slightest, but she was sure it was happening. At one point, she asked me if I wanted to ditch Austin and stay in the shops. She said it was safer. I was on my best behavior partly because there was this other bitch on Clara's right who was rocking a bow and arrow, like, one of those compound ones they use for hunting. I didn't want to mess with that. Austin told her that we had whatever they needed, water or food or other stuff. Clara said "thanks but no thanks" and we started heading back, but it was obvious one of the girls from up the Golden Road was following us, trying to figure out where all our shit was. We gave her the slip, but it took a bit of time.

The ointment worked, but the next few days were like that. We would go find some people and ask them what was up, and they would act all paranoid like we were there to cut them up or something. Everybody wanted something, but nobody wanted to pay anything, and everyone just wanted to know where our stash was. And they all said stay away from the Pirates. Everyone said that, man, every single one. Some people who were cool earlier were not cool now. I mean, we even went back to the Circus, and no one was around and they had put up all these Halloween decorations that made it look all haunted. Everyone was closing up shop and hunkering down, and we were by ourselves and starting to get a little nervous. Austin was especially nervous because, this is going to sound stupid, but his charm wasn't doing it anymore. He could turn on the smooth and give them as many pearly whites as he wanted, and people couldn't get past how terrified they were. It was like those movies where people go to foreign countries and no one can communicate on basic stuff. It was like that. I don't mean to be gross, but when you can't sell rubbers to a park full of horny twentysomethings, shit is seriously fucked up. Plus, they all kept trying to follow us back to our stash.

We kind of got paranoid too. Austin's idea was to start putting little packets of food and water in places in case we needed to hide for the night or something, so he started doing that. There were a couple nights there where he would be gone all night, and I would be just terrified out of my mind in that big empty room with all this stuff in it. I would smoke a little to calm down, and it kind of did the trick, but after a while even that was a problem in case someone smelled the smoke, so we quit that, too. One night, he was gone from six at night until, like, lunch the next day, and he told me there were people who knew he was in the area who were just waiting him out and it was really scaring him. Everyone knew who he was, and everyone knew he had stuff. He started carrying one of the handguns with him. I did too.

It just got a little worse, every day, and we got really good at hiding. I remember, one time there was a group of Pirates who came through the ride. They were so loud we heard them before they set foot in there, but the room we were in, it was one of those places where if you didn't know it was there you could miss it. Plus, Austin and me, we put up bunches of fake moss and vines and shit so it was even harder to find. I don't think they ever got close to finding us, but just hearing those dudes talk . . . that was enough to, like, elevate it. They were talking about their part of the park and how the dead bodies they hung up were doing. I remember hearing one of them say, "The bitch, she's starting to bloat but that Deadpool near the ride, he's still the same" and then they laughed about it. After they left, I kind of accepted for the first time that there were people who would kill us if they could, and I cried. I'm not proud of it, but I cried, and Austin wasn't sure how to react. He held me and told me it would be OK, but I could tell he was full of shit. I knew him. He was scared too.

The night he didn't come back, I wish I could tell you it was different than the other times, but it wasn't. Eight hours went by and I kept telling myself, he's coming back, and we're going to hunker down and ride this out, and then four more hours went by, and I started panicking a little more, and by the evening I was a wreck. The next morning, I knew he was gone. I smoked, I drank what we found, and just got good and fucked up and cried for a couple of days. I would go back and forth between hoping he . . . never mind. This ain't about me. This is about Austin. And Austin disappeared one night, and I never saw him or heard from him or even found out what happened. That's part of why I'm talking to you. Somebody's got to know. There's got to be somebody who can help. This guy, this great guy who was the light of my life, was either killed or died on accident or something, and someone's gotta know. This can't just be one of those things that never get solved. Someone's gotta know, and if they know, all I can do is what Austin did to those girls who gave us the first aid stuff. I can say please, just like Austin said please to those girls. Please, help me figure this out.

I will tell you one more thing. Once the weed and the booze wore off and once I kind of got done crying and ate something and got my head on straight, I realized something. I was angry. Time was, before I started working there, that I could be a hard-ass bitch, and when I quit my crying, I realized I *was* an angry, hard-ass bitch and I was sitting on a shitload of guns.

INTERVIEW 11: CLARA ANN CLARK

Gift Shop Manager, Leader of the ShopGirls.

I don't know how many people you've interviewed, but I bet you aren't going to hear too many people say this. Ready?

I was my best self, leading those girls. I reached my full potential. I was a hard-charging, badass leader, and I pushed girls to fight when they would have otherwise been victims. I was in charge of the Golden Road, and I didn't give an inch to anybody. I didn't know I had it in me, and I left part of my soul in that park, but I got something back. Something that's changed my life for better and for worse. Mostly better.

I was in a kinda sorta leadership position before the hurricane. I had worked the summer before at several different shops along the Golden Road, depending on the current promotion. The regular gift shop, called the Fantastic Every Day Shop, that was where I landed most of the time, and it was a friendly enough place. I never had to work at the camera store or the donut shop. They both had wicked high turnover and that's where I first heard the term "The Yellow Dick Road" to describe what most people thought of working the shops. You can still find the "Yellow Dick Road" Facebook page online where they all shared stories of shitty behavior by customers. But it was OK for me. Not great, by any stretch. It wasn't what I wanted to do with my life, but it paid fine, and I didn't have anything better going on, so I came back the next summer, the summer when it all happened. Since I came back for a second summer, they immediately put me in charge of a few things, so that's how I knew everyone. I would arrange for deliveries and do schedules, and I was called a "manager" even though I never had any real power beyond handing out coupons to people who complained enough about the right sort of things.

So, I kind of knew everyone who worked in the shops. Now, this isn't an official thing, and if you ever talk to Ritchie Fresno, ask him if this is true, but I always understood that the gift shops were staffed at least 90 percent by girls. You hear rumors about why. Some said it was better for sales, which was probably true, some said market research showed you wanted females up front in hospitality for this reason, for that reason. I don't know why they did it, but it was true. Most of the shops were run and staffed by girls. After a while, you don't question it, just like you don't question the process for everything. There was a very strict way they handled the shops, and while everything sort of made sense, they made you follow the rules whether they made sense or not. Everything was "regimented." That's the word they kept using. You also heard rumors that the gift shops made, like, ridiculous profits and that they were one of the main engines of growth at the company. I don't know. I had to move a lot of boxes and do a lot of time sheets, that's the sort of thing I knew about. And dealing with customers. My first summer I wasn't far enough up the food chain, so I had to deal with anyone who got so angry they demanded to see a manager, and usually it was some overstressed mom or douchebag dad who'd been out in the sun too long. You gave them a coupon, you pretended to apologize, and that was usually it. Like I said, not so bad.

But there was this one time I want to tell you about. It'll make sense in a second. This one time I get the call that there was an angry woman up front and I went up there and she immediately starts just screaming, "I won't be treated like this" and "What are you all, idiots?" and worse stuff than that, and when I tried to give her the items for free, she wouldn't stop. She was off on some sort of rage thing and couldn't be talked down. At that point, I calmly ask the cashier to call a 117 for the store, which meant we needed security, but that usually takes a couple of minutes, and in the meantime, this woman has turned ugly and personal. She starts yelling at me about my hair and about how ugly I am, and when I say, "Ma'am, help me understand how we can help," she shot back, "You're too stupid to figure it out! I heard the other girls say so. They're talking behind your back. You're an awful manager." For some reason, that really hurt and I started tearing up a little bit, and the second she saw my crying she went in for the kill. At one point she sounded like that bully from *A Christmas Story*, making faces and yelling, "You gonna cry now?" and calling me a "weak-kneed pussy," and it was just so over the top. Security shows up, and I fill out the paperwork, but I couldn't shake it. I had lost it in front of some staff members and I had let that woman get under my skin enough to where I broke down. It was the sort of thing I never talked about after that, even to my mom, but I remembered it. That woman's face would show up before I went to bed and before I got in the shower, and I just thought, this is something I'm going to have to live with. I figured I'd have to move on with this kind of . . . I don't know, this hidden thing that caused me pain and that got to me more than it should have.

I've always sort of been like that. I've had bullies in middle school, I got pushed around a couple times before I figured out how the gift shops worked, and before this all happened, I had, honest to God, said to myself, "You're going to have to toughen up or this stuff is never going to stop." I mean, it wouldn't have helped me with that psycho woman in the store, but it was something I needed to really work on. Turns out, I wasn't the only one who needed to toughen up.

You've heard about the crowd that just sort of milled around outside the shelter along the Golden Road, right? People were kind of goofing off, and that one kid climbed on the buildings and fell off? I swear to you, the second that kid's skull hit the ground, it was like someone flipped the fear switch. Inside the shelter it was kind of scary, but unless you were claustrophobic, you knew it was worse outside, and you just sort of rode it out, right? Once it became clear that the chain of command wasn't happening and these kids didn't have anyone to tell them what to do, that was when all the pent-up anxiety and fear, they couldn't hold it back any longer. Some of these kids had never made a decision without help, ever. Others were freaking out because they couldn't get on their phones and check in with people. That was a big deal. Long story short, most of the girls on the Golden Road just collapsed. Then that fucker Hockney showed up and did the only merciful thing I ever saw him do, and the fear took on a different flavor. At first it was panic that something bad was going to happen. After that kid's head was turned into chunks and his blood was pooling in the gutters, it was much more "something like that is going to happen to me," and then the mind goes from there.

I didn't see it happen, Hockney and the stanchion. I wasn't far away, though. I was actually trailing Mr. Garliek at that point, trying to figure out what in the hell I was supposed to be doing, and he was running around and yelling at anyone he thought he could get away with yelling at. Seriously, he yelled when people tried to leave, he yelled at people standing around, he found some maintenance guys and yelled at them like a maniac, like this was somehow their fault. Any time anyone tried to get a solid answer out of him about what we were supposed to be doing, he would fly off the handle and start yelling things like, "You should know what to do," and "Didn't you read the manual?" He was starting to sound like my crazy lady in the shop, so I ducked away from the three or four managers who were following him and walked over toward the shops just in time to hear the clang. The "clang heard round the park," right? Sam Garliek, he heard it too and he was still puffed up and acting in charge until he saw what happened. The dead body shut him up pretty good, and he began walking pretty fast toward the center of the park. I didn't see him again for a week, which was just as well. From what I saw of him and how he handled himself, an arrow somewhere above the neckline wouldn't have been a waste, if you follow me.

OK, OK, I know I'm not getting to the good stuff, but I need you to know one more thing about me, OK? Sorry. OK. One more thing. I . . . I kind of hate people. Seriously, I've thought about how to phrase this and the best thing I can say isn't, "I'm not a people person," or something like that. It's that I hate people. Some persons, individual persons, I like and love, but when you get eight or more together in a group, I hate that. I mean, *hate* that. I hate cliques, I hate crowds, and the only reason I got anywhere in retail is that I was always moving around. I had a purpose. My idea of hell is being one of those people in the middle of those crowd shots you see in concerts, you know, where fifteen thousand people are watching some band or something. But it's not just the number of bodies; it's that a person gets stupid when they become people. They are easily convinced of things. So I guess if my story had a heading, like, in your book, it might be "How Clara stopped hating people because they started doing what she said." Or something less wordy that doesn't make me sound like a controlling bitch.

So there's a dead body on one side of the Golden Road, and a big crowd gathered around it, and in that crowd there are at least four girls just sobbing and crying. I chalked it up to the car crash syndrome, where if you see a car crash, you feel bad but are desperate for a good long look. These girls were getting their good long look, and I think they were starting to regret it. Two girls I recognized from one of the stores, they were holding each other, and I don't know what it was, but that pissed me right off. I went over there and pulled them apart and said, "Why are you looking at that guy? Is he going to get any deader?" and they were taken aback by that. Rightfully, I think. Then I said, "Do you want something useful to do?" and both girls immediately nodded their heads yes. They weren't speaking yet, and they were sniffling, and one of them had snot running down her top lip, but they both nodded their heads. I said, "You both work in Fantastic Ts & More, right?" and they did, so I told them to go protect the place. Make sure no one made off with any of the merchandise. I said, "Make sure the pop and the snacks and all that are safe too. If anyone tries to take anything, you get in their face. Do you get me?" I wasn't sure at the time where I got the phrase, "Do you get me?" Later on I remembered it was from military training scene from the movie *Starship Troopers*.

The last thing I told those girls was, if you see anyone who works at the stores along the Road, tell them the same thing. Tell them the stores are off-limits. No one is taking anything out of the stores, and I kind of left it at that. A lot of the girls were in pairs or threes. I didn't have anyone I was really close to at the park. At home I've got a few close friends, but in the park I did a lot of things by myself. I mean, I always had someone to eat with and I didn't go to movies by myself very often, but I spent a lot of weeknights in my dorm room in FresnoVille by myself, which is fine. Like I said, I hate people. I decided to take a stroll through the crowd to see if there was anyone I recognized that I could tell to go to a store. I didn't have a plan. Not really. I just saw that giving these girls something—anything—to do was better than having them stare at a dead body on the road. I found a girl here and there, but about twenty minutes later, when I came back, I saw the shops were all staffed. Better than that, I saw at least two groups of guys get kicked out of stores on the Golden Road. They would immediately start going another direction and started going from store to store and talking to the girls, and they all asked me some variant of the question, "What do we do next?" After the third or fourth time, I went to one of the shops that sold these cheapo watches and I grabbed, like, forty of them and started handing them out. I said, "Keep your posts until 7:00 p.m., then meet in the center of the Golden Road." That gave me a couple hours to figure out what the hell I was going to say.

During those few hours, I thought I'd better figure out just how bad things were, so I walked north through the Circus and saw the road to the dorms was flooded. I didn't want to circle the entire park, so I started pumping people for information. Anyone I came across, I made it seem like I really needed to know about the condition of the park, and they all pretty much told me the same story—we're flooded, we're not going anywhere, hunker down, and did you hear about the dead guy? Yeah, I had heard about the dead guy, and then it kind of hit me, the dead guy was what was freaking everybody out, and in order to rally these girls and stop them from acting all helpless, the best thing to do was to have them face their fears. Then, what I was going to say started to take shape, and I found a shop that had paper and a pen, and I started writing it down. Seven o'clock rolled around, and the girls all came out. It was raining at that point, naturally, and when we all gathered, there were thirty-six of us, all cold and wet and most of all freaked out. I told them if they had keys to lock up and then to follow me, and I led them to the dead body. I told them if they had phones to make a video and five or six of them did. Then I gave them my speech.

Here's what I had written down. I made a few changes as I went, but you get the gist.

> "Thank you all for coming and for standing your posts. It might seem like an empty gesture, but believe me, it's anything but. I called you all here to take a look at this guy *[point toward body]*. I know you've all seen him, but I want to you to take a real good look at him. What do you notice? His head's pretty much smashed in. That much is obvious . . ."

I remember there were a few girls who kind of snickered at that line. It seemed odd at the time, but I get it now.

> ". . . but what else do you see? Do you see his clothes? His shoes? If you were to forget, for a split second, that this was a dead body, would he look like anyone you know? Can you relate to what happened to him? Can you see yourself doing something stupid to get a laugh and ending up dead in this park? Can you picture that?"

At this point I had the girls' attention, and I vividly remember two sensations. One was a feeling of power. I felt like they were hanging on to my every word. The second was a sense of purpose. They were looking to me for answers, and damn it, I had them. It sounds stupid now, but this was the first time in my life I felt like a leader.

> "I see my older brother, Bo. He's a goofball. He would climb on a building in the rain for a laugh. I'm different than he is, but how far away am I from doing something like that? Something stupid that could get me hurt? Something stupid that would get me killed?"

I paused for effect and I remember the only sound was the rain. The rain and my voice.

> "I have an idea. That's all it is, an idea, but it's an idea that if we all buy in, might help us from doing something stupid. It gives

us someone to be accountable to. It gives us a sense of purpose while we're here, and in case you haven't seen for yourself, we're going to be here a while. I hate to be the bearer of bad news, girls, but we are flooded on all sides, and it is not likely that we are getting out of here in the next forty-eight to seventy-two hours."

I had no idea if this was true or not, but I wanted to sound authoritative, like I'd done some sort of research they hadn't done.

"During that time, or however long we end up being here, I propose that we live by two rules. They're simple rules. They're basic rules. But they are rules that just might keep something bad from happening to us. Rule one: This is our space. These stores are our stores. No one takes anything, no one breaks anything. These stores are going to be one thing they don't need to repair at the end of this thing. This is a good idea, I think, because it gives us something to do. It gives us a purpose. And it gives us everything we need. There are three restaurants and two snack stations here—that's enough to feed us for a month. And it's ours. It's not anyone else's. The shops belong to the girls who run them."

I've shown this speech to a few people and they've commented that this sounds really harsh at this point in the crisis, and I agree. It was kind of harsh, but I want you to know where my head was at. A lot of these girls were young, they were getting their first taste of freedom a lot like college freshmen, and they reacted in a bunch of different ways. Some of them were party animals, some of them were overly social and always on their phones, some of them were kind of withdrawn, like me, and some of them were homesick. I went to summer camp for years and years and I saw the counselors deal with homesick kids. What you do is, you give them an activity. You give them something to do. So yeah, at this point it sounds like a call to arms, but that's not what I was thinking. I was thinking, all these girls need a rallying point, and here it is. We were going to defend the shops.

> "Rule two: We take care of each other. This one is harder. I don't know all of you. I know some of you, and I know that some of you don't particularly like me. I've heard some of you say that I'm not an effective manager or that I allow customers to walk all over me."

This was less a statement of fact and more me taking my weakness and acknowledging it, diffusing it. I don't know to this day if what that lady who was screaming at me, if what she said, was true. It didn't really matter then, and it doesn't matter now, because I was setting up an idea. I was making it sound like I was an average schmo, just like them, instead of their immediate supervisor, which I was.

> "I can't make you respect me, and I can't make you respect whoever is standing next to you, or that girl across from you on the road right now, or anyone else in this circle. I can't. But what I can do is make a promise that if you fall down, I'm going to help you up, and if you're thirsty and I have water, I'm going to give you some of mine. If I know first aid and you're hurt, I'm going to help you, and if you need a shoulder to cry on, mine is here, without judgment. I know this sounds dramatic, but this is a dramatic fucking situation we find ourselves in . . ."

A bit of well-placed profanity never goes awry if you pick your spot with care. Stephen King novels taught me that.

> ". . . and if you are that shoulder or that bottle of water or that first aid to a fellow ShopGirl, then I promise you we are going to get through this no matter how bad it gets. We can't control

what else happens in this park. We can't control when rescue is going to come. But we can take care of the shops, and we can take care of each other. That's what we can do. Or . . . or . . ."

I actually wrote that in to make sure I paused.

". . . we could end up like this guy. What do you think?"

Then I folded up my soggy piece of paper, stuck it in my pocket, and opened the floor. We stayed up all night that night trying to figure out how our little tribe was going to work. That's the words we kept using, "little tribe," because of that Nirvana song. Well, the live version of that Nirvana song. Never mind. We stayed up, and we hashed out who would eat when, how we would take care of the shops, and how everything was going to go down. One of the first things we decided, and it was a really hot-button issue, but we came to a consensus, was that the dead body we had gathered around would stay in the street. I know it sounds gross, but the idea was that it was both a symbol that would scare bad guys off and a symbol of what would happen if we didn't take care of each other. Morbid? Yes, but how did I put it? This was a dramatic fucking situation. The remarkable thing, now that I think back on it, is no one ever questioned my leadership. After that night, we were a group. There were fights and there were hard feelings and there were girls who didn't like each other, but no one ever said, "This is stupid." To be honest with you, that's the reaction I expected. I thought one girl would laugh or break the mood or something, but it never happened. We became a group, and it was like wet cement that set. The day after our all-night "how is this going to work" meeting, I heard one of our tribe talking with a couple of stragglers who weren't in their section yet, and she said, "I'm with the ShopGirls."

OK, now onto what you want, right? The lead-up to the Council. The first week was all about setup. We figured out when we were going to eat, when we were going to sleep, who was manning which stores, and, most importantly, we went around to the rest of the park and figured out what everyone else was doing. We sort of had an informal "come hang out with us" agreement with the Robots . . . um . . . the folks in Fantastic Future World. Can I go with the tribe names at this point? I mean, you know where all this is headed, you know the shorthand. Everybody knows this shorthand. My fucking mother knows the shorthand at this point. Hehe, Stephen King.

The Robots and the Fairies were closest to us, so it was cool until they locked themselves down after Elvis, who was an awesome guy before the hurricane, had something happen to him. I never figured out what exactly happened, so all I got was rumors stacked on rumors wrapped in more rumors. You'd be amazed how quickly rumors can grow and get out of hand when kids don't have the constant distraction of their phones to check every twelve seconds. There was talk of severed heads and that his girlfriend had her head cut off and that Elvis had been raped by the Deadpools and the Pirates had red glowing eyes and all kinds of garbage, but I was able to figure out a couple of things. One, there was a violent element in the park, and it was west of the Exclamation Point; two, people were scared; and three, the Fairies had no idea what they were doing. We would have taken in some of their folks if we had the resources. Most people, they had gone back to the part of the park where they felt comfortable, and some of them had really good leaders like Elvis and, I later found out, Riley. Jesus God Almighty, what that poor woman had to deal with. It was fight from the word "go." But some leaders weren't nearly as good, and that was the Fairies. They were just sort of there, and when they got threatened, they hid. And they were found. I . . . OK, I heard a story of the Pirates crossing over into Fairy territory, three at a time, and dragging girls off as they screamed. I never saw it myself, but that was a pretty standard story. I don't know if it's true or not, but given what we ended up going through after the Council, I can say it's in line with their character.

So we've got threats of violence out in the park. By that point I had a few girls, seven of us all told, who were sort of acting like a board of directors. They were never elected, it just sort of happened. They said, and I agreed, that we needed to pay attention to defense, and I happened to know that we had six bow and arrow sets in our inventory. Not toy ones, real ones, that were retailed at $1,100, and we figured they would sell because of all the movies right now where girls use bows and arrows. What are there, like, seven series of movies where there are badass girl archers? Turned out there were at least three badass girl archers in our group and another four who were good enough to take lessons from the good ones, so the Archer Corp was born. Basically, one archer would patrol the rooftops during the daylight. We put them on top of Fantastic Holidays Forever because it was tall, and no one was sneaking up on you there. Plus it was a hell of a view. The idea was, if threats showed up, the archers could take to the rooftops and make them think twice. And of course, after that, girls wanted to know how to fight if they didn't have bows and arrows, so we set up self-defense classes taught by this girl named Randy . . . actually, I think her name was Amanda but she went by Randy, and she basically taught police-style tactics. Go for the eyes or the balls, use their weight against them, that sort of thing.

It was a good thing we did that, too, because the first raid came just six days after we all left the bunker. It was at night, so I'm still not sure who it was, but I have my suspicions. Someone else must have gotten their hands on the inventory sheets, because the raiders showed up at Fantastic Film Gifts and Autographs and started ransacking the place. A few of the girls heard the ruckus, woke everyone up, and we all marched shoulder to shoulder to the store, and I rapped on the glass and told them to come out. There was this long pause, and remember, it's pitch black except for our flashlights, and they came out running. I don't think they figured there would be nearly as many of us as there were, because they hit the wall of ShopGirls full speed. That was the only thing that saved them. The girls, God love 'em, they kicked, and they scratched, and they grabbed, and there was screaming, and by the time it was clear they had gotten away, the girls were all so jacked up we could have burned down the whole park, the whole state of Florida, and good riddance. We were all fine aside from a few bruises, and one girl was super excited. She kept saying, "We gotta get back to the commons, you've gotta see this!" and when we got back, we lit the lanterns, and she stands on one of the couches and yells, "I got his fucking ear!" and holds up this bloody ear and everyone just screamed and danced and whooped and hugged each other and . . . I don't know. We all felt like sisters. We all felt like badasses. It was one of the greatest nights of my life.

Like I said, I was my best self when I was leading those girls. Part of me still hates "people" but I loved that group. I still do. They were my girls, they were my family, they were my army. And given all we were up against later on, I can tell you we put up one hell of a fight.

INTERVIEW 12: CHASE POUNDER

Ride Line Supervisor, Pirate.

It was clear from the first couple of days that everyone in our section was on borrowed time.

I tried to get things organized. And when that didn't work, I tried to help protect people. And when that didn't work, I tried to join another group. And when that didn't work, I strongly contemplated suicide. Looking back, I'm glad I didn't go through with it. At the time, there wasn't a guaranteed painless way to do it. Any option I considered could have gone horribly wrong and left me in more pain than I was sure to face from the Pirates. Now that I'm out of the park, I know that there are ways of healing from trauma. I am on that road, but I guess the best way to put it is that I have lived through some shit. As part of that healing process and getting all my cards on the table, I'd like to be very honest with you. This is hard for me. I'm not going to lie, this opens me up to possible legal issues. But I'm going to tell you because I have decided there must be a reckoning. There's no other way I can move forward, so if I have to take some lumps because of this, so be it.

I will spare you the details about life working at the park. I was a college student making money in the summer, and I stayed on because I needed to sock a little more away before I went back to school. I was not thrilled with my job working the Fairy Flight ride. It was endless little girls and boys all day long. When you work the line, you get to see the worst of people, or at least that's what I thought. Breaking up fights was not an uncommon occurrence, and I started lifting weights in the FresnoVille gym after my first week because it was pretty clear I was going to be throwing my weight around on a semiregular basis. I remember talking about my job to people back home as if it was *so hard.* Looking back, it might have been the biggest adversity I had ever overcome in my life up to that point. On occasion, some entitled and stressed-out parents would yell and maybe push me because the line was too long. That was it. That was my big struggle that defined me as a person.

I remember one time there were these two guys who got into a fight in line. By the time I got to them, they were trying to punch each other, both their wives were screaming the worst type of language you can imagine, and both of them were filming the fight with their phones. Hundreds of kids were hearing a woman shriek, "Die you fucking cunt!" as loud as she could while the other one was screaming, "This is going on YouTube! This is going on YouTube!" Then I show up and try to break up the fight and ended up getting hit on the side of the head really hard. Sure enough, the woman uploaded the video like she said she would. A bunch of the comments were about me getting hit. "That asshole deserved it" and "FantasticLand employee goes down like the bitch he is!" . . . that sort of thing. I thought that was hard to take at the time. There weren't any camera phones during the time the park was flooded, but I guarantee you, it was a thousand times worse.

There's a misconception I've read in a bunch of places that it was mainly girls who worked in the Fairy Prairie, but that is not the truth. There were lots of guys there, and some of them were really able to handle themselves. I learned crowd control from a few guys in the Fairy Prairie and learned what to look out for—sudden movements in a line, people who looked like they were trying to conceal something, that moment that turned a loudmouth with a temper into a physical threat—all that sort of thing. Somc of thc guys had great stories, too, and after hours we would sit around the dorm rooms and drink and talk like they were war stories. There were some good guys in there. If things had gone differently, we could have been a player in the tribes, not that being a "player" was something to aspire to. What I mean is, if we had organized we could have protected ourselves and our people. As things were, no one wanted to try to survive a hurricane surrounded by glitter wings and bedazzled skirts.

Another thing I've heard over and over again is, "Once everyone got out of the shelter, they all went to the section of the park they worked at." That's not true either. People went where their friends were, and a few people, not many, thought far enough ahead to go where there was a better chance of food or safety. Most everyone found their friends and that's where they went, full stop. That's how we lost most of the guys in the Fairy Prairie. It was a combination of guys not seeing the Pink Palace as a place where they felt really secure and our section not being very tight-knit. It happened really quickly, and it wasn't hard to understand why it happened, but it made me immediately nervous. It was like I had missed some important meeting where friends in other sections of the park were handed out, and all the guys I hung out with, they were gone, and I was sitting there with no backup. The first couple days after the storm, I was starting to get antsy. It was mainly girls in the park, and right away we were . . . getting threatening signals, I'll put it that way. There were a lot of guys, and they were always guys, who would just walk through like they were getting a good look at the place, and when someone went up to them, they would calmly walk back the other direction. They never said anything. That was the worst part. They just wanted to see what was going on, and it wasn't much. Then, little by little, things started getting worse.

I had multiple opportunities early on to go to another section of the park. I didn't. I promised I would be honest with you, so here it is: I didn't leave for two reasons. One was I thought I could get laid. How's that for honest? I had a couple of girls squarely in my sights, and by the time it was clear that sex was about 150 places down on my list of priorities, it was too late to leave. The second was that I had a misguided sense of duty. I have no idea where it came from. I felt like even though it was pink and frilly and for little girls, I felt like this was where I was comfortable, and if lines had to be drawn, this was the side of the line I was on. I can't explain it to you better than that. I wish I could.

One morning we found two knives jammed into the eyes of the Princess Fairy on top of the Fairy Flight ride. There was no noise the night before and no explanation, but it was the biggest sign in our section, and the message couldn't have been much clearer. The sign was wooden and painted, which . . . you kind of have to understand the story of the Princess Fairy to get it, but they were woodland creatures that were big on natural habitats, so there weren't any huge neon signs or anything. Lots of wood and fake leaves and plants, that sort of thing. I wasn't in charge at all, no one was really up to that job, but I decided I wanted to climb up and take a closer look. When I got up there, the knives had notes attached to them saying things like, "Get ready, 'cause here we come," and "A pirate takes what he wants." I shoved them in my pocket and decided not to show them to anyone. That was a mistake, looking back.

During the first few weeks in the park, as it sort of settled in that rescue wasn't coming any time soon, there were no rules. People came and went, and sometimes they stayed other places, so I can't pinpoint for you when the disappearances began, but I can tell you when they got more brazen. At one point, I had been talking to my friend Marissa, who was a ShopGirl, and hearing all her stories about how there was a raid and all that, when I get back to the Prairie, I see this guy sort of leading this other girl named Charlotte north along the road that leads to the Exclamation Point. I called out to her, and when she turned around, she was crying. I think I said something like, "What's up?" and she sort of shook her head at me. The guy who was leading her turned around and said, "Hey." Then there was this long pause and he said, "I'm taking her." I sort of had a hard time registering that, so I just stood there, and Charlotte, she hung her head and wouldn't make eye contact. Finally I was able to muster up a, "take her where?" and he said, "Anywhere I want. You aren't going to stop me." Then he grabbed her and kept walking.

I wish I could tell you I regret not standing up for Charlotte. The truth of the matter is, all the bad things that happened, they were going to happen anyway. I could have beaten that guy to a pulp and saved Charlotte and mobilized all the people in the Fairy Prairie and we could have rallied like the ShopGirls and it wouldn't have made a difference.

None. We were already targeted, and we were already done. We were seen as weak, not just by the Pirates but by everyone else who had come by and found us disorganized and kind of in shambles. Plus, that guy was right. I was used to separating fat tourists and taking abuse from soccer moms. I wasn't sure what sort of fighter I was. Not really. Not yet.

After my encounter, I ran back to the main restaurant, Canary Fairy's Confectionaries, where we were all staying because it was cooler in there because of the stained wood motif, and told them what had happened. Basically, our group can be summed up by how they reacted. Some of them cried, and some of them sank into their own corners or went back to reading books or whatever, and those who I could get engaged, they threw out idea after idea after idea about what we should do to fight back or make peace or hide somewhere or join with another group and a million other ideas. In the morning, six of our group had left; I found out later they'd gone to other groups. We still had over twenty-five people, give or take, and nobody was really panicking yet, even though we were bleeding people. Even the criers had calmed down, so I didn't freak out until two guys showed up that afternoon.

They both had red bandanas around their heads, and they never stopped grinning the entire time they were there. They came up to the door and knocked. I don't remember who answered the door, but when it swung open, they were really to the point. They said, "We're going to be taking a bunch of your food from the snack bars. You're welcome to stop us." Then they shut the door, and we could hear them whistling and moving around outside. Immediately, the group started talking about what we should do and how we should stop them. We argued and argued and after a while, I finally laid it out there. I said, "This is simple. They are two guys. If we all go out there right now and threaten them, we can get them to leave," but of course no one agreed with that. Finally, I started walking around to see if I could find six or eight people to go with me if I decided to go out there. I came up with four. By the time we had worked up the guts to go out there, they had completely cleaned out one of the snow-cone booths. That was a big deal because snow cones are nothing but flavored water, and water was kind of a big deal, especially in the later days of the park. And they had taken all of it. There were something like two thousand bottles of water in the store room, and they had managed to load it up, probably on some carts or something, and take it while we argued about how to stop them. They left another note, with another knife, that said, "See you soon." At that point, it occurred to me that these guys were giving us weapons. Later that night, we realized they had taken another of the girls.

That night, I was sleeping on a pile of empty potato sacks that never actually held potatoes but were there for decoration, and I thought, tomorrow I'm going to go to Fantastic Future World or somewhere and see if I can get in with them. But first, I figured, I needed a way to protect myself. I had seen this guy hanging around whose name was Austin, and he was the kind of dude who could get you anything you needed, so I figured he could get me a gun if I was lucky and I don't know what else if I wasn't that lucky. He always had options. I . . . I had squirreled away some money at that point. I had taken it from the cash registers and from the count room because I thought we would be rescued quickly and I could keep the cash on me or something. The first couple of days I honestly thought I was going to make out with enough money to maybe buy a car. The security cameras were down, the drawers were open. It just . . . it didn't feel like stealing. It felt like something the park would have to deal with because of the hurricane. Plus, I was stuck in the park with dangerous people all around me and no way to contact the outside world. Call it hazard pay.

I tried to find Austin most of the next day and wasn't able to. I spent most of the day in another really long, drawn-out discussion about what to do about the guys who had come and taken a bunch of the water. I swear to you, one of the arguments was, "Why is this such a big deal? It's raining all the time. Let's just put out buckets and we can drink out of that." I felt myself beginning to lose it, so I walked away and a girl named Tia followed me out. She said that she was scared and was worried they were going to take her, and that's when I sort of lost it. I remember yelling at her, "You should be scared. They are going to take you unless we do something to stop them," and she started sobbing, so I cooled off and told her the name of a couple of girls I knew on the Golden Road. I told her go up there, admit she was scared, but be strong and tell them everything that's been going on. Tell them we probably won't be here too much longer if this keeps up and to get ready. There are going to be refugees, I told her.

I slept away from the group that night, high up in the scaffolding of the Fairy Flight ride, and I figured out my next few steps. I put finding Austin at the top of the list, and then I was going to head over to the Robots, where I knew a few people. If that didn't work, I was going to head up to the World's Circus. I've always been a rational guy, so I didn't believe any of what I had heard about all the dead bodies up there. It just didn't track with me, so that was step two. That was as far as I got in my head because I started hearing screaming from the restaurant. God, I wanted to stay up there. I wanted to wait and cover my ears until I could see sunlight coming from the little corner of the room that fed into the gift shop. I wanted to hide. To be fair, I should have hid, but movement down below made that impossible. There was someone running around the guts of the ride, and I couldn't see them, and they didn't know I was there. I had this big iron tool that I had taken from one of the repair shops. It was the closest thing to a weapon I could find, and by that time, I had a pretty good idea of the layout of the place.

I was able to figure out two things, even though I couldn't see what was going on. The first thing was there was only one of them. I knew it was a guy by the way he moved and the way he was breathing heavily. The second thing I knew was that this guy was walking along the tracks where the fairy carriages move along the ride. I could hear a very particular clang when he walked. It was this sort of tinny but hollow sound. He was toward the beginning, so I started crawling down as quietly as I could, but it wasn't nearly quiet enough. He heard me but couldn't figure out where I was, so he started talking to me. He was one of those guys, full of bravado, just like the ones who had come to take the water. I remember he said, "You can have the first shot. Come on, give me a good one. One good one, right in the face," and he got angrier and angrier as he said it. Then he started calling me names and yelling at me to come out. I was about ten feet above him and was as quiet as I could possibly be, but after calling me a coward and a few other things, he got really quiet and I knew he was listening for me. Suddenly there was the clink noise, like metal hitting metal. Then another one. Then another one, and then something hit me in the leg. It stung a bit, but I kept quiet. Then a second one hit me a lot harder, in the stomach, and I let out a grunt noise, and he had found me. He was throwing bolts he had gathered from the ride, from what I could tell. Heavy ones.

This guy, whoever he was, tried to find a way up to me in the dark, and I suddenly heard him yell, and I heard him hit the floor. Then there was a scuffle, and I knew I had to move. I climbed down to the rails of the ride and pulled out my flashlight. When I turned it on, I found Austin beating one of the Pirates with the butt of a handgun. I've always heard about pistol whipping, but you don't really understand it until you see it. It's pretty damn brutal. You're never sure what parts of your memory are real or not, but I swear to God I saw a tooth go flying through the beam of the flashlight, and when I did shine a light on the guy, his mouth was all bloody. The Pirate, he was sort of begging for mercy by the time I got the light on them, saying things like, "Stop, please." It was the "please" that stuck in my memory. So polite. I held up my hands to show Austin I wasn't going to hurt him and he got it immediately. We weren't close, but he knew me. I was able to ask Austin what was happening over the moans of the guy he was beating, and Austin said, "The Pirates are cleaning you out." He must have figured from my stunned silence that I didn't get it, so he said, "They're taking all your food and all your water and all your people," and that did it. I remember asking how many of them there were, and he just sort of shook his head and said, "We need to find a way out of here," and that's when he was tackled by two other Pirates, and I remember getting hit in the head with something and feeling simultaneously sick and sort of . . . a very rough, scratchy sort of pain before I kind of stumbled around and hit the ground.

Again, you never know if what you remember is real or not, but I remember being dragged out of the ride. I remember it because I was sort of panicked. I knew there were these two huge bolts on either side of the ride's entrance where the gate shuts when it's closed, and if I was dragged over those, the back of my head would get torn open, and they would never know. I had this very vivid image of leaving a trail of blood, so I tried to verbalize it, but I couldn't take in enough air to make a loud noise. I do remember trying to say something but just feeling really sick again. That's when things get a little clearer, because I remember hearing a bunch of cheers and turning my head. The Pirate leader, Mr. Hockney, he had Austin's hands tied behind his back and was up in his face yelling. It took me a minute, but he had found a gun on Austin, and he wanted to know where the rest of them were. Austin was talking really fast, saying there were more guns but he would never find them, and if he wanted the stash, they needed to trust each other. I'm still lying on the ground when Mr. Hockney says, "I only trust men who have spilled blood with me or for me. You don't fit either of those categories," then he winds up and hits Austin in the side of the head with the pistol. When he did that, the gun went off. Everyone just froze and looked to see where the bullet had gone and there was this long beat. I remember Austin had an odd mix of fear and suspense on his face. I expected someone to start screaming, but one of the Pirates walked up to Mr. Hockney and showed him his shirt. The bullet had grazed it, near as I can figure, because I didn't see any blood or other damage. The Pirate, I later learned his name was Armand, just showed Mr. Hockney his shirt. That was all. It was the smallest thing, but Mr. Hockney completely lost his temper and turned back to Austin and started beating him with the gun and then with his feet, stomping on him as hard as he could on his chest and then on his head. After about thirty seconds, he motioned for one of the Pirates to pick him up, and Austin was jerking strangely, like his head was on a wire and someone was pulling it hard from one direction. Everyone sort of drew back and he fell to the ground and he started twitching. He was facing me, and I remember looking into his eyes and thinking, "No one's in there." It was like a seizure, only worse. It was like a seizure you don't get up from.

I remember, very clearly, Mr. Hockney panting, red-faced. He said, "I didn't mean to break him like that. But no one takes a shot at us, right?" The Pirates sort of half cheered and someone yelled, "He's in misery, sir," and Brock heard that and said, "We can't have misery around here, now can we?" Then he walked over and shot Austin at least six times. I lost track after the fourth shot, they all blended together. Austin wasn't facing me after they shot him, and I didn't have time to look at his body as the Pirates pulled me up and we started walking. It was obvious we were headed back to the Dead Man's Cove, where I was pretty sure they were going to kill me or hurt me. I remember hearing some of the girls from our group making that sound when you try not to cry but you can't help it, that sort of sorrowful sob through hands pressed against the mouth. I said earlier that dealing with line jumpers and family men with tempers was the entirety of my hardship up until this point. The thing that surprised me was, as they dragged me away toward the Pirate part of the park, I was oddly calm. Detached, I think I would call it. Part of my brain was screaming, "They're going to kill you, they're going to torture you," and that was very much on my mind, but panic wasn't part of the equation. Maybe that had to do with not being able to fight back if I wanted to.

I must have passed out at some point, because I remember having this really vivid dream about water. I don't remember all of it, but I was in an inner tube floating down this creek like I did in the summers with my grandparents, and things kept reaching up to try to grab me. Hands kept touching my feet whenever they broke the surface of the water, and right before I woke up I remember one of the hands grabbing onto me. When I woke up from that I was inside the Cannon Splash, which is one of two rides they have in that section of the park. The Cannon, it's a water ride, but before the big drop, there's this section where your little pirate ship sails through a village and through a secret pirate cave with jewels and alcoves and jails. It's pretty easy to recognize because the other ride in the park is set on a pirate ship and doesn't have nearly the ambience of the Cannon, which is one of the most popular rides in the park. I knew immediately that's where I was because I was surprisingly lucid when I woke up. I remembered what had happened and where I likely was, and when I saw that I was in a jail cell I was able to put it together fairly quickly. Plus there were three girls in there with me, only one of whom I knew. It was Charlotte, but I could barely tell. She had bruises all over her face and one of her eyes was almost swollen shut. I sat up and when I didn't feel as sick as before, I asked her what happened to her face. She said, "I won," and then whistled really loudly and yelled, "*He's awake!*" One of the girls had a phone and she took a photo of me, half groggy. I remember it showing up somewhere online after we got out of the park.

A couple of Pirates immediately showed up and unlocked the door. It was a real working cell, which makes no damn sense if you ask me. Why would you create a real cell in a theme park? I've heard it was some sort of nod to authenticity or something, but whoever built it was out of their mind. I felt ridiculous being held in a real jail in a fake pirate ride, but before I could dwell on it too much I was dragged out of the cell and down a long hall with water sloshing on my right side. I remember looking at the other cells as they dragged me down the hall, and I saw most of the "prisoners" had been worked over. One had a big black eye, another had a bandage over her cheek and was bruised all over her face. After about thirty-five steps I started to hear a lot of chatter, and then we went into the main room of the ride, which was lit with artificial light. Somehow, this ride had limited power. The light was still soft, but it was the first time I'd seen electric light in a couple of weeks. The main room had a big pool on one side but otherwise was in a bowl shape. Most of the Pirates were about twelve feet above me along the edge of the bowl. The floor was dirty and covered with dust, which was fake, because the floor was concrete, not stone. I remember thinking how stupid it was that this real thing was happening on this fake floor.

Mr. Hockney stepped forward, and everyone immediately quieted. He stared right at me and said, "I have heard you don't like fighting. Right now you have no choice," and everyone started yelling. They brought one of the girls from the Fairy Prairie over; I didn't remember her name then. She looked very scared, but there was a guy and a girl on either side of her, rubbing her shoulders and encouraging her like a trainer would encourage a boxer. Mr. Hockney held up his hand and said, "Membership to the Pirates is something you earn. You get what you want by taking it. The only thing keeping you from our brotherhood is the person in front of you." Then he just let that hang in the air. I wasn't even aware he wanted us to fight, but I figured it out when the girl charged me and threw her shoulder into my stomach and knocked the wind out of me completely.

In the past four hours or so I had been pelted with bolts, knocked unconscious, dragged, and jailed, and I don't know what it was, but when that girl tried to barrel me over, that was the last straw. I felt awful but I didn't go down, and when I got my chance to fight back, I was angry and ready. I grabbed her by the waist and tossed her has hard as I could to the right. She landed just short of the water, and I was over to her before I knew what I was doing and gave her a kick as hard as I could into her chest and shoulder. She didn't roll like I thought she would, but she did let out a scream, and at that point it registered with me that everyone was cheering. They were wild and abandoned. I remember focusing on one of the Pirates, just for a moment, and seeing a long line of spit dangle from his mouth as he screamed. Right next to him was a girl who was yelling so loud her face had gone beet red and strands of hair had fallen into her mouth. My opponent was on her feet now, and I picked up a handful of fake dust and threw it at her face. It hit the mark, and her hands went to her face and I hit her, full strength underneath her right cheek. I didn't even know why I was fighting. I didn't want to be a Pirate. I've talked to my therapist about it, and she suggested I was so happy to have power over anything that I took full advantage of the situation. That's a small consolation after you've felt your fist break a poor girl's cheekbone.

She fell back, holding her face, but didn't go down, and it was at this point the anger really started to overtake me. I charged her, and she turned and ran. I caught her and threw her into the water and dove in after her. The water was fetid and gross but I didn't notice. I was in a rage, and the girl was too scared to fight back. I punched and I punched and by the time I was done, she was unconscious. At that point, I came to my senses a bit and threw her body back onto the land and stood, dripping. My shirt was torn, and I realized my cheek was bleeding. She had scratched me at some point. Mr. Hockney was already down on the main level with me and was walking toward me. He had a knife in his hand, but I didn't feel threatened. I remember what he said, exactly. I'll never be able to forget. He was a man of few words but the words tended to stick with you. He said, "She went into this knowing the stakes. She was afraid and didn't want to be afraid anymore. She said she would fight, and maybe she would die, and that was OK." He put his hand on my shoulder and handed me the knife and told me, "Put her at peace, brother."

At that point, and I swear this is true, the gathering of Pirates started singing. It started as a low chant and grew and grew. It was a song I would grow to know well. They sang:

A pirate gets what he wants
and what he wants he gets
He'll spill blood for his brothers
A pirate never quits

Over and over they sang, a little louder each time. I was shaking now. I remember tears, but I don't remember the sensation of crying, but I do remember the violent shaking of my hands. I looked at Mr. Hockney, and I stammered, "I don't know where to stab," and he put his hands over mine and helped me guide the knife. He put it over her heart and he whispered to me, "Together, my friend," and I closed my eyes and together we pushed down. I pushed until I felt the cloth of her shirt and then some of the warm blood, and I remember her thrashing around a bit and . . . the worst was when I heard her death rattle, the wet choke that comes when you can no longer swallow, and I heard her lose control of her body and fill her pants. I could smell that and the metallic tinge of blood, but her eyes never opened. I'm thankful for that every day. Through it all, Mr. Hockney held my hands, and when we finally stood up after it was done, he hugged me, and I hugged him back as hard as I could. I grabbed on to him like he was the giver of life itself and when we broke the embrace, he held up my hand and said, "Chase Pounder is a Pirate!" and everyone called back, "A Pirate never quits!"

I took a while to recover, emotionally and physically, and the Pirates gave me the time I needed. I had food and a room, I had brotherhood and entertainment. I saw Pirates treat people cruelly, but I never had to do anything like that first night. It was like I was baptized in blood. That's what my friend Kyle called it. I was immediately accepted and

I have never felt so accepted anywhere in my life. And I did . . . other things later. Things I wish I hadn't. I helped Mr. Hockney set up the cannon. I cheered as people beat each other to death. I saw other people in the exact same situation I was in. I saw beggars and criers, and I was part of the group that charged the ShopGirls near the end. I screamed for blood until drool ran out of my mouth. I took an arrow. I have a scar. But those don't stay with me. The two things that stay with me are my inability to bring the group in the Fairy Prairie together and one long look I took at the girl I killed before they took me away. I remember thinking I would trade places with her if I could. I still think that. Right now, I wish it had been me that died on that floor. I wish I didn't have to live with my failure and her face and the things that I did. Every day I want to die. Every day.

Honest enough for you?

INTERVIEW 13: SAL MCVEY

Parade Dance Troup/Guest Relations, Pirate.

Dude, I've been to concerts, I've been to Tijuana and seen a donkey show, I once partied after-hours in a pot dispensary with an entire women's volleyball team from Texas, so I can tell you, definitively, I have never been to a party half as fun as the one Brock Hockney threw. That. Was. A. Fucking. Party. At least, until that whole cannon thing. But even then, man, it was never boring. Not for a second. I just wish we had our phones there to put it online. It would have been epic.

I cannot tell you how many people have come up to me and asked, "How could you be part of a group that killed people and raped people and stabbed people," and all that bullshit. That's why I wanted to talk. I'm not going to jail, I've struck my deals with prosecutors, what's done is done. I've got talk shows falling all over themselves to have me on. Why not tell the truth and why not get a little cheddar out of this whole thing, right? But you? I'm talking to you to set the record straight because there's a lot of bullshit out there. A lot of people think we were monsters. Not true. Not even close.

First thing I want to clear up is that nobody raped anybody, and if they did it didn't come from Brock or anyone else in charge. If rape happened, it was one person who decided that was a good idea. I heard of stuff like that happening here and there, but it didn't happen in the Cannon Splash and it didn't happen with other Pirates cheering on. I, like, totally understand how something like that would get out there. We did raid the Pixies and take all their members, and most of them were girls, but I'm being dead honest with you, man, rape wasn't part of this thing. We had a lot of girls in our ranks, too. It wasn't a big deal. You can believe me or not, but no one was looking to rape anybody. Brock said it wasn't how things were going to work. I remember this one dude we called Jackpot because he wore this stupid Las Vegas shirt almost every day, he was all, "Pirates raped during the 1700s," or whatever, and Brock said, "We've got other things to worry about without having to deal with STDs and pregnancies," so everyone backed off that idea. People listened when Brock spoke. That's true. Now hookups, that's a different story. You ever heard the idea that women are attracted to power? That's totally true. The stronger you were in the group, the more girls would just hang on you. Trust me. I know.

This one girl named Lilly, she wouldn't leave me alone after a while, and I had to get a little rough with her until she got the message to leave me alone, but I never forced myself on her. Hell, she was begging for it, and a couple times I was bored, so I would hit that, then I would have to push her off me. It's like, just because we screwed once doesn't mean I want you around me every second, right? So then I get interested in this other girl, whose name was December. Seriously, her parents named her December. Who does that? I don't know, but she was really hot, and she and I go to the bottom floor of the Cannons where the cells are, and we're going at it and Lilly shows up and takes a swing at me with a big piece of wood she found somewhere. Then she starts hitting December, and they get into this fight, and one girl is naked, and before long there are a dozen guys watching this fight. It was a blast, but afterward Brock took me aside and said, "You need to respect your women. Next time it won't turn out so well." And I took the hint. That sort of shit doesn't stand, so I dropped them both, and they both found other guys, and I found another girl, and things were fine. I wasn't the only one who had that sort of thing happen, and I wasn't the only one Brock talked to, but he never had to talk to someone about something more than once, and Brock said, "Respect women." So we did. The thing that's crazy, now that I think about it, was how much drama there was and no one was even beefing on

Facebook or anything. It was all old-fashioned "I heard it through the grapevine" type stuff.

OK, the second thing I want to clear up is the fights. I heard, like, over a hundred people died in the park while we were stuck there. That may be true, but not many died in our fights. I can count three that died that way, and one was a freak thing. But the fights, they were awesome. Let me ask you this—have you ever been without your phone, your TV, or anything for longer than, like, two hours? It's a fucking nightmare! I remember after we all gathered in the Cannon, there was this moment where everyone was like, "OK, now what?" and there was nothing to keep us entertained. I'm not kidding, man, it's like going through withdrawal. Some people started picking at the grout in the walls and then another guy started talking to the first guy about the grout in the walls. It was literally so boring we were talking about the walls. You can call Brock a monster if you want, but he was one smart dude. He knew everyone was bored out of their gourd, so the third night he started the fights. And this wasn't like *Fight Club* where one guy fights another guy and everyone hugs. This was full-on wrestling style, man. He would pick two guys to fight, and if Brock picked you, you had to fight, that was the rule. Then he would start hyping it up. He would go, "This one guy has got a great hook, but this other guy, he's a madman," and he'd start playing them against each other, so when you showed up that night after lugging bottles of water and food and shit all day, you were pumped to see this fight. Then a night would pass, and the next night it would be two different guys. Then, later on, we started gathering up the prisoners and making them fight. In some ways, that was even more entertaining, because you were never, ever sure what was going to happen. It could be an all-out brawl or one person beating on someone who was crying the whole time. Either way, it was a show, and we all got really into it.

I'm off the hook now in terms of going to jail, so I can tell you about the times people died, if you want to hear them. Keep in mind, most of us had never seen a dead body yet. The first time it was after we pissed off the Deadpools. Brock had been going on and on about how we had to defend what was ours and pumping us up with his Code of the Blade and all of that, so the first night out when we caught people in our gift shop, we were all really high off it. We found four people and we were going to make two of them fight to join our group, and before the fight could even happen, we brand the one guy and he goes to brand this girl, and it all goes tits-up, and she's screaming and bleeding and you could just feel the air go out of everybody. This guy, I forget his name, he fucked up this simple thing and everyone kind of trudged back to the Cannon feeling like absolute shit. When we get in there, the first thing Brock does is take off his shirt and just deck the guy hard in the face, and then he said, "Now you know you're in a fight. To be fair, you get one shot at me," and the guy starts whining and crying and trying to talk his way out of it despite Brock saying over and over, "This is happening. Start fighting," and when he wouldn't Brock just started hitting him. After each punch he would yell, "Are you going to fight now?" just over and over again. *Bam!* "Are you going to fight now?" *Bam!* "Are you going to fight now?" and he eventually beat the guy unconscious. Then Brock, all covered in sweat and some blood, just slid the guy into the pool of water next to where we held the fights, and the guy drowned. There weren't even any bubbles. Then Brock gave this big speech about how this was the situation we are in. The punches are coming, he said, and if you don't fight back, you don't deserve to breathe. It was kind of an important moment for everyone. A couple minutes later, we saw all the bubbles come up at once, and we knew the guy was dead.

What's the Code of the Blade? That's the rules Brock set forth for the group, and he was serious as hell about them. There was the Code of the Blade, which is about how the Pirates acted, and then the Rules for Survival that came later. He made us all memorize them; in fact, I just said one just a second ago. There were four rules:

1. A Pirate is not afraid in public.
2. A Pirate respects himself and the chain of command.
3. A Pirate does not steal from another Pirate.
4. A Pirate fights for what he has or he does not deserve to draw breath.

That last one, he was super big on that. No one takes what you have, and no one takes what we have. He saw that as an honor thing. He didn't care if it was a bottle of water or what. What's yours is yours, and no one takes it. Where was I on the bodies? Oh yeah, number two.

The second one was a little more sad. We had a few people who would come in from time to time because we kind of got a reputation quick. Our whole thing was, "We take what we want, and don't give it back," and some people took issue with that, as you can imagine, but most of the park understood that we were strong, and that attracted some desperate types. One day this girl, whose name was Jenny, she shows up and immediately wants to talk to Brock, and he spent a lot of time with her. A lot of time. Then one day, she's going to fight this dude who we picked up along the Prairie Fairy. She's got Pirates helping her, getting her ready, and she gives a good show, but the dude just kind of unloaded on her. He was a good fighter, and she didn't stand much of a chance. The dude, who later became a Pirate, he had ninety pounds on her, easy, and after she was down, Brock and this dude went down there and killed her. We could tell by Brock's tone that this was a big deal. I don't know who it was, but someone started chanting the "Pirate Never Quits" anthem from the park, and we all picked it up. It was sad, but at the end of the day, it was one of those really big bonding moments. Everyone remembers that night.

The third one, that was just a freak thing. Kenny Pot, he hung out with Jackpot, but his name was Kenny so we called him Kenny Pot, and he told us he smoked weed all the time before he got trapped in the park, he hit his head really hard on a sharp piece of concrete during a fight, and we had to put him down. It was sad, but it didn't hurt morale much.

So, what else do you want to know? You want to know about Brock, right? Everyone wants to know about Brock. He's the goddamn mystery of the media, isn't he? He's the puzzle everyone is trying to solve. There's nothing to solve, man. I'll tell you the only two things you need to know about Brock. He got us organized and got the rules set really fast, I mean really fast. He had guys on his side from the second he came out of the shelter and the Rules of the Blade and all of that, they were always just there. If you want my "expert analysis" on why so many people joined the Pirates right away, that was it. The rules were clear, the leader was clear, and he was strong, right off the bat. The second thing you need to know about Brock was he was the craziest and the most dedicated and the hardest and the strongest of us. He was built like a brick shithouse, and he could straight up take anyone in the park. He was ripped, he was focused, and he was the best of us. It's easy to follow a leader who knows what he wants and has a good chance of getting it. There's nothing else you need to know.

OK, one more thing. Everything he said came true. He said people would start coming after our territory and our resources. They did. He said people would be begging to join us. They were. He said our enemies were everywhere, and you bet your ass they were. He said everyone would be scared of how strong we were, and we were the ones with the targets on us.

We were.

But that's just it, man. We were one crew against the entire park, and it was like that when it started, and it was like that when we were all sick and there were bodies rotting and the Point went down and created a sea of broken glass. They were always against us. If you weren't a Pirate, you wanted to kill the Pirates. It was that fucking simple, and because it was that fucking simple we all had a purpose, some of us for the first time in our lives. It wasn't hard to kill when the person you're killing has a knife to your brother's throat, you know? And we were brothers. Even the girls who were in our group, we called them brothers, and no one seemed to mind. I'm going to have a hard time describing this, but a lot of us came from decent families, but that's different from having brothers. My mom, she loves me, but I would never stand shoulder to shoulder with my mom and fight someone trying to take my food or my water. It was different than most of us had ever felt before. We worked really hard during the day and sweated with each other, then we cheered each other on in the fights, and sometimes we fought each other in a brotherly spirit, and we slept in the same building and we were bonded tight and that made everything so much better. We were "sewn together out of blood and love," Brock once said. I was closer to these guys than my own brothers. I still talk to some of them to this day.

Brock's brother? We never talked about that. Never. In fact, Brock wasn't that big a talker, but when he gave a speech, you sat up and you listened. I only thought he was full of shit one time and I learned my lesson there. He said he had seen the Freaks in the World's Circus and that no one was to go north of the Point. He said it was too dangerous. A few of us, Mark and Raoul and I, we thought that had to be bullshit. Nothing scared Brock, and nothing scared us, so one night while we were making runs to and from the Fairy Prairie and taking all their stuff, we stashed our stuff in a building somewhere and went to check it out. Brock had said there were bodies "strewn on the ground." I remember that because I had never heard the word "strewn" before, and there were murderers around every corner and traps and all sorts of shit. We figured, at worst, there was a body and maybe, like, a net in a tree, so we were cautious about it, but we certainly weren't scared.

When you come up on the World's Circus, there's this big entryway with clowns and elephants and jugglers on it, and when you pass through there, it's kind of a long way until you get to the first ride. Basically, there's a big empty space they used for gathering and sometimes for live performances. They had street performers and singers and stuff like that who would stop in the middle of that area and perform and then go somewhere else and perform twenty minutes later. Anyway, there's this big space after you go through the entryway. We get there expecting to see something, and there's nothing there. I remember it was late afternoon, so the sun was setting, but it was overcast and raining so there wasn't a whole lot of light. We were squinting really hard, looking for all this carnage, and there's just nothing there, man. Nada. And that, that right there, was the eeriest thing I had seen up until that point, because everywhere in the park there was garbage or voices or some sort of evidence that someone had been there, but between the entryway and the first ride, there was nothing. It even looked clean. That was not normal and we started to sweat a little bit.

We didn't even notice anything all that gruesome at first. The way the section is set up, you go through the big open performance area, there's a kiddie ride on your right, and then this big circus tent in the center that leads to the other rides. The tent wasn't lit up, so it was hard to see much of anything. As we got a little closer we started hearing, like, circus music. What do they call that thing . . . a calliope? Is that it? That thing that goes *do do doody do do doot doot doo doo*, that thing? We start hearing it, only it's not the song we're used to hearing, it's something in more of a minor key. I couldn't place it at all, but there were, like, kids chattering underneath it, and that was when we really started to sweat. And then it got louder. At this point, the three of us, me and Mark and Raoul, we were starting to get closer to each other, just out of nervousness, until we were basically touching. That's when the spotlight came on.

It made this sharp sort of half-swoosh, half-crack noise, and the light was as wide as the big entrance to the tent, and then we could see it. There were two bodies hanging from their necks above the entrance to the tent, like some sort of fucked-up curtain, and there were bloody-looking chunks of I don't know what hanging between them. Seriously, it was like a dead body curtain and then we could see more stuff inside. I saw a severed head and Mark swore he saw a band saw, like the kind his dad had in his garage, with blood all over it, and Raoul swore he saw someone's skin stretched out over one of the tents like that one scene in *Silence of the Lambs*. You know the one, with the security guard who had his skin stretched out like wings? Raoul said he saw that, and his face was white enough to where I believed him.

I have no shame telling you we took off. We ran, man. Got. The. Fuck. Out. Of. There. And as we're running, we see them. There were two guys, dressed in these gruesome dark masks, there were bones sticking out and stuff dripping off them, and they were both holding machetes. I shit you not, man, bloody guys wearing gross masks with machetes. There were two of them, and they were both coming from one side of the entryway like they were coming back from a hunting trip, and they had a sack. No, seriously, they had something in a sack. That sack had something moving in it, man. Look, I can see from the look on your face that you think I'm exaggerating or something, but no. Not even close. This memory is as vivid as my first blow job, you feel me? These guys were real, and they had real machetes, and they had something in that bag, and all three of us ran like we'd never run before. I ran track in high school, and I left all those records in the goddamn dust, I swear.

Once we were clear and huffing and puffing, we all agreed to tell Brock, to come clean about it. He understood. No punishment, corporal or otherwise. In fact, he told us to tell the others. Spread it around, he said, that there are different kinds of enemies out there—normal people and barbarians. And we did. We told everyone, and a few of our guys went to check it out for themselves, and they all came back with similar stories. That place was condemned, man. If they wanted to fight us, fine, but they were going to have to come to us. We weren't going to go to them. Not no way, not no how.

So what else? So, the Council of Pieces. You want to know about the Council of Pieces, or, as I call it, our finest hour? All I can say is God bless Johnny Fresno, man. That dude was such a stickler for authenticity that we had real swords and real jails and, most of all, real black powder. I'm getting ahead of myself. I imagine all the others are going to tell you the same thing, but Sam Garliek, in all his glory, shows up one day outside our gate and he . . . God, this is funny . . . he's actually yelling "Parley, parley," like that fucking means anything. Like he's in a pirate movie or something. I remember Raoul turned to me and said, "That's French for 'I'm a pussy, please don't stab me.'" He laughed hard about that. Jackpot went out to meet him, and Garliek just kept yelling that word until Jackpot smacked him in the head, hard, but with an open hand, and asked him what he was blathering on about. He said he wanted to talk to whoever was in charge, and Jackpot made an X on the ground with his foot and said, "You leave this spot and we break your face," then went to get Brock.

They talked for a little while, and Sam handed Brock a piece of paper, and that was it. That night at dinner Brock told us that we had been invited to a summit. He said it was being called, "The Summit of Peace," and that got a really good rolling chuckle going throughout the group. Then he read the whole thing on this piece of paper.

Author's Note: Here is the text of the letter, recovered from the Executive Offices.

FantasticLand Employees,

I understand fighting over food and water. I even understand fighting for territory. But murders? Dead bodies? Is this befitting of your position with FantasticLand Inc.? You used to bring joy to children and families, now you're killing each other? How is this possible? What message does this send?

All is not lost. I would like to call a meeting at 1:00 p.m. tomorrow of all the park sections at the Exclamation Point in the center of the park. I would call this meeting mandatory, but I think we are all intelligent enough to understand this goes beyond your employment. This is about our survival. The best chance we have of being rescued in a timely fashion is to pool our resources, not hang people from the lampposts. Please, this cannot continue. You are destroying this park and any chance at its future operation. We can survive together under one central authority. I believe this. You should too.

Please bring as many people as you see fit. There will be NO VIOLENCE at this meeting. We will figure this out and find rescue.

—Sam Garliek
Acting Park Manager

That shit was hilarious. So funny. I'll let someone else tell you about how it went down. I wasn't so involved with that.

Last thing, the bodies, right? Why did we hang bodies from the lampposts? That was something that just sort of happened. I remembered when a couple of those Robots came around looking for trouble, we gave it to them, and then the Deadpools came at us, and we fought them off too. We were all rallying afterward, and we wanted to just give them a big, fat middle finger, man. We wanted them to see a giant "fuck you" every time they looked in our direction. So we strung up that one woman we killed, and believe me, that did the trick. It was no big thing, really. It wasn't hard. It wasn't gross. We didn't feel bad about it. The only problem was later on when she started to leak. She had invaded our space, she had tried to hurt us, and we hurt her. Simple. I honestly don't know why it didn't happen more. And when those other motherfuckers killed a Pirate, they started doing the same thing, man, and it hurt, and it was ugly but we understood it. We fought hard, and we drank hard, and we partied hard, and we loved hard, and when one of ours fell in battle, we felt it hard, but that's what it was about, man. That's why we were Pirates. We were the kings of FantasticLand and no one could take that away from us.

INTERVIEW 14: GLENN GUIGNOL

Fire Breather in the World's Circus, Head of the Freaks.

All of this might be my fault.

Not, directly. Heavens no. I'm not a killer, nor did I do any killing during my incarceration in the park. But the escalation, the jump from mild-mannered children of suburbia to little stabby stabby monsters, you could make a reasonable case that I did that. Again, not my intent, but an understandable result. The one aspect of this thing I keep rolling around and around in my mind and can find no clarity on is why, in the name of all that is good and right, didn't anyone remember that we were coming up on Fantastic Fright Nights?

Every story you've heard about gory discoveries in the World's Circus is true, or at least the initial report is. I've made my living in part from the idea that when people experience a shock or see something horrific, that's not what scares them. It's what they don't see that really twists the blade. If you want to truly scare someone, you need to jolt them to attention and let their twisted little imaginations do the rest. The greats understood that. Hitchcock, Lynch, Craven. People say suspense is terrifying, but they're not correct. You must be given a framework and jolted to attention for the fear response to start manufacturing its own nightmares. That's all we did. We had the framework, which was being trapped in the park. We had the jolt, which was the gore. Once that was in the mix, people began to get genuinely afraid of us, which meant they left us alone. Which means we won, in a very real and tangible sense.

We would have decked the entire section of the park in guts and gore anyway, but the fighting within the park lent it a sense of urgency and in some ways spurred us to do our best work. Before the real blood started to spill, most of the people who made their way to the World's Circus were content to be the stoner poets of this specific disaster. One of my wards, a fellow named Deckland, was a small-time drug dealer who had hidden his stash in the mechanical systems of the Three Ring Swing ride, so marijuana was abundant. Deckland, the boy wonder of the brain that he was, had imported a particularly strong batch and found ways to cut it to make it last longer. To most of the Freaks, as we quickly dubbed ourselves, Deckland's resourcefulness was enough to make up for the terrible sin of being named Deckland. The result was that, for the first few weeks, the best adjectives to describe our group were damp, high, and relatively happy. There were some good-natured complaints about not being able to get online, and I admit I felt that as well, but you'd be amazed how halfway decent weed can make a bad situation into an extremely tolerable one. I'm convinced it would have stayed that way until the weed ran out if it weren't for Mr. Springer and his call to arms.

Elvis to his friends, but Mr. Springer to me, we never meshed. In fact, quite the opposite. I have a strong personality and an even stronger work ethic. I'm passionate about my art and my craft and expect that ethic in those I work with. The long hair and the multiple tattoos fool a lot of people, and part of that is on purpose. I am aware of how I present myself. But if you work for me, I expect dedication, and I expect sweat. If I don't get it, I have been known to come down on people. Mr. Springer, he had the opposite philosophy. He very much wanted to be your friend, not your boss, which was a precarious situation for a man who was supposed to be your boss, not your friend. When I needed something from Mr. Springer for our show or for Fantastic Fright Nights, I could count on him spending forty-eight hours with his thumb up his ass before getting to work, and it drove me mad. And from what I can gather, I was of a sort that irritated him all the way to his greasy black hair. If we were oil and water, the oil was on fire, and the water had been frozen into razor-sharp shards of ice. Every time I had to interact with him, I prepped for battle and he did the same.

Given our history, it came as no surprise to me when several of my Freaks saw him throw a lit bottle of liquor at our circus tent, nor was it a surprise when the bottle failed to break on the tent and spilled flaming liquor all over the ground. He threw a breakable bottle at a cloth tent. That, in and of itself, describes the man we're working with here. It bears mentioning at this point that we had already put up a bit of a display, more for our own amusement than anything. It was a classic severed-head arrangement, inspired by season one of *Game of Thrones*. The heads were in a line and . . . well, they were fake, of course. The World's Circus is where all the accoutrements for the Fright Nights are stored. We had severed heads and literal gallon drums of fake blood and entrails and makeup and costumes and other severed bits. The circus was where we did the mazes off to the north and the presentations in the small theatrical space near the entryway for Halloween, which was a month or so away when the storm hit. All the horror paraphernalia had been catalogued and disinfected and was ready for use. So, yes, fake. Fake, fake, fake. Like I said, I have yet to murder anyone, even though I was in the middle of the Hipster Killing Fields, and I meant what I said. To my knowledge, none of the Freaks murdered anyone either.

Getting back to Mr. Springer, after his attack befitting his intelligence, I simply walked up to him and asked what he thought he was going to accomplish. I believe I phrased it, "What fucking idiot thing are you trying to accomplish, you callow turd?" I remember, because I really enjoyed the juxtaposition of "callow" and "turd." I have my moments of poetic flair, however profane. He didn't appreciate it, though, and began screaming and bellowing on about murders and how he had to stop us, and then I noticed there were several employees from the Fantastic Future World behind him, all trying to light their bottles of alcohol. My response was to walk over to the display, grab the head nearest to me, and overhand it straight at the moron. He caught it, and between holding a polyurethane head and me screaming about how goddamned stupid he was, it sank in, and he told his people to back down.

Since I was surrounded by young men and women who had decided to stay high for as much of their waking day as possible, all was forgiven, and he was immediately shepherded into the tent, where he told us his story. Apparently he and his lady friend had been attacked by Pirates, defended by Deadpools, everything was going to hell, and everyone needed to fight back. Then he had the temerity to recruit from my population. He said numbers were going to be important, and we all had to band together. At this point, I began doing some calculations. Most of my group were not going to go with him, content to stay out of trouble's way, if possible, but we were going to lose a few here and there. I immediately started targeting those with experience that I needed. Shady Ned, whose name I never actually knew but was a wizard with an airbrush, Jellica West, who I trusted with some pretty big projects, and several others. I went around while Mr. Springer went on ad nauseam and made damn sure the people I needed weren't going to leave. There were variants on the theme, but basically I told them, "Don't leave. I have a plan." And they didn't.

Once Mr. Springer got all the yelling out of his system, I made a big show of going over, giving him a forearm shake, and telling him his group was welcome here, and we were not going to hurt anyone. Then I told him we were going to make this place look really scary, and, if he would, he could try to help us build a legend. I instructed him to tell everyone not to come here. That we were demonic, that we hunted children in the night, that coming past our gate meant putting your blood and your flesh at risk, that we had turned savage. He was really spooked by what he had seen from the Pirates, so he agreed. I don't want to give him any credit at all, but I think he understood. We were going to appear fearsome; we were going to puff our plumage as big as possible and hope no one noticed we were nothing but some artists and stoners. Then, after his group left, we got to work.

The first thing I did was find Mr. Powers, who worked in maintenance. I had heard the maintenance folks had set up camp in the tunnels, and I could not blame them one iota. The tunnels run all over the park. My theory was if this gambit worked and we could convince those who had turned violent to stay away, then the maintenance folks might feel more comfortable camped out under our section of the park. I was able to track him down fairly easily, and we had a great conversation. Turns out, the flooding in the park that was keeping us from mounting any sort of evacuation was also starting to take a toll on the tunnels. They weren't flooding, but they were damp, it was dark, and the workers were finding it more and more unpleasant. He liked our plan, had heard some of the stories, and agreed to move his camp in our direction as much as he could. Mr. Powers—he kept asking me to call him Charlie, and I never would—he was an eminently reasonable man. He also volunteered some of his staff to help with our gory little decorating project.

Once work started and I fell into my old work habits, those who had worked with me before followed suit. Those who hadn't, they got with the program. The idea was to create a real-life haunted park, but we couldn't just sling gore everywhere. That was tackiness, not camouflage. In the design phase, we decided that drawing people in was important and that giving them both a jump scare and a shot of gore was the best way to go. We did some research on what was visible from what vantage point. Where would people approach us from if they were curious? If they were attacking? If they were hostile? It wasn't until fairly deep into the process that I realized that in creating a subterfuge, we were also creating both a warning system and rudimentary defenses through various elements of the design. We were hunkering down, and the power of creation was glorious.

When we were done, if you approached by day, we had actors and electronic elements that would make you think twice about coming up to the tent. Mr. Powers, he had the market cornered on generators, fortunately, so we could run deterrents of all sorts from loud noises to jump scares and even a serious weapon or two. We had a machine that was initially meant to sling a dummy from a hiding place into the open. We disabled the safety apparatus on that and made it launch a couple very big, very sharp pieces of wood. We decided that was the last line of defense if intruders made it to the tent, kind of a "you've seen the scares, now here's the real thing, motherfucker" sort of finale. It worked every time and would do some serious damage to three or more people, by my estimation. Turns out I was right, but that was much later on.

Turning the World's Circus from an amusement into a human butcher shop, albeit a fake human butcher shop, that was only half the battle, as they say. We needed to build the backstory, so we schemed and came up with a plan there as well. Under the cover of night, we would go and leave little clues around the park as to what we wanted people to think we were up to. One example was a bloodstained note from one of the Robots begging for help. It said things like, "If it's a good day, I stay whole. If it's not, I lose a finger, a toe, or an ear. They're running out of small things to cut off me. Please help." It was that sort of thing. As an aside, I love how that letter runs on pure fear and how the logic of someone writing a letter with no fingers doesn't even enter into it. To put it another way, people are dumb, in my experience.

Sure enough, about two days after we finished, we got to test it out. One of the more rational ShopGirls had heard our story, and she and two of her friends walked right through the gate around lunchtime. Typically, we were more effective if you had some shadows and darkness going, but our actors more than picked up the slack. As they approached, a couple of them started very softly whistling to each other, which, of course, had been agreed upon. Then they started circling around and making banging noises. That, coupled with the various gory decorations, had them scared. Then we hit them with the music. One of the advantages of being a man in your early forties who works primarily with younger adults is they have no frame of reference for your pop culture, so I was able to pipe the first twenty seconds of "Mr. Tinkertrain" by Ozzy Osbourne over the small sound system we had cobbled together. It's this minor key circus-style opening before the guitars come in, and it features children playing in the background. In reality, it's a song about a serial child molester, but such were Mr. Osbourne's muses, I suppose.

With the music and the movement and the gore and the banging, they didn't make it within a hundred feet of the tent. I was a proud papa. A proud, ghoulish, gory papa.

We continued to make tweaks as we went along, and it got better and better. I can honestly say it's some of my best work, given the restraints and the circumstances. When Mr. Garliek came with the invitation to his summit, he didn't make it nearly as far as the ShopGirls did.

He started yelling about authority and any other damn thing that came into his head that helped him deal with his fear, but it was obvious we had him where we wanted him, and we did not relent. We did not drop the act, we did not break character, and by the time he dropped his note and ran . . . well, let's say there was evidence that he had urinated when he did not wish to urinate. I don't think I've ever felt quite so fulfilled by my work. I brought the invitation to the group, and they decided we would break character this one time and show up, but I would do so in a suit and tie and say as little as possible to maintain some mystique. The decision was made after a great amount of discussion as well as a fair amount of rifling through the wardrobe available to us. You'd be surprised what you can find in the costume department aside from large foam heads.

That's the story up until the Council of Pieces and it's a fairly simple one. So. Now I have nowhere else to go. I have to go . . . there, which is where I assume you were actually headed all along. If I must, I must, and I will begin this way. I have no problem living amongst macabre decorations and settings. It's in my DNA, so it seems. But after a while, all the fake blood started to get to some people, and they would talk to me about it. Mr. Powers was particularly affected and told me frequently how our project gave him the creeps. I would always be reassuring and tell them this was for our safety, and it was the easiest way to avoid a fight. More and more, what people were reporting wasn't a simple case of the creeps but something different. They reported seeing something . . . two somethings, actually, and their reports were similar enough to where I began to take notice.

The story would go like this. They were always in an area without many people, which is big red flag in terms of credibility, and they would get a sensation as if they were being watched. They would become hyper-aware and begin looking around, and they wouldn't see or hear anything. Then they would decide to move back toward the rest of the group from wherever they were, and they would see two figures in their path, usually off to the side, but obvious enough to where they wanted to be seen. They were dressed in dark clothing and had modified a few of the masks we use for Fantastic Fright Night to include pieces of what looked like bone. The effect, according to reports, was to create an evil warthog sort of thing, which is kind of a brilliant design aesthetic. Very few designers go for that warthog thing, but they're terrifying creatures. The two warthogs, let's call them, would then slowly advance. They would take their time and would never break into a run. They never responded when spoken to, and they never showed any interest in anything except advancing on whoever they had cornered. Of course they were carrying weapons, and the reports always varied. One person said they had modified blades from table saws, big ones that they had fashioned grips for so they could swing them. Others said it was simpler, like machetes. The one that got me was when one of my Freaks said he had tripped on something as he tried to retreat, and it turned out they had strung some sort of trip wire and started advancing on him more quickly. He got away, but I know true fear when I see it, and the guy who had this encounter was straight terrified. I was also concerned, because if these two were indeed what they seemed, they were trying more advanced hunting techniques. They were developing as they went along.

Do I believe they're real? Of course someone was out there doing something, and if you give it any thought at all, there are only two rational explanations. Either someone was taking what we did in the World's Circus and pretending to be crazy and violent in order to keep people away or . . . the other thing. Either way, the Warthogs never bothered me and, aside from a few stories, never bothered my people that I could tell. Once the battles really got going and raids were a daily thing in most sections of the park, people would go missing on a fairly regular basis, so if you want to make it seem like the Warthogs were out there, picking people off and blaming it on the other tribes, that's certainly an argument you could make. I know that we kept a close eye on our people, and most of them got out of the park safely. It was the same way with the Mole Men, which was my least favorite tribe name. We tried to keep to ourselves, not make allies, not make enemies, and survive as best we could. By and large, it worked.

I will say this about the mysterious figures in the masks. They did us a big favor. A huge favor. Everyone thought the Warthogs were somehow associated with us and that we were controlling them. I will tell you, face to face and on the record, that we had nothing to do with them. They weren't our personal hit squad, they weren't agents of fear, and they weren't the product of some sort of evil ritual. You'd be amazed at the sort of mumbo jumbo some people take seriously. I don't know who they are, and I don't know what they did.

Here's what I do know. We won. We outsmarted everyone. If you set aside what happened at the Council of Pieces, we had the highest rate of survival of any of the tribes, we were in the least amount of conflict, and no one from our side was prosecuted for crimes, because we weren't forced to commit any. I've read, extensively, all the think pieces and all the writing on what happened in FantasticLand, and I've fixated on one idea. A writer from the *New Yorker* set forth the idea that by pretending to be the most violent, we saved ourselves but created more violence in the park. I think that's right. I don't think it's a bad thing. I think we set everyone against each other because they were afraid of us and what we were eventually going to do. We bluffed, and everyone raised the stakes, and no one ever called us, to beat a card metaphor into the ground.

When you take into account what happened at the Council of Pieces, I find what we were able to accomplish pretty fucking remarkable.

INTERVIEW 15: LOUISE MUSKGROVE

Cashier at Hero Haven Comics, Deadpool.

Riley said she had a bad feeling about the meeting. She said nothing good would come of it. We were heavy into the back and forth with the Pirates at this point, and there were lots of injuries, and a few people had been killed, so everyone was already weary and sad, and it was starting to feel hopeless. Nobody objected when Riley said, "Let's do this." If I had spoken my mind at that point, I would have said something along the lines of, "No shit, nothing good is going to come out of this. You are seriously understating the issue," but that wouldn't have gotten us anywhere. We had fought the Pirates to a stalemate, and the meeting was a way forward. We weren't sure forward to where, but it was forward.

Sam Garliek, that little shit, he went around and gave invitations to everyone like he was a princess throwing a tea party. I'm surprised he didn't include a fancy envelope stuffed with glitter. You know who he reminds me of, especially after we all got out? He reminds me of Wormtongue, from *Lord of the Rings*. You know that dude? Whispering in the ear of a king with bad idea after bad idea. Only difference is the only king he was whispering to was in his own head. He thought he still had some sort of authority. Nope! No authority at all. Any authority he had disappeared the moment Brock Hockney killed that guy with that stanchion. All bets were off after that, in my estimation.

When that asshole called his "Meeting of Peace," we had been there for . . . God, what was it? It was really hard to tell time in the park because all you had was the pitch black of night and the gray of the day, and they all sort of melded together after a while. Plus there were no clocks other than watches we might have had on, and most people figured early on, what's the point? It's not like there was a schedule to keep, plus if you wear a watch for too long in the humidity, you get a rash. Time wasn't much of a force in the park, is my point. If I had to guess, I'd put it at three or four weeks that we had been stuck. I remember we were all sick of the limited food options, I remember that. I remember it was after we made the mistake of all getting really hammered on the booze from the Muscle Man Grill and when we woke up, one Deadpool girl was missing. Let's put it at three and a half weeks. In that time, we'd figured out a few things. First, we figured out the Pirates were aggressive, but they weren't terribly tactical. They always came at us from the same direction, it was always a frontal assault, so we fortified a couple of walkways with some broken glass and nails, and that did the trick. They had never flanked us before the meeting, so even though every day or every other day we got some sort of assault from the Pirates, we were pretty solid on our situation. Everyone else seemed to be leaving us alone, and our threat was to the southwest. If you kept your eyes in that direction, you could see what was coming.

Second, we had basic first aid. There were two girls who ran a first aid tent near the center of the park but well past the Exclamation Point, nearer to the Golden Road. I really respected those girls for a couple of reasons. They were good, as far as I could tell, but they made a point of saying that they treated everyone and that their medical tent was not a place to fight. The effect was huge. All of us still had nightmares about what happened to Tom, so it was very nice to have someone we knew we could go to for help. We had only lost two other Deadpools at that point. There was the one girl who disappeared after we all got shitfaced and then there was Steven, who was the sweetest guy. He . . . he got separated. No one was really sure how, but we found him beaten to death and hung over one of the wooden traffic barricades we had put up between us and the Pirates. They laid him out and blew this whistle one of them had. After that, a couple of us, not me but others, actually went over there and took a bunch of their food, and they said they stabbed one of the Pirates in the stomach. I noticed the food was from the Fairy Prairie, but I didn't say anything. To be honest, there were so many rumors floating around about getting rescued and who had done what and even, like, serial killers on the ground, that you couldn't believe anything.

So when we get this invitation from Sam, the consensus was sort of, "Well . . . it's worth a shot." Yeah, a shot. There wasn't even that much discussion. Riley picked four people she wanted to be there with her, for protection, and that was it. At the time, I was taking a break from college, but I was thinking of going back to be a journalist, so I decided I would lobby to be on the "Council of Peace" crew. I'm not much of a fighter, I'm kind of slight and not too aggressive, so Riley wasn't having it, but I sort of begged her. I said this was going to be a big part of the story of this disaster, and I wanted to be there. She finally ended up taking me. She said, "You want to record what happens so bad? Then show up, sit in the corner, and don't say anything. Take notes and stay on our six." I remember vividly, her saying, "Stay on our six," and then I could come. I had this diary I had been taking notes in, and I had a bunch of pens, and I was ready.

Want to know the real tragedy? I had seven GoPro cameras, a bunch of other equipment from the marketing department, and more phones than I could possibly use but no way to charge them. I could have shot this thing from every angle, I could have miked the whole thing, I could have made a documentary that would have made Werner Herzog jealous if I only had a way to charge the equipment. I wasn't the only one freaking out about this. Every single day someone would get frustrated because if they had a camera they could have gotten a hundred thousand likes or favorites or upvotes or whatever, but we had no way to record what we saw and no way to get it out there. Some people got really mad about it, to the point where they would throw things. Have you ever had that sensation? Knowing you were sitting on a gold mine if you could just get a charge for five goddamn minutes? It's frustrating as hell. But it was pens and notebooks. It was better than nothing, but not much.

The invitation Sam had sent said everyone was supposed to meet at noon at the Exclamation Point in the center of the park. Asshole didn't stop to think that not everyone had a working timepiece, you know? It also said he would serve as the "moderator" and that order "would be enforced," which was the part that was making everyone nervous. What the hell did that mean? Had cops shown up and we hadn't seen it? Did he have guns? Was there a bunch of employees who were following him? Was it a trap? Everyone had a theory, but like I said, Riley was convinced this was the way forward. So, on a humid, rainy late morning, as close to noon as we could figure, we all set out for the center of the park.

We were not the first ones there. Someone had set up a big table with this really fancy white tablecloth with all this beadwork on the fringes. I know it was from one of the restaurants, probably the Fantastic Underground which was ridiculously fancy. It was getting rained on, and I remember thinking how the manager, whoever he or she was, would likely lose their shit if they saw their tablecloth covering a couple of picnic tables or whatever and getting rained on. There was a lot of stuff like that in the weeks after we got stuck in the park. I remember one Deadpool taking apart a lemon squeezer they had in a lemonade stand and putting the spiked squeezer part on the end of a stick and taping it there. It wasn't sturdy, but he carried it everywhere, like he was a mid-level warrior with a mace. All I could think of was how that lemonade stand was ruined forever. Anyway, someone had set up this long table, and there were people already sitting around it.

I made up my mind right away that I wasn't going to stay on Riley's "six," and I was going to find a spot where I could hear everything and write down as much as possible. I was going to capture the mood and the atmosphere but most importantly what people said. Over the summer I had been practicing my own bastard form of shorthand, and I was OK at it, so I figured this would be the thing, right? I could tell news people, "I was there, I took notes, and this was what happened." I looked around and there was no place that made sense to set up until I looked up at the Exclamation Point. Even if you've never heard of FantasticLand, you've heard of the giant Exclamation Point in the center of the park. I figured it was kind of, I don't know, symbolic maybe. I would be taking the history of the park from the symbol of the park. Plus there was a service ladder that led to some scaffolding that some of the painters had left up the night before the storm hit. It was maybe twelve feet up. It was the best place to be by a country mile.

I climb up there and then people really start showing up. The ShopGirls were already there. Clara Ann, I knew her as a friend of a friend, she was already sitting there like she owned the place and had four girls with her. Two of the girls had bows and arrows slung over their backs. I began to see why some people were serious when they said, "Be careful of the Golden Road." This was the first evidence I had ever seen of their archers, and it was kind of scary. The Robots, Elvis and his crew, they were there when we showed up. They were talking with these guys who were still wearing their maintenance work clothes. I had heard of the Mole Men, but they were really hard to track down, so it was cool to finally see one of them. Later I got to know Stu Dietz a little bit. He reminds me of my uncle. He was standing next to this taller guy who turned out to be Charlie Powers. He was hard to miss because he was bald as bald can be, and tall. You don't see that combination too often except in horror movies.

So it was us, the ShopGirls, the Mole Men, and the Robots gathered around the table, and everyone was talking and seemed to be having a good time. Then, like all at once, everyone realized that the only groups left were the Pirates and the Freaks and maybe what was left of the Fairies or Pixies—people called them different names. Once everyone realized that, the mood got darker. We had been fighting the Pirates for weeks, they had killed our people, and the Freaks . . . everyone had heard stories, and the stories were bad. Like, blood-on-the-walls, guts-on-the-floor kind of bad. We heard the Freaks before we saw them. This odd, tinkling music started playing over some speakers somewhere and then repeated, and the third time we heard it we saw two guys in these fancy dress suits wearing gimp masks walking toward us. In front of them was this guy with this black beard and long hair and a bunch of tattoos. I wasn't sure what I was expecting, but if they meant to creep everyone out, it worked. They looked like they had knives hidden somewhere and no one wanted to meet their eyes.

Chatter kind of stopped after they showed up, and then we waited. And waited. Maybe ten minutes later, Brock Hockney shows up. Just him. He's dressed in a T-shirt and jeans—he has no hat, no sword, nothing. He wasn't even wearing boots. He had high-tops on, and he was chewing on what looked like a toothpick. It was the exact opposite of the Freaks, except they sort of looked like they had rehearsed it and Brock looked . . . he looked confident. Like he was exactly where he wanted to be. He walked up to the table and sat at the far end, away from everyone. So you had the Robots and us and the Mole Men in one cluster with their backs to the Exclamation Point, the Freaks on their own side, and then Brock sitting by himself, and no one within ten feet of him. The Pixies or the Fairies or whatever, no one ever showed. That answered that question.

Sam, he was there the entire time, too, but no one was talking to him. He kicked it off.

Author's Note: What follows is Louise Muskgrove's transcript of the meeting, translated and edited by Ms. Muskgrove.

Sam Garliek: I want to thank everyone for coming. I know not everyone at this table gets along. Showing up is a good first step. Thank you. *[long silence]* It's obvious things have gotten out of hand. There have been deaths. There has been violence.

(Unidentified Robot): What the fuck do you know about it, dweeb? *[chuckles]*

SG: OK, that was uncalled for. Whoever said that, you don't think I've gone through hardship? You don't think this whole thing has been tough on me?

Charlie Powers: It was tougher on that Francis girl in the shelter.

SG: Shut up, Charlie.

Stu Dietz: Whether or not you killed that girl, everyone thinks you did.

SG: I didn't kill anyone, but . . . that's not why we're here. We're here so we *stop* killing each other. This behavior is off the rails, people! What do you think is going to happen to this park if word gets out that its employees were fighting and killing each other? What about . . .

[Sam is hit with a rock in the shoulder, to the verbal approval of everyone at the table.]

RILEY BOYD: Shut the fuck up, you weasel.

SG: I will not shut up. *Stop it!* This is important. I don't care if you don't like *me [Sam is drowned out by shouts of "we don't."]* . . . keep going. It can't keep going. We are going to be rescued any day now and what . . .

CLARA ANN CLARK: About that, Sam. What's the fucking holdup? *[More cheers and yelling]*

SG: I have information! I have information. I have a radio that picks up broadcasts. Some of you do too. You hear what's going on out there, everyone is doing what they can, but this storm is really, really bad. It's been twenty-five days or so and . . .

ELVIS SPRINGER: There has to be something you can do. Some sort of message you can send, man! This is a completely unacceptable situation.

SG: . . . look, I can say "any day now" until I'm blue in the face, but you all know they're eventually going to get around to us. We're eventually going to get out of here. I want you to think about what happens to you, not him or her or the person you're fighting, but *you* when we get out? *[Silence]* Do you think you're going back to school? How about going to jail? Huh? How about a cell where you live for twenty years because you killed someone? How about that?

GLENN GUIGNOL: We're already in a cell. It's just a big one.

SG: That's a bad attitude, sir. A very bad attitude. I don't care who you think you are or what you think you're doing, eventually the cops are going to come. They're going to be here with guns, and you're going to have to put your hands up and face the fucking music, people. And the only thing we can do, the only thing we can do right now is to work together and not make this any worse than it already is.

CAC: He's right, you know.

SG: You will be held to account for what you've done and not by me, and not by this company, but by the police. Your families will hear about what you did here. Your mothers and your fathers, they will hear about this. You will be brought to justice.

Brock Hockney: Justice?

SG: Because the law is still the law . . .

BH: *Justice!? [Silence]* There is no justice here.

SG: There will be justice later, is what I'm saying, Mr. Hockney.

BH: Justice? For who? For the company that brings home billions of dollars off of our sweat? For the suits who haven't walked the park in years? For you?

SG: I . . . I mean, there will be consequences for how you've behaved. There will be reports and, and, investigations . . .

BH: I wish you could hear yourself. You think you're any different from us? What about Ms. Francis, Mr. Garliek? What about that poor girl who only wanted reassurance that her leader had her best interest at heart?

SG: *I didn't kill that girl!*

BH: *What about my fucking brother?*

SG: That . . . that was unfortunate.

BH: *[flipping up the tablecloth]* So is this.

At that point, the loudest sound I had ever heard consumed everything, and all of a sudden I was falling off the scaffolding. The ground was coming at me before I knew what was coming, and I managed to get my forearm up to my face, and the other one underneath my stomach. I landed partly on my feet and then got tossed onto my front, so it could have been a lot worse. Once I hit the ground, I kind of waited for the waves of pain, and boy howdy did they come. My cheek and part of my face hurt like a bitch, and both my knees were screaming, but the most concerning thing was I couldn't hear. It was all ringing. I thought for a second I couldn't see as well, but it was just the dust, and when it started to clear . . . it's one of those memories that is so clear and I'm so sure of . . . I'm more sure of what I saw than anything I've ever seen in my life.

The tables were splintered and thrown everywhere. The only part of the meeting setup that was the same was where Brock was sitting, but he wasn't sitting at a table. It was a cannon. A goddamn cannon, like from a pirate ship. They had shown up early and set a really nice table for everyone to meet at and no one questioned who set it up, and no one looked under the long tablecloth. The Pirates brought a cannon to the meeting and shot straight at the leaders of the tribes. I've given this some thought, and even if someone had seen it, would they have said anything? Would they have believed it was a weapon, that it was dangerous and not some sort of prop? Probably not, is my guess, but it's just as likely no one even noticed the damn thing. Get this straight: I hate the Pirates. I stone cold hate that group, but . . . what balls. They hid a cannon in plain sight.

The cannon had been pointed square at the Exclamation Point, which was why I had fallen from the scaffolding. I followed the path from the cannon to the Point, and that's where I saw the first body. I don't know who it was to this day, because their head and a large chunk of their torso were just gone. I saw blood, sure, but I also got to see inside that poor person. I saw rib bones, that's what I remember most, but there was also, like, viscera. I didn't know that word until I left the park and heard it on news reports, but that's what it was. Guts pushed together into, like, a paste, I guess. I remember the blood standing in stark contrast to the gray in the sky because of all the cannon smoke. I looked a little further down the line of fire and Elvis from the Robots, he had taken off his shirt and was holding it to Charlie Powers' head, most of which was gone. He was trying to stanch the wound of a guy who was missing a large part of his head. I remember, he had one eye and it was rolled up and his mouth was wide open in this gruesome sort of . . . I don't even know what to call it. He was dead. Super dead. Deader than dead, but Elvis was holding his shirt to his head like you do in the movies. You know, "keep pressure on it," that sort of thing. I guess there's no right way to react in that situation.

I followed the line of fire the rest of the way to the Exclamation Point and noticed the cannonball had ripped part of the base completely away. There were chunks of brightly colored plastic and glass everywhere, and there were three or four people who had gathered around the base, Mole

Men and Robots I would guess, and they were just in pieces. It was just a mess of blood and glass, and I remember one woman holding her head and screaming, but I couldn't hear her. I was looking at all of this, and I still couldn't hear, which is why I didn't notice what was going on around me. The Pirates had shown up and had started killing people.

That's not entirely accurate. The Pirates had shown up and started fighting, but they had the element of surprise, and even though I couldn't hear, it was clear they were winning. I saw some of the Mole Men scatter in one direction, and the Freaks were running in another direction, and some of the Deadpools, they were straight up hand-to-hand fighting Pirates who were armed with swords. They were using chunks of table and chairs and anything else they could find to block the swords, and it all seemed very desperate. Sometimes it worked, and sometimes other Pirates would knock them off their feet or knock whatever they were holding out of their hands, and the stabbing would start. Once one of the Pirates got their blade in someone, others ran up out of nowhere and would just start stabbing as fast and as hard as they could. I saw it happen three times, three different people just getting stabbed and stabbed, and their faces first being all intense and then rolling into that same death grimace I had seen on half of Mr. Powers's face.

After the second stabbing, I realized I was in danger, and I was on the wrong side of the park. I couldn't retreat to the Hero Haven, so I took a long route north and tried my best to keep on the perimeter of it all. I succeeded well enough and actually bumped into a ShopGirl archer who was pretty mad that I threw off her aim. I watched her put an arrow into a Pirate's leg, and the dude just dropped and started screaming. My hearing had started to come back.

At that point, I was in full flight mode. Once I felt safe enough, I turned my back to the thing and just fucking ran for the common room in the Hero Haven. I was the first to make it back, and I quick told everyone what happened and told them to get off their asses and grab their weapons, the attack might be coming. But of course it never came. No cannon, no horde of Pirates. Nothing. No one. No one came back. Not Riley or any of the four who went with her. It was just . . . nothing. After a while, when it became clear no one was coming home from that meeting, you could feel the room just totally deflate. Everyone lay down with their weapons that night, but no one slept. Not that night. I forget where and how the "Council of Peace" became the "Council of Pieces," if it was a bad joke or what, but by the time everyone woke up the next morning, that's what everyone was calling it. I feel bad about it, but when I was staring into the darkness that night, I didn't think about the blood or the death or any of that. I was thinking about how I would have killed for a camera. What I could have shot, it would have been legendary.

Before everyone turned in, a group of us decided to go back and at least get a look at the scene before the sun set completely. We weren't anywhere near the Exclamation Point when we could see the bodies hanging from the wire that had once supported the Exclamation Point.

INTERVIEW 16: STUART DIETZ

FantasticLand Maintenance, Mole Man. Interview 2.

I was sitting next to Charlie when that fucker fired that cannon. I'm lucky. I didn't get hit, and I don't remember much. When that sort of thing happens, it doesn't register right away. I remember one time when I was a kid, I was riding my bike with some buddies, and I jumped over this dirt pile and wiped out and ended up busting my leg. It was a, what do you call it, compound fracture, where the bone sticks outta the skin, and I remember seeing it happen and not feeling a damn thing. The only thing I remember, clear as day, was the feeling that "this is strange and should not be happening," then I saw the blood and freaked out like you do when you're a little kid. That's what it was like after that cannon fired. I remember my ears ringing, and I was blown out the back of my seat, and I landed with my back to Charlie. He took the brunt of it. I . . . see, I gotta give Hockney credit. He knew what he was doing. The cannonball, that was plenty damaging. That blew some folks clear apart. But it was when it hit the Exclamation Point that it did a bunch of little damage. The Point is a mixture of fiberglass and regular glass and wood and chunks of metal and whatever the hell else they put into it. When that metal ball hit, it was like setting off an entirely separate bomb, right in front of everyone. I couldn't have planned it any better, that destructive bitter asshole.

I was blown out of my seat and onto the ground, and that spared most of my body from any serious harm. I caught a piece of wood in the shoulder. Nothing serious. That and I had a bit of bursitis before, and now I can barely hear out of my left ear. The guy next to me, most of his head just blew apart. When they finally got me out of that godforsaken park, I had a minor blood infection from my shoulder. Don't ask me how that happened, and don't tell me God works in mysterious ways. If He's up there, I want an answer to that one.

I'll spare you the gory details of the immediate aftermath unless you want to hear about 'em. What do you need to know, anyway? I sat up, some people had chunks of stuff in them and were bleeding and screaming, and I saw Charlie and saw what was left of his head hanging from a string of skin and muscle on his neck. There. Gory enough for you? I was in that "this is strange and should not be happening" phase I was talking to you about, and what knocked me out of it was when Lucy, she worked in maintenance and was really good at painting, which we did a lot of in the park, she ran up and grabbed me, and she was crying. She grabbed me and cried "help" really loud and I saw she was being chased. This guy had a sword and he was running toward her. Something inside me clicked and it was like going from a dream or something to being really focused. I kicked a metal folding chair toward the guy with the sword running at Lucy, and sure enough it tripped him up. He fell on his face, and the sword went tumbling out of his hand. I looked at Lucy and she gave me a look that said, "I'm OK," and we both started looking for other guys from our group.

Before Charlie got a cannonball to the face, he was really high on this whole "Council" thing. He was telling us it was our chance to come out of the tunnels, even though we could kind of do that whenever we wanted. We were friends with the Robots and with the Deadpools and even with Glenn and his guys. They had a brilliant thing going, scaring everyone like that. Charlie said if we were friends with three of the five or six groups, then things couldn't be as bad as everyone was saying. We stayed away from the Pirates because we had seen bodies hanging from the street lamps, and the ShopGirls were their own thing. If you went up to them, you had to have a reason. That was how it worked. But old Charlie, he was convinced this was going to work, and he told anyone who wanted to come up and watch to come up and watch. About fifteen of us took him up on that.

I was kind of Charlie's right-hand man at this point. He was the one who everyone looked to for the decisions, but me and this guy named Tomas, we were kind of his brain trust. He ran most of the big decisions by us, and we both really disagreed with him on this. He wasn't the kind of guy who made up his mind and that was that, you know? He was more the "listen to everyone first" kind of guy, but on this one, he wouldn't hear me or Tomas out. I thought it was a bad idea because that little shit Sam Garliek was leading it. Tomas, he thought it was a bad idea because one group or another was going to show up armed, and that would make everyone on edge, and something bad could go down. Charlie didn't agree with either of those and told everyone to show up, so when Lucy and I were running back toward the tunnels I was able to see who made it and who didn't. Nine of us made it, six of us didn't. I saw two that died in the cannon blast, which meant four of us got caught up in the fighting. I remember we all retreated to the tunnels after it all went down, and I was just muttering over and over "goddammit Charlie." Just over and over. I knew it was his fault for not seeing something like this coming. I mean, no one saw that cannon coming, but he should have known something like this was going to happen.

As we sat there in the tunnels, waiting to see who came back and who was dead or worse, I remember Lucy and this other lady whose name I never learned, they just both grabbed onto each other and were openly sobbing. After a while it started getting to a few of us because they weren't calming down or nothing, they just kept sobbing. It became this chorus of "shut ups" and them calming down and someone defending them, and then they'd start up again and the whole thing would play back out. After a while, I kind of remembered what it was like when my kids would throw a fit and nothing ever got better until someone with a cooler head came in, so I went to them and I crouched down and I said, loud enough for everyone to hear, "Ladies, Charlie is gone. He was a good guy, but he had the wrong idea. We need to focus on something new. We need to focus on getting us rescued." That calmed them down pretty quick, and . . . I don't know, it just sort of reframed the thing. This bad thing happened, and it happened because we had been doing things a certain way. Now we were going to try something different. It seemed like a good idea, given what had just happened.

That night, back in the commons, we started planning. Everyone stayed up. If they weren't participating, they were listening and drinking coffee, and I heard people talk that night that I had never heard talk before. Everyone had an idea, and at the end of the thing, we came up with a list of five things we needed to do, and they ranged from really easy, like shooting off all the flares in the emergency kits at once, to really complicated. The biggest one, the one that made the most sense and was going to be the hardest, was taking down the Exclamation Point.

Here was the thinking. The Exclamation Point at the center of the park was about three hundred tons of glass and concrete and fiberglass and other shit. Tons and tons. It was also seventy-five feet tall and about thirty-five feet or so across. In other words, everyone in the park would see it was gone, but so would, like, satellites and Google Maps and all that shit. Someone was figuring out where and how to send aid, and if the Point went down, that was at least a curiosity. That was something that needed a closer look, even if the resources were stretched thinner than a fat guy's tighty whiteys from fifty pounds ago. Everyone agreed that if we took it down, someone would come, and if someone came and saw all the bodies hanging from the light posts and blood on the Golden Road, then help would come.

It was a good plan, but it had some problems, obviously. Most obvious was how the hell do you do it? It's not like we could Google "how many pounds of TNT will bring down a national landmark" or anything, even if we could get on the computer. My hope, when we were planning it out that night, was that Brock's little outburst had damaged the Point enough to where we would just need to give it a little nudge and, you know, *timber*, which meant we had to go out there and take a good look at it. I want you to keep in mind, we weren't rough and ready to fight whoever was out there. A lot of us were older and just trying to make an extra buck or two, and next thing you know we were in the middle of this bullshit. There was a large bunch of folks who just wanted to sit in the dark and wait this out, and I can see where they were coming from. In all the time we were in the park, no one bothered us, really. Any problems we had were after we went up and interacted with people. But still, I wanted a look at what happened, so the next day, with no sleep and my ear still hurting like a bitch, I went back out there.

I came up from the tunnels as close to the Point as I could, which was by a family restroom about a hundred yards away from where I wanted to be. I kind of poked my head out and looked around, and the first thing I noticed was how dead it was. No pun intended. There wasn't a soul out there. Second thing was that it wasn't raining for the first time I could remember since Sadie cold-cocked us. The ground was still wet, and water was dripping from everything, and it was cloudy, but it wasn't raining. I figured it was a good sign.

I stayed close to the buildings at all times because I figured it was a bad idea at this point to be more exposed than I had to be. I was really close to the Point, probably twenty-five yards or so, before I noticed the bodies hanging from a wire. A lot of people mistakenly thought that wire was some sort of high-tension deal that supported the Exclamation Point, but that wasn't true. It was a line they used to hang banners for special occasions. Signage, basically. If they had a corporate event, that's where they would put up the WELCOME AMERICAN BUTTHEADS LLC sign so they felt good about giving us their money. That's where the bodies were hanging from. The Point, it was supported by a heavy concrete base and then by various other mechanisms, but not by any sort of wires. I can see where people make that mistake, but the bodies, they were hanging from the welcome sign wires.

I had to walk under the bodies to get to the damaged part of the Point's base. I kind of forgot my "no exposure" rule because I wanted to see if I knew anyone up there. Turns out, I didn't. It was a couple of kids. Two of them looked like Deadpools, and I heard later one of them was Riley, who was their leader. I had met her a few times, but the bodies were pretty mangled. I'm not surprised I couldn't figure out who it was. I'm not a guy who's been to war, but I've seen enough of those History Channel documentaries to know a real body from a Hollywood one. They never get the angles right in the fake bodies. The real ones sort of have this odd, loose angle thing going on where they bend in ways no one is supposed to bend. I remember looking at a couple of the bodies and seeing their arms and other parts bent and thinking, "That's the real thing."

One of the kids up there, he was looking pretty bad, like he was going to give way at any second. He was hung by his neck. You, um, you do the math. I remember thinking that if I was this kid's mom, I would never want to hear about how my son's head came off, and so I'll shut up about it. When I finally made it to the part where the cannonball hit, it was the oddest thing. The cannonball had basically taken out a little less than a quarter of the base and kept going into the park. To this day, I don't know where it stopped. I would guess somewhere in the Fantastic Folks from History ride, based on the big fucking hole in the side of its facade, but that's just a guess. I took a look, and there was good news and bad news. The good news was that it was pretty messed up from a structural standpoint, but the bad news was that it was not nearly messed up enough. You could have run a truck into the thing and it would have stayed up, which meant we had to move to plan B, which was explosives.

I did a few quick measurements and headed back, but as I was rounding the corner near the family restroom area, I looked back and I saw that this girl had been following me. She was by herself, just standing about fifty feet away from me, and she was armed. I could see she was holding two shotguns, one in each hand, and had an even bigger caliber something or other in a holster on her back. I didn't know what to do, so I sort of raised my chin up to acknowledge that I saw her. She didn't move. Not an inch. So I got my ass back underground. I don't know what that was about either and kind of don't care to know. A woman with a bunch of guns is usually something I get behind, but I don't know. Let's leave it there.

Everyone was really glad to see me when I got back, but I was ready for bed, so I hit the sack. I'm like that. When I'm done, I'm done. It takes an act of God to wake me up. When I finally got up about five hours later, our people had found a few TNT demolition blocks from who the hell knows where. Turns out there were a couple of construction projects slated at the park that needed some minor demolition, and that's where they found them. I'm not good with explosives, but Tomas had learned a little about demolition in the army. When I told him what we were dealing with and gave him the dimensions, he wasn't sure it would work. He said we were only able to find so much TNT and we would need so much more TNT and yadda yadda. Some other folks put their heads together and they figured it out, or at least figured it out enough to where they thought it was worth giving it a shot. The idea was we would go out there with whatever equipment we could find, like jackhammers and sledgehammers and such, and make a hole in the base to put the explosives in.

It did not escape us that this would make a lot of noise that would be like ringing the goddamn dinner bell. Plus, it would be kind of an operation. It would take generators for the jackhammers, and we'd be throwing chunks of concrete everywhere, so we had a bunch of discussion about that. We spent a day gathering the materials and then, the second night after that stupid fucking meeting, the wind picked up and started blowing something fierce, and the rains started up again, and Tomas put on a hard hat he had found and said, "It's time." And he was right. The wind would cover up a lot of the noise, the rain would discourage folks from coming out, and not a single one of us hadn't worked in the rain before. It was the perfect time, and we hadn't even planned for it. The only problem was it was dark, so we'd have to use extra gennies for a lighting setup, which we also had. We did a quick vote, and almost everyone wanted to risk it, and everyone who didn't kind of got what we were thinking. So we went.

I don't know if you've ever worked construction, but there's a reason no project has ever been on time or under budget. We get out there, and immediately the bodies scare off a few people, and the generators are working but one of the jackhammers doesn't like the rain, so we're down to one, and Tomas is operating that himself. Then the lights went out, so we had to figure out what was wrong there, and when we couldn't, we just ended up shining flashlights on Tomas as he drilled as best he could. This ended up being a good thing because I heard later on that a couple of Pirates had seen the lights and come out to investigate but couldn't find us in the dark. I don't know if that's true or not, but I do know the longer we were out there, the more nervous I was getting. We were working fast and we were working wet, and it sucked, but we had a plan. It had probably been an hour or so when I heard the first gunshots.

There's no mistaking a gunshot, not even in heavy wind. I didn't think there was a gun in the entire godforsaken park until I saw that woman armed to the teeth a couple days before. Then, *blam*! There were guns, and they were being fired. Tomas heard it too and stopped drilling and kind of looked at me and I looked at him, and he yelled over the wind, "We've got to get this done." And he was right. We had been at it for a long time, I had no idea where to get more gas for the gennies since the filling station on grounds was flooded, and I wanted out of the fucking park. I just really wanted out. So did Tomas. He had a wife and three kids somewhere, and he wasn't looking after them during a very dangerous time because he was stuck in FantasticLand. So I give him a nod, and Tomas starts drilling again.

He finally gets close enough, and he's got the demo blocks just about in place, and the hole is too small for one of them. He's working it, very gingerly mind you, and all of a sudden I hear someone yell, "*Run*" and I start hearing the yells. I shine the light away from Tomas for a second, and I see most of my people running like hell and just a handful of Pirates, maybe four or five of them, beating on the folks they'd been able to catch. I've heard a few of those assholes saying they enjoyed the atmosphere of living by an honor code or some such shit, but where's the honor in holding down a fifty-year-old grandmother and beating the hell out of her in the rain? I'm sorry, I just don't get it. And, I'll be honest with you, I got kind of upset. So when one of them came at me I took the butt of my flashlight and bashed him over the head with it and he dropped. The others were too busy with whatever they were doing, so I stomped the kid hard in the face to make sure he'd stay down and turned the flashlight back to Tomas. He about had everything the way he wanted it and nodded to me. I turned back around to see the kid and I caught his feet as he was being dragged away behind a knickknack shop a few feet away. I would have followed up to figure out who was taking him and why, but Tomas had grabbed my shoulders and motioned that we needed to get to the detonator. The fuses were all set, and we were ready to blow this thing.

Our plan was to run back to the tunnels where we had set up the detonators and blow the thing from a safe distance, with the added safety of being underground. While we were running back, I heard all sorts of things. There were screams, there was yelling, there was even another gunshot. My mindset at that time was "head down, keep moving," and I was able to do that. Adrenaline helped 'cause I'm pretty sure I covered that distance at a dead sprint. Once we got down there, we were missing a few folks, I think four people were not in the tunnel, but we decided to blow it anyway, because if we didn't, someone might fuck with the explosives and the plan wouldn't work, so we went ahead and pressed the button.

A couple things happened after that you're gonna want to know about.

First thing. Big thing. Tomas was thinking these were quarter-pound TNT demo blocks. They were one-pound blocks. Asshole never read the side of the things; he just thought he knew what he was dealing with because that's what he'd trained on in the army. He had done all the math on destroying the base and not accounted for three fourths of the explosive power he was dealing with. It was right there on the side of the fucking blocks: one pound. He didn't bother to look, so the boom we were expecting? It was less like a boom and more like the Four Horsemen of the Apocalypse farting in unison. The tunnel rocked to the point that we thought it was going to cave in, but it held. There was shit falling from the ceiling like you see in movies. We had earplugs in, but it wasn't nearly enough for how close we were. The shockwave shattered all the lightbulbs, not that they worked anyway, but it's never fun when sharp glass falls from the sky. Plus, and I don't want to get into this too much, but we probably killed some folks. I don't know who, and I don't know how, but we were amateurs dealing with explosives, and that's about as smart as kicking a hungry lion in the balls. I honestly cannot tell you who we killed, if we killed a bunch of our people or a bunch of the Pirates or what. Either way, I don't feel good about it. An explosion is a bad way to die. I still feel really bad about that.

Second thing. Also a big thing. We were aiming to destroy the base and send the Exclamation Point falling in one direction. That didn't happen. Basically we blew the base to kingdom come along with a good part of the Exclamation Point. No one saw the explosion and lived to tell about it, so I can't say for sure what happened, but I do know at the end we had a hole where the base used to be, and about a third of the Point was blown to shit. Just gone, replaced by a million fragments of fiberglass and what not. The only part you could still ID as the Point was the curve of the top, which is the biggest part of the thing. That survived. There were also big chunks, but I'll be damned if I knew what part of the Point they came from.

Last thing. The idea was for us to knock the Point over. That way, if someone looked down on the park, they might see the Point on its side and see it as a call for help. That was our intention—to get attention and get rescued. We certainly got attention, but not from anyone we wanted. There was already a big fight after Garliek's dumb-fuck meeting, but after we blew up the Point and folks saw there were explosives in play, that's when things took a turn. A bad turn. Like it wasn't bad enough already, but now we had little armies, and they were starting to panic.

If history teaches us anything, it's that armies and panic are a bad combo. A really bad combo.

INTERVIEW 17: ANONYMOUS

Author's Note: For reasons concerning legal liability and possible retaliation, the subject of this interview has requested anonymity. I have been able to clear her credentials as a member of the park staff and confirm several key events through various means and sources. I cannot confirm every detail of her story and usually stay away from anonymous sourcing, but I have chosen to include her interview because it gets at a very important part of this story during a period about which many refuse to talk or were not present for the events described.

We were holding our own until those idiots blew up the middle of the park. The supplies were holding out, we were able to scare off anyone who came by looking for trouble, and most of all we had each other. We were sisters, and we were ready to fight for each other. That all changed after the explosion. That was the hardest thing to accept, the absolute hardest thing to get over. You, like, put your life in someone's hands, and you sleep in the same communal area with them, and you believe in them and love them, and all of a sudden they get scared, and no one trusts each other, and it stops being a club and starts becoming an army. That sucks. That really sucks. I killed people and watched them choke on blood and scream, and we stabbed them, and that doesn't haunt me like Clara Ann haunts me.

We lost three girls in the explosion, a girl named Hera who was just awesome and fun and another girl we called Sam. Ten minutes after the boom, Clara yelled at everyone to take stock, count heads, check our weapons, and make sure this didn't get worse like it did at the Council of Pieces. I remember she would yell, "Be ready," at the top of her lungs, like she was Paul Revere. She would run up and down the Golden Road shouting, "Be ready," and stepping over Paul and yelling and yelling. Paul? Paul the Puddle. It's a bad joke. It's what we started calling the body in the middle of the road—that dude Brock killed, like, the second day—because he was starting to kind of melt. Not melt, but he was wet all the time and part of him was bloating and other parts were just gross and gooey. He was a landmark. "Meet you at Paul in fifteen minutes," that sort of thing. But Clara, she was in full panic mode, and you could hear it in her voice, and everyone responded. Probably two minutes after she started yelling, we were all at our posts ready to kick ass.

No one came. We sat there, our ass cheeks clenched, bruising for a fight, and no one came.

There wasn't even any screaming or anything. Just smoke from the boom and, after a while, the sound of rain. Rain rain rain rain rain. I swear to God I still wake up feeling wet. Your hair was always stuck to your face, and your feet were always cold, even when it was hot, and it was just terrible. After the boom, Clara Ann made it a rule that someone had to be on guard twenty-four hours a day, on the roofs, waiting for an attack, so there were times standing on that roof was like taking a cold bath with your clothes on. All the girls got coughs, and one girl's feet got so damp stuff started growing on them. It was terrible, and people started to, like, ask Clara Ann if we could lighten up a bit. No one had to be on the roof at four in the morning. Not even the Pirates were that motivated. But she started insisting, and then when that didn't work, she started yelling. And things were just about to reach a head when the first raid came.

It happened right after lunch, in broad daylight. We were eating cheese spread and rock-hard scones because someone had made just a ton of scones before the hurricane hit, when we heard a screaming sound. All these girls who weren't with us were running toward the

Road with sticks and a few swords, and behind them were three girls pulling the cannon. If we hadn't seen the cannon, we might not have known who was coming at us, but the hardware made it obvious: these were Pirates and Fairies who had become Pirates. If they hadn't started screaming before they got to us, they might have made it farther. Hell, shoot the cannon to announce yourself, if that's the way you want to go, but no. They came at us yelling like they were Vikings or something. It was really stupid if you ask me, and at that point we were so glad to have something else to focus on that we let them have it. They wanted blood? Come and get it, assholes. We were pissed off and sick and bored and itching for a fight.

Our archers, they were up first; they had thirty-five arrows between them and each of them had a name. We had three archers, and they each had a spot on the rooftops that they could get to in about forty-five seconds on a good day, so it goes like this. We hear the screaming, saw the cannon, we hear Clara Ann yelling "Be ready," and before the first set of Pirate girls gets to our buildings, the archers are screaming "Simon! Nick! Edgar!" as they're firing off the arrows and yelling the names of the arrows as they let them go. From there, it's all screaming and blood.

We were armed pretty well. We got the arrows from a sporting goods store on the Road, and the rest of us had hockey sticks and baseball bats. You'd be surprised how badass you can be with a tennis racket. We even had, like, armor. Football shoulder pads and knee pads and stuff. All the girls grabbed their gear, and to her credit, there was Clara Ann, right at the front, with a big piece of jagged metal she'd found and wrapped a bunch of tape around it so she could use it as a sword. She called it Tetanus; it was kind of nerdy that she gave it a name, but it was funny when she did it. I remember, I was next to my friend Scottie, and when you have nothing to talk about for hours and hours you talk about what it would be like if you have to run at someone and fight them, like we were sure was going to happen. Scottie always said she thought everyone would run right up to the person they were going to fight and then they'd look at each other and realize how stupid that was. "Maybe we'll all start laughing," she said. She was wrong. By the time your legs are pumping and your arms are swinging, any thought or higher brain function is gone. I've been a "nice girl" most of my life, but, goddammit, I wanted to get my fight on. I wanted some scars on my skin and some dead bodies at my feet.

I got them both by the time I left the park.

I had a baseball bat. It was a metal one, and I carried it everywhere. It was my constant companion, and I started to call it Cap. Like, kneecap someone. Ever heard that? That's what I was thinking, and everyone seemed to think it was a good name for a bat. I also didn't wear any guards or pads or anything because I was thinking the best thing to do if you ever got into a fight was move, move, move. I ran it in my head a hundred times before it happened, and I remember thinking, "What would you go for?" Like, if I had to fight someone, who would I choose? I figured I would choose the person who was standing still. Who had no momentum, right? And that, turns out, is totally right. The ShopGirls, we ran into the crowd and it was like, the first person who wasn't running past you was the person you took a swing at, and the first girl I saw, she had this really nasty scar on the side of her face. Really nasty, like, "she got it in the park and it wasn't healing right" sort of nasty. She was looking at another set of girls fighting, and I took Cap and without any fanfare just fucking bashed her in the head. I heard it connect . . . this is going to sound really gross, but you know when you're hitting a ball and you know you "got all of it"? I got all of that girl's head, and she went down. Then it was like, great, who's next?

The good news was when our archers started hitting the Lady Pirates—that's what we called them because we thought it sounded like a high school basketball team—when the arrows started hitting the Lady Pirates they lost about a third of their numbers. They ran at the first sight of blood, which makes sense. We spent most of our time on defense, trying to stop people attacking us, so we noticed when things started getting serious, about a third of any group would just stop fighting and leave. Sometimes they ran, but I was on the roof once and it was more casual than that. It's like, they lost interest and started wandering around. So already they were down to about twenty girls, and we had a lot more than that swinging bats and rackets and other stuff. A few of the smart ones figured out we were going to win and started running, and the last ten girls or so . . . we laid them out. We knocked them out or we went over and made sure the arrows had done their job . . . and I remember this really well, Clara Ann walked over to one girl who was yelling and screaming about her arm and stabbed her in the head with Tetanus. Then she, like, twisted the sword around in the girl's head until she stopped kicking around. It took a lot longer than I thought it would, but at the end, there was our fearless leader, bloody sword in her hand, leading us to victory. She never let us forget that.

They never did anything with the cannon. I don't even know if they knew how to fire it.

We ended up killing four girls, five with the one Clara Ann killed, and injuring seven more. The ones we hurt, we showed mercy to them, helped them up and sent back to the Pirate Cove as soon as they could walk. We didn't lose anybody, but a couple of girls had gashes and stuff that needed medical attention, and Scottie sprained her ankle running toward the battle. That night was the party you would expect within reason, because we were all sick to death of being stuck in the park by then. Clara Ann got up and gave us a speech. She said we needed to send a "don't fuck with us" message to the Pirates and anyone else who wanted to hurt us. Turns out, the Pirates got it loud and clear, because the next day they tried to hit us with cannon fire. It started in the afternoon when we heard a boom and actually saw the cannonball fly over us and into the swampy part of the grounds past the Golden Road. Then, like, half an hour later, another one was way short. I'm not sure it made it out of the Pirate Cove, and the girl on patrol at that time said she heard a lot of yelling from there. My guess is they fired it at the Deadpools, but I don't know that for sure. It would make sense, though. I mean, they were right there staring them in the face every day, and we were a bit of a hike.

That night, one of the guys from the Deadpools, his name was Daniel, he shows up and he asks to meet with Clara Ann. He's holding Riley's sword, which was a big deal, I found out later. He and Clara Ann talk, and after about half an hour she comes out and asks me and two other girls to come into her "office," which is actually just a section of the uniform center. It was me and a girl named Kristen, who I liked, and another girl named Drew, who I didn't. Clara Ann said she had met with this guy, Daniel, and they both agreed we needed to take out the cannon before the Pirates got too good at firing it and started hitting buildings and hurting people. No one had any idea how to dismantle a cannon, but the idea was to take a small "strike team" and go into the Pirate Cove and then figure it out as we went. I must have had an "are you fucking kidding me" look on my face because Clara Ann started yelling. She yelled about how it was so important to take out this weapon and how I shouldn't be selfish, and if we were going to survive this someone needed to do this. I remember, clearly, it was the first time someone used the word "if," not "when." At that point, though, it made total sense. It felt like we were never leaving and that this was the world we're dealing with now.

She pushed me to go with the "strike team." She pushed hard. Kristen and Drew, they were kind of hesitant too, but we could all tell Clara Ann was going to yell even more if we didn't do what she wanted, so we said yes. That night the four of us met with Daniel and two other Deadpools and got our weapons together. Immediately, it was clear we were coming at this from different places. One girl Deadpool, I never did learn her name but she had lots of freckles, she was all, "I've killed one Pirate and I'm going to kill a bunch more," and was, like, stroking this small knife she carried with her. Drew and I shot each other a "who is this crazy bitch" glance. The other guy Deadpool was a bit more chill, but you could tell he had seen more than his share of shit. They had a back way to get in to the Pirate Cove, which involved climbing up through the back of the fake town that was the backdrop for the Main Street area. From there, the entire plan consisted of "find the cannon and make sure it doesn't work anymore." That was it. Oh, and "kill any Pirate you see," according to Freckles McStabby. And, even though we're operating under one of the dumbest plans ever devised, it worked at first. The cannon was right there in the middle of town, completely unguarded, and there isn't anyone hanging out anywhere we could see. We kind of hang out for twenty minutes or so, and wonder of wonders we don't see anyone, so we start talking about what we're going to do. Do we pull the wick out? Do we knock off the wheels? We have no idea. Not one. The best we can come up with is, "Let's go look at the thing, and if anyone comes out, have them chase us back to the group and we'll stab them." Another brilliant plan.

Freckles and Drew decide they're the ones who are going to go down there, so they jump down from our hiding place and just waltz up to the damn thing. No resistance, no nothing. They fiddle around for a while and run back to us. They have no idea what they're doing. They said, "We could take the wheels off, but the Pirates would just put them back on," and Daniel says, "What are the chances of us rolling it off the main road and into one of the big ponds over there?" The Pirate Cove had a couple of decorative ponds near the entryway and we were, like, a few hundred feet away from one of them. If it sank to the bottom of one of those ponds, they'd never get it out. But it would take all of us. After a bunch of back and forth and arguing, we decide to go for it.

The cannon was a big bastard, but once we got it rolling, we were able to get it moving at a good clip. I couldn't believe how well this was going until we just about hit the edge of the water. That's when we got noticed. We heard shouts from a couple of Pirates who had seen us. They were a ways back, but we could see there were about eight of them running in our direction. Immediately, everyone chooses which way they're going to go. Freckles pulls out her knife and gets ready to fight. Drew looks around for someone to tell her what to do. To Clara's credit, she kind of stepped up. There was a layer of bricks and a hill separating the ground we were on from the overflowing pond, so Clara Ann looks back and yells, "Push!" and we start pushing as hard and as fast as we possibly could. We got it right up to the edge, and thank God the ground leveled off a bit after the hill, but we couldn't get the damn thing over the layer of bricks. We tried three or four times. Clara Ann jumps down and starts pawing at the bricks and soon we're all down there, pulling at them with everything we can while the Pirates close in on us. I get the first brick up because I plunged my hands under the dirt, not aiming at the brick itself, and soon we had made enough headway to push the cannon into the pond.

It was a glorious moment. That second the wheels went past their fulcrum, the barrel pitched forward and the whole thing just went *spoosh*. It was fantastic. Daniel, the Deadpool leader, he had this giant grin on his face, and Clara Ann actually looked happy for a second. If a fairy showed up today and said, "You need a happy memory to make you fly," that's what I'd pick, that stupid fucking cannon hitting the water followed by looking at the Pirates and seeing the understanding on their faces. They looked like little boys who were about to cry. Then they looked like pissed-off men who wanted to kill us. We turned and ran, and thank God we still had enough distance on the Pirates that we could make a few turns and hide. We hid in an abandoned taffy store called Fantaffy. All seven of us were able to run in the back or duck behind counters. We could hear the Pirates looking for us, but they lost interest pretty quickly because they wanted to see if they could save the cannon. Spoiler alert, they couldn't.

I hid behind the counter and was waiting for the all clear when I heard fighting noises in the back where the other kids were hiding. It was me and Clara Ann and Freckles and that other Deadpool guy behind the counter, and Clara Ann and I jump up and run back there to find Daniel standing over Drew, working on making as big a hole in her neck as he could with a knife. He had grabbed a knife from the back of Fantaffy and . . . holy shit, it was bad. He had stabbed her in the side of the neck, by surprise, I would guess, and was working to make that hole as big as he could by, like, wiggling it, and apparently it wasn't cutting and Drew was still thrashing around. Then I hear a noise behind me and Freckles and Clara Ann are going at it, grabbing onto each other and fighting as hard as they could. I didn't see Kristen, the other girl who had come with us, and the Deadpool guy whose name I never got, he looked as dumbfounded as I did. I remember taking a beat and then taking Cap and taking a good hard swing at Freckles. I hit her right in the back of the head, even though she was wrestling with Clara. Cap's aim is always true.

So Freckles goes down, and Daniel looks up from cutting my friend's neck open and runs at me with a knife. I don't have enough room in the small kitchen to really get a good windup going, but I wing Daniel pretty good in his arm, and by then Clara Ann is on him. She didn't bring Tetanus with her, but she did have a knife she found in the sporting goods store and she lunged for Daniel, who was holding his arm from where I hit him, and stabbed him through his right eyeball. Or left eyeball. Right to me, left to him. Either way, bad deal for him. He does a sensible thing and runs out of the back room and out the door, yelling. Clara looks at me and said, "I'll look at Drew. You finish this girl." She said her name, but I forget what it was.

I hadn't knocked Freckles out. Not completely. She had half rolled over, and she caught my gaze out of the corner of her eye. She knew it was coming, and I knew I was going to do it and it was this weird . . . I don't know, let's call it understanding. It was like, through her eyes and the look on her face, she let me know that this was going to suck for me, but not as much as it was going to suck for her, and I think I got a little bit of an apology in there, I think. Maybe I'm making too much of it in my mind. Either way, a second after we had that moment, I beat her to death with my metal baseball bat. I didn't stop until her head was a very different shape from when I started. Blood wasn't enough. I needed to make sure . . . I needed . . . I needed to get it out. The frustration of being trapped in the park and my friend just getting murdered for no fucking reason, I swung and I swung and I swung, and by the time I was done Freckles was a pink mess and fuck her. Fuck her. I was doing this to her but she did it to herself and fuck her.

The guy, the other Deadpool, he had run for the hills by the time I was done. Drew, she was dead. We never did find Kristen. I like to think she ran off and made it out of the park and met a sweet guy, and now they're married and thinking of starting a family. Something worse likely happened to her, but I don't know what. I just know something worse happened to me when we finally got out. The girl, Freckles? I was having a really bad day, and I looked her up. I knew just enough about her to find her on Facebook, and wouldn't you know it, her account was still up. I got to learn all about her. *Alllllll* about her. I know the name of her pets, I know the name of her boyfriend, I know what she wore to prom. Sometimes I think of her wearing her prom dress, only her head is bashed in. Fuck you, Facebook.

While Clara Ann and I were trudging back to the Golden Road, I asked her, "Why did they do that?" Things had gone really well and we had just given the Pirates a high hard one. No one had to die, but instead there was blood and bodies in the back of a taffy store for no reason. I was on a rant, going on and on about how they had gone savage or how they were hardly people anymore, and Clara Ann yelled at me to shut up. Then she said, "I get it. They killed because they knew if they didn't, we would." And I start back up, saying, "You're crazy, we would have left them alone," and Clara walked up, really close to me so I could smell her breath and really make out her eyes, and she said, "Well, now you know. Don't you?" And then she started double-timing it back to the Golden Road.

That fucked me up like nothing has ever fucked me up before or since. What she was telling me is that, if we were never rescued, we were going to keep killing and killing and killing each other until there was just one person left on a mountain of bodies. The tribes would kill each other, and when there was no one left to kill, they would kill their ranks, and Clara Ann had already played it out in her head and was ready. She was right. By this point, with the talk of murderers in masks and that crap in the World's Circus and the explosion and everything, everyone was feverish, everyone was violent. I thought a lot that night about how we got here. How did we get sick like this? Would we ever get better?

There was no big celebration when we got back that evening. We told the story, sure, but there was no celebration. That night the Pirates came again, this time in full force. They were mostly guys. We fought them. We lost five girls that night, they lost two. It was a bad night, a bloody night, but I was in such shock from what happened in the taffy store that the whole thing was . . . easier? Is that what I want to say? Easier? I grabbed Cap, and I swung and swung at some Pirates. Maybe I killed one, but I know I hit two pretty good. Maybe they're both fine right now and are gay lovers in the Caribbean, I don't know. We never did get raided by the Deadpools. The Pirates came back a few more times, and during one raid, I got a huge gash on my arm. There's the scar. Just like I wanted. I was really detached at this point. Outwardly, I was all "we are the ShopGirls," but really, no one else gave a shit about us. Our leader would kill us if she could. Every single group, they'd kill us if they could. It's one thing to think that and it's another thing to see your friend getting carved up in the back of a fucking taffy store, *a fucking taffy store*, by someone you thought was your friend or at least your ally. We had just done great things together. That's the part that stings. I'm babbling.

I dealt with the whole thing by pulling in. I went through the motions we had set up. I cried in private and Cap and I were strong in public. We got raided, I think, three more times before they finally got us out of there. But if I went inward, Clara Ann, she went out. She was constantly alert, constantly yelling, constantly trying to keep everyone safe and not caring about who she upset in the process. At one point, another ShopGirl came to me and asked if we should start talking about assassinating Clara, and I told her, let her do her thing. Find a way to cope with it and let her do her thing, because she knows more than you about this situation. And she had her moments as a leader.

I only told Scottie the details of what happened to Drew, and she cried with me. She died during the second or third raid, I can't remember which. I found out because the Pirates lined up the bodies they were able to kill right along one of the far streets, and we had to figure out whether to leave them or do something with them. We ended up leaving them. What the hell did it matter? What would we have done, anyway? Plus, and this is what I learned during my time in the park, collecting the bodies would have just been one more chance for someone to kill you.

INTERVIEW 18: JASON CARD

Retail Cashier.

My daddy took me out hunting every year when I was a kid. I never got a taste for it, but I learned a couple a things. Hunting isn't about shooting a deer or a quail or whatever you're hunting. It's about putting yourself next to the animal so you can shoot it. Most of it is waiting, and when you're not waiting you figure out where you can go so when you do wait, you come across the animal. You make noise, you move too much, nothing's comin' anywhere near you, and you go home with an empty truck. That's lesson number one.

Once all that bullshit started going down and it started getting dangerous, I decided instead of jumping around and trying to find someone to kill, maybe I'd just wait this whole thing out. My mamma, she calls me a "skinny little fart," God love her, and I'm not much help in a fight. Found that out the hard way. There's not a lot of oomph behind any punch I'm gonna throw, so I figured the best thing I could do was find a spot where things were a little calmer and set up camp there. I remember telling myself this was just a storm of a different kind, and if I was smart, I would wait for it to blow over, just like the last one. That's how I found myself in the Dreamland.

There's a ton of hotels around FantasticLand, but only four are officially part of the park. There's the Mighty Maiden, there's the ElectroLounge which is all future-y, there's the GetAway, which is more geared toward adults, and then there's the Dreamland, which is the expensive one. It's the one that has the walkway straight to the park, like you seen in airports, only outside, and it's all enclosed, so you step out of the hotel lobby, go on this speedy walkway, and step off at the park. When it was working, it was pretty slick. The Dreamland, it's the one with the huge main entrance with the chandelier made with all those interlocking pieces of different colored glass. The one with all those big LCD screens and super-fast Wi-Fi that doesn't matter even a little bit when the power dies? It was the one that started at $450 a night. That one. After things started getting hairy in the park and it was clear the violence wasn't a one-time thing, that it was going to keep happening, I stuffed everything I thought I needed into a backpack I had and I slogged there in water up to my waist. I had heard that a couple of people had tried heading out to find help, and I'll tell you that's a fool's errand, man. I nearly froze to death walking to that hotel, and you could see it from the front of the park. Also, that water wasn't what you call clean. It was a nightmare, it smelled like shit, and there was so much gunk floating in it I felt like I was in that scene in *Star Wars*, the scene with the trash compactor? That's what the water was like leading up to the hotel, man. Just gross. Highly, highly gross.

Once I made it there and found a way in, which involved some broken glass, I saw the main lobby was flooded and basically ruined, but this hotel was thirty stories at forty rooms a story, meaning I had my pick of soft, comfortable beds and rooms that locked from the inside. I was safe, and if you got used to the smell from the bottom floor, which I never really did, it was comfortable enough. It was definitely comfortable enough if you're just sitting there waiting for rescue. Plenty of food, too. There were restaurants on the third floor and on the roof, so I didn't even need to go to the nasty bottom floor unless I really felt like it. And I usually didn't. A week in I was pissing over the balcony into the lobby whenever I had to go. It was kind of beautiful.

Plus, and this was the big thing for me, no one else had thought of this! No one. I was it, man. I was resident *numero uno* in this hotel, man. What do they say in church? Alpha and omega. I was pretty tempted to go back to the park and find some other friends of mine and bring them back with me so they could take a piss off the balcony, but it would have meant another trudge through that disgusting water, and after a while I got pretty used to being alone. No lie, I had this "last man on Earth" thing going where I filled my days pretty well with gathering stuff from the kitchens and going through luggage and bunches of other stuff. You'd be surprised how many dildos people bring on vacation, man. I was surprised to find any, but I swear, man, every third suitcase had a vibrator or a big ol' dick in it. Without fail. I also found, like, weed in one of the suitcases. That came in handy. I found some weapons that I kept in whatever room I was in just in case I needed to fight my way out, that's what I was thinking. I even found books to read. Tons of books, man. I read, like, fifteen books by flashlight at night because there was nothing else to do once it got dark. I don't want to sound like no sissy, but walking around a giant, waterlogged hotel with no lights anywhere, that shit is for the birds. Not fun, not doing it. I'd rather stay in a room and read a spy book or something. For a while I was reading a series about a spy, well, he was more of a special agent type who was strong and tough and all but was more patient than everyone, and that's how he beat them. Those were my favorites. I must have gone through seven or eight of those. I never really had time to read before, so it was kind of a nice change.

Living in a place like that, I got really tuned in to the noises that places made. I knew you couldn't hear the sloshing of the water in the lobby if you were above the third floor, I knew the smell was worst on one, two, and seven for some reason. I knew how quiet it got. It was really quiet, man. Really quiet. I was kind of thankful because it meant that if something happened, like us getting rescued or some numb-nuts firing off a cannon, that I would hear it immediately. Big noises were like a big shift in my world, but when you're in there long enough, little noises got to be pretty big, too. When I first heard from my two little buddies, they didn't talk. Not a peep out of them. They were quieter than mice fucking on cotton, but just because I'd been there so long I knew they were there. I knew.

It was, I would say, about three weeks in when they first showed up. I heard them on the first floor, heard them come in. It was one afternoon, early, and it was just a few splashes outside and a bit of rustling and a few more splashes is all. I swear to you, I heard the splashes and stopped what I was doing and ran out into the main area that overlooked the lobby and I saw two people coming in. I was on fourteen or so when I heard them, so I didn't get a look at them, but they made that move where they looked up and then looked at each other and even from super high up, I could tell they saw me. There was also something weird-looking about them, so I gathered my gear and hightailed it up to the high twentys somewhere and kind of regrouped. Someone else was in here, and the chances of them being friendly weren't real good. So I decided what I was going to do was to keep as quiet as I could and try to get more info. I was going to be that spy guy from the books and find out what I was dealing with before I did anything. I was going to be patient, man. I was going to beat them.

I had been there long enough that I knew the service entrances front and back, so I could keep a pretty good eye on things while staying out of the main areas, but these new visitors, they must have had the same idea I had, man, because they were just as quiet as I was. I figured they'd be loud and bring their friends and I would find a hidey-hole somewhere, but while I was trying to listen to them, I think they were trying to listen to me, too. The thing was, I had been doing it longer. The one girl—one was a guy and the other was a girl—she had a cold or something and sneezed every so often. Even when you try to stifle a sneeze it still makes a little *poof* sound, you know? Most of the time, when she would sneeze, it would be a few floors down or a few floors up. It was never all that close. I was kind of getting more and more nervous as time went on and they didn't say anything or introduce themselves. It left me time to think that they had bad ideas about what was going to happen when we finally did meet. I kinda figured they were scared, but as time went on, that wasn't what was happening. I was looking for them in a huge hotel, and they were looking for me. And I was starting to get scared, man. I don't mind admitting it. I don't spook easily but I was spooked, scared, and a little freaked out, even.

One night, out of the blue, the banging started. Remember me telling you how I would lock myself in a room at night and feel pretty safe until the sun came up? Well, one night about a week or so after they got to the hotel, they just started banging on doors once it got dark. I'm sure you've had folks tell you how dark it got out there? I think that goes double for the hotel. We didn't even have stars overhead, and then, one day, I'm sleeping without saying a word or making a noise for a long-ass time, and I hear *bang bang* at around floor three. I'm in a suite up on eighteen, right? I mixed it around so I was on different floors and different styles of rooms, but the banging started on three and I counted it. They hit every room. Sometimes I would hear a *bang*, and a second later the door would hit the back of the wall and other times the door would be locked and you'd just hear them banging on it.

Real quick, when the hotel lost power all the doors automatically opened because no hotel wants a bunch of guests trapped in their rooms, right? I started to realize that the doors that were locked, they were the ones I had slept in because once I shut the door, the lock reengaged for some reason. Sure enough, I started doing the math in my head about where I had been and where they were and the locked doors were all places I had slept. Then I was trying to figure out if there was a pattern, and there was because I have this thing about odd numbers. Don't like them. Stay away from them if I can. So when they got to the fifth floor it was *bang!* and then you'd hear the door hit and then another *bang!* and nothing. I don't know what they were trying to do other than get me to make some noise, which I didn't. I stayed quiet and they banged on doors for about three hours by my count. They made it up to twelve before they packed it in. So then, I'm thinking, do I find another room? An odd-numbered room? A room I'd been in before? I know the locks reengaged, but I had this thingie from the front desk in my bag that could reopen the locked rooms. Should I use that? Suddenly, everything was a mind game, man. Everything was a "if I do this, what happens" sort of thing in my head. I started getting nervous, and that's when I started making mistakes.

The first big screwup happened in the kitchen of the restaurant on the top of the hotel. It was lovely during the day. Just prettier than a picture, man. I knew where the food was, and I was a little nervous and moving a little fast, and my arm bumped a row of pots that was above one of the sinks, and suddenly all of them just started falling, one after another. It was more noise than I'd heard in a long time, and I heard a quick little "fuck" come out of my mouth before I grabbed the food and took off. The restaurant up top, it only had one way in or out, so I immediately ran out there, and then there's only two stairways, one for the public and another for staff, and I used the staff entrance and just moved down as quickly and as quietly as I could. I swear to you, man, it wasn't thirty seconds later I heard them up there, and they were talking and yelling. I was far enough away to where I couldn't make out what they were saying, but I could tell it was a frustrated yell sort of thing. Shortly after that, I started hearing them everywhere. They would tromp around, they would leave and come back, they would pretend to leave to see if I'd come out, and of course, every other night or so, they'd start banging on doors again. To call it creepy was the understatement of the fucking year, man. I was scared pretty much all the time.

One day, I actually saw them leave out the main floor. I was in the fourth floor laundry, which is pretty hard to find if you're not looking for it, and I hear splashing in the main floor. I was kind of sick of hiding all the time, and I was in some sort of mood, so I decide to sneak a quick look, and I go to the ledge overlooking the main lobby, and there they are, one guy and one girl in these fucked-up pig mask things, leaving out the front. The girl turns around, looks right at me, and makes this really big, exaggerated waving motion, just to make sure I knew they saw me, and then off into the muck they went. It would be friendly if they weren't dressed like killers from the movies and hadn't been hunting me for a while, man. That killed any bravery I had been saving up right quick, and I was up on twenty-one again to hide out. The next night, the banging started again.

After that I started hearing really nasty noises at night, like they weren't shy about making noise anymore. I couldn't figure out what the hell they were doing down there, and I had a suspicion that if I poked my head out for a gander, one of them would have been ready to . . . I don't know. Catch me? Kill me? Well, fuck me if I was going to find out. I just heard noises that did a number on my head. There was banging and there was sawing, I knew those two sounds. Then there was this wet sort of thwacking noise, I don't know what that was. And then a sawing one night. No idea, but that one sort of got to me. Then, one night, clear as day, there was the male voice who was begging and screaming. I couldn't hear what he was saying, exactly, but it was obvious something was happening, and whatever it was, the guy was none too happy about it. That sort of took it all to a whole new level. The way I figure it, one of two things was happening. Either two crazies were putting on a show to try to get me down to where they were, or they were . . . you know . . . batshit crazy psycho murderers who were finding people in the park and dragging them to the hotel and butchering them alive. Not to put too fine a point on it. I kind of made up my mind that night that I needed to find out which one it was.

The first time I heard the guy screaming and begging, I didn't work up the nerve to get out of the room. It wasn't easy, sometimes, because of curiosity and all, but I stayed put. Then the next afternoon I didn't hear the screaming, but I heard a power tool, and it was louder than anything they'd used before, probably a chainsaw by the sound of it, and my brain started doing the math. I figured I was up high, on seventeen at that point, and I had a pair of binoculars I had found in the same suitcase as this huge rubber dong. At least one of those weirdos was down there in the main lobby running the machine, whatever it was, and the second one, if he or she was on the lookout for me, where would they be? My guess would be about middle of the road, maybe on ten. Maybe a little higher because if I showed up between the two of them, they would have a pretty good shot at tracking me down. I figured I was high enough to go for a peek, and after a while I talked myself into it. I had a serrated knife hung on my belt and I could have brought a baseball bat or a hockey stick or something, but I figured if they saw me, I would want to Road Runner it back to the room or to a hiding place or something. That was my thinking, I guess.

I was in a room about twenty feet away from the main hallway, where you could see all the way down to the flooded first floor if you stuck your head over the railing. Using what I had learned over the last month or so about keeping quiet, I snuck up and peered over the edge. I don't know exactly what I saw because I never got a good look. The second my head peeked over the top, I heard someone on the first floor give a loud whistle, and suddenly I see her. The girl with that fucked-up mask on, she's on my floor. I don't know if it was luck or it was them planning or whatever, man, but the main hallway was in the shape of, like, a rectangle, and she was on the other side of it. My head did the math. I knew I could run up to seventeen in about three minutes if I was really booking, and homeboy was probably already on the way, so I knew I needed to get the hell out of there. The stairways were on the sides, and the girl hadn't taken off after me. She was kind of hanging out to see which way I decided to go. I tried cutting right, and she mirrored me, totally. Then I cut left and the same thing. This was also the first time I got a clear look at either one of them. She was skinny and probably faster than me and was wearing all black except for her mask which was, like, this weird mix of circus and animal and gooey shit. It's hard to describe, but it looked a lot like painted meat with a horn or two where there shouldn't have been a horn. I could have probably made it to the stairs, but then what? Then she's maybe twenty-five feet away from me, if I'm lucky, and coming for my blood with that scary-ass mask, man, and God knows what else. I was probably two minutes away from being double-teamed, and they had me. They had waited for me, and they had put themselves next to me, and I came out. I felt totally stupid, man. Like a total bonehead. The last straw was when she gave me that same wave she gave me earlier, like she was saying, "See, told you we'd get you."

I was out of options, so I went back into my room, locked the door, and moved every piece of furniture there was against it. I moved the beds and the TV and the dressers, and by the time they started knocking, I couldn't even see the door. The knocking was all quiet-like at first. Then it stopped, then the chainsaw started. In the room, I had my knife and I had a good bit of food and drink, so I was hoping I would have the chance to, like, wait them out, but no luck. They were coming in. My only hope then was that I could cut them as they tried to get in, maybe hurt them enough to leave me alone. Then my eyes went to the window.

Here was my thinking. I was twenty floors up. I had a choice between two crazy motherfuckers armed with a chainsaw trying to get in and either a twenty-foot drop to the next floor or figuring something else out, I didn't know. So, as quietly as I could, I took the screen off the window and rolled it out as far as it would go while the chainsaw was cutting the door in the background. I cannot tell you how happy I was to see that floor eighteen was suites and had big white wrought-iron balconies. Sturdy bastards, too. Thought was, if I could drop two stories, not kill myself or break my leg, and do it without Thing One and Thing Two knowing I wasn't in the room, I could wade back through the muck and get back to the park. It was time to check out, I figured.

Turns out, hotels don't like you opening windows long enough to drop out of them, so I took the hockey stick and broke the window in the quietest way you can break a window. I don't know if they heard it, and at that point, I didn't really care. They had carved out the top of the door and were working on one of the mattresses. I also tied one of the sheets to one of the bed frames and propped it against the window, so it would hold if you didn't jostle it too much. I figured it was about a fifteen-foot drop and with the sheet I cut it down to about twelve. In case my colorful language ain't conveying it, that's a fucking long way. That's "I shouldn't be doing this" long. No, that's "what the fuck am I doing I'm going to die right now" long. That's what it is. So I climb out the window, I shimmy down the bedsheet, I say all the prayers I remember, and I aim myself, and I drop. Well, obviously I made it. I'm talking to you, ain't I? I don't want to brag, but the worst of it was I scraped my arm kinda bad and had a huge bruise on my leg the next day. That's all.

All the doors open from the outside, so I rip open the door, hoping their chainsaw would cover up my footsteps. Hell, truth of the matter was I was sick of creeping around and being quiet. I wanted to move and to thump around and yell. I wanted to give them the finger on my way out the door, but the two crazy masked assholes, they were so intent on getting that door down I was able to break a window, drop two floors, and slam down seventeen flights of stairs and out one of the service entrances without them ever turning off the chainsaw. They never even, like, stopped and said, "What's that noise?" I was sloshing through thick, nasty-ass water on my way back to the park before they knew what happened. I have fantasies about them getting to the other side and screaming in disappointment like the bad guys do in the movies, just letting out a big *YEAAAAAARG* with their hands up in the air.

Sometimes the deer gets away, right?

Of course, the park was no picnic, but it was a damn sight better than getting hunted by psychos. There are some folks who tell me the Warthogs, that's what they call them, they tell me I'm either making this up or that no one was actually killing anyone else like that. They believe the tribes were fighting but not that there were killers out there doing it for, like, fucked-up joy, right? I don't know, man. I never saw any bodies for sure, and it makes sense that they were trying to flush me out, but you don't take a chainsaw to a man's door unless you've got serious business on the other side, is what I'm saying. If I hadn't vamoosed out that window, they'd be wearing my skin on their faces, is my best guess. I don't know what to make of them. I don't know if they were two absolutely crazy motherfuckers who found each other or if they went crazy in the park or if they were just playing or what. No idea. And something tells me if I did know, I'd wish I didn't.

So, let me ask you what you make of this. I still have my wallet and everything. I like to think I didn't leave anything behind in that hotel. I decided on telling you what happened in part because it makes me seem like kind of a ninja badass, but the other thing is, whoever was behind those masks . . . they figured out who I am. I get postcards from them, about once every month or two. I know it's from them because these postcards, there's nothing written on them, and the only place I ever saw them was in the hotel. They're super cheesy, too. They've got a picture of the Dreamland tower and the words "Fantastic in Every Way" on it. Sometimes the postmarks are closer to me, sometimes they're further away. Shit, man, I've moved three times since I got out of that park and the postcards always know where I am. What do you make of that?

Are they coming for me, or are they just saying "hi"?

INTERVIEW 19: GEMMA ALBERS

First Aid Station Chief.

If you take the number of people that I helped while I was stuck in the park versus the number of people who were hurt because of me, I think I come out about even. The whole thing was senseless, I've accepted that. It took me a long time to come to "senseless." For the longest time, it felt more like I was responsible for the deaths of about twenty people. That's a pretty heavy burden, and it took a long time to let it go. Since I got out, I've been able to focus on the good I did, but it's a struggle. Every day, it's a struggle.

I don't mean to be rude, but do you know what "first aid" refers to? It's the first line of medical care, with the implicit understanding that one will then proceed to the next level, where a trained medical professional can deal with them if that is what is called for. At no point is first aid supposed to solve "every medical problem anyone has ever had ever," and it certainly isn't "field hospital for an amusement park full of sick and injured people." That was not part of the job description, but it's what I ended up doing.

Let me back up—there were supposed to be seven of us, that's what the protocol called for. Seven first aid workers, functioning as a team to meet all the needs of the employees until rescue occurs. But five of them who were supposed to stay, they piled on the buses and never gave us another thought. I felt for the longest time like I was the one who stayed, and I was the one who should be called a hero. I don't think that anymore. I should have gotten on the bus. I should have run, but I didn't, and it was just me and Morgan, this twenty-one-year-old girl we had hired just a month or so earlier. I had been on the job for two years and thought it was a pretty good gig. There were a lot of scrapes, a bit of heat exhaustion, that sort of thing. Plus, and I cannot stress this enough, there were trained doctors and RNs on hand who knew what they were doing and who could take over when my skills were exhausted. Guess what? When the hurricane hit, they all ran or didn't come into work, too. So it was me and Morgan kind of looking at each other, thinking, "This could get really bad really fast." And it did.

The tunnels? About a dozen sprained and broken legs and arms. Then we started getting rashes, lots of them. We were in the heat of Florida, and it never stopped raining, so no one ever got truly dry, and next thing you know, people were coated over 40 percent or 50 percent of their body with red bumps and later gray and green bumps. It was really gross. People didn't have the good sense to try drying off first, so they would come to us wanting a cream or something, but we went through the supply of ointments and creams in the first three weeks. So then we started seeing infections where people scratched their rashes until they bled, and then the pustules would scab over but the rash would still be there, so you wouldn't have just a rash on your skin, you'd have an infection and a fever and maybe even a blood disease—genius. This one kid came to me with red streaks under the skin headed straight from his arms into his chest toward his heart. I'm no doctor, as I told everyone *every day*, but I knew I was probably looking at a dead guy unless I started him on antibiotics. We had run out of antibiotics before we ran out of ointment.

We're out of antibiotics and we're out of ointment, so what do these morons do? They start fighting with each other and sending me battle injuries. Then the fighting got bad, and I started having to go to patients. For most of them, there was very little I could do. Sure, I could stop bleeding. Sure, I could clean and dress a wound. But then what? Then they need the next level of care is what, and that was something neither Morgan nor I could come anywhere close to providing. So all these Pirates or ShopGirls or Robots or whatever are looking at me expectantly, like, "Please save our friend," and there's nothing I can do. The bleeding would start up again, or the wound would get infected, or the rash would come back, and there was nothing to be done. It was a . . . it was a shitty situation. There. I said it.

I remember this one poor guy, he came to us early on because he had punctured his face on part of a ride or something, I forget exactly. He had a decent-sized puncture wound, but he didn't even need stitches. It wasn't bleeding. I gave him some Neosporin and told him to keep that on there as much as he could and he should be fine. Four days later his friends bring him back in, unconscious. His face had swelled to where he could only see out of one eye, and the smell coming off his wound was this sick, kind of thick and meaty smell, not at all like the "almond" smell they tell you about in training that means infection has set in. A hospital could have saved his life. He had me. So we used antibiotics and kept him in the little triage center we had set up, and he died anyway. His fever got worse, and one morning he was gone. Now take that story and apply it to kids swinging sharp rusty metal pieces at each other, and you get an idea of the sort of thing I was dealing with.

Can I tell you a little bit about Morgan? I feel like I owe it to her. She deserves a lot of credit. She and I didn't much like each other when we started working together. I'm kind of direct, and on the job I'm all business. She was skinny and cute and always had a text message to answer instead of prepping the trays or refilling the supplies. She was 100 percent a social creature, and while that's good for working fast food, you have a million things to do at a first aid station and not much time to do them. So we didn't hit it off. But what I found as I kept working next to Morgan was that she had an inner strength I didn't have. The more hot water she was in, the cooler she became and the more efficient and effective she got. I kind of operated on one level. She had slow, which was her speed most of the time, but then she could dial it all the way up to Super Morgan, where she could change IV drips and set casts and twenty more things at once. She was the one who kept my head in the game when I wanted to give up. And she was the one everyone wanted to see when they came in.

We slept in the hut on a couple of cots we moved out of the shelter. Because of that and our proximity to both the Golden Road, the Exclamation Point, and where the Robots had set up camp, we got a front row seat to some of the raids. We could tell when the violence was escalating because we heard it, and if it wasn't pitch dark, we saw it. Most nights it was fine. Morgan and I would either collapse onto our cots, exhausted, or if we were lucky, we would get to play cards or talk or even sing a little bit before bed. I play guitar and was kind of a Christian camp kid growing up, so I had my guitar in my locker at the park, and every now and then that came in handy. I would sing to folks who were suffering, and I like to think that helped. Still, like I said, Morgan was the one with the bedside manner, the popular one. Which was fine.

All of the tribes wanted her for their own. The Pirates offered her a room with a view and "the best looking guys in the park." Charming. The ShopGirls offered her weapons and sisterhood, the Robots tried to play it cool, but they were really hot to have her, and the Freaks, they were doing their own thing. Even sweet old Charlie from the Mole Men would come up from time to time, ask for our help, and then slyly suggest how great it was down in the tunnels. We kind of shrugged him off, but everyone wanted their in-house first aid person. But we decided that we had to remain neutral with this whole tribes business, and we were going to apply what care we could evenly and on a first come, first served basis. That was sort of working until Brock Hockney fired that cannon. After that, the tribes only looked out for themselves, so it was much, much harder to provide what little care we could.

After the hurricane hit, we set up a first aid station near the center of the park, not far away from the Exclamation Point. There was a hut they used to sell sunglasses out of, and it worked fine for our purposes. We could see who was coming from every direction and what condition they were in, and we had a big awning to keep people directly out of the rain. Every day, someone from one of the tribes would ask Morgan or me to be part of their group. We always had the same answer: "We are caring for everyone in the park." You could track how bad things were between tribes by how many times we had to say that. Three meant things were pretty bad and four times meant there was some fear behind it. Begging usually came after that. I was kind of hard about the whole thing, but Morgan would put her arms around people and say things like, "I know you're scared, but everyone is scared, and there has to be some place everybody can go for first aid." I saw her give some version of that speech probably forty times. Then folks started getting more insistent.

It was the Pirates who started it. I bet you could have guessed that. Brock Hockney came to see us himself, which was kind of a rare thing, because everyone at the park knew who he was, and I knew some ShopGirls in particular who were gunning for him. He waltzed up, casual as you please, and basically said he didn't care which one, but one of us had to come be the property of the Pirates. He didn't put it like that. I think he used the term "exclusive contract," like it was a transaction instead of an implied kidnapping. Luckily for us, he said we had a couple hours to make up our minds, and when some Pirates came back to "fetch" us, they found a couple of the ShopGirls and a couple of the Robots hanging around, and the implication was clear. We were neutral. Our little sunglasses hut was Switzerland. Everyone at the park got our bumbling attempts at medicine. Of course it didn't stop there.

Morgan was the one with the bedside manner, so it makes sense she was the one who was kidnapped. We slept together in the hut, and when they came for her, I was able to make enough of a ruckus to where a few barefooted ShopGirls heard and came running. They went after the Pirates and were able to get to them and to Morgan before they got across the threshold of Pirate Land or whatever they called it. Then, of course, the ShopGirls said we couldn't treat Pirates anymore, and we gave them "the speech." They sort of spit some threats at us, but deep down they understood, I think.

The thing was, we didn't just have the training—we had all the supplies. I would say we had 70 percent of the medical supplies in the park, which we moved to the hut really early on. So, of course, people started coming and robbing our supplies. Every tribe except the Mole Men and the Freaks did it at one point or another. Some were really brazen about it; others at least tried to make it seem like they weren't stealing. Then we had a lot of people who begged. “Please help me,” “please help my friend,” “it hurts so bad.” We didn’t have pain medication beyond ibuprofen, so with a large number of cases we had to really work to get the “we can’t do anything for you” message through their heads. Some people didn’t take too well to that. It was the stress, I would tell myself, not anything personal. But then they started getting violent, and that’s a lot harder to rationalize. Morgan had her wrist sprained when a Robot grabbed it particularly hard, and a Pirate straight-up broke my nose. After that, Morgan and I had conversations about folding up the tent, but the thing was, we were doing some good, too. When there was no more ointment, we figured out how to mix up a paste that wasn’t half bad at treating rashes, using what supplies we could scrounge up. When we walked through parts of the park, we would get “thank yous” by the dozens. We got so many kudos that I started to think maybe our abilities were being built up a little much. Then after about three weeks, when we were sucking wind and running on fumes, we kind of, sort of started an armed conflict.

There was a Pirate, of course it was a Pirate, getting treated for a small stab wound to the arm. A Deadpool walked up looking for something. I never figured out what, because they started punching each other and knocking everything over. I’d seen fights before in school and in the park, but this was a little different. This wasn’t “I’m fighting to prove something,” this was “I’m fighting to kill you.” It was so violent that we didn’t feel like we could handle it ourselves, so Morgan had found this bell, and every time we rang it, someone would come and help. We rang the bell and twenty seconds later we had two ShopGirls and a Robot there, and instead of asking how they could help, they grabbed the Pirate and held him down and they all took turns beating him and beating him. I remember, after every kick or punch he would try to get up, he would curse worse and worse, calling them every name in the book, until he started to gargle. I recognized that there was fluid—probably blood—in his lungs and that even if they stopped, they were probably going to kill him. The Pirate, I never caught his name, had a friend who had run off when the fighting started. By the time he got back with a few other Pirates, the first guy was dead. They beat him to death in the street, and I will remember this forever, they had taken turns kicking him in the head until they saw brain matter. It didn't take nearly as long as I thought something like that would take.

Then, of course, the Pirates made threats, and the other group made threats, and the long and the short of it was the Pirates swore they would shut us down. I am a religious person, so I prayed that night that moods would cool and we would be left alone, and sure enough, for two weeks after that, we were left alone, and Morgan and I continued playing "Dr. Quinn, Medicine Women." That's what we called it because we were working with so little. And, as was our decision, we did not deny care, such as it was, to anyone. No one got turned away. The robberies even slowed down. I had no idea why this happened, so I attributed it to prayer. Then, toward the end, about four or five weeks into this whole thing, we got a visit from Mr. Hockney again. I later saw a worse side of him, but one-on-one he was always very cool and respectful to me. He walked in, flanked by about eight other Pirates, and said, "One of you ladies is coming with me. There will be no further discussion on this topic." Then sat back in his chair and waited for us to talk.

Morgan launched into the speech, and the second she said the phrase "Everyone receives care," Brock gave a little nod, and one of the Pirates took out a lighter and lit a stick he had been holding behind his back. It was dipped in gasoline or something flammable. I hadn't smelled it because, to be honest, the cornucopia of smells polluting my nose was one of the fresh hells of that place. One day it would be 80 percent rotten hot dogs and 20 percent feces, and then another day it would be some other decaying meat and mold, and if we were lucky we got a sickly sweet smell out of the Fairy Prairie as all their snow cone machines started to leak. I didn't smell the gas, and before I could say anything, they were lighting our tent on fire. I was never thankful for the weather in that place except for that day, because the tent was wet and had been for some time, so it took a while to light. For a second there, it was almost comical, that young man trying to get something to light and failing two or three times. It was less funny when he pulled out a pocket bottle of lighter fluid and sprayed it right on the tarp. That got 'er going. The tent was supported by a big fake palm tree that you could find in several sections of the park, and Morgan, bless her, immediately jumped up on top of the tarp and started trying to put the fire out. At that point, Mr. Hockney looked at me and said, "I want the one on the roof. She's got balls. Kill the other one." Then a couple of the Pirates started coming toward me.

I . . . I like to think that my faith and my upbringing had helped me keep my fear at bay. Through four or five weeks in that place, I had faced blood and bones and no supplies and bullies, and I did it without ever freaking out. I had cried, twice, but that was over . . . other things. I don't want to lie to you and say, "I had never been frightened before," but I can confidently and truthfully tell you I had never been frightened *like that* before. The thing that did it was seeing the details of these boys' faces. They were shiny and had a bunch of acne. They had scraggly beards. I remember the smiles underneath and how completely ugly they were. They were ugly all the way down. I didn't pray right then, I was too afraid, but the Lord works in mysterious ways. Sometimes those mysterious ways involve an arrow that misses your head by inches but hits one of the advancing Pirates square in the chest.

I saw the one Pirate go down, said a quick "thank God," and immediately ran outside to both get out of the way and to see if there was anything I could do to help put out the fire. By then, the ShopGirls were firing more arrows, and the Pirates had drawn swords and run toward the girls who had fired. Outside the tent, Morgan had actually climbed on top of the tarp of the hut and was beating at the flames with a bloody towel we hadn't washed yet. I screamed, "What are you doing?" and she yelled, "If this tent goes, those assholes win!" For Morgan, it was the principle of the thing, I suppose. Like I said, she was strong. So strong. She was unbiased, but she was not a fan of the Pirates. As she kept beating at the flames, I noticed there were a lot more than eight Pirates. There were more like twenty or twenty-five who must have been nearby or hiding, and they were all gathered around the guy with the arrow in his chest. I saw Mr. Hockney hold up a sword, and they all screamed as he brought the sword down. Later I learned this was part of the deal with the Pirates. If you were mortally injured, all your friends gathered around while you were put out of your misery. It's a bunch of savage nonsense if you ask me, but I saw it happen with my own two eyes.

Then the Pirates turned their attention to the ShopGirls. There was one archer and three others who were armed but had started retreating. Four more Pirates brandished sticks and set them on fire. Then I heard Mr. Hockney say, "Burn them out," and the Pirates started walking toward the Golden Road, which wasn't far away from our hut.

Before they could get very far, the rest of the ShopGirls came out. By this point, they were in ragged shape and looked . . . well, they looked like they were ready to go to war. I remember thinking *a ponytail can only do so much*, and then I thought *who am I to talk? I probably look worse.* I could see two archers on the roof and it immediately became clear that they were going to start firing, so I jumped up on the flaming roof as fast as I could. My thought was if they were firing, I wanted to get behind the plastic tree, and I couldn't do that down on the ground. Plus, maybe I could help with the fire. I pulled Morgan toward the tree, but she wasn't having any of it. The fire wasn't spreading quickly, but it was spreading, and she was doing everything she could think of to beat it back. I noticed she had lost her rag, and it was on fire, so she was trying to bail water that had collected at the top of the tarp into the flames. I should have helped her, but I took cover. At that point I heard a lot of yelling and looked toward the Golden Road to see the Pirates charging the ShopGirls, but then I realized it was more than just the ShopGirls. I recognized Robots and Deadpools there, too. The Deadpools, I had heard their numbers were below twenty because of the consistent Pirate attacks, so there was an alliance, apparently. I got to see the two groups, the Pirates and the three tribes fighting together, running at each other. And then, chaos.

I can only tell you flashes of what I saw. Any sort of "this happened, then that happened" would be me imagining things. There's no story here; it was just a bunch of folks hacking away at each other. I used this word before but it was barbarism. I saw a girl I had seen at a Bible study hit a guy in the head with a baseball bat, and I saw his head tilt sideways at an odd angle, which meant part of his spine was broken. I saw two people on fire trying to put each other out in immense panic and pain. I saw three Pirates standing over a girl, stabbing her and pulling at her flesh, and then, one second later, one of the Pirates get an arrow high up on his neck. I remember one boy crying and screaming as he was stabbed, yelling, "NO, NO," over and over again like it would somehow stop his attackers, like he was losing a game and just realized how much was at stake. I remember seeing a sword fight, an honest to God sword fight, between Brock Hockney and the leader of the ShopGirls, I don't remember her name. It's very different when the two combatants are actually trying to stab each other. There's nothing pretty about it and there's a lot more cursing. Hockney, I remember, had all he could handle because the ShopGirl, she was savage and fierce and just swinging and swinging. I didn't see how that fight ended, but I could also tell that all around them, the Pirates were winning most of the fights they were in. They fought in clusters of two and three, and they were better prepared and seemed to . . . I don't know how to put it . . . they seemed to not be fighting scared. They were clearly the aggressors and everyone else was trying not to die.

I didn't get to see that much of it because the fire had spread. Once it hit the main section of tarp, it really picked up. Morgan had joined me behind the tree, and we gave up on the tarp. We tried to jump down, but the problem was there wasn't a good place to jump off. I hadn't realized how high up we were. We ran from one spot to another, and while we were making up our minds, we heard the first set of gunshots. It was a really quick series of pops, and then a pause, and then another series of pops. I was just above two Pirates getting ready to stab some guy I didn't recognize when I saw one of them just drop. It was as quick as a light turning off, just *pow* and he went to the ground. I didn't see any blood or anything, just his body drop in this odd way. Then I heard another round of pops, and the other Pirate was on the ground, and was screaming for help. At one point, I heard him yell something about bleeding out, and I looked over the edge, and his leg was covered in blood, and I thought I saw some spray, which is never a good sign. Then the pops continued, and more Pirates went down. No one seemed to know where they were coming from, but somebody was somewhere shooting Pirates, and they were doing a pretty good job of it from what I could tell. Morgan and I finally committed and jumped off the top of the tent, and she landed funny on her ankle. As I was getting her up I heard a weird noise, kind of like a really fast *zip* of air, and didn't think much of it until Morgan and I got out of harm's way.

We ran to one of the concession stands just off the World's Circus and we both kind of collapsed. You've probably guessed by now that she was shot, but it was more of a graze. It caught her outside thigh a bit, and there was some blood but nothing serious. I started to take her pants off to look at it, and she stopped me and said, "It'll be fine. Let's just watch." So we did. We sat down, hidden by a glass case that used to hold candy, took some deep breaths, and watched our tent, which had been our home for something like five weeks, burn. And Lord, how it burned. At one point the entire tent was ablaze, and the hot air underneath it swelled, and the whole thing just took flight, a flaming tarp, and it flew for about twenty feet and landed on the ground and continued to just burn and smoke. It was beautiful. And of course the blaze was the backdrop for the fighting, which had ended really quickly after the shooting started. Pirates were dragging their friends back to the Cove, and everyone was helping someone. It was kind of like the fever broke at that moment. There had been so much blood and so much hate, and then someone with some guns came in and changed the outcome of a battle, and it felt, to me, like everyone lost their taste for killing each other after that. There were no more shouts of "revenge," no more battle cries. It was quiet until those cops came in a couple days later. The tarp was still smoldering when they got there.

Morgan was fine. We still keep in touch. We kind of hid out for the rest of our time in the park and didn't worry about fixing anyone else. Besides, we were out of absolutely everything. There was nothing more we could do, so we watched the tarp burn, then played cards and talked like this terrible thing hadn't happened.

Like we were civilized again.

LETTER FROM THE FLORIDA NATIONAL GUARD

From: The Public Affairs Department of the Florida National Guard
The Desk of Sgt. Steven A. Scott
St. Francis Barracks
82 Marine Street
St. Augustine, Florida 32084

To: Adam Jakes
Reporter

Regarding: Rescue of FantasticLand Facilities

Mr. Jakes,

I have been assigned the duty of answering your questions regarding the Florida National Guard's operations in the rescue of 207 souls from the FantasticLand amusement park in the wake of Hurricane Sadie. While we have deemed a formal interview with command inappropriate at this time, I have been cleared to answer the written questions submitted last week. You will find the answers attached. Your interviews and the reporting you have done thus far have influenced the amount of information we are providing. The information was gathered from multiple sources throughout the National Guard, but we will not be providing attribution at this time. I will be your liaison should you care to have further contact.

Our answers are underneath the questions posed. Good luck with your reporting.

How was the situation at FantasticLand presented to the National Guard initially?

The Florida National Guard was involved very early on in rescue efforts in the wake of Hurricane Sadie. In our coordination with the Red Cross, we began with the coastal regions and worked our way inland, as the coastal regions suffered the most structural damage and the greatest loss of life. As we worked inland, we had many reports of violence. These reports were treated seriously and each was dealt with in the order of proximity and severity of the reports.

In the case of FantasticLand, we were alerted to the need for assistance from the Volusia County sheriff's office on November 12. At this point in rescue operations, the abilities of the National Guard were outmatched by the need of the residents of Central Florida. The destruction has been well documented. Over twenty-five thousand servicemen and women from all branches of the military were deployed in the state during this time period. Given that FantasticLand was very far inland, and stores of food and water were available, it was not deemed a priority location. Those who remember taking the call from CCS roughly five weeks into the disaster remember the call sounded urgent and that the reports were "fantastical." We were told to bring as many personnel as we could spare. Initially thirty-five rescue personnel entered the park. Hours later, another two hundred were dispatched.

Was the FNG told by FantasticLand management to not send rescue personnel to the park?

During our rescue efforts, we put out a call to different businesses and corporations with property and employees in harm's way. The reason for these calls was to prioritize our rescue efforts. FantasticFun responded to our information request and put the FantasticLand property as a low priority. The reason they gave was, "There is enough food and clean water for the employees on site. We feel there is no immediate danger." We responded accordingly and prioritized other sites.

What was the situation when the FNG entered FantasticLand?
We were given a report by the Clark County sheriff's office that there was evidence of violence in the park and that force might be necessary to subdue perpetrators of that violence. We responded with full-body armor and assault weapons. As has been well documented through leaked images in the media, we did encounter several bodies immediately upon entering the park and found many more as we continued our sweep. Everyone in the park was led out in handcuffs, and other federal agencies, including the FBI, were contacted to help sort through the events that had transpired. We met no resistance from any individual inside the park. More than two hundred survivors were taken to a processing facility in Daytona Beach and remained there until authorities decided whether or not to hold them on criminal charges.

Why was it necessary to take the survivors out in handcuffs? Were you met with resistance?
See the above explanation.

Can you tell us anything about the body camera video that was uploaded the day after the FNG entered the park?
The person or persons who uploaded that video have been identified and properly disciplined.

Can you give me a timeline of the day? I'm specifically interested in what portions of the park were visited and in what order.
Personnel from the FNG entered the front of the park using transport specifically designed to handle standing water up to five feet. Access to

the main entrance featured roads that were not available in other, more heavily wooded sections of the park. Once inside, we assessed the scene and immediately sent for reinforcements and specialized personnel. Our forces waited at the front gate for backup to arrive, and then the park was searched. Medical personnel had been called and arrived shortly after our initial reinforcements. Every single survivor in the park required some form of medical attention, with a range of issues beginning at skin irritation and ending with mortal gunshot and stab wounds. There is no way to account for the order in which the sections of the park were visited. The operational strategy was to send personnel to every section of the park and once the main population was cleared out, to do a more extensive search for survivors.

Was the Dreamland Resort a target of the initial operation? If not, when was it visited, and did it stand out in any way?
The Dreamland Resort was part of the second wave of operations and was not visited until the day after the initial rescue operation at the park. There were three dead bodies in the hotel, but the condition of the bodies was unremarkable based on what we saw in the rest of the park.

Did the FNG take part in determining who to hold after the initial rescue?
We did not. I would refer you to the FBI, the Clark County Sheriff, and other local law enforcement on that issue.

Can you help me put this rescue operation in perspective in terms of size, scope, and cooperation among agencies?
In order to get at the root of your question, context is needed. The FNG and every other law enforcement and aid organization was overwhelmed by the damage and need created by Hurricane Sadie. Every agency, every department, and every individual were stretched to their absolute limit by the needs of the survivors of this storm. Many in our ranks worked

two to three twenty-four-hour shifts at a time before taking twenty-four hours off and going back to work. Collapse due to exhaustion was not uncommon. With that in mind, once the scope of the casualties was clear to the sheriff, we were called, and once we assessed the scene, we called in seven other agencies to help with the effort. Needs ranged from criminal investigation to hazardous waste disposal to large-scale medical aid, none of which we are specifically trained to provide. In the end, over ten agencies were called in. There were many rescue efforts due to Sadie that were bigger and several others that required this level of interagency cooperation.

From your perspective, how did FantasticLand management and ownership respond in the immediate aftermath of your rescue efforts?
The ownership of FantasticLand was immediately helpful, and their staff was able to assist us in our search efforts in the park. They recognized the seriousness of what had happened and reacted appropriately.

Can you tell me anything about the reactions of the survivors upon rescue?
While we did not encounter violence upon entering the park, there were individuals who were reluctant to exit. At no point did any of our personnel threaten force, and the small pockets of resistance were diffused quickly and through verbal means. Upon our initial sweep, we saw dangerous conditions throughout the park and removed everyone for their safety.

That being said, there were many who were grateful to be rescued. We saw tears of gratitude and of relief as their ordeal ended. Many were eager to talk about their experiences to us and to other agencies. I can also tell you they were very happy to be dry and in different clothing.

Was there any management inside the park you were able to identify?
No, there was not. We were told later that Mr. Sam Garliek was in charge of the shift, but he was one of the last people removed from the

park. He had locked himself in a manager's station off the main entrance and had not come out for roughly two weeks, by his account.

I have multiple reports of a single park employee who secured the weapons locker full of guns. Did you see many gunshot wounds upon entering the park?
As previously stated, we treated many gunshot wounds. We also found a cache of guns on the grounds. As you are well aware, Sophie Ruskin was charged with many of the shootings in the park but had dozens of park employees attest to her innocence. We found no physical proof to tie the shootings to anyone, and now that the case is out of the courts, there is very little hope of finding and punishing the shooter or shooters responsible.

How long were the employees who were initially released held in custody?
All the agencies involved had a large mess to sort out, so the answer varies. They were free anywhere from forty-eight hours to six days after the initial rescue operation.

How did your personnel react after the rescue of the park?
You may attribute the following quotes to PFC Amy Poland, who was in the first wave and who has agreed to release this quote to the media.

> The initial challenge of clearing so many people from the park was so large that the larger implications of what happened didn't sink in until much, much later. During the operation, it was all about finding the survivors and getting them to the next step in the rescue process. It's much easier to ignore bodies hanging from lampposts when you have an explicit mission and other members of your team counting on you.

We worked for days on end and rested when we could. When the job was finally done, the media had descended and we were asked many times how we "felt" going in there. It was still impossible to say because we hadn't had any time to process what we had seen. Now that we are months and years removed, I have a greater perspective and I can say that, as a mother, what we saw was truly terrifying. To think our young people are capable of what we saw chills the blood for a very long time.

How would you compare the response of the FantasticLand employees with others who were trapped by the hurricane for a long period of time?

This is an excellent question and one that gets to the heart of this tragedy.

The FNG responded to needs in dozens of communities up and down the Florida coastline. In some cases, flooding was worse than it was in FantasticLand. After several of these towns, we noticed a trend developing. Those who were stranded for some time would most often respond in one of two ways. Either they would bond or they would separate. Bonding led to joint efforts at survival, and hard-to-execute programs like food and water rationing and emotional support were able to be delivered within the community, oftentimes to a masterful degree. When people bonded they tended to stay alive longer.

Those who separated did not benefit from the pooling of resources or talent and would often become desperate. It was not uncommon for the Florida National Guard to have to sort out attacks and murders, all of which we handed off to local law enforcement. The difference between the cases we saw and FantasticLand was the speed of the separation and then the subsequent rush to violence after that separation. The death toll in the park was grim. No one disputes this. But based on what we saw and how long they had to fight, it is a minor miracle that the body count wasn't much higher, which brings us to an interesting idea: The employees of FantasticLand both bonded and separated. That makes the case unique.

To elaborate, the employees enjoyed all the benefits of pooled resources and all the land mines of separation, and since they had more and better resources to share, what they were able to accomplish was much greater and much worse. We've never seen a case like it, in all honesty.

We hope this helps.

Sgt. Steven A. Scott

INTERVIEW 20: TRAVIS BARNES

Former Lieutenant in the Florida National Guard.

I don't remember where I got it or how or even why I turned it on. By that point, I had worked thirty-six hours in a row, and most of the mental faculties I had left were in service of not tripping over my own feet and shooting myself. Honestly, I don't know where I got the body camera or why, but I do remember turning it on before I went into FantasticLand.

No, wait. I do remember. I took it from some cop in one of the towns we were in. He thought it didn't work anymore, that it had been ruined. I saw the tiny little camera was in a waterproof cover, so I asked him to give it to me, and he did. I think that's how it happened. Honestly, I'm hazy on the whole thing. We were going from town to town, and I was seeing some of the most heartbreaking stuff I'd ever seen in my life. Dead babies, folks eating their pets, that kind of thing. I remember in one town, we went through this restaurant that we were told had survivors in it. We get there, and it's crickets. Nothing. There had been gangs in this particular town that formed when it didn't look like help was coming, so we had our guns drawn, and we were ready to throw down if need be, but there was no one in the joint. After searching about five minutes, I hear one of my crew yelling and run back into the kitchen where there are twenty people jammed in this huge walk-in freezer and they're all dead. Apparently they were in trouble and hid in the freezer, thinking they could get out, and they couldn't. There were a few men, but it was mostly women and kids. It wasn't so bad to look at, but just the thought of having to watch your kid freeze to death, saying, "Mommy, I'm cold," and "Mommy, I can't feel my fingers," knowing they were going to die . . . that's what haunted me. Take that and multiply it by the fifty-two towns we went through before we got to that stupid theme park and subtract any meaningful sleep and you get the idea where my head was at.

I had started turning the body camera on every time we all drew our weapons. See, we were not a combat unit. We weren't hardened, muscled badasses. We were volunteers who could hold our own, but . . . I don't know. I don't want to say we weren't trained for this, because we were, but I will say we never in a million years thought we'd have to do something like this. And after moving from town to town, not sleeping, it was a recipe for disaster. Someone was going to fuck up and badly. So the body camera was kind of for me. If something particularly egregious went down, I wanted documentation. I wasn't alone, by the way. There are other videos out there. I was just dumb enough to upload it.

So we're going from town to town to town, and some aren't so bad. The folks need help, and there's plenty of injuries to go around, but all in all, they've done pretty well for being cut off from civilization for a little over a month. And then some towns, we go in and it's *Mad Max*. There are gangs, and they've gone a bit out of their minds, and there are bodies, and they've sometimes done things with the bodies like hung them up. I remember in one town someone had duct taped severed arms onto more than a dozen street signs. I have no idea why someone would do that, or where he got the arms. Or what he was trying to get at. Or . . . just . . . after like, six, wouldn't you stop? Why keep going? Anyway, at that point, you have to just clear the area and look at the State Patrol guys and say, "You're no longer in danger. Good luck figuring out what the hell happened here." I don't envy anyone who had to clean up a mess like that.

We had been told, "Get to FantasticLand when you get there," so we hadn't been avoiding the place, but we weren't rushing there, either. We had a way of prioritizing our communities—it was an equation that involved how far inland they were, the population, likelihood of food and water scarcity, stuff like that. FantasticLand was in the middle of a bunch of areas that had fared pretty well, and we were all of the attitude of "we'll get there when we get there." But then our CO called and said my unit was to drop what we were doing and get over there quick as we could. He also said there was evidence of violence, and so we were ordered to treat folks as hostile until we knew different. I know that might sound harsh, but you have to understand what we'd been through. The second town I went into, I forget the name, I had to shoot a guy who was coming at me with a knife. And the eleventh town. Forgive me for being in a draw-first sort of mood. I was never far from my rifle and with good reason. I'm going to leave it at that.

We got the call on whatever day it was, early in the morning, and we weren't far. I remember we were just north of the park, and we had started to notice how bad the flooding was. See, people think the flooding was all one level, but that's not the case, not even close. Some cities had water up to your ankles, other up past your ass. I've been told it has to do with topography and water tables and infrastructure and all that. I don't know, man. I own a body detailing shop when I'm not a soldier. What I do know is everything around the park was flooded and flooded badly, and you let that water sit for a couple of weeks and it's nasty and disgusting. The sewage was the worst part. If I got paid by how many turds had floated by me when I was hiking through flooded areas, I wouldn't be talking to you. I'd be somewhere high up in the mountains where I'd never have to wade through shit ever again. The flooding was bad, was what I'm getting at.

We roll up on FantasticLand in the morning, about an hour after the sun came up, because the only thing worse than dealing with desperate, half-crazed people is doing it in the dark, and we're expecting the worst. Like . . . I don't know. Each place was different. Maybe they'd come at us with a cotton candy machine or something, but it was really quiet. We ended up meeting up with another battalion of Florida National Guard members that we knew were coming, and there were about forty of us total, which was a big number at that point. Our forces were split up from the coast all the way to Georgia. Also by that time, we had been supplied with hip waders that fit over our uniforms, but I don't mind telling you they didn't work worth a shit. We all had rashes and boils and I don't even know what from wading through that water for so long, but we still wore them. The downside of the waders was they slowed you down once you were out of the water. That comes into play later.

We wade past all the topiaries—I remember there were four huge Exclamation Points on either side of the main entrance that were carved out of trees—and then into the park. It's got this long main road before you can go any other direction, so we start walking it, and I'm in about the middle of the pack when I remember to turn my body camera on, but before I get the chance, this kid comes running up to us with his hand in the air. This isn't on the video, but I remember him just singing our praises to the heavens. Turns out later it was that kid who stayed in the hotel all that time, Jason something. He came out of one of the stores in the front and sort of half jogged, half stumbled toward us, saying, "Thank God, thank Jesus, thank God," over and over and over again. He was mumbling, trying to tell us six things at once. I saw that in a lot in the other towns, and I saw it a lot that day. A lot. The best thing to do with someone in that state is to get handcuffs on them so you're damn sure they're not going to hurt you and then sort it out later, and that's what we did. I remember he had a huge grin on his face when someone in the back of our pack led him away. I thought at the time he was grinning like an idiot. I've heard his story since. That guy was not an idiot.

After that, I turned the camera on. I'll walk you through the video.

Editor's note: For formatting purposes, we will describe the scene on the video and follow it with Mr. Barnes's commentary.

0:58—The video shows a group of Florida National Guard troops in full combat gear with their weapons raised in front of the camera. The camera is in the middle of the group. The camera views the body of "Paul," the employee who fell off the building and was killed by Brock Hockney and is now in an advanced state of decay. Someone offscreen says, "Jesus, is that a person?"

At that point, we knew it was going to be a tough one. I had seen decayed bodies before. You'd be surprised at what humidity and rain can do to a body. Man, I've seen people who were in rough shape, I had even seen bodies as bad at this one, but it's never something that becomes commonplace, you know? It's the sort of thing that sticks with you. Other than that poor son of a bitch, I can tell you it smelled terrible in there. When I was talking to one of the survivors later on, he said he didn't notice, so they must have gotten used to it, but to us it was this toxic mix of sewage and decaying food and some sort of chemical, I don't know what, but it had this really acrid top layer to it. One of my friends mentioned later that whatever was causing the smell, there had to be a lot of it for it to hang around in such a wide open area.

1:42—The first survivor comes into view. She has been identified as Claire Hostetler, a ShopGirl who was most likely an archer for the group. Her hair is long, dark, and stringy, and she's holding a dingy rag to her arm. The troops yell at her to get down. She is crying her entire time on camera.

Yeah, that's the other thing they do. If someone has been in the muck for a month and we get there to rescue them, it's either a million miles an hour or they shut down and you can't get a word out of them. That's pretty typical, honestly. That girl, she didn't say a word as they put the cuffs on or led her to the back. It's creepy, yeah, but not uncommon.

2:04—Girls begin streaming from the shops in pairs and groups of three. Almost all of them appear to be nursing injuries and helping those who are more seriously injured. One of the troops suddenly yells "Holy shit!" and guns are raised.

In the space of twenty seconds, we went from helping one girl to the back to being surrounded by girls who looked like that spooky chick from *The Ring*. Then Tony, he's in the front, I hear him yell, and this is the first time my sleep-deprived brain makes the connection that I'm wearing a body camera and somebody is going to want to see this when I'm done, so I run to the front and there's this row of bodies. They're all girls and they're laid out, I think there were a dozen or so *[there were seven—ed]*, and they were all hurt in various ways, but each one of them had their head bashed in. Then someone had put ropes up, like those velvet ropes they use for crowds, and hooked them on those big gold-looking things with the heavy bases. By the looks of it, that's what had been used to bash the heads in. It was pretty brutal, more brutal than most of the things we saw. The thing that stuck with me was, why lay them out, you know? Why would you do that unless you are totally off your gourd or some sort of monster?

7:16—The ShopGirls are cuffed and moved to the back of the line. The troops are moving up past the flaming tarp when an unidentified soldier says, "Isn't there supposed to be a big Exclamation Point here?" and another unidentified soldier says, "Who do I look like? Ritchie Fresno?" The group is then split into smaller groups. Some head toward the Fairy Prairie and Fantastic Future World while others, including Barnes, head toward the Pirate Cove and the Hero Haven.

At this point the group had already splintered a bit and a few of us had stayed behind to help with the survivors. I knew it was going to be a while before we were reinforced, but I knew someone had called it in and there would be more help coming eventually. Like I keep saying, we had been through this before. One time there was this trailer park that had erupted into all-out war, and there were hundreds of people on both sides trying to kill each other, so there were a lot of bodies and a lot of injuries, too. We had to wait two days for the Red Cross to get their shit together and send out some ERVs *[Emergency Response Vehicles—ed]* and for transport to show up to get people out of there and into a processing station. Of course, in the meantime, these rednecks are still trying to kill each other, so we lost probably another seven or eight people waiting for help to show up. I was really hoping this wasn't going to be one of those cases, but everyone was stretched way past their breaking point.

We come up on the Pirates first, and I don't know what you've heard, but it wasn't so bad. There were no bodies in sight, the streets were not running red with blood. It looked fine. It even smelled a little better than the other parts of the park.

13:15—Members of the Pirates are seen coming out of various buildings, each with their hands up. Brock Hockney is the first to reach the soldiers and he surrenders willingly, as do the rest. Some of them are injured, and they look unwashed, but there are no tears, and none of them say a word.

Of course, we found some terrible stuff when we actually went down into the ride where they were all living, but when we rolled up, they came out in a group with their hands up and didn't give us any trouble. Look . . . I mean, we found stuff, yeah. I wasn't part of that group, but they pulled some bodies out of there. They found a whole bunch in the areas behind the rides, like fifteen or twenty or something *[it was seven—ed]*, but they were all so decomposed from the water it was hard to ID them. But if you ask me, the Pirates didn't seem as bad as everyone made them out to be later. They were the easiest part of my job that day. They were a hell of a lot easier than the next group.

23:12—The Pirates have been processed, and the group comes up on the Deadpool camp and walks around the barriers of trash cans, pallets, and other items that had been erected. Immediately, a woman comes running at them holding a sword. When confronted with the soldiers, she immediately drops her sword and runs to the group, yelling, "I was ready to die. I was going to die today," and other variants over and over.

That girl, I remember her name. Jill Van Meveren. After we got our initial sweep of the park done, I ended up sitting with her for a bit. She went on and on about how she thought every day she was going to fight and live, and that last day she said she knew it was over. She said something about the day: "This is done," which, in her head, meant she was going to die. Apparently there had been some sort of big fight the day before, and she told me, "When that was over, I knew this was over. I knew I didn't need to hang on anymore because it was done." Again, that wasn't anything I hadn't heard before, but she put it really well, especially for a younger person.

The camera doesn't show it, but the thing I remember most about that section of the park was it was really quiet. We had a few more people come out, right after Jill did, but they were all really beaten up and could barely make it. One of them actually stumbled toward us like he was a zombie or something. I heard later that he was stumbling because he had an infection in his foot so bad it had started snaking its way up his circulatory system and toward his heart. A few antibiotics and he was fine, but the doctors said this kid shouldn't have been able to walk with the condition of his legs, but he did. He saw us and knew we were the way out, and he did what he shouldn't have been able to do. That was new. That kid, whoever he was, he held on a long time. I respect the hell out of that.

28:30—The group moves on to the World's Circus. There is video of two masks that look like the ones worn by "the Warthogs" on the ground near the entrance.

Yeah, that. I have no idea if those are the masks or not, but I can tell you I talked to a couple folks who went into the hotel right across the way from the entrance, and they told me they had seen some shit. Keep in mind, I'm basically passing along rumors here, but I heard them from people who had spent the past three or four weeks with no reason to make anything up. I pulled apart frozen bodies huddled together as they died. I wouldn't make that up if I hadn't done it. So, what I heard was there were booby traps all over the first floor. There were trip wires, holes dug in weird places, and it all led up to this sort of makeshift stage and there were body parts all over it. This dude said there were parts of at least three bodies that he could make out. Maybe more. He said, I remember, you never know how good you are at putting together that particular puzzle until you have to.

The official line was "we found nothing unusual." I can see why they did that. It's a damn sight better than "they were butchering people in the hotel lobby." I can't imagine that would do much for the FantasticLand stock price, right? Plus, I don't like thinking about who might be out there. It gives me the creeps.

31:03—Approaching the World's Circus gate, the group of survivors made up of Freaks and Mole Men are sitting in a line. Glenn Guignol says, "It's about fucking time."

That guy, man. He's no one I'd be friends with personally, but you got to hand it to him. We got them in handcuffs and sent them all out toward the entrance, and when we went through what they had created, it was really spooky and well done. I had an assault rifle in my hands, I *knew* it was all fake, and it still creeped me out. I was super impressed. A lot of them made it out. I went with that group to get them processed, and that's the last piece of video you'll see, me walking with these survivors through the wreckage of the Exclamation Point. No one was in a really talkative mood, which I can totally understand. We saw a few more bodies scattered, and this really weird thing happened when we got near the main entrance. Right off the shops someone had laid out all these bodies, and they were in our way so we had to, like, walk around them. The thing I remember was everyone sort of did it in their own way, you know? Some looked at the bodies and were very careful not to step on them, one guy was saying prayers, and most of them just looked straight ahead at the exit. I can't say I blamed them.

After we got everyone out on the first sweep, we went back in and started going building by building, which was harder than you'd think it would be. Some people were so sick they couldn't walk. I talked to one of the med guys afterward, and he said it was a mix of hypoglycemia and waterborne illnesses and some blood diseases and a whole host of other crap. We were going through that pink girly part of the park at one point and had just gone through one of the buildings off the main road that was, like, an employee locker room. We had just left, and one guy wanted to light up a cigarette and his lighter was dead, so he goes back in there and hears this whispering and follows it to a little crawl space behind the couch, and there's this girl there. She's skinny and sick and so weak she couldn't even call out loud enough for us to find her. I remember this guy just coming out of the building with this frail, thin girl in his arms, and she's grabbing onto him with everything she has left and was whispering something to him, and he whispered back and was moving as fast as he could toward the med vehicles. He came back about twenty minutes later, and there were tears in his eyes. We asked him what she said, and he said, "She was just saying 'mommy' over and over and over," then he started crying, and we had to deal with that. There were a few of those. These kids were sick even though they had food, and they were killing each other even with enough to go around, right?

I heard reports that all the "good food" had gone bad and they were stuck eating cotton candy and sour cherry balls and all that crap. I don't buy it. Yeah, the meat and everything had spoiled, but there were energy bars and restaurants full of starches, and they could have gotten by a little better, if you ask me. I saw people during the cleanup from Sadie stretch a little bit of food a long, long way. There was no real reason things had to get this bad.

So, the big question—why did I upload the video? Easy. I was paid. I had a feeling what I had was worth something, and I was one of the only ones smart enough to actually turn on a video camera. And I was totally right. I put together a thirty-second teaser and sent it off to all the news outlets, both the big ones and the online ones with big readership. I'm not going to tell you how much I made, but it was enough to make it worth my while. Yes, I was officially reprimanded, and yes, I've had a lot of people saying things like, "You're profiting off the blood of these poor kids," and stuff like that. Yes, I received a dishonorable discharge for the FNG, and a bunch of people think I'm an asshole. Think that if you want. My daughter gets to go to college. Plus, you're paying me to be in your book. Don't forget about that.

I didn't kill these kids. I was just smart enough to make some money off it. I don't lose any sleep from it. None at all.

INTERVIEW 21: EMMET R. KELLEY

Assistant Prosecutor for Florida's 15th Judicial Circuit.

Son, I'm sure I don't have to tell you, politics can be a bitch. A capital B, ball-bustin', no-holds-barred bitch, yes sir. If you get into the game at all, you gotta know eventually that bitch is coming for you, and when she got me she tuned me up good and proper. That's why I'm talking to you.

See, I was the lead prosecutor for Florida's 15th District for six years. That may not seem like a long time, but I spent my whole life getting there. Private practice, Chamber of Commerce dinners, kissing the right asses, contact after contact, political dinners, eventually landing a job in the office and working my way to lead. Pretty traditional. Then you get a high-profile batch of cases where the law isn't on your side, and suddenly you're "ineffective" and "incompetent" and . . . let me get this quote right here, "so dumb someone should throw a toaster in the shower with him because he's too stupid to live." The Internet, apparently, can also be a bitch.

All right, then. Let's back up. Like anyone, I was shocked and saddened by the response to Hurricane Sadie, but it really was a monumental job to get everyone out of their various communities. There was flooding further inland than anyone had ever imagined. Looked like Al Gore had a point after all. Next thing you know, towns with no infrastructure for flooding had people needing help and no way to get to them or help them, so they had to wait. They waited for the National Guard, and they waited for the Red Cross and boy howdy, they waited, and in the meantime there was violence and death all around. All around. Sadie hit us in September, and the first batch of cases started hitting two months to the day after she made landfall. They weren't open-and-shut prosecutions. They were rough stuff. Murders where there were no reliable witnesses and basically no hard evidence, assaults that could have come from any number of perpetrators, thefts where chain of custody made no logical sense. We lost a lot of cases at first.

We had our winners, though. Jameis Clay, I put him in jail forever. That was the cannibal case where this mean-looking SOB killed five women and ate them. Honestly, I didn't have much more to go on from an evidence standpoint, but I did have witness after witness who were positively sure of what they saw, and I had a defendant who . . . how should I put this delicately . . . you could picture taking a bite out of your arm. That make sense to you? It's easy to prosecute someone for monstrous acts when the fella in question looks a lot like a monster. My thinking shifted a bit. After five or six cases, people were getting sick of the trials. Some of the media coverage dropped off. We could actually present a case without blonde bimbos on TV squawking about us twenty-four hours a day. We started to win here and there, and I had a good strategy going, which was to make the monsters seem as much like monsters as I could. If someone was big and scary, play that up. If they had a temper, be damn sure to get them riled. If they were creepy, make them seem like the creepiest sumbitch in the Sunshine State. And it was working, yes sir. I was getting a conviction here and conviction there. My boss wasn't on my ass all the time. Which, unfortunately, brings me to FantasticLand.

I saw the video, same as everyone. But instead of running to my computers and blogging about it or vlogging about it or smogging about it or whatever the hell everyone does, I got a sinking feeling, like I had eaten something rotten and it was time to pay the dues. The part that really got me nervous is when they started hauling out petite teenage girls who had, if you believed the squawkers on TV, ripped people apart with their bare hands. It was tough to believe that the freshman rush at Florida State was capable of killing people. Then you got these kids, just out of school, green as green could possibly be, and the TV was saying "*They're killers! They're killers!*" I knew what was coming before it hit my office. When it finally got there, it was worse than I thought.

You ever seen that one movie . . . what was it . . . the one where Denzel Washington was trying to figure out who robbed a bank? I can't remember the name, but one of the big twists at the end was all the robbers pretended they were customers and they all vouched for one another so at the end of the day the cops knew who did it, but they had no way to prove it because there was reasonable doubt built into the crime. You ever see that? Anyways, that was the case here. I know, for sure, that I have at least three murderers dead to rights. The evidence says it's them, their enemies say it's them, but their friends are all, "No, Bambi over here was so innocent and actually she was feeding deer and giving everyone hugs the whole time," and suddenly you're served a hot steaming plate of reasonable doubt that a jury is going to eat faster than my momma's biscuits. It happened over and over. Me or one of my team had a good case, and her friends from FantasticLand, who were all celebrities at this point in one form or another, they got on the stand and cried and begged for their friend, and we would lose. Or, as I heard over and over again from my boss, we'd "blow it."

I'll tell you the one the bugs the hell out of me, sir. The one that keeps me up at night, the one I hope I'm able to not think about when I have my proverbial dark night of the soul. Sophie Ruskin. The girl with the guns. I had two of the kids in the park, nice kids by all accounts but maybe tied up in some bad actions in the park, I had two of them tell me she shot them. That she would strut around the park showing off her guns, and then when the fighting started toward the end, she started shooting. Shot a bunch of boys in that park, killed a few of them, too. The boys from the . . . what was it . . . the Pirates, they all saw her and identified her and testified against her, the whole kit and caboodle. Then the defense brought up witness after witness after witness after witness, and they all had exactly the same story—it was dark, there was a shooter, and it was a man. A boy. A fella. It couldn't have been her, because the shooter was some guy wearing a hooded sweatshirt no one could see. And you could tell, *you could tell* they were full of shit because their stories weren't 100 percent straight. There were slips here and there, and they all used exactly the same language. I used that in my closing statement. "They all have exactly the same story, told in the exact same way," I said. The jury didn't care. No conviction. She shot a bunch of people and is free right now.

At this point, most everyone from FantasticLand is going free. Pirates are going free, those gals with the bows and arrows, they went free, that guy with all the severed heads, he never made it to trial. We dropped it because it was hard to get at actually what he did, but a fella with that many tattoos is probably up to no good. But he was free. I'm getting yelled at on a daily basis, my boss just red-faced, screaming, saying, "We're failing this office," and "We're failing the people," and "Your ass is on the line, here." Like I didn't know that. I've had enough blowhard bosses to know when the shit is sliding downhill, and from what I hear the governor was involved in the yelling, which means I got it twice as bad when it got down to me.

Politics being the bitch she is, I made my play. I promised, publicly, convictions of Brock Hockney and of Sam Garliek. They were the bogeymen of this deal in the media. They called Brock the "Pirate Monster," and Sam, since he was supposed to be in charge and they found him hiding in an office somewhere, they called him "coward" and "weasel" and a whole host of other things. I remember seeing a T-shirt around town with his face that said FANTASTIC ASSHOLE on it. I admit, I smiled. It was cute. So that was the play. Convict both Brock and Sam or say sayonara to my legal career. So we got to work.

To be honest, I thought Brock was going to be easy and Mr. Garliek was going to be the slippery one. Turns out it was the other way around. Whatever happened in that park, the people who were with Brock were with him till the bitter end, yes sir. He had people who were still fighting for him and calling in favors from their parents and all sorts of stuff. Mr. Garliek, by contrast, had been abandoned. No one was making any excuses, no one was fighting on his behalf, and there were T-shirts on the street calling him an asshole. He could have saved a baby from a burning building on national TV, and it wouldn't have made a dent in how much people hated him. If he showed up on a desert island with a sandwich and a rescue boat, most people would try to beat him to death with the sandwich. People hated him. His lawyer, a really sweet fella named Roger Anderson who was in over his big bald head, told me as much. Told me, "There's no way we're getting a fair trial here or anywhere." I told him, "Seems that way, what do you want me to do about it?" He said, "Cut us a deal."

I kinda chuckled at that because I needed both of them to avoid being taken out back and shot, and I told Roger so, but he was insistent. He said, "I have something," and I pushed him, and you know what he had? He had video. Sam Garliek had set up battery-powered video cameras in three locations around the area where they had that big meeting, the . . . what did he call it . . . the Parts of the Council or whatever it was. They were small, and after all the blood had dried, he went back and picked them up.

The consequences of this action are twofold, sir. First off, it cemented a win for me on Brock. No matter what else happened, the jury would see three angles of him shooting a cannon off into a crowd full of people. Once they saw that, game over. It was very likely they would convict him of killing Kennedy if I charged him with it. That was done, done, done, I don't give a good goddamn what his cronies said on the stand. But that left the matter of Mr. Garliek. Cooperating with us boosted his character. It made him seem more in charge. His argument, "I did everything by the book, and no one responded like they were supposed to," suddenly seemed a lot more leaky. The idea of him killing that Francis girl in the dark seems less plausible. Plus, ol' Rog Anderson asked for immunity. I told him no way that was going to happen, so he asked for a deal that would reduce the charges against Mr. Garliek. I don't remember off the top of my head what they all were, but there was wiggle room there. I was leaning toward saying yes, but before I did, I decided to go see Brock for myself, just to get his side of things. I knew Mr. Garliek was a coward, but I thought maybe this Brock character was misunderstood; he got a little excited and he deserved a chance. Turns out I was, uh, I was wrong about that.

Brock got a good amount of media attention after everyone got out of the park, so he was removed from the general population almost immediately. His attorney, John Dahlstrom, he's a friend of mine. We'd been golfing before and ran in the same circles, and while we liked each other outside the courtroom, we had a reputation for absolutely going for each other's throats when it came time for trial. We both understood that and basically respected each other, so when I called and said I wanted to come and talk to him and Brock, he said that might not be such a good idea. I asked him why, and he said, "Brock isn't very good with people." I pressed him, and it turns out John was pretty sure Brock was one of those well-heeled psychopaths like you see in the movies. One who was real charming until they stuck you in the gut.

But I pressed the issue. I told John something had happened that they needed to consider, which is Florida lawyer code for, "I probably have you by the balls." So he sets up the meeting, and I drive down to Big Pine, wait in the waiting room, and after a bit, this broad-shouldered towhead comes in, sits down, and proceeds to stare at me until John makes his way to the table. It was maybe ten seconds, but that's a long time to stare at someone. It wasn't the greatest first impression. It creeped me out, to be honest.

Mr. Garliek may have been a weasel, but he had the right idea. I should have brought a video camera, because I cannot, I mean, *cannot* do justice to our conversation. It wasn't necessarily what was said, though that was bad enough, but how he said it. The tone, the way he stared, it was both . . . attractive and repulsive. I had gone into the meeting expecting a thug, and what I got was more Hannibal Lecter. He was creepy, I think was the best way of putting it. Creepy and totally convinced of his own righteousness and superiority. He treated his whole incarceration as an inconvenience and saw his actions in the park as a gift to mankind. I am not exaggerating, sir. And he would drop little violent rejoinders into the conversation. I remember at one point, I was playing a bit of hardball with John, telling him he didn't have a leg to stand on, and Brock chimes in, "I've seen people without a leg to stand on. In my experience, there's a lot more blood." Then he sat back in his chair, all satisfied. I grew up in the church, sir. I've served communion and the whole thing, but I don't think I'd ever been confronted with . . . well, I'll just say it . . . with evil like that in my life.

On the drive back from Big Pine, I really got to thinking. Since Hurricane Sadie slammed into us, I had gained twenty-five pounds, my darling wife and I were on the outs, we hardly talked anymore, and I was getting regular tongue-lashings from everyone from the governor on down. It was a rough patch, to be sure, but I really got to thinking. Some of these kids did terrible things. The stuff their attorneys told me in confidence, it would chill your blood. Yes it would. But why were they hurting each other? Was it out of self-preservation, as many of their attorneys argued? Were they in a situation where this sort of behavior was normalized? Or were they confronted with a monster and had to fight and stab and whatever else they had to do in order to survive that monster? And I came to a conclusion. I decided on my ride back that my career wasn't as important as Brock Hockney going to jail. Forever.

When I got back to the office, I let my team know what I was planning, and nobody threw up any roadblocks. I went to Rog that afternoon and I told him we'd take the deal, we'd reduce the charges against Mr. Garliek if he provided the tapes, and that would be that. Rog jumped at the chance, and forty-eight hours later, Mr. Garliek fought his way past an entire army of reporters, looked the judge in the eye, pled guilty to seven misdemeanors, and walked out with a huge fine and time served. When he walked out, the reporters were so shocked they almost forgot to ask questions. Mr. Garliek got in a car and was gone before too much of a hubbub could be made. Fifteen minutes later, I was in my boss's office. I laid it all out. He asked for my resignation, and I gave it to him, yes sir, I did. And that was the end of my legal career. But they got Mr. Hockney. That video, which leaked after the trial, everyone sort of got it. Even John Dahlstrom. He gave it his all, but you can tell when a defense attorney's heart isn't in it. Besides, what defense do you come up with against video of your client shooting a cannon into a crowd? Tough defense, that one.

I get asked a lot how I could let Sam Garliek go, and I want to speak to that just a bit, if you'll permit me. I can say, now that I'm not an official anymore, that I flat-out don't like that guy. John and Brock, they tried to sell me on the idea that Sam was the mastermind behind the whole thing, that he had a roving gang of thugs who did what he wanted and the whole "tribes" thing was a backlash against that. Personally, I don't think Sam was that smart. I think he was a poor leader who was in over his head and panicked. Then he hid. Then he sold everything he had to save his own skin. That's not a hero in my book, though you talk to him and he'll tell you different. At the end of the day I had a choice to make: convict the coward or convict the monster. There's no doubt in my mind I made the right choice. No doubt. I sleep like a baby. Plus, from what I hear, Sam Garliek is getting what he deserves in the outside world. I mentioned the T-shirts with his face on them, right?

So, that's that. Of course, I made out OK after getting fired. I got hired on TV as an "expert commentator" so fast it made my head spin, and I made enough money to make it OK. My wife, she's a principal at a local middle school, she makes OK money too, so we don't want for anything, really. I still comment fairly regularly. I had a producer tell me he liked my laid-back way of speaking, which I think is a nice way of saying I speak stupid enough for everyone to understand. I don't care. I dropped the weight, I fixed things with Janet—that's my wife—and I'm doing what I want. I don't go to Chamber dinners anymore. I haven't played golf in a year. I always hated golf. I'm starting to get involved in politics a bit, but on my terms and on the legal side.

I'm not giving that bitch another bite at my behind, that's for sure.

INTERVIEW 22: BROCK HOCKNEY

Character in the Pirate Cove, Leader of the Pirates.

Author's Note: I interviewed Brock Hockney at the Big Pine Key Road Correctional Facility, where he will likely spend the rest of his life. I have included the interview in its entirety, as Mr. Hockney was not willing to tell his story, like my other interviewees. However, I believe his responses to my questions shed light on the man many call the "Pirate Monster of FantasticLand." Our time was also limited due to requests from his attorney.

ADAM JAKES: Good morning, Mr. Hockney. I'm Adam Jakes, a reporter, and I'm writing a book about FantasticLand and what went on there. Thank you for meeting with me.

[Silence]

The best thing I've found to do in conducting these interviews is to let people tell me their stories. I can kind of jump in to clarify things, but what your lawyers and I would love is for you to just start talking and give us your side of the story. So, we can start before the hurricane hit. What did you do in FantasticLand, Brock?

[Silence]

Do you not want to tell me?

Brock Hockney (to his attorney, John Dahlstrom): What is this?

John Dahlstrom: I think this could really help, Brock.

BH: Help what?

AJ: By telling your story and letting people hear your side . . .

BH: I understand the concept, you fucking sand mite. What I'm asking my attorney is what he's thinking this will help. Will it make an appeal more likely? Will I get better privileges in here? What's the endgame?

JD: Public sentiment, Brock. We've talked about this.

[Silence]

BH: I don't agree, but I didn't finish in the middle of the pack at Florida State. Ask, then.

AJ: The other people told me their story.

BH: They did?

AJ: Yes. They did.

BH: And when they spoke of me, did they make me sound like "other people"?

AJ: No, Brock, they didn't. They made you sound charismatic and violent. They made it sound like you were the poster child for this whole mess.

[Silence]

AJ: How about we try this: what did you do when you started working at FantasticLand?

BH: I worked.

AJ: Worked doing what?

BH: I dressed up as a Pirate and made little kids happy.

AJ: Did you like doing that?

BH: Yes. It paid well and it was rewarding.

[Silence]

AJ: Why did you sign up for Operation Rapture?

BH: Money. And I liked the concept.

AJ: What do you mean, the concept?

BH: I mean I like the idea of being one of the people responsible for the park after everyone else ran. I like being responsible.

AJ: I'm not trying to bait you, Brock, but you have to see how some people could see that as a contradiction, given your actions in the park.

BH: Let me ask you, Adam, were you in the park after the hurricane? You were, what, a ShopGirl? A Fairy? Of course you weren't. You weren't in the park, so when you say something like, "your actions in the park," you have to see how that would make me upset. Yes?

AJ: Yes, Brock.

BH: Also, we've never met before, Adam. I understand, Adam, that you're trying to foster familiarity, Adam, but we've never met and we surely are not on a first-name basis, are we? Adam?

AJ: I take your point.

BH: So we've established that you don't know me, and the only thing you think you know is because other people have called me names and made claims about me. If you were on the other side of this table, would you conclude, reasonably, that the person asking the questions was at best rude and at worst disrespectful and antagonistic? Like they were itching for a fight, almost?

AJ: Again, I take your point.

BH: You take my point . . .

AJ: Mr. Hockney.

BH: Thank you. Ask.

AJ: What can you tell me about your time in the emergency shelters as the hurricane was passing through?

BH: I can tell you it was crowded and unpleasant.

AJ: Anything else?

BH: Oh, and dark. It was frequently dark.

AJ: And that's the story?

BH: I'm answering your questions. If you have a specific question, Mr. Jakes, ask it.

AJ: I have a lot of questions but not a lot of hard evidence. It's not like anyone made it out of there with their phones.

BH: Funny you should mention that.

AJ: How so?

BH: I would look into that angle if I were you. I've never been much of a social media person myself, but one of my biggest challenges as a leader was breaking that particular habit in my peers. When you are used to constant stimuli and then have it taken away with nothing to replace it, people act in all sorts of interesting ways.

AJ: What sort of responses did you see?

BH: The biggest thing I saw was a lack of purpose. Kids wandering around, not sure what to do with themselves. If I can say this without sounding like a cult leader, it made them far more susceptible to suggestion. Actually, I take that back. I don't think it was suggestion, I think I was the one who found a way to harness the epic boredom of a hundred bored young people. When you're used to expending a certain amount of energy presenting yourself to strangers, imagine the appeal of someone saying, "Come over here. Use that energy for something that matters." The people who joined me, Mr. Jakes, were simply thrilled to have a place for their passion.

AJ: Really?

BH: I think so. I also think you're still trying to establish rapport. That you're working up to something. If you have a "hard question," go ahead and ask it. I have places to be.

AJ: All right. I heard your brother died in the tunnels and that you two were very close. These same sources told me it wasn't something you talked about on many occasions but that it came up at the Council of Pieces.

BH: Council of Pieces? I've never heard that term. It's delightful.

AJ: I have a source telling me you invoked your brother before firing the cannon.

BH: I see. So you want me to admit to firing the cannon?

AJ: No, Mr. Hockney, everyone I've interviewed agreed that you did that. I'm more interested in your motivations.

BH: And revenge for my dead brother seems like a nice, tidy storyline to you, does it?

AJ: It's something people could understand. That's all we're trying to do, understand.

BH: And selling books is a nice by-product.

[Silence]

BH: Not to be baited, then, are you? All right, yes, my brother died in the tunnels. Yes I was very bitter about it and remain so to this day. If the protocols in the park were the least bit thought through, my brother would be alive. But if he hadn't died, would I have led the Pirates? I would like to think that yes, I would have. I'm a natural leader, and I had the best ideas. I have no idea whether I invoked my brother's name at the . . . what was it . . . Council of Pieces? Damned if that doesn't have a ring to it.

If you want to know how my brother's death informed the situation, it led me to believe the situation was extraordinary. It made me believe, rightfully, that all law had been dissolved.

AJ: Says the man in jail.

BH: Says the man in jail with no possibility of parole. Interrupt me again and I'll jump across this table and have at your fucking windpipe. I bet I can get it out of there before the guards stop me.

JOHN DAHLSTROM: Brock . . .

AJ: I apologize for interrupting, but I want to dwell on this idea of extraordinary circumstances. What led you to believe that rules didn't apply, to put it indelicately?

BH: Management. Pure and simple.

AJ: Management?

BH: If management couldn't provide people with the most basic of needs, or, indeed, if they kill someone who is questioning their leadership choices, all bets are off, are they not?

AJ: You're referring to Sam Garliek and that Flynn girl?

BH: Among others. It was common knowledge that he killed her in the dark. You said that I was the "poster child" for what happened in the park. You're wrong. Sam Garliek killing that girl was where control was officially lost. After that, what else was there to do but protect oneself? There were also other rumors and innuendo. He was the lead manager before the hurricane, but he certainly wasn't alone.

AJ: What else did you hear, sir?

BH: Murder, intimidation, bullying, rape, sodomy, torture, you name it.

AJ: Really?

BH: I heard one story about a girl in the shelters going to Mr. Garliek's little Command Center because she was having a nervous breakdown. The stress of the situation was more than her helicopter parents ever prepared her for. She was hyperventilating or some such thing, and when she went to management to beg for help, she was pulled into a dark room and gang raped by three of Mr. Garliek's underlings. Because they could. Now tell me, Mr. Jakes, do you believe this story?

AJ: If you're asking, sir, it sounds like the sort of thing my reporting would have uncovered by now.

BH: Maybe you're not a very good reporter. I know Sam Garliek is a liar.

AJ: Regardless, since we're in the thick of it, Mr. Hockney, can I ask about the incident with the injured man and the stanchion?

BH: Ask.

AJ: Everyone I've interviewed has described seeing or hearing about the moment where an employee fell from a rooftop and was very badly hurt. You then killed the man with a stanchion. It was described as a mercy killing. It is one of the core, solid events everyone has described or had described to them. Did it happen?

BH: Possibly.

AJ: Possibly?

BH: It sounds like something I would have done.

AJ: Come on, Mr. Hockney.

BH: Watch your tone, please.

AJ: You're right. I'm sorry. But can you see how that answer is difficult to accept?

BH: You have proven yourself capable of manners, but that doesn't mean I give even a fraction of a shit about your emotional state.

AJ: Then let me toss another one at you, please. I spoke with a woman named Jill Van Meveren who was a Deadpool . . .

BH: Really? Some of them made it out? Hmm.

AJ: Yes, they did. She said you and several other Pirates cut off the hands of another employee and afterward left a stanchion as a word of warning. Like it was the calling card of the Pirates.

BH: That's what they thought?

AH: Yes

BH: They're very perceptive.

[Silence]

John Dahlstrom: Brock, it's OK to talk about this one.

BH: What if I'm not in the mood?

JD: Brock, please . . .

BH: On the advice of my attorney, here's what I recall. When I came out of the emergency shelters I was, understandably, upset. I was upset at the leadership of the park. I was upset at the death of my brother by easily preventable means. I was upset at my circumstances. When I saw the poor gentleman on the ground, clearly suffering and clearly wounded beyond the skills of our most gifted medical practitioners, I took a heavy metal stanchion and hit his head with it until I saw what I thought to be brain matter. Then I stopped. There was an audience, and that audience should feel ashamed of themselves for not taking action when it was crystal clear there was action to be taken.

AJ: You're saying someone else should have killed him?

BH: Mr. Jakes, what other option was there? The man was suffering. But they were afraid, weren't they?

AJ: What do you think they were afraid of?

BH: If I had to guess, I would say they were scared of "getting into trouble." You'd be surprised how long it took some to realize no one was going to swoop in and impose order. I remember explaining that to one gentleman in particular who argued that someone might record it and put it online. The look on his face when he realized no one was watching was a sight to behold. Freeing these men and women of their fear was just as much an act of mercy as putting that poor dying man out of his misery.

AJ: I don't think anyone disputes the killing as an act of mercy. But why the public forum? Why the overt violence? Was this man's death something you wanted the other employees to see?

BH: Like, to intimidate them?

AJ: I suppose.

BH: If that was the effect, it was unintended. I was, quite frankly, in a fog. Not to dwell on it, but my brother had just died because no one could keep the lights on and no one knew to keep an inhaler handy. Action, especially action that was so clear-cut, felt like the right thing at the time. Sincerely, Mr. Jakes, I have no more for you on the topic than that.

AJ: There is one more question on the killing, if you'll permit me. I've looked extensively into what public records I could find of your past. There is no history of violence. You were in two fights, both in middle school, and both were low-level affairs.

BH: Yes.

AJ: What I'm wondering, Mr. Hockney, is how you go from no violence to killing in such a short period of time?

BH: That's a good question. John, don't you think that's a good question? Mr. Jakes, it goes back to circumstances. You asked me how my brother's death affected me. To repeat myself, it told me the circumstances were extraordinary. We were in a situation that was going to push us, to test us, to challenge us in ways we had believed we would never be tested. We were at war, sir. War against management who had shown themselves ready to kill and war for survival. There is only so much food and water.

AJ: There was more than enough food and water to go around.

BH: Only so much goodwill, then. Do you think my little incident with the stanchion led others to fear for their lives?

AJ: I know that to be the case.

BH: Well, I cannot be held accountable for how people interpret events. Fair enough?

AJ: Yes, thank you. I'd like to move on to the formation of the Pirates, if I may. One of the employees I interviewed said she witnessed you kill the man with the stanchion, and that motivated her and her friends to organize.

BH: Why didn't she stop me?

AJ: Pardon?

BH: I'm making an assumption here, but I would imagine this woman described the incident in brutal terms and said something like, "Someone should have stopped him," right? My question is, if she was so afraid and so traumatized by my act of mercy, why didn't she stop me? Either before or after, it doesn't matter.

AJ: I can't speak for her, Mr. Hockney, but most people would likely not stop someone who had just bludgeoned a man to death.

BH: Maybe that should change. Maybe a bit more accountability is in order.

AJ: But you can see how this might have escalated people's fears about being in the park.

BH: Again, Mr. Jakes, I am not responsible for how events are interpreted.

AJ: All right. You worked in the Pirate Cove. Was it natural for you to gravitate back there after leaving the emergency shelter?

BH: Very much so. There didn't seem to be much else to do, to be honest. Plus you feel more comfortable in familiar environments.

AJ: And others that you worked with, they were there as well?

BH: More than just them. After the incident with the stanchion, my recollection is that I had ten to fifteen people following me to the Cove. And we started talking.

AJ: About what?

BH: A variety of things. We introduced ourselves, obviously. Some were Pirate Cove workers and some were not, so there were tours. We talked about our time in the emergency shelter and about management's shortcomings. Some of our new friends went and brought others they thought would like the environment. Before you knew it, we had a merry little band.

AJ: Were they initially looking to you for leadership?

BH: That's a curious question, Mr. Jakes. Why must there be leadership, especially since the leadership in place already failed us?

AJ: But you were unquestionably their leader.

BH: I never presented myself as such. I had ideas that others seemed to enjoy. At some point, it became obvious that a loose set of rules were going to have to be established, and the group looked to me to do that. The rules . . . I want to talk for a moment about our rules. It was vital that the rules be simple, clear, and most importantly absolute. Clear boundaries, clear penalties. Now, this might seem a little, what's the word, hokey to anyone who wasn't in our situation, but what we needed was a code of honor. That's what I worked on, a code of honor. If I might brag for a moment, we had full buy-in. To a piece, all the men and women from my area decided this code made sense to follow.

AJ: Right, the code. Let's see what I can remember . . . A Pirate is a brother, and a brother is worth spilling blood for, a Pirate does what he knows is right, a Pirate fights for the cause, and . . . what was the one about stealing?

BH: You're missing a few, but you have the gist. A Pirate gets what he wants, but not from another Pirate. That was the most obtuse of the rules, but we made sure it was understood. You don't steal from other Pirates, period. We had a court set up where people brought their grievances. Once word got around that we had zero tolerance for stealing, it sank in pretty fast.

AJ: Is that how that Deadpool ended up losing his hands early on?

BH: I've been instructed not to talk about that one.

AJ: I see. And is the code how the Deadpools ended up being attacked almost constantly? Or how bodies ended up hanging from lampposts in the Pirate Cove?

BH: Those are two separate questions and it sounds as if you're a bit indignant there, Adam.

AJ: I'm not going for an indignant tone, but I have to ask about the more fantastical things that I've heard.

BH: All right. Lay them on the table.

AJ: I heard the Pirates beat intruders to death. I heard the Pirates would take people, that they took everything and everyone from the Fairy Prairie for their own ends. I heard a story about fights to the death for the entertainment of the Pirates. I heard a good-natured duo initially tried to flee the park and may have been murdered after they returned in desperate need of help. I heard phrases like, "The Pirates got them."

BH: Well, surely, Mr. Jakes, there would have been evidence of such barbarism when the National Guard showed up.

AJ: I respect your point, sir, but while you may have a body-cam video of the end of this thing, I have interview after interview after interview of people telling me all manner of gruesomeness attributed to you and the Pirates. Murder after murder, with the bodies often put on display in some way.

BH: And do you believe them?

AJ: Honestly? Yes. I believe things got out of hand and the Pirates did whatever they wanted to whoever they wanted.

BH: *[Laughing]* Oh, the things you don't know.

John Dahlstrom: Brock, stop now.

BH: If you had been there, Mr. Jakes. If you had only seen.

JD: Brock, as your attorney, please stop talking. Mr. Jakes . . .

BH: Ever been curious about what human flesh tastes like?

JD: BROCK!

[At this point, we still had ten minutes left of interview time scheduled. I was asked to leave the room until they could confer. I was asked back with five minutes left.]

John Dahlstrom: We have time for two more questions, Mr. Jakes.

AJ: All right. You have admitted to firing the cannon at the Council of Pieces . . .

BH: Still a great name.

AJ: If intimidation wasn't your goal as previously stated, what was your goal?

BH: To kill people.

[Silence]

AJ: Anything else?

BH: No. I wanted casualties. Got them, too.

AJ: Why?

BH: Are you sure that's what you want your last question to be? I'm being generous with you, Mr. Jakes, because "anything else?" is technically a question. But what the hell, I'm in a good mood. I wanted to test a theory I've had since childhood. It goes like this: If people are stupid and weak enough, you can point a cannon at their face, and they will refuse to believe it's there. I now have substantial evidence on the matter.

AJ: All right, Mr. Hockney. Last question. In the media, you have been portrayed as a monster. Jury members in your trial took twenty-two minutes to convict you. Obviously you are the single person who has borne the most blame, legally and in the court of public opinion, for what happened inside FantasticLand. Do you feel that's fair?

BH: It doesn't matter if it's fair or not, does it?

AJ: Does it?

BH: You wouldn't have lasted long, sir. I see you as a Deadpool. That sound about right? Clinging with your friends as we pick you off one by one, pretending you're up to the challenge but knowing in your heart that we would be there soon and we were going to take what we wanted and there's nothing you could do to stop us? You asked me if it's fair that I'm portrayed as a monster. I go back to something I asked you fifteen minutes ago. Who stopped me? I'm not overly tall, nor am I overly strong. Two men could take me, yet no two men stood up. Would you have stood up to me, Adam? Or would you have stood by as I walked by with a bloody stanchion? I know where my money's at.

I'll leave you with this since I'm about to give my attorney a well-earned coronary. Sometimes you have to fight, sir. There are times in life where unpleasant things are happening, and if you don't fight you might as well be meat. Those who kill can smell those who are ripe for slaughter, and if you don't stand up, if you don't punch and kick and rip and tear, what good are you? You wouldn't have lasted long, Mr. Jakes. If you don't know what I just told you, if you don't feel it in your bones, then that's all you are. Bones. If you'll excuse me.

Brock Hockney has not given another interview. His lawyer says he is unavailable.

INTERVIEW 23: RITCHIE FRESNO

Owner of FantasticLand.

Let's get this out of the way now. I'm not my father.

You don't want to know how many times over the years I've been exposed to the "Legend of Johnny Fresno." Teachers, principals, roommates, potential employers, fuckin' romantic partners, man. All of 'em. They come at you with this "your dad was America's Dreamer" sort of bullshit and then they look at you like, "What you got?" Turns out what I got was a shark-like business sense and a pack-and-a-half-a-day American Spirit habit. That's what I got.

You want an example? Sure, man. I tell this story all the time, but it bears repeating. I'm at this party in college; there's drinking, there's weed, there's loud music, and I'm approached by this hot little chica, gorgeous big brown eyes and this sweet rack, and she is instantly overly friendly toward me. Like, I'm not even trying, man, and she's like, "Let's go upstairs," and I'm like, "Hells to the yeah let's go upstairs." So we're making out and clothes are coming off, and by the time I get her pants off I realize she's wearing FantasticLand panties. They were bright yellow with the Exclamation Point on them, and when she sees that I see her panties, she throws me on the bed, gets on top of me, and yells, "Fuck me, Johnny Fresno!" It totally creeped me out, and I got out of there. She was, like, a groupie for my dad. That's kind of a great metaphor for my life. The lineage gets me into the party, but then, brother, things tend to go sideways.

You know, if I would have told a reporter that story a year ago, you would have had to watch out for falling board members. They would have jumped out of the fucking windows on the top of the thirty-second floor, man. But since I sold and I'm no longer in the mix, the gloves are off, as they say. I'm off the leash, so not only can I tell you what happened in the boardroom after the hurricane because no one was smart enough to get an NDA out of me, but I can tell you what happened while I'm atop a pile of cash that I could never possibly spend in this life. After what my dad put me through when I was a kid, I have no problem spilling the beans.

What was I put through? Just like I told you. How do you think life shakes out for you when your dad is the Dreamer in Chief, the guy whose name is as big as Walt Disney or Steven Spielberg? You are constantly, in every little action and moment, judged against that monster of a legacy, and there's no escape from it. Try to be the good child, you'll never be good enough. Try rebellion on for size, and it doesn't matter, man. The press wants you to be the bad seed, and anyone you'd hang around with, they never actually accept you into the group. You're the guy with all the money. That's what I've been to every social group I've ever been a part of, the rich guy. At least now I'm on boards where they're honest about that sort of thing.

So I wandered, man. I tried on a bunch of personalities. I was a punk, then I was an angel, then I believed in God, then I played tennis, of all fucking things, then I found where I fit—business school. I had a knack for it, plus when I started doing well, my dad's right-hand man Ollie Tracks stepped in and mentored me, and he did a good job, if I do say so myself. He taught me about all the nasty bits of running the park, that part Dad didn't want to think about. Truthfully, I think he was happy to have an ally with the Fresno name. It's my legal name, by the way. I'm half Lebanese, from what I can tell. Dad never wanted to claim we were anything other than white, but . . . hello! I'm the darkest guy on all the boards I serve on. I don't even tan.

Regardless of never fitting in, I was always a bright cat, so I graduated high school, got my degree in business from Dartmouth, pulled some strings and got into the Harvard Business School, and by then I had found other folks who were in my same boat. Things calmed down on the personal front, and I really sank my teeth into business school. I got a rep pretty early as a left-leaning badass, which was sort of a rare thing. I cared about workers but was relentless in pursuit of best practices. The thing I wanted people to know was that if you were front line I was your friend, and if you were management, I was going to get the best out of you if it meant leaving your corpse smoking and bloody in your office. Once you were in the upper echelon, you were my bitch, man. I would work you hard, and then I would go to the bar and laugh at you. That's the rep I got, it's the rep I wanted, and it ended up working well for FantasticLand. Up to a point.

See, the dirty little secret of FantasticLand was that we were insanely profitable and we actually had less to work with than Disney or Universal. Our footprint was significantly smaller, our brand not nearly as well known, and when I took over, our finances were pretty bad, man. If dad hadn't kicked the bucket, the park might well have closed. I took over as CEO, and Ollie was my right hand until he died, but before he did, we were able to completely 180 the park, from loser to lean, tight, and profitable. I had presidents calling me, man, wanting to know how I did it, and if I could do it for this business or that business. I always listened, but at the end of the day I just wanted a cold beer and a hot lady, you dig? That's kind of how I got my second rep as a party boy, but I never really partied, per se. I was a regular at a bar and I was always solid at work at 7:00 a.m. Always.

Let me set the stage for the hurricane. Phil Mueller, the head of personnel, that guy was a beast and a half. He talked slow and was easygoing, but that guy demanded the best and got the best, so we were buds. He had a brain for analytics, unlike most older dudes, and I loved him for it, so he figured out the best way to move folks in and out of positions, he knew when traffic peaked at the park and how to put the best employees where they needed to be, and he was just an all-round super dude. I trusted him, so when he came to me with Operation Rapture, which Trolly had pitched to him before he passed on, I was onboard because it was Phil. No other reason. Plus, it sounded like a decent plan to put a skeleton crew in the park to protect the property. On paper, great idea, man.

So Sadie, that bitch, she hits, and I call Phil, and he assures me, like, "Yeah, everything went off without a hitch, we'll check back once the storm passes." Then the power goes out. Then the power stays out. Then the power stays out and we are in the middle of a national nightmare with my park in the center of it, and there's literally no way to get to the park without a fleet of helicopters or a Jet Ski or super-duper hip waders and an Olympic athlete's respiratory system. And I kept on Phil, man, I told him, get it done, get with the National Guard or whoever, make contact, and he kept on saying, "Red tape, red tape, red tape," every damn time I talked to him. By the time we were in the second week of the thing, I was writing most of the park off, man, I figured there was no saving most of the infrastructure. Good thing I had a monster head of insurance, because we actually made money in the case of a total Act of God-style loss. America, man. What can I tell ya?

I called an emergency meeting of all the VPs the day after the hurricane passed, and it went fine, as these things go. Then after a week I called an emergency meeting of the board. I told them we're out of contact with the park, we have this protocol in place, and we were going to hope for the best till the lights came back on and everyone was cool. Everyone was chill. So we wait, and we wait, and then I start getting reports.

The first report was from Phil. He said he had received a call from one of the emergency sat phones. There were only three of them in the park. It was Sam Garliek, who was the guy in charge of the shift and the guy Phil had given the keys to before he ran for the hills. He said things were going to shit and there were dead bodies. Phil, being Phil, exploded at the guy and said, "Fix it or I'm going to stick my foot up your ass until you taste shoe polish," and apparently, from what I've heard, Sam did something that ended with a bang, if you catch me. Then the next report I got was a few days later from my IT guy, saying the Exclamation Point was gone, and I was like, "What do you mean gone? It's five and a half tons of fucking concrete and fiberglass and shit," and he was like, "I'm looking at our satellite feed right now, and it's not fucking there." And sure enough, it was gone. So that's when I stepped in.

I have zero contacts in the military, but I know dudes who do, so I was about seven phone calls in when I learned someone had told the military that things were hunky fucking dory in the park, and they had all the water they needed, and go ahead and save other people. I don't know, to this day, what idiot from my company made that call, and if I ever find out I'm going to beat them with the nearest heavy implement, man. I'm not a violent dude, but I have seldom been as upset as I was when I heard that. So I'm on the phone, pumping every contact I have, and it's not going anywhere. Then I finally get something done, I sit back, and then the reports start coming in. And they're bad.

I remember one time when I was a kid, I saw my dad totally break down. It was over the dumbest thing, too. He was crying because he couldn't build a giant restaurant in the park. He was so exercised over not being able to see the ocean from high up that this mighty man, this pillar of American innovation and imagination, was crying in our goddamn kitchen, man. I never knew why. I think the closest I ever came to understanding it was when I heard there were bodies on the Golden Road and bones in the gift shop. It was like, this thing, this all-encompassing thing that had been my torment and my motivation and my pain and my work and my identity and my triumph, I knew in that split second that it was done. I knew it would capture everyone's imagination and that it was impossible to contain, and I knew, in that moment, that the park was going to close and not reopen, man. I knew it. But that didn't mean I was going down without a fight.

I told Phil and everyone else who was worth a shit to start gathering information from every source they possibly could. I got the board together. Four hours later everyone was in the same room—I didn't want to risk a teleconference—and I laid it out. Things had gone bad in the park. Kids were killing each other. At that point, I had two photos and some scary-ass reports about heads on spikes and whatnot. Now, remember, we had seen violence before now because of the hurricane. Communities were cut off, and some of them started shooting each other, but—and I don't want to sound racist or anything—it seemed like what you read about gangs, you know? It didn't seem . . . God, what's the word . . . it didn't sound horrific. It sounded like people shooting other people, which is easy to forget about.

You know what's not easy to forget about? Fucking dead bodies in an amusement park. That's not easy to forget about.

The board, at this point, they totally let me down. Fear, I've learned, is never a good place from which to operate, and you've never seen as many rich assholes go as deathly white as they went when I laid it out. They knew what I knew, in their hearts, but then they just started making the dumbest decisions you could imagine. They actually said words like "cover up" and "suppress" and they meant it, man. They didn't understand that the cat was already out of the barn, or whatever. That there was no way in hell the media wasn't going to bite onto this as hard as they could and that the public wouldn't lap up every detail. It was picture perfect for twenty-four-hour news, man. It was a breaking story with gory photos that could distract people from the awful response to the hurricane while at the same time letting them feel superior and outraged. It, like, hit all the fucked-up news sectors you wanted to hit. But the board was, like, obstruct-obstruct-obstruct. And when it became clear that wasn't going to work, they were all spin-spin-spin, and when *that* didn't work, I threatened to quit the company my dad built if they didn't start acting like men and own up to this. And they didn't.

I don't want to get into the weeds, man, but the entire plan seemed to be "don't say anything," which was an impossibility. We had media camped out at our building and news reporters saying things like, "There is no response from FantasticLand management" six times an hour, twenty-four hours a day. I begged them, I threatened them, I yelled at them, I cajoled them, but fear is a powerful thing. Fear is so powerful; it takes Ivy League–educated dudes and turns them into scared little schoolgirls. I don't remember the exact moment I said "Fuck this," but I remember that when I made the decision to leave this mess that was my father's legacy, I moved fast. I put out feelers to buyers and had the thing sold so fast the board hardly had time to react. I was done. I went on the news and made my famous "FantasticLand is overseen by cowards" speech, and then I was done. Gone. Outta there. Bridge burned all to hell, man. I don't regret it for a second.

A lot of people have asked me why I sold a multibillion-dollar company for $700 million, well below market value. Easy. I was already getting paid seventeer million dollars a year as owner and CEO, and that's without the profits from the park, which were easily in excess of a billion dollars a year. Of course we put a lot of that money back into the park, but we aren't publicly traded or anything. Dad owned the park, and when he died he left it to me, man. I had the keys to the empire, and I wanted out, so I sold. And now, I'm a regular at a bar, I've learned a couple of musical instruments, I'm married, and life really isn't bad, man. I'm in the best shape of my life. I'm richer than Midas. I travel where I want, when I want. I still get calls from presidents. My life is better than yours, it really is. And I don't have this god-awful mess to clean up.

Why do I think it happened? Hell if I know. Throw a bunch of kids into a toxic mix like that, man, and nothing good is coming out, but that's not my fault or the fault of anyone in the park. I did tour the grounds, though, one time before they knocked the whole thing down. I got to see it all shabby-like, and it was tough, I don't mind telling you. By the time I went through there, the blood had been all cleaned up, obviously, but I spent a couple hours just walking. I remember, at one point I found a cannon in one of the ponds, and I stood and looked at it for, like, ten minutes, and I was just thinking and thinking, "How did that get there?" And I tried to come up with a scenario where someone thought it was a good idea to throw a cannon in a pond and I came up with nothin'. I guess I'm gonna have to read your book, huh?

I don't mind talking about how painful it was. Even with all the cleanup they had done, when I walked through the empty park my mind filled in all the blanks, man. I knew the basic gist of the story by then, so it wasn't hard to imagine Pirates and Robots or whatever it was, fighting and killing each other. To be honest, it only reinforced my decision to sell. The park was tainted, man, and it had to go.

I didn't watch when they demolished the park. Couldn't stand it. I spent the day watching sports and getting blind stinking drunk. But, to be honest, what the hell else were they going to do? It was no longer FantasticLand, now it was Slaughter Land or Brock Hockney Did This At This Place Land. It wasn't FantasticLand. Sadie blew her away, and those kids dug the grave where she landed. I didn't watch because, and you're gonna get something out of me here, part of me always loved the place. I have this, like, Technicolor memory of the first time my dad bought me a candied apple in the World's Circus. I remember the way the sun shined off the caramel coating, I remember the sun and the smells of food and sunscreen, I remember hearing giggling and happiness all around, man. Most of all, I remember my dad beaming at me, like he knew he had just given me the perfect memory. Then I grew up and was a hard-ass for the company, but there's part of this tubby old drunk who never let go of that little boy.

So, yeah, I'm not a big fan of what they're planning to do with it. A park where people can pretend to join a tribe and fake fight with other visitors. That's fucked up on a very fundamental level.

They'll probably make their money back in a year and a half or so.

AFTERWORD

As a reporter, I'm already uncomfortable with appearing in this reporting as much as I have. The Brock Hockney interview, in particular, is painful for me to read. However, after my editor pushed me to write an afterword to wrap up what my reporting uncovered, somehow the idea didn't feel as self-indulgent as I feared it would. There are so few conclusions to what I found, so much detail but so little new information, a wrap-up might provide the reader with some sort of absolution, some sort of point. In other words, I have one more chance to tell you why I think this happened, why the young people of FantasticLand started down a path that led to an amusement park bathed in blood. I get a chance to tell you why, so maybe you won't feel so fascinated or so scared.

On this front, my dear readers, I can offer no real help or comfort.

The events that transpired in FantasticLand were senseless. There was plenty of food. There was plenty of water. There was more than enough room for everyone to ride out the extended period after the storm in peace and comfort. There was no reason this had to happen. If I have found one new fact in all my reporting, it's that I believe many who were involved have come to accept this. The Brock Hockneys of the world aside, I think once the media storm died down and the online "What tribe are you?" quizzes all fade from the most-viewed page lists, a profound sense of sadness has set in. Sadness at the lives lost, but also sadness that it came to this in the first place. What I sensed in my interview subjects was sadness, with maybe a twinge of embarrassment at how easily FantasticLand resorted to violence and how quickly we ate it up.

Even though I don't have any answers, my editor would kill me if I didn't at least share my theory. If there's one question I was asked more than any other over the course of my reporting, it was, "Why did they start killing each other so quickly?" Of course, I can't answer this question for every employee who found themselves trapped in "The Place Where Fun Is Guaranteed," but many of them expressed or implied a disassociation with reality while in the park. In some ways, that makes perfect sense. The park was *supposed* to transport visitors to a different place, but in this case it seems the effect was only heightened. Some said it was the lack of people where they had only seen crowds that made the whole thing feel unreal. Some said their heightened emotional state and sudden change of diet put them in a fog. And, of course, there was the young man from the Robot tribe who told me, "Nothing in the park was Facebook official." Not to be glib, but I think the Robot has a point. We would be naive to discount the role of technology in the "battle for FantasticLand." The young people were accustomed to constant stimuli in a safe environment and suddenly they found themselves, like so many in the past, suffering from "intense boredom punctuated by moments of absolute terror." They were used to sharing every aspect of their lives, and when the most exciting and noteworthy of circumstances befell them, there was no way to share it. I'm not smart enough to know exactly how, but that had to have a profound effect.

It's safe to say that sadness and shame tainted FantasticLand immediately after the news broke and long after. The park never reopened after the storm. Demolition began six months to the day after the first photos from the park leaked. Ritchie Fresno's sale of the park was unprecedented in its speed and in the amount of litigation that followed. The new owners have not shared their plans for the space, particularly after an idea to build a monument/amusement park based on the "Battle For FantasticLand" was met with derision from every right-thinking person in the country.

While good taste might have prevailed in that case, we remain positively fascinated by FantasticLand. Some employees have parlayed their temporary fame into more substantial work. Jill Van Meveren now works as a security consultant, for example. Sophie Ruskin has a podcast. Glenn Guignol appeared on the last season of a monster makeup reality competition show. Books have flooded the market. TV shows dedicated to the event routinely receive top ratings. There are T-shirts you can buy at the mall. In this way, FantasticLand will never die.

Nor will it die in the minds of those who lived through it. I have a confession in our final moments together. In the author's note at the beginning of this book, I told you about Alice Barlow, one of the archers for the ShopGirls. I told you about her social media page and how her mother was isolating her daughter until she could find some solace. After that piece was written and most of the reporting was put to bed, Alice's mother contacted me and said Alice wanted to talk. She wanted to unburden herself, but was unsure how much of her story she could tell.

I traveled to the small farming town in Oklahoma where she lived on a hot July day, the climate change that produced Hurricane Sadie fully on display as the mercury pushed 103 degrees. Her mother welcomed me and led me to Alice's room. It was just as I had pictured it. Alice was on her bed. Her mother introduced us and quietly shut the door, leaving a silence as deep as any I've experienced as a journalist. I introduced myself. I told her what I was doing and who I had spoken with. For a time, there was happy chitchat about mutual acquaintances. How was Clara Ann doing? Elvis made it out? That was great! Then I asked her about her story.

She didn't get far.

This is going to sound trite, but as that young woman sobbed and sobbed and as her mother ran in to console her and as I watched the seconds tick on my digital recorder—two minutes, five minutes, seven minutes—I could not help but feel intense anger. I was mad at the people who took the "What tribe are you?" quiz online—if the person who wrote it were there, I would have read them the riot act. I was mad at the people who want to turn the former FantasticLand into an "experience" where tourists can relive the battle. I was mad at the toll that this slaughter took on those who survived. Mostly, I was mad at myself. Alice

Barlow was not ready to talk to me. She would never be ready. But I wanted to know. We all want to know. How many did you kill? How did it feel? What were the Pirates like? Did you ever meet Brock Hockney? We all want to know, and watching that girl sob brought the weight of my guilt crashing on my head. I started to cry too. I wouldn't be human if I had not.

At the end of the day, this project left me with the sense that I was not the reporter I imagined myself to be. Yes, I was able to convince most of my subjects to tell their stories, but in the end, what have we learned? That violence lurks in all of us? That we are easily led by those with less than the purest of intentions? To always check how much TNT you're using?

I don't know. I wish I did. I wish I could tie this up in a bow. I wish I knew why Alice Barlow could hold and protect that baby duck and shoot arrows into her fellow employees two months later. I wish I knew, but I don't.

None of us do.